LOVECRAFT
COUNTRY

LOVECRAFT COUNTRY

⊱ A NOVEL ⊰

MATT RUFF

HARPER
An Imprint of HarperCollins*Publishers*

HarperCollins books may be purchased for educational, business, or sales promotional use. For information, please e-mail the Special Markets Department at SPsales@harpercollins.com.

FIRST EDITION

Designed by Jaime Putorti
Copyright for images: cajoer/Shutterstock, Inc.

Library of Congress Cataloging-in-Publication Data has been applied for.

ISBN: 978-0-06-229206-3

20   ov/LSC   10 9 8 7 6 5

FOR HAROLD AND RITA

LOVECRAFT
COUNTRY

LOVECRAFT COUNTRY

⌐⊟⌐

JIM CROW MILE—A unit of measurement, peculiar to colored motorists, comprising both physical distance and random helpings of fear, paranoia, frustration, and outrage. Its amorphous nature makes exact travel times impossible to calculate, and its violence puts the traveler's good health and sanity constantly at hazard.
—The Safe Negro Travel Guide, *Summer 1954 edition*

Atticus was almost home when the state trooper pulled him over.

He'd left Jacksonville two days before in a secondhand '48 Cadillac Coupe that he'd bought with the last of his Army pay. The first day he drove 450 miles, eating and drinking from a basket he'd packed in advance, stopping the car only to get gas. At one of the gas stops the colored restroom was out of order, and when the attendant refused him the key to the whites' room, Atticus was forced to urinate in the bushes behind the station.

He spent the night in Chattanooga. *The Safe Negro Travel Guide* had listings for four hotels and a motel, all in the same part of the city. Atticus chose the motel, which had an attached 24-hour diner. The price of the room, as promised by the *Guide*, was three dollars.

In the diner the next morning he consulted a road atlas. He had another six hundred miles to go to Chicago. Midway along his intended route was the city of Louisville, Kentucky, which according to the *Guide* had a restaurant that would serve him lunch. Atticus considered it, but any inclination to further delay his homecoming was overwhelmed by a desire to put the South behind him, so after he finished breakfast he got the basket from his car and had the diner cook fill it with sandwiches and Cokes and cold fried chicken.

Around one p.m. he reached the Ohio River, which marked the border between Kentucky and Indiana. As he crossed the water on a bridge named for a dead slave owner, Atticus cocked his arm out the window and bade Jim Crow farewell with a raised middle finger. A white driver coming the other way saw the gesture and shouted something vile, but Atticus just laughed and stepped on the gas, and so passed into the North.

An hour later along a stretch of farmland the Cadillac blew a tire. Atticus wrestled the car to a safe stop at the roadside and got out to put on the spare, but the spare was flat, too. He was frustrated by this—he'd checked the spare before setting out, and it had seemed fine then—but however much he frowned at it, the spare remained resolute in its flatness. A Southern tire, Atticus thought: Jim Crow's revenge.

Behind him for at least ten miles there was nothing but fields and woods, but looking ahead on the road he could see, perhaps two miles distant, a cluster of buildings. Taking *The Safe Negro Travel Guide* with him, he started walking. There was traffic on the road, and at first as he walked he tried waving down vehicles that were headed his way, but the drivers all either ignored him or sped up to get past him, and eventually he gave up and just concentrated on putting one foot in front of the other.

He came to the first of the buildings. The sign out front said JANS- SEN'S AUTO REPAIR, and Atticus thought he might be in luck until he saw the Confederate flag hanging above the garage entrance. That was almost enough to make him keep walking, but he decided he had to try.

Inside the garage were two white men: a little fellow with a peach- fuzz mustache who sat on a high stool reading a magazine, and a much bigger man who was bent under the open hood of a pickup truck. As Atticus entered, the little man looked up from his magazine and made a rude sucking sound between his teeth.

"Excuse me," Atticus said. This got the attention of the big man. As he straightened up and turned around, Atticus saw he had a tattoo of what looked like a wolf's head on his forearm.

"Sorry to disturb you," Atticus said, "but I've had some trouble. I need to buy a tire."

The big man glared at him for a moment, then said flatly: "No."

"I can see you're busy," said Atticus, as if that might be the problem. "I'm not asking you to change it for me. Just sell me the tire, and I'll—"

"No."

"I don't understand. You don't want my money? You don't have to *do* anything, just—"

"No." The big man crossed his arms. "You need me to say it another fifty times? Because I will."

And Atticus, fuming now, said: "That's a Wolfhound tattoo, right? Twenty-seventh Infantry regiment?" He fingered the service pin on his own lapel. "I was with the 24th Infantry. We fought alongside the 27th across most of Korea."

"I wasn't in Korea," the big man said. "I was at Guadalcanal, and Luzon. And there weren't any niggers there."

With that he bent under the truck hood again, his back both a dismissal and an invitation. Leaving Atticus to decide which way he wanted to take it. The collective indignities of the past months in Florida made it a closer call than Atticus liked. The little man on the stool was still looking at him, and if he'd said anything or even cracked a smile Atticus would have gone in swinging. But the little man, perhaps sensing how quickly he could lose his teeth even with the big man to protect him, did not smile or speak, and Atticus stalked off with his fists at his sides.

Across the road was a general store with a pay phone on its front porch. Atticus looked in the *Guide* and found a listing for a Negro-owned garage in Indianapolis, some fifty miles away. He placed the call and explained his predicament to the mechanic who answered. The mechanic was sympathetic and agreed to come help, but warned that it would be a while. "That's OK," Atticus said. "I'll be here."

He hung up and noticed the old woman inside the general store watching him nervously through the screen door. Once again, he chose to turn and walk away.

He went back to the car. In the trunk beside the useless spare was a cardboard box filled with battered paperbacks. Atticus selected a copy of Ray Bradbury's *The Martian Chronicles*. He sat in the Cadillac and read about the "rocket summer" of 1999, when winter's snows were melted by the exhaust from a Mars-bound spacecraft. He imagined himself aboard, rising into the sky on a jet of fire, leaving North and South behind forever.

Four hours passed. He read all of *The Martian Chronicles*. He drank warm Coke and ate a sandwich, but mindful of the gaze of passing motorists, he did not touch the fried chicken. He perspired in the breezeless June heat. When his bladder could no longer be ignored, he waited for a lull in the traffic and went behind a sycamore that grew by the roadside.

It was after seven o'clock when the tow truck arrived. The driver, a gray-haired, light-skinned Negro, introduced himself as Earl Maybree. "Earl, just Earl," he insisted, when Atticus tried to call him Mr. Maybree. He lifted the replacement tire from the rear of the tow truck. "Let's get you back on your way."

With the two of them working together it took less than ten minutes. The simplicity of it, and the thought of the afternoon just wasted for no good reason, started Atticus fuming again. He stepped away from the car to compose himself, pretending to study the sun now hanging low on the horizon.

"How far do you have to go?" Earl asked him.

"Chicago."

Earl raised an eyebrow. "Tonight?"

"Well . . . That was the plan."

"Tell you what," Earl said. "I'm done for the day. Why don't you come home with me, let my wife fix you a real dinner. Maybe rest awhile."

"No, sir, I couldn't."

"Sure you could. It's on your way. And I wouldn't want you to leave Indiana thinkin' it's all bad people."

Earl lived in the colored district around Indiana Avenue northwest of the state capitol building. His house was a narrow wooden two-story with a tiny patch of grass out front. When they arrived the sun had set and clouds were blowing in from the north, hastening the darkness. In the street, a stickball game was in progress, but now the mothers of the players were calling them inside.

Earl and Atticus went inside too. Earl's wife, Mavis, greeted Atticus warmly and showed him where he could wash up. Despite the welcome, Atticus was apprehensive sitting down at the kitchen table, for many of the obvious topics of dinner conversation—his service in Korea; his stay in Jacksonville; today's events; and most of all his father in Chicago—were things he didn't really care to talk about. But after they'd said grace, Earl surprised him by asking what he'd thought of *The Martian Chronicles*. "I saw you had it in the car."

So they talked about Ray Bradbury, and Robert Heinlein, and Isaac Asimov, all of whom Earl liked; and L. Ron Hubbard, whom he didn't; and the Tom Swift series, which Earl had loved when he was young but which embarrassed him now, both for the books' depiction of Negroes and for the fact that as a boy he hadn't noticed it, despite his father's repeated attempts to point it out to him. "Yeah, my pop had some problems with my reading choices too," Atticus said.

Mavis said little during the meal, seeming content to listen and to refill Atticus's plate whenever it was in danger of being emptied. By the time they finished dessert it was full dark and rain was drumming on the kitchen window. "Well," Mavis spoke up at last. "You can't drive any farther tonight in this." Atticus, past the point of even token resistance, allowed himself to be led upstairs to the spare bedroom. There on the dresser was a photograph of a young man in uniform. A black ribbon had been tied around a corner of the frame. "Our Dennis," Mavis said, or so Atticus thought. But as she began to put fresh sheets on the bed, she added: "He died in the forest," and Atticus realized she was talking about the Ardennes.

Atticus lay in bed with a book Earl had offered him: more Bradbury, a short story collection called *Dark Carnival*. It was a nice gesture but not really the best bedtime fare. After reading one story about a vampire family reunion and another, very strange tale about a man who had his skeleton removed, Atticus shut the book, gazed for a moment at the Arkham House imprint on its spine, and set it aside. He reached for his trousers and got out the letter from his father. Reading it over again, he touched a finger to a word written near the bottom of the page. "Arkham," he whispered.

The rain stopped at three in the morning. Atticus opened his eyes in the silence, unsure at first what country he was in. He dressed in the dark and crept downstairs, thinking to leave a note, but Earl was awake, sitting at the kitchen table with a cigarette.

"Sneakin' out?" Earl said to Atticus.

"Yes, sir. I appreciate the hospitality, but I need to get home."

Earl nodded and made a little shooing gesture with his cigarette hand.

"Tell Mrs. Maybree thank you for me. Tell her I said goodbye."

Earl made the shooing gesture again. Atticus got in his car and drove off through the dark and still-damp streets, feeling like the ghost in whose bed he had slept.

By first light he was well to the north. He passed a sign reading CHICAGO—52. The state trooper was parked on the shoulder on the opposite side of the road. The trooper had been napping, and had Atticus come even five minutes earlier he might have passed by unnoticed, but in the pink dawnlight the trooper sat up blinking and yawning. He saw Atticus driving by and came fully alert.

Atticus watched in the rearview as the patrol car made a U-turn onto the road. He got the Cadillac's registration and bill of sale from the glove box and put them on the passenger seat along with his driver's license, everything in plain sight so there'd be no confusion about what he was reaching for. Lights flashed in the rearview and the police siren came on. Atticus pulled over, rolled down his window, and as he'd been taught to do in his very first driving lesson, gripped the top of the steering wheel with both hands.

The trooper took his time getting out of the patrol car, stopping to stretch before ambling up alongside the Cadillac.

"Is this your car?" he began.

"Yes, sir," Atticus said. Without taking his hands off the wheel, he inclined his head towards the papers in the passenger seat.

"Show me."

Atticus handed him the documents.

"Atticus Turner," the state trooper said, reading the name off his license. "You know why I stopped you?"

"No, sir," Atticus lied.

"You weren't speeding," the trooper assured him. "But when I saw your license plate, I got worried you might be lost. Florida is the other way."

Atticus gripped the wheel a little tighter. "I'm going to Chicago. Sir."

"What for?"

"Family. My dad needs me."

"But you live in Florida?"

"I've been working down in Jacksonville. Since I got out of the service."

The trooper yawned without bothering to cover his mouth. "Been working, or still working?"

"Sir?"

"Are you going back to Florida?"

"No, sir. I don't plan to."

"You don't plan to. So you're staying in Chicago?"

"For a while."

"How long?"

"I don't know. As long as my father needs me."

"And then what?"

"I don't know. I haven't decided."

"You haven't decided." The trooper frowned. "But you're just passing through, here. Right?"

"Yes, sir," Atticus said, resisting the temptation to add, "if you'll let me."

Still frowning, the trooper shoved the documents back through the window. Atticus replaced them on the passenger seat. "What's in there?" the trooper asked next, pointing at the basket on the floor.

"What's left of my lunch, from yesterday."

"What about in back? Anything in the trunk?"

"Just my clothes," Atticus said. "My Army uniform. Some books."

"What kind of books?"

"Science fiction, mostly."

"*Science* fiction? And this is your car?"

"Officer—"

"Step out." The trooper moved back from the door and placed a hand on the butt of his revolver. Atticus got out of the car, slowly. Standing, he was an inch taller than the trooper; his reward for this impertinence was to be spun around, shoved up against the Cadillac, and roughly frisked. "All right," said the trooper. "Open the trunk."

The trooper pawed through Atticus's clothes first, patting down the sides of his duffel bag as if it too were a black man braced against a car. Then he turned to the books, dumping the box out into the trunk. Atticus tried not to care, telling himself paperbacks were meant to be abused, but it was hard, like watching friends get knocked around.

"What's this?" The trooper picked up a gift-wrapped object that had been at the bottom of the box.

"Another book," Atticus said. "It's a present for my uncle."

The trooper tore off the wrapping paper, revealing a hardbound volume. "*A Princess of Mars.*" He looked sideways at Atticus. "Your uncle likes princesses, does he?" He tossed the book into the box, Atticus dying a little as it landed splayed open, bending pages.

The trooper circled the Cadillac. When he opened the passenger door, Atticus thought he was going after *The Martian Chronicles*, which was still up front somewhere. But the trooper came up holding *The Safe Negro Travel Guide*. He thumbed through it, at first puzzled and then astonished. "These addresses," he said. "These are all places that serve colored people?" Atticus nodded. "Well," said the trooper, "if that doesn't beat everything . . ." He squinted at the *Guide* edge-on. "Not very thick, is it?" Atticus didn't respond to that.

"All right," the trooper said finally. "I'm going to let you go. But I'm keeping this guidebook. Don't worry," he added, forestalling the objection that Atticus knew better than to make, "you won't need it anymore. You say you're going to Chicago? Well, between here and there, there's *no* place that you want to stop. Understood?"

Atticus understood.

The main office of the Safe Negro Travel Company (George Berry, proprietor) was in Washington Park on Chicago's South Side. Atticus parked in front of the Freemasons' temple next door and sat watching the early morning pedestrians and the drivers going by, not a white face among them. There were streets in Jacksonville where you'd rarely see a white person either, but this street, this neighborhood, was home—had, once upon a time, been Atticus's whole world—and it soothed him like nothing save his mother's voice could. As he relaxed, the ball inside him unwinding by slow degrees, he reflected that the state trooper had been right: Here, he needed no guide.

The travel office was still closed at this hour, but Atticus could see a light on in the apartment above it. Rather than ring the buzzer, he went around to the alley and climbed the fire escape to knock at the kitchen door. From within he heard the scrape of a chair and the rasp of the door bolt. The door opened halfway and Uncle George peered out warily. But when he saw who it was he cried out "Hey!" and threw the door wide, drawing Atticus into a tight embrace.

"Hey yourself," Atticus said laughing, returning the hug.

"Man, it's good to see you!" Stepping back, George gripped Atticus by the shoulders and looked him up and down. "When did you get back?"

"Just rolled in now."

"Well come on inside."

Entering the kitchen, Atticus was struck by the funhouse sensation that had dogged him on his only other visit home since joining the military. Though he'd reached his full growth—just—before enlisting, in his strongest memories of this place he'd been a much smaller person, so that the room seemed to have shrunk. When his uncle had shut the door and turned to embrace him a second time, Atticus realized George had shrunk too, though in George's case that just meant they were now the same height.

"Is Aunt Hippolyta home?" Atticus asked, curious to take her measure as well.

"No," said George. "She's in Wyoming. There's this new spa opened up near Yellowstone, run by Quakers if you can believe it. Supposedly open to everyone. She's checking it out." Early in their marriage, Hippolyta had volunteered herself as a scout for *The Safe Negro Travel Guide*, specializing in vacation resorts. Initially she and George had traveled together, but these days she most often went alone, leaving George home to care for their son. "She'll be gone at least a week. But I know Horace will be glad to see you, once he wakes up."

"Horace is still sleeping?" Atticus was surprised. "School year's not over already, is it?"

"Not quite," George said. "But today's Saturday." Laughing at Atticus's reaction to this news: "Guess I don't have to ask how your trip was."

"No, you don't." He held out the book he'd carried like a broken bird from the car. "Here."

"What's this . . . Ah, Mr. Burroughs!"

"Souvenir from Japan," Atticus said. "I found this bookstore outside the base in Gifu, guy had one shelf of books in English, almost all science fiction . . . I thought that might be a first edition, but now I think it's just old."

"Well-traveled," George said. The book fell open to the bent pages; Atticus had done his best to flatten them, but the creasing was permanent.

"Yeah, it was in better shape when I bought it."

"Hey, that's OK," George said. "Should still read just fine." He smiled. "Come on, let's put this in the place of honor." He headed for the bedroom he and Hippolyta shared with their best books.

Atticus followed him partway, stopping outside the apartment's other bedroom to look in on his cousin. Horace, twelve years old, lay on his back with his mouth open, his breath wheezy and labored. There was an issue of *Tom Corbett, Space Cadet* beside his pillow and more were scattered on the floor.

A short-legged easel desk faced the wall opposite the bed. A sheet of construction paper on the desk had been divided into panels containing scenes from an intergalactic adventure: Negroes in capes, wandering through a Buck Rogers landscape. Atticus studied it from the doorway, head tilted as he tried to pick up the thread of the story.

George came back down the hall. "He's getting really good," Atticus said, keeping his voice low.

"Yeah, he's been trying to talk me into starting a comics line. I told him if he saves up enough of his own money, I might go in with him on a *small* print run . . . So, you hungry? Why don't I get him up, call your father, and we all go out to breakfast together. You seen Montrose yet?"

"Not yet," said Atticus. "And before I do, there's something I need to talk to you about."

"All right. Go make yourself comfortable, I'll put coffee on."

While George busied himself in the kitchen, Atticus went out to the front parlor, which in childhood had served him as both library and reading room. The bookshelves were divided into his and hers, Aunt Hippolyta's interests running primarily to science and natural history, with a smattering of Jane Austen. George gave a nod to respectable literature but reserved his deepest passion and most of his shelf space for the genres of pulp: science fiction, fantasy, mysteries and detective stories, horror and weird tales.

Atticus's shared devotion to these mostly white-authored genres had been a source of ongoing struggle with his father. George, as Montrose's older brother, was largely immune to his scorn and could always tell him to keep his opinions to himself. Atticus didn't have that privilege. If his father was in a mood to debate his tastes in reading, he had no choice but to oblige him.

There was usually plenty to argue about. Edgar Rice Burroughs, for example, offered a wealth of critical fodder with his Tarzan stories (was it even necessary to list all the problems Montrose had with Tarzan, starting with the very idea of him?), or his Barsoom series, whose protagonist John Carter had been a captain in the Army of Northern Virginia before becoming a Martian warlord. "A Confederate officer?" Atticus's father had said, appalled. "That's the hero?" When Atticus tried to suggest it wasn't that bad since technically John Carter was an ex-Confederate, his father scoffed: "*Ex*-Confederate? What's that, like an ex-Nazi? The man fought for slavery! You don't get to put an 'ex-' in front of that!"

Montrose could have simply forbidden him to read such things. Atticus knew other sons whose fathers had done that, who'd thrown their comic books and *Amazing Stories* collections into the trash. But Montrose, with limited exceptions, didn't believe in book-banning. He always insisted he just wanted Atticus to think about what he read, rather than imbibing it mindlessly, and Atticus, if he were being honest, had to admit that was a reasonable goal. But if it was fair to acknowledge his father's good intentions, it also seemed fair to point out that his father was a belligerent man who enjoyed having cause to pick on him.

Uncle George wasn't much help. "It's not as if your father's wrong," he said one time when Atticus was complaining.

"But you love these stories!" Atticus said. "You love them as much as I do!"

"I do love them," George agreed. "But stories are like people, Atticus. Loving them doesn't make them perfect. You try to cherish their virtues and overlook their flaws. The flaws are still there, though."

"But you don't get mad. Not like Pop does."

"No, that's true, I don't get mad. Not at stories. They do disappoint me sometimes." He looked at the shelves. "Sometimes, they stab me in the heart."

Standing in front of those same shelves now, Atticus reached for a book bearing the Arkham House imprint: *The Outsider and Others*, by H. P. Lovecraft.

Lovecraft was not an author Atticus would have expected to like. He wrote horror stories, which were more George's thing, Atticus preferring adventures with happy or at least hopeful endings. But one day on a whim he'd decided to give Lovecraft a try, choosing at random a lengthy tale called "At the Mountains of Madness."

The story concerned a scientific fossil-hunting expedition to Antarctica. While scouting for new dig sites, the scientists discovered a mountain range with peaks higher than Everest. In a plateau in the mountains lay a city, built millions of years ago by a race of aliens called the Elder Things, or Old Ones, who came to Earth from space during the Precambrian Era. Although the Old Ones had abandoned the city long ago, their former slaves, protoplasmic monsters called shoggoths, still roamed the tunnels beneath the ruins.

"Shiggoths?" Atticus's father said, when Atticus made the mistake of telling him about this.

"Sh*oggoths*," Atticus corrected him.

"Uh-huh. And the master race, the Elder Klansmen—"

"Elder *Things*. Old Ones."

"They're fair-skinned, I bet. And the Shiggoths, they're dark."

"The Elder Things are barrel-shaped. They have *wings*."

"But they're white, right?"

"They're *gray*."

"*Pale* gray?"

After some additional teasing in this vein—and a more serious sidebar on Mr. Lovecraft's willful misconceptions about evolution—Montrose let it go, or seemed to. But a few nights later he brought home a surprise.

Atticus's mother was out with a friend that evening, and Atticus was alone in the apartment, reading "The Call of Cthulhu" and trying to ignore a strange gurgling in the kitchen sink. He was actually relieved when his father came home.

Montrose started in right away. "I stopped by the public library after work," he said as he was hanging up his coat. "I did a little research on your friend Mr. Lovecraft."

"Yeah?" Atticus said, without enthusiasm. He recognized the perverse mix of anger and glee in his father's voice and knew that something he enjoyed was about to be irrevocably spoiled.

"Turns out he was a poet, too. No Langston Hughes, but still, it's interesting . . . Here."

The typescript his father handed him was like a cheap parody of one of the arcane texts from Lovecraft's stories: an amateur literary journal, produced on an ancient mimeograph and bound between stained sheets of cardboard. There was no title page, but a tag on the cover gave its origin as PROVIDENCE, 1912. How it had ended up in the Chicago public library system Atticus never knew, but given its existence he wasn't surprised his father had managed to find it. Montrose had a nose for such things.

An index card from the library catalogue had been used as a bookmark in the journal. Atticus turned to the indicated page, and there it was, eight lines of comic verse by Howard Phillips Lovecraft.

The title of the poem was "On the Creation of Niggers."

Sometimes, they stab me in the heart . . .

"Getting reacquainted with old friends?" George said, appearing with the coffee.

"Yeah." Atticus slid the book back into its place and took the cup George offered him. "Thanks." They sat, Atticus feeling a wave of exhaustion wash over him.

"So," George said. "How was Florida?"

"Segregated," Atticus replied, thinking as he said it that it wasn't the right word, since you could apply it just as well to Chicago.

But George nodded. "Yeah, I didn't think you'd like the South. Didn't expect to see you back so soon, though. I figured you'd stick it out there at least through the end of the summer."

"I figured that too," Atticus said. "And I was thinking I might try California, next. But then I got this." He showed George the letter from his father.

George recognized the handwriting on the envelope immediately. He nodded again. "Montrose asked me for your mailing address."

"He tell you what he was planning to write me about?"

George laughed. "You kidding? He wouldn't even admit he was *going* to write you. Just told me he thought he should have the address, 'in case.' It's been like that since you left: He worries about you, wants to know everything I know, but Lord forbid he should say so. So he'll slip it in, casual, when we're talking about something else: 'Oh, *by the way*, you hear anything about that boy?'"

"'That boy.'" Atticus made a face.

"Hey, if he used your name it might sound like he cared. And even that much is an improvement. That first year you were in Korea, he wouldn't even ask. He'd come over for dinner and wait for me to volunteer the information. And if I didn't volunteer, he wouldn't say anything, but he wouldn't go home. He'd stay here till ten, eleven, midnight if that's what it took, waiting for me to bring up the subject of you. Drove me crazy." George shook his head. "So what did he write to you about?"

"Mom," Atticus said. "He says he found out where her family came from."

"He's still obsessing on that? Huh."

Atticus's mother, Dora, had been the only child of an unmarried woman. Her father's identity was a mystery and a taboo subject. Her mother, disowned by her family, had in turn seldom spoken of them, as a result of which Dora knew little of her maternal grandparents other than that they had lived in Brooklyn and came originally from somewhere in New England.

Montrose, who could trace his own roots back five generations, had sworn to find out more about Dora's ancestry. At first, when he and Dora were courting, he had intended this as a sort of love offering, but by the time Atticus was born, it had become a purely selfish pursuit and one of a long list of things about which he and Dora fought.

Atticus could remember lying in his childhood bed, listening to the two of them argue. "How can you not want to know?" his father would say. "Who you come from is part of who you are. How do you just let that be stolen from you?"

"I know where the past leads," his mother would reply. "It's a sad place. Why would I want to know it better? Does knowing make *you* happy?"

"It ain't *about* happy. It's about being whole. You have a right to that. You have a duty to that."

"But I don't want it. Please, just let it go."

Atticus was seventeen when his mother died. The day of the funeral, he'd found his father pawing through a box of his mother's keepsakes. Montrose had pulled out a photograph of Dora's grandparents—the only image of them she'd possessed—and removed it from its frame so he could read something written on the back. Some clue.

Atticus had snatched the photo from his startled father's hands. "Let it go!" he'd shouted. "She said let it go!" Montrose, rearing back, had recovered quickly, his fury more than a match for his son's. He'd struck Atticus hard enough to knock him to the floor, then stood over him, raging: "Don't you *ever* tell me what to do. *Ever*."

"Of course he's still obsessing on it," Atticus said now, in answer to George's question. "But the thing I need to ask you—you say Pop drove you crazy. What I'm wondering is whether you think he might have finally done the same to himself." He read aloud from the letter, struggling a bit with his father's handwriting: "'I know that, like your mother, you think you can forgive, for*get*, the past. You can't. You cannot. The past is alive, a living, thing. You own, *owe* it. Now I have found something, about your mother's . . . forebears. You have a sacred, a *secret*, legacy, a birthright which has been kept from you.'"

"Legacy?" George said. "Is he talking about an inheritance?"

"He doesn't say exactly. But whatever it is, it has something to do with the place that Mom's people supposedly came from. He says he needs me to come home, so we can go there, together, and claim what's mine."

"Well, that doesn't sound crazy. Wishful thinking, maybe, but . . ."

"The crazy part isn't the legacy. It's the location. This place he wants me to go with him, it's in Lovecraft Country."

George shook his head, not understanding.

"Arkham," Atticus said. "The letter says Mom's ancestors come from Arkham, Massachusetts." Arkham: home of the corpse reanimator

Herbert West, and of Miskatonic University, which had sponsored the fossil-hunting expedition to the mountains of madness. "It *is* made up, right? I mean—"

"Oh, yeah," George said. "Lovecraft based it on Salem, I think, but it's not a real place . . . Let me see that letter." Atticus handed it to him and George studied it, squinting and tilting his head side to side. "It's a 'd,'" he said finally.

"What?"

"It's not Arkham, with a 'k,' it's Ardham, with a 'd.'"

Atticus got up and stared at the letter over George's shoulder. "That's a 'd'?"

"Yeah."

"No. A 'b,' maybe . . ."

"No, it's a 'd.' Ardham, for sure."

"Man." Atticus sighed in frustration. "You know, for someone who talks so much about the importance of being educated, you'd think he'd learn to *write* clearly."

"It's not his fault," George said. "Montrose is dyslexic."

This was news to Atticus. "Since when?"

"Since ever. It's why he had so much trouble in school. Well, one reason. Your grandpa Turner had the same problem."

"Why didn't I know this?"

"You mean, why didn't Montrose ever tell you?" George laughed. "Figure it out." He grabbed a road atlas from one of the bookshelves. After consulting the index in the back, he turned to the map of Massachusetts. "Yeah, here it is."

Ardham, marked by a hollow dot signifying a settlement of no more than 250 people, was in the north-central part of the state, just below the New Hampshire border. An unnamed tributary of the Connecticut River looped south around it; the map showed no direct road access, though a state highway intersected the tributary nearby.

"Sorry," George said, as Atticus frowned at the map. "Your dad hasn't lost his mind. Maybe you should have called before you drove all this way."

"No, it was about time for me to come home," Atticus said. "I guess I'd better go see him. Find out what this 'birthright' is all about."

"Hold on a second . . ."

"What?"

"Devon County," George said, tapping a finger on the map. "Devon County, Massachusetts, that rings a bell . . . Huh. I wonder. Maybe this Ardham is in Lovecraft Country after all . . ."

"What are you talking about?"

"Let's go downstairs to the office. I need to check my files."

George had begun publishing *The Safe Negro Travel Guide* as a means of advertising his travel agency's services, and though the *Guide* had ultimately become profitable in its own right, the agency—now expanded to three locations—remained his primary business and source of income.

The agency would book trips and tickets for anyone, but specialized in helping middle-class Negroes negotiate with a travel industry that was at best reluctant to accept their patronage. Through his network of contacts and scouts, George kept up-to-date files not only on which hotels allowed Negro guests, but which air and cruise lines were most likely to honor their reservations. For those wishing to vacation abroad, the agency could recommend destinations that were relatively free of local race prejudice and, just as important, not overrun by white American tourists—for nothing was more frustrating than traveling thousands of miles only to encounter the same bigots you dealt with every day at home.

The files were stored in a back room. George flipped on the lights as they entered and reached for something atop a cabinet beside the door. "Check this out," he said to Atticus.

It was a road atlas, the same edition as the one upstairs, only this copy had been extensively illustrated with brightly colored drawings. Atticus recognized Horace's handiwork: Some of the boy's first art experiments had involved sketching cartoons onto gas station maps. Horace really had gotten good at it, though, and as Atticus paged through the atlas, it dawned on him that what he was holding was a visual translation of *The Safe Negro Travel Guide*.

Major Negro population centers like Chicago's South Side were represented as shining fortresses. Smaller neighborhoods and enclaves were marked with towers or oases. Isolated hotels and motels were inns with smiling keepers. Tourist homes—private residences that lent rooms to Negro travelers—were peasant huts, or tree houses, or hobbit holes.

Less friendly parts of the country were populated by ogres and trolls, vampires and werewolves, wild beasts, ghosts, evil sorcerers, and hooded white knights. In Oklahoma, a great white dragon coiled around Tulsa, breathing fire onto the neighborhood where Atticus's father and Uncle George had been born.

Atticus turned to Massachusetts. Devon County was marked with an icon he'd seen in numerous other places in the atlas: a sundial. Standing beside it, casting his own shadow over the gnomon, was a grim Templar holding a noose.

"Victor Franklin," said George, who'd been rummaging in file drawers while Atticus looked at the atlas. He waved a typewritten sheet he'd extracted from a folder.

"Who?" Atticus said.

"Old schoolmate from Howard. I don't think you ever met him, but the past couple years he's been running the Grand Boulevard office for me. Last September he went back east to visit his folks, and I asked him if he'd take a side trip through New England to check out some new listings for the *Guide*.

"One of the places I sent him was in New Hampshire. Another school friend, Lester Deering, moved up there to open a hotel. Place was supposed to be up and running already, but Lester had some problems with the local contractors and had to delay—the day Victor came by, he was over in the next town, trying to hire a new electrician to finish the wiring. So Victor shows up and the hotel's not open, nobody's around, and when he tries to rent a room at a motel down the road—"

"No vacancies."

"Right. Not for him. So he said to hell with it, and decided to head back down into Massachusetts and spend the night at a tourist home.

"So he started driving south, and by the time he crossed the state line he needed to pee. He could have gone to a gas station and asked to use their restroom, but the way his day had been going he could guess how that would turn out, so instead he decided to pull over and go in the woods.

"As soon as he got out of the car, he got nervous. The sun was going down, he hadn't passed another car in miles, and he hadn't seen another colored man since Boston. But he had to go, so he stepped into the woods, just far enough to be out of sight if anyone did drive by. And he was in the middle of his business when he heard something thrashing around farther out in the trees."

"Shoggoth?" Atticus said.

George smiled. "I don't think Victor would know what that is, but his thoughts were definitely leaning in that direction. 'It was big, whatever it was,' he told me, 'and I wasn't interested in finding out how big.' So he zipped up in a hurry and ran back out to the road, which is where the real monster was waiting for him.

"County sheriff," George said. "Victor had been so focused on whatever it was busting branches out in the woods, he never even heard the patrol car drive up. It was just there, parked behind Victor's Lincoln. And the sheriff was leaning against the Lincoln's front hood, holding a rifle. Victor said when he saw the expression on the sheriff's face, he had more than half a mind to turn and run. He said the only thing that stopped him was the certainty he'd be shot in the back if he did that.

"Instead he put his hands up and said, 'Hello, officer, how can I help you?' The sheriff started right in with the usual Twenty Questions: Who are you, where are you coming from, why'd you stop here? Victor answered as respectfully as he could, until the sheriff cut him off and said: 'So what you're telling me is, you came all the way from Chicago to piss in my woods like some animal?' And Victor was trying to come up with an answer to that that wouldn't get him shot in the face, when the sheriff asked another question: 'Do you know what a sundown town is?'

"Victor told the sheriff yes, he was familiar with the concept. 'Well,' the sheriff said, 'you're in Devon, which is a sundown *county*. If I'd caught you here after dark, it'd be my sworn duty to hang you from one of these trees.' And Victor—he said he was so scared he was *calm*, you know that feeling?—Victor looked up in the sky, and he couldn't see the sun above the trees, but there was still light, so he said: 'It's not sunset yet.' And then, he said, he very nearly fainted, hearing how those words sounded coming out of his mouth, like he was giving sass . . . But the sheriff just chuckled. 'No, not yet,' he said. 'Sunset today is at 7:09. You've got seven minutes.' 'Well then,' said Victor, 'if you let me go on my way, I'll be out of the county in *six* minutes.' 'Not going south, you won't,' the sheriff told him. 'Not unless you speed. And if you speed, I'll have to pull you over . . .' 'I'll go back north, then,' Victor said. 'That *might* work,' the sheriff said. 'Why don't you try that and see what happens?'

"So Victor went to get in the Lincoln, terrified that the sheriff was just toying with him before putting a bullet in him, and then when he opened the car door he had another thought, and he looked at the road and looked at the sheriff and said, 'Is it legal for me to make a U-turn here?' And the sheriff smiled and told him, 'It's a good thing you asked that. Ordinarily, I'd consider a U-turn to be a violation, but if you say please, I might let it go just this once.' So Victor said please, and the sheriff ran out the clock some more thinking it over but finally said OK. So Victor got in the Lincoln and the sheriff got in his patrol car and they both turned around, and Victor went back up the road at just under the speed limit with the sheriff riding his bumper the whole way. He made it into New Hampshire with about thirty seconds to spare."

Listening to this story, Atticus felt a number of different emotions, but one of the strongest was embarrassment. He'd been so upset by his own encounter with the Indiana state trooper, when the trooper hadn't even drawn his pistol. "So the sheriff let him go then?"

"The sheriff stopped at the state border. But the road ran straight for another half mile, and when Victor looked in the rearview he saw the sheriff get out of the patrol car and train the rifle on him. He got his head down just in time: The sheriff shot out his back window, and one round came straight through and starred the glass above the steering wheel, right at eye level. Victor kept it on the road, though, and kept his foot on the gas. He went a whole other county without slowing down before he was sure the sheriff wasn't chasing him. Then the shakes hit him so bad he nearly ran the Lincoln into a ditch."

"How'd he get home?"

"Through Canada. Quebec border guards had some questions about the bullet holes, but they let him in, and he was able to get the glass replaced in Montreal. And when he finally got back here, he typed up this report"—George waved the sheet of paper again—"saying he couldn't recommend Devon County for inclusion in *The Safe Negro Travel Guide*."

"Well, thanks for the warning, George," Atticus said. "But you know I can't tell Pop that story. It'd just make him even more determined to go."

"Yeah, I know. I wouldn't tell him about the shoggoth, either."

Atticus's father didn't answer the buzzer at his apartment building. Atticus rang a second time and the landlady, Mrs. Frazier—who at eighty-two could still hear a pin drop anywhere on her property—came out to see who it was. She reacted as George had done, embracing Atticus and welcoming him back, but when she'd finished fussing over him she told him his father wasn't home and hadn't been for nearly a week. "He went off with a white man, last Sunday evening just before dark."

"A white man?" Atticus said. "You mean a policeman?"

"Oh, I don't think so," Mrs. Frazier said. "He wasn't wearing a uniform, and he looked a little young to be a detective. And he drove a very fancy car—silver, with dark windows. Never saw one quite like it before."

"Did this man give his name?"

"No, and your father didn't introduce him. But your father did tell me you'd be coming home soon, and he said you'd know where to find him."

"Mrs. Frazier, did my father seem . . . OK?"

"Well, you know your father . . . I wouldn't say he was in a *good* mood, but it was the least angry I've ever seen him in the presence of a white person."

Atticus borrowed a spare key from Mrs. Frazier and let himself into the third-floor apartment. He stood just inside the door, adjusting again to the change in scale; the flat, never large, now felt cramped and claustrophobic. The front room was home to the magic couch, which folded out into the bed where Atticus had used to sleep, and the Frankenstein Victrola, which Montrose had built himself, installing a modern turntable, radio receiver, and speakers into an antique phonograph cabinet salvaged from the flames of Tulsa. Atticus looked with new knowledge at his father's record collection, which crowded the shelves on the walls. The collection contained not just music but spoken-word albums: speeches, lectures, audio plays.

Atticus was surprised to see a television set. His father had long resisted that, saying he'd save his money for the day Negroes had their own broadcast stations. Maybe *Popular Mechanics* was offering build-it-yourself TV kits now.

He turned and went into the narrow hallway that ran past the tiny kitchen and bathroom to his parents' bedroom in back. A pair of doorless, shallow hall closets had been fitted out with more shelving. A number of these shelves were still stenciled with Atticus's name, but all of his old possessions were gone—thrown out, in fulfillment of a threat made by Montrose when Atticus announced his intention to join the U.S. Army. Atticus, who'd already removed his few prize belongings to George's for safekeeping, had taken the threat in stride. When his father turned from words to fists, Atticus had taken that too, promising himself this was the last time Montrose would lay a hand on him.

But their big fight had come later, in the summer of 1951, when Atticus returned home on leave following his first combat tour. Enough time had passed for both Atticus and his father to regret at least some of what had been said and done. There was no formal reconciliation and certainly no exchange of apologies, but when Atticus appeared un-expectedly at his father's door one morning, Montrose had let him in, that single act speaking volumes.

Their unofficial cease-fire lasted less than a day. That evening Atticus got a call from a reporter at *The Chicago Defender* who wanted to interview him for a series of profiles of Negro soldiers. Atticus was flattered, but Montrose became livid when he heard. "What's wrong with you?" he said. "Bad enough you nearly throw your own life away for a country that hates you, now you want to inspire other young men to make the same stupid mistake?"

The progression from words to blows was quicker this time, with Atticus determined for once to give as good as he got. Looking around the back bedroom, Atticus could still see cracks in the plaster where he and his father, grappling, had slammed into the walls. Incredibly, it was Montrose who'd broken off the fight, right at the point where they were about to start doing serious damage to one another. Atticus had walked out, vowing never to return, but in his own gesture of restraint he'd left the reporter's phone number behind and had not, then or afterwards, allowed himself to be interviewed about his service.

"Ah, Pop," Atticus said now, sighing. He ran a hand over his head and looked at the bed, tempted. Instead of lying down, he went to the kitchen to get himself a drink of water. That was when he saw the note on the refrigerator door. It was just one word, scrawled on a piece of scrap paper. Atticus recognized the "d" for what it was now, but in his head he still heard the name of that other town, the one that existed only in Lovecraft Country.

He phoned George. "You going after him?" George asked.

"Yeah, I guess I'd better."

"All right, I'll go with you."

"You sure?"

"Yeah, of course. We can take Woody." Woody was George's station wagon, a Series 22 Packard with inlaid birch trim and side paneling. "Just give me a few hours to find someone to watch Horace and take care of some other things."

"OK," Atticus said. "But listen, George, in the meantime, you know anyone I could ask who might know about this white guy Pop went off with?"

"You could try over at the Brothers. If he's really been gone since Sunday, he must have asked for time off, or they'd have called me to find out where he was."

The Garvey Brothers Print Shop—actually owned by a Jewish couple, the Garfields—handled all the printing for George's travel agency, including runs of *The Safe Negro Travel Guide*. Montrose worked for the Brothers as a machinist, maintaining and operating the presses and doing occasional tune-up work on the shop's two delivery trucks.

Atticus drove over to the shop and spoke to the weekend supervisor, who confirmed that Montrose had taken his two weeks' vacation early, claiming it was a family emergency. The supervisor knew nothing about any white man, though.

Atticus had better luck at Denmark Vesey's, the bar where his father sometimes went after work. The bartender on duty, Charlie Boyd, had been working the evening shift a week and a half earlier when a white man had come in—a rare occurrence, Vesey's being the sort of establishment most Caucasians would only enter in search of trouble or a bribe.

"Guy was in his early twenties," Charlie said. "Brown hair, blue eyes, sharp dresser. I don't think he was a cop, but he had that attitude, like of course he could just walk in here. And he wasn't afraid of Tree." Tree was the bouncer, six-foot-six and so dark-skinned that even other Negroes sometimes did the white man's double take when they saw him.

"This guy talked to my dad?"

Charlie nodded. "Came right up to him. And you know your dad, he's like, 'Who the hell are *you*?' but this guy says, 'Mr. Turner? We spoke on the phone,' and hands him a business card." Charlie shrugged. "Maybe he was a lawyer. Maybe that's how he could afford that car."

"You saw what he was driving?"

"Tree did. Silver four-door sedan with tinted windows. Tree didn't recognize the make, but he figured it must be foreign. And real expensive."

"What did this guy and Pop talk about?"

"That I don't know. After he gave your dad his card, the two of them went over to a booth. They talked for maybe fifteen minutes, then the white guy got up and left. Your dad sat there a while longer, finished his drink, and then he left too. And that's the last time I saw him in here."

"And when was this?"

"Wednesday night before last."

Montrose's letter to Atticus had been postmarked the following day. But sometime between Thursday and Sunday night, Atticus's father had decided not to wait for a reply.

Continuing to puzzle over that, Atticus returned to the apartment.

Exhaustion hit him again and this time he surrendered to it, flopping on the bed in his father's room and napping into the afternoon.

The phone woke him. It was George, calling to say he still had some errands to run but would be ready to leave by six. After he hung up Atticus checked the fridge—finding nothing among the week-old leftovers he wanted or dared to eat—then wandered, yawning, into the living room. He stepped idly to the window and parted the curtains.

This was a mostly middle-class block, its resident strivers eager to take part in the American dream of consumerism. Often frustrated in that pursuit, they spent their hard-earned dollars where and how they could: on furniture and appliances for their too-small apartments; on fine clothes for church, and for those theaters and nightclubs that would grant them admittance; and on luxury cars that, if they couldn't be driven safely through the countryside, at least made a statement parked by the curb.

But even on this street of Cadillacs, the car parked at the corner stood out, bespeaking a whole other order of wealth and privilege. Sleek, low-slung, and vaguely sinister, it was a car that would surely be named after a predator. Its silver skin and trim reflected the afternoon sun coldly, suggesting winter rather than summer. Its windows looked not just tinted but smoked, a seemingly solid black that offered no hint of who or what might be inside.

Atticus wasn't the only one to take note of it. A group of boys passing on the sidewalk stopped short beside the car, jaws dropping. One of them reached out to stroke it; as his fingers brushed the metal body-work, he let out a squawk and yanked his hand back. The other boys laughed. After some double-daring, another boy stepped up to place his palm flat on the car hood . . . and jumped back shrieking. The boys broke and ran, laughing in panic.

By then Atticus was moving too. He threw on a shirt, trousers, and shoes, and ran downstairs. It couldn't have been more than two minutes, but by the time he reached the sidewalk, the silver car had vanished. He looked up and down the street, in vain, then stared at the empty space where the car had been, wondering if he'd dreamed it.

Atticus arrived at George's to find a short, slender woman in a sundress standing guard over the Packard.

"Letitia?" he said. "Letitia Dandridge?"

"Atticus Turner," Letitia said, feigning disappointment at his uncertainty, for she'd seen him coming a block away and recognized him instantly. But then she laughed and opened her arms.

Growing up, the Dandridges had lived west of State Street in a poorer section of the neighborhood. Letitia's older sister, Ruby, had used to babysit Atticus, and her brother, Marvin, had worked part-time at the travel agency. Letitia, a year younger than Atticus, had for a while been the only girl member of the South Side Futurists Science-Fiction Club, which met after school in George's parlor. Eventually Mrs. Dandridge had put an end to that, insisting that Letitia stop wasting time on foolishness and start earning her keep like her siblings, after which Atticus rarely saw her.

"'Titia Dandridge," he marveled. "So what have you been doing with yourself?"

"Oh, you know, same as you. Out in the world, having adventures."

"Yeah?" He smiled. "Less fighting, I hope."

She shrugged a shoulder. "I could tell some stories."

"And you're back here now?"

Letitia nodded. "You heard Momma died last year?"

"I think Uncle George might have mentioned it in a letter. I'm sorry."

"Yeah, I missed the funeral," she said, in a tone Atticus might have used to describe missing a bus. "I think Momma was pretty mad at me for that. I started having a real bad run of luck."

Atticus kept his expression neutral. Mrs. Dandridge had worked in a beauty parlor, but her real business was telling fortunes and putting people in contact with their dead relatives—talents granted her through some vaguely Pentecostal arrangement with Jesus. Atticus wasn't sure what he thought about all that, but he knew Letitia took it seriously. "So you came back home to . . . make peace with her?"

"More like I ran out of choices," Letitia said. "I've been staying with Ruby while I come up with a new plan. She thinks I should get a job as a maid up on the North Side, but *that's* never going to happen, so . . ."

"So what are you doing here? Did George ask you to watch Horace?"

"No, Ruby's going to look after Horace. I'm going with you."

"You are?"

"Partway," George said. He came out of the building lugging a grocery bag and a clutch of canteens and walked around to the open back of the Packard. "We're going to give Letitia a ride to her brother's place in Springfield, Massachusetts. That gets us within fifty miles of Ardham. We'll catch our breath there, then go find Montrose."

"Do we know how to get to Ardham?" Atticus asked.

"That's the other reason we're stopping at Marvin's. He's working for the *Springfield Afro-American* now, so I asked him to do some research for us. He's going to get us a map of Devon County and see what else he can dig up."

Having stowed the food and water, George consulted a checklist, ticking off items: mattress, pillows, and blankets; spare tire and jack; spare gas; road flares; first-aid kit; flashlights; reading material . . . "Looks like we're all set," he concluded. "I'll drive the first leg. Who else wants to sit up front?"

Atticus and Letitia exchanged looks, grinning, kids again for a moment. "Letitia can ride shotgun," Atticus said. "I'll stretch out in back until you're ready to change drivers."

"Now, now," said Letitia. "It's a big front seat. Room for all three of us, if you want." Playacting again, she slipped her arm in his, arched an eyebrow. "*I don't mind.*"

The North Korean guerrillas were night fighters. By day they buried their weapons and hid themselves in plain sight among the civilian population. More than once while riding past a rice paddy, Atticus had studied the farmers in their cotton pajamas and tried to guess which of them would, come dark, trade his hoe for a rifle and bayonet. But if there was a trick to spotting Communist infiltrators, Atticus never learned it.

White people in his experience were far more transparent. The most hateful rarely bothered to conceal their hostility, and when for some reason they did try to hide their feelings, they generally exhibited all the guile of five-year-olds, who cannot imagine that the world sees them other than as they wish to be seen.

All of which is to say: He knew right away there was going to be trouble in Simmonsville.

It was a pleasant enough journey up to that point. They crossed Indiana, Ohio, and northwest Pennsylvania without incident. George knew the location of every Esso station along their route, so there was never a problem finding a restroom when they needed one. At their second stop, around midnight, George gave Atticus the driver's seat and crawled into the back to get some shut-eye. Letitia propped a pillow against the front passenger door and slept curled up against it, now and then kicking Atticus in the thigh as if to keep him from nodding off at the wheel.

By sunup they were in Erie, Pennsylvania. They had a hot breakfast at Egg Benedict's, a café recommended by the *Guide*—a recommendation George reaffirmed, jotting an entry in a pocket notebook. Afterwards Letitia insisted on taking a turn at the wheel. The Packard was almost too big for her—she had to scoot forward to reach the pedals—but she handled it just fine, though her heavy foot on the gas made George nervous. Atticus, dozing in back, heard his uncle urging her to slow down, slow down, no need to give the highway patrol any excuses. But Letitia told him not to worry, it was Sunday, and Jesus surely wouldn't let anything happen to her until she'd had a chance to make up for missing church. George was still trying to answer that logic when Atticus fell asleep.

When he woke they were at a truck stop in Auburn, New York. George went to refill the canteens and Letitia took an apple from the grocery bag and got out to stretch her legs. Atticus, without thinking about it, grabbed a banana.

He was standing beside the Packard rubbing sleep from his eyes when he heard laughter coming from over by the diesel pumps. A truck driver and one of the pump jockeys were grinning at him and elbowing each other in the ribs. Atticus looked at the half-eaten banana in his hand and felt his face get hot. For roughly the millionth time in his life he asked himself, Is there any way I can just ignore this and get on with my day? and he reflected that it was the minor slights that were the hardest to let pass. Then the jockey began thumping his chest and hooting like an ape, and Atticus tossed the banana aside and put up his fists.

But before he could step to, a pyramid of oil cans stacked by the pumps collapsed with a crash. The jockey dropped his gorilla act and ran to stop the cans rolling every which way. One got under his foot and he slipped, taking a hard pratfall. The truck driver burst out in fresh laughter and several other customers joined in. Atticus didn't laugh, but he decided to consider the insult paid. He lowered his hands and turned away and saw Letitia strolling back towards the car, no longer holding her apple.

They got under way again. Atticus drove and Letitia lay in back with her chin propped in her hands, looking pleased with herself. George, reviewing his travel notes, said that he wanted to stop in Simmonsville for lunch. "There's a restaurant there called Lydia's that I got a good report on. As long as we're passing by I thought we'd check it out."

"Where is this?" Atticus asked. George showed him on the map: Simmonsville was a flyspeck in the dairylands south of Utica, a region that, in Horace's atlas, would probably have been populated by cattle-devouring trolls who picked their teeth with the bones of unwary motorists. "You really want to stop in the middle of farm country? Why don't we just keep going till we hit Albany?"

"No, I hear you," George said, "but the guy I got the tip from said the woman who owned the place couldn't have been friendlier. Told him to come back anytime."

It took them another hour and a half to get there, driving east on the state highway that was sometimes four lanes but more often two. Along one of the two-lane stretches they saw a billboard announcing the upcoming grand opening of the New York State Thruway. The announcement was illustrated with a cartoon of a white family literally flying to their destination in a bubble-top hover car. "Look, George," Atticus said. "It's the future."

At the Simmonsville junction a volunteer firehouse had been erected between the two road branches. A shirtless blond muscleman in tan canvas pants with gray suspenders sat on a bleached wood chair out front, soaking up the sun and puffing on a cigarette. He watched the approaching Packard with interest, eyes narrowing when it chose the road into Simmonsville.

"It's a red brick building," George said, focused on his notes. "Should be on the left-hand side, on the far end of town." Atticus, who'd caught the fireman's look and read the message there, said nothing, only watched in the side mirror until the firehouse was out of sight behind them.

The road ran south past scattered houses before curving east onto an abbreviated main street with half a dozen shops. The shops were all closed and the street was deserted except for a kid on a bicycle doing lazy figure eights in front of a feed store. Next to the feed store was a vacant lot with a fence thrown up around it to form a small paddock. A big brown mare stood forlornly inside, flicking its tail at the cloud of flies that rose from the dust.

Beyond the paddock was an uninviting pile of whitewashed brick with SIMMONSVILLE DINETTE hand-painted on the plate glass window. "That must be it," George said.

Atticus eased the car to a stop but kept it idling. "I thought you said it was called Lydia's."

"It's the only brick building," George observed. "And it's in the right place." He gestured at the road ahead, which ran on between open fields. "End of town."

"I don't know, George. I don't like the looks of this."

"Ah, come on. You know better than to judge a book by its cover."

"A book can't refuse you service," Atticus noted. "Or spit in your water glass."

But George was insistent, so against his better judgment Atticus pulled into the gravel lot on the east side of the building. He parked the Packard facing outward and left the key in the ignition, just in case.

The dinette was small, just a few tables and a counter with a grill top in back. There was only one customer, a man in a porkpie hat who sat at the counter, mopping gravy off a plate with a crust of bread. He looked around as they came in, his eyes turning to slits in a fair imitation of the fireman. The teenaged boy behind the counter had the opposite reaction, his eyes going wide as if George, Atticus, and Letitia were Green Martians who'd teleported in from Barsoom. This look of startlement lasted for all of a second before being replaced by a mask of poorly feigned indifference: the white man's double take.

"Hello there," George said, with an exaggerated friendliness meant to stress that they came in peace. "We're just driving by today, and we thought—"

The customer slammed his hand down on the counter, making his plate and the counterboy jump. He stood up, adjusted his hat, and made for the door, looking as though he might steamroll Letitia, who was in his way. But she stood her ground and at the last moment he sidestepped, only brushing her shoulder as he went past and out.

"So," George said to the counterboy as if nothing had happened, "do we just seat ourselves?" The counterboy blinked and his Adam's apple bobbed up and down, which George chose to interpret as a yes; he took a chair at the table nearest the door.

"George," Atticus began, then sighed and sat down too.

Letitia remained standing, flicking something invisible off her shoulder. "I'm going to use the ladies'," she announced. She headed into the back of the dinette, even as the boy came out from behind the counter carrying menus. He did a little dance to keep from colliding with her, knocking over a napkin dispenser with one flailing arm.

"So what's good?" George asked, picking up the menu that the counterboy dropped in front of him. "What do you recommend?" The boy just blinked and swallowed; Atticus was beginning to wonder if there was something wrong with him beyond the usual. "Tell you what," George said. "Why don't we start with some coffee?"

Looking both relieved and freshly startled, the boy retreated behind the counter. He set up cups and saucers and was reaching for the coffeepot when a phone rang. The boy turned towards the sound, paused, and turned back towards the pot. The phone rang again and he repeated his two-step of indecision, this time managing to somehow sweep the cups onto the floor. He stepped back from the shattering of crockery, threw up his hands, and on the third ring went running into the back. Atticus watched him go. He heard the phone being picked up and heard the boy say softly, "Hello?" So at least he wasn't a mute.

Atticus looked at George. "You got a good report on this place, huh?"

"It was from a few months ago," George said, shrugging. "Obviously the place is under new management, or something."

"You think so?"

"Yeah, OK, but we're here now."

"Doesn't mean we have to stay. We get back in the car, we could be in Albany in ninety minutes."

"Nah, we're here, let's just order."

"George—"

"We're *here*," George said. "And we have every right to be. I'm a citizen. You're a citizen—and a veteran, for God's sake. Our money spends as good as anyone else's."

"I hear you. But this citizen likes to get value for his money, and if the food here is anything like the service—"

"Hey, that other guy cleaned his plate . . . Anyway, I'm hungry. Let's give the nervous kid a chance."

But the nervous kid was taking his time coming back. For that matter, so was Letitia. Growing restless, Atticus leaned back in his chair and stretched. His knuckles brushed the wall, and he noticed that the dinette's interior brick was coated with the same whitewash as the exterior. He looked up: The ceiling was bright new wood, unpainted, except for two rough support beams, thick as phone poles, that were slathered in white. He checked the floor, next: new linoleum, inexpertly laid down.

"Hey George," Atticus said.

"Yeah?"

"You remember that time when I was little and you and me and Pop took that trip to Washington, D.C.?"

"Sure, of course I do. That's where I first met Hippolyta, remember? But what makes you think of that now?"

Looking at the wall again, Atticus repeated a trivia question from that long-ago road trip: "Why is the White House white?"

"War of 1812," George said. "British soldiers put the executive mansion to the torch. Then later when the slaves rebuilt it, they had to paint the walls white to cover up the . . ."

". . . the burn marks," Atticus finished for him, as the fire truck pulled up in front of the dinette. The man with the gray suspenders was driving; another fireman and the customer in the porkpie hat were in the cab with him, and two more men were riding on the sides of the rig.

George slid his chair away from the table. "Back door?" he suggested.

"Might be better to make a stand here, take them one at a time as they come in," Atticus said.

The firemen formed a skirmish line beside their vehicle. Gray Suspenders was armed with a fire ax and one of the other men had a baseball bat. But before they could rush the dinette, something caused them all to turn and look back the way they'd come. They stood motionless for a moment, and then the man with the bat walked west out of view. Another man followed him, and another, and finally the guy in the porkpie hat, leaving only Gray Suspenders beside the truck with his ax lowered and his arms spread in a gesture of dismay.

Atticus and George were leaning towards the window trying to see what was going on when Letitia returned at long last from the ladies' room, moving calmly but swiftly. Her forehead was beaded with sweat and there was dust in her hair. "Time to go," she said.

She didn't need to say it twice. They slipped out the front door and ran for the car, George and Atticus both glancing over their shoulders at the mare now loose in the street, rearing up kicking at the men who surrounded it. The man with the bat stepped too close and took a hoof in the ribs.

George yanked open the passenger door and slid across the front seat to the driver's side, Letitia and Atticus piling in after him. Atticus was pulling the door shut again when Gray Suspenders belatedly noted their departure and let out a shout. George gunned the motor and drove out of the lot in a spray of gravel.

They sped east through the fields. While George kept an eye on the rearview, Atticus threw a questioning glance at Letitia. "The counterboy ran out the back," she explained. "But before he did, I overheard him on the phone talking about these scary Negroes who'd taken over the restaurant. I thought we might need a diversion."

"We may need another one," George said. The fire truck was chasing them. George gripped the wheel and gave the Packard more gas. "Letitia, honey," he said, "would you do me a favor and reach, real careful, under my seat?"

The gun was a .45 Colt revolver, reassuringly large. Atticus nodded. "I was hoping that was on the checklist," he said. He held out a hand, but before turning the revolver over to him Letitia swung out the cylinder, verified that all six chambers were loaded, and snapped it closed again.

"Try not to kill anyone," George said. "But see if you can get these fools to back off."

"I'll do my best," Atticus said. He gave Letitia another look, then took the gun and turned to roll down his window.

A shiny blur caught his eye. Across the narrowing field to their right was another road, and a silver car with smoked windows was racing along it, running neck-and-neck with the Packard.

"George," Atticus said.

"I see it," George said. The two roads converged at a crossing up ahead, but with the fire truck coming up behind them he couldn't slow down. Instead he pressed the accelerator all the way to the floor and laid on the horn.

The silver car sped up too.

Atticus thumbed back the hammer on the Colt and fired a warning shot high across the field. This brought no reaction from the silver car, but as the gun's report faded away there was a second, thinner pistol crack from behind them. Porkpie Hat was leaning out of the fire truck, holding his lid on with one hand and aiming a snub-nosed revolver with the other.

"Hell," George said. Letitia shut her eyes and whispered urgently to the Lord. Atticus leveled the Colt at the silver car.

At the last second, the silver car gave way. The Packard roared through the crossing and the silver car cut in behind it with a squeal of brakes, skidding to a halt directly in the path of the fire truck. The truck bore down on it, horn and siren merging into one long bray.

The truck swerved. To Atticus looking back it seemed that it swerved too late, but in the instant before impact the whole vehicle jolted sideways as though some external force had given it a shove. It missed the silver car by a hand's breadth, then cut back across the road, out of control, and crashed through a fence into another field. He glimpsed a fireman catapulting through the air even as the truck was swallowed by a great billowing cloud of dust.

The silver car remained in the crossroads. In a moment it too had disappeared behind the dust blowing across the road, but before it did, Atticus saw it flash its headlights, just once, as though it were winking at him.

A childhood bout with polio had left Letitia's brother, Marvin, with a withered left arm, but he insisted on carrying her bag inside for her. The little house smelled pleasantly of a stew that had been simmering since noon, and hot bread, fresh out of the oven. Within minutes of their arrival they were seated around the kitchen table, saying grace, and the first taste of the food lifted their spirits so much that when Marvin asked how their trip had gone, they all burst out laughing.

They told him the story of their adventure in Simmonsville, George and Atticus both praising Letitia for her cleverness in releasing the mare. "Like having our own Indian scout," George said. "And a lucky thing, too."

"Now, now," said Letitia, blushing.

But by unspoken agreement, they did not mention the silver car or the wreck of the fire truck. And Atticus, knowing his and George's journey wasn't over, never fully relaxed. When Marvin brought out dessert—homemade blueberry pie and vanilla ice cream, every mouthful of which sapped the will for further travel—Atticus began casting glances at the clock on the wall. It was already after four.

Marvin took the hint. Leaving his own pie and ice cream unfinished, he went into another room and came back with a notepad. "So I did that research you asked," he said. "I'd heard stories about Devon County before, but I never realized just how strange a place it is." Consulting his notes: "The county seat, Bideford, is named for a town in England where they held one of the country's last witch trials. That was in 1682—a woman named Temperance Lloyd was convicted of having intercourse with the devil, who appeared to her in the form of a black man. They hanged her, along with two other women."

George raised an eyebrow. "You're not saying Bideford, Massachusetts, was founded by witches, are you?"

"More like the witch hunters. A number of the families who settled Bideford in 1731 were related to the prosecutors in the Temperance Lloyd case—and proud of it. The town developed a reputation for being unusually backward-looking, even by eighteenth-century standards. During the War of Independence, the citizens of Bideford sided with King George, and in 1795, the mayor of Bideford was arrested by the state militia for continuing to hold slaves more than a decade after the Massachusetts Supreme Court declared slavery unconstitutional. Then a few years after that, the state tried to consolidate Devon County into Worcester County. Most of Devon went along, but Bideford and three other neighboring towns refused to be assimilated, and eventually the legislature threw up its hands and decided to let them be. Ever since, it's been like the land time forgot—inbred, insular, clinging to the past tooth and nail."

"And they don't like Negroes," Atticus said.

"They don't like outsiders, period," said Marvin. "But yeah. I found a lot of stories in our news morgue about travelers getting attacked in Devon. Lot of missing person reports, too." He looked at George. "That stretch of highway your friend Victor was on? Not a healthy place for a colored man to be driving, day or night."

"What about Ardham?" George said.

"Ardham's more of a mystery. It was settled around the same time as Bideford, but none of the local histories say by who, or who lives there now. I couldn't find any news clippings on it at all. I was going to call the registry of deeds and see about property records, but they aren't open on weekends and I have a feeling the Bideford office might not be all that helpful anyway."

"Never mind the property records," said Atticus. "Can you tell us how to get there?"

"I think so. Here, reach me that map tube from up on the refrigerator."

They cleared the dishes and unrolled the map of Devon County on the table. The centers of Devon's four towns formed a rough box around a forest called the Sabbath Kingdom Wood, with Bideford at the southwest corner. The unincorporated community of Ardham was a fifth point near the top of the map; it was nestled in a small open area bounded on the north by nameless hills and on the south by the Connecticut River tributary, identified here as the Shadowbrook. A bridge crossed from Ardham southeast over the water and a road led into the Wood on the far side, but within a mile the road faded out, as though the mapmaker's pen had run dry. Seven or eight miles to the southwest, it reappeared, crossing Torridge Creek into Bideford.

"This is the most detailed map I could find," Marvin said. "Most don't even hint at a road through the forest, but it exists. It's unpaved, and it loops and branches and dead-ends, but it's drivable, and it will get you to Ardham eventually. Or so I'm told."

"Told by who?" Atticus said.

"A friend at the state census bureau. Devon County's reputation being what it is, I thought he might have some stories, so I called him at home this afternoon. Turns out he'd spoken with the census taker who visited Ardham in 1950. It was kind of a to-do: On his first try, the census taker turned back halfway through the woods because he thought he was being stalked by a grizzly bear. He came back a week later with a park ranger from Mount Holyoke."

"Did he say what Ardham was like?"

"The census taker compared it to a medieval farm village. Big manor house up on the hillside, cottages and fields down by the water. Pretty as a postcard, but the residents weren't any friendlier than the people in Bideford. At the manor, no one would come to the door, and the folks in the cottages threw rocks at the car."

"Well," said George. "I'm sure Montrose will have them won over by the time we get there."

"What about that sheriff?" Atticus asked.

"Oh, yeah." Marvin flipped open his pad again. "Eustace Hunt—he's only been sheriff a few years, but the NAACP's got a thick complaint file on him. Forty-five years old, unmarried, former Marine drill sergeant from North Carolina. He moved to Bideford after he was discharged."

"I thought they didn't like outsiders."

"He's a special case, sort of a prodigal son. The Hunts were one of Bideford's founding families, but in 1861 a bunch of them got secession fever and went south to sign up with General Lee. Sheriff Hunt is descended from one of the survivors of Pickett's Charge."

"And proud of it," Atticus guessed. "You sure there isn't some other way into Ardham? Like maybe a nice quiet back road over those hills from New Hampshire?"

"Not that I know of," Marvin said. "Sorry."

"So what do you want to do?" George said.

"Well, I don't know about you," said Atticus, "but I've had my fill of rednecks for one day. And from what Marvin says, it sounds like it doesn't matter whether we go before sunset or after. Either way, the sheriff's not going to be happy to see us. So maybe the smart move is not to let him see us."

"You mean go after dark?"

"I'm thinking early morning. Say we leave here around two a.m., roll through Bideford around three while the witch hunters are all sleeping. Once we get in the woods, we'll see what that road is really like, and either keep going or find a spot to hide from the grizzlies until sunup. Knock on the manor door for breakfast."

"Sure," George said, and laughed. "That'll work."

Then Letitia said: "I'm going with you."

She'd been quiet so long they'd almost forgotten she was there.

"What?" said Atticus. "No."

"Definitely not," said George.

But now Marvin was laughing. "Uh-oh!" he said. "Somebody just got a message from Jesus."

Letitia scowled at him. "Now why would you want to go and say a blasphemous thing like that? Why? And you . . ." She turned to Atticus and George. "Didn't you just get done talking about how lucky you were to have me with you today?"

"We did, and we were, and we're grateful, honey," George said. "But—"

"And didn't I tell *you* the Lord would keep me safe? You really think it's just luck you're the beneficiary of that?"

"Oh, here we go," said Marvin.

"You really think it's an accident I just *happened* to need a ride to Springfield?"

"Accident or no," Atticus said, "you don't need a ride to Ardham, and you're not getting one."

"Atticus—"

"No, Letitia. It's bad enough George and I have to go. This isn't just some racist backwater, it's . . . weird."

"All the more reason not to refuse a gift of Providence."

"'Gift of Providence,'" Marvin said. "And *I'm* the blasphemer." He started laughing again, sliding his chair back when Letitia tried to kick him under the table.

But Atticus and George weren't so easily moved.

Letitia slept in Marvin's room that night, while Marvin took the living room davenport and George and Atticus grabbed a few hours' rest on a pair of spare mattresses in the basement. George went straight to sleep, but Atticus stayed up reading till almost midnight.

When the alarm woke them at quarter to two, Marvin was already making coffee. Atticus sat in the kitchen while George went to run his checklist on the car again.

"Letitia's awake," Marvin said, unprompted. "I heard her moving around. But I don't think she's coming out to say goodbye."

"Sorry if we got your visit off on the wrong note."

"No, that's my own fault, for teasing her. She's here to borrow money from me," Marvin explained. "She hasn't said for what yet, but I know it's going to be for something the Lord wants her to do, which means He wants me to make the loan, right? Trouble is, I'm a cynic who mocks divine Providence, so I think now she's got it figured that helping you is the price God wants from her in exchange for softening my heart." He shook his head. "It was Momma who taught her to think that way. Letitia's more sincere about it than Momma was, but still, it *annoys* me . . ."

Atticus, not knowing what to say to this, drank his coffee.

"Anyway," Marvin concluded, "she'll get over it as soon as she figures another angle. God's will is flexible."

George came back in. "Ready as we'll ever be," he said.

"You want a cup before you go?" Marvin asked.

"Nah, that's OK, I don't think I'll have any trouble keeping my eyes open. And I'd rather not have to pee in the woods."

"All right, then," Marvin said. "Stay safe. Stop by on your way home and let us know you're OK." He looked at Atticus. "Letitia and I will be praying for you."

George drove. Their route north took them through white Springfield, and as they were stopped for a light near the city limits a police cruiser drove up alongside them. George kept his eyes on the road ahead and Atticus did likewise. When the light changed, the cruiser waited for them to go first and followed them to the city line. Once it was clear they were leaving town the cruiser turned back without stopping them, but given their rationale for being abroad at this hour, they couldn't help taking it as a bad omen.

"Bideford's a lot smaller than Springfield," George suggested. "Police night shift is probably just a deputy with his feet up at the station house."

"Yeah, that sounds good," said Atticus, feeling foolish. "Keep saying that."

The highway was deserted and they made good time. Around quarter to three they passed the turnoff for New Salem. George abruptly killed the headlights and pulled onto the shoulder.

"What?" said Atticus.

"Could just be the willies," George said, "but I feel like there's still someone behind us."

They sat in the dark looking back at the road junction, which was illuminated by a lamp strung on a utility pole. No other vehicles appeared. "The willies," George affirmed, not sounding terribly convinced.

A few more miles and they came to a sign announcing DEVON COUNTY. At a crossroads a few miles after that they turned onto King Street, Bideford's main thoroughfare. From Marvin's map they knew it was possible to reach the Torridge Creek bridge without passing through the town center, but they'd decided it was better to take the most direct route rather than risk getting lost on some side road.

Once again they found cause to question their reasoning. Whatever other aspects of progress the citizens of Bideford had rejected, they clearly had no problem with electricity: Floodlights on the front of the town hall, county courthouse, and several other buildings turned a two-block stretch of King Street bright as day. The intersection at the center of this bright zone featured Bideford's only traffic signal, which turned red as they approached it.

They sat waiting at the light feeling horribly exposed, even though, as on the highway, they seemed to have the road to themselves. George drummed his fingers on the wheel and nervously scanned the empty sidewalks. Atticus peered up at the darkened windows above a corner barbershop; lowering his gaze to the shop itself, he spied, taped to the inside of the glass, a faded campaign poster for the States' Rights Democratic Party, with the stern white faces of Strom Thurmond and Fielding Wright giving him the evil eye.

The traffic signal turned green. George goosed the accelerator, the squeal of the Packard's tires too loud in the three a.m. stillness. They rolled past a squat brick fort on which the words DEVON COUNTY SHERIFF'S DEPT. were illuminated by yet another floodlight, George and Atticus both shrinking down in their seats until the building was behind them.

King Street ended at the creek. They turned right onto Bank Street, a narrow lane that ran behind a pair of small factory buildings. A white man loitered by the back door of one of the factories, having a smoke. When he saw the Packard come around the corner he tossed his cigarette and stepped out into the middle of the lane, raising an arm to shield his eyes. "Wakely?" he called. "That you?" George and Atticus sat frozen as if they were the ones caught in the headlights. "Wakely?" the man called again. He came towards them, slipping a hand into his trouser pocket. "Who is that?" He started to walk around the driver's side and George goosed the accelerator again, the man crying out "Hey!" and stumbling back against the guardrail that ran along the creek bank.

They almost missed the turn onto the bridge, which was unmarked and unlit, but Atticus saw the gap in the guardrail and said, "Here." A tap of the brakes, another squeal of tires, and they were passing over the creek in a wooden tunnel. The road on the far side was blacktopped for the first dozen yards, but then like the ink trail on Marvin's map the blacktop faded out, leaving a rutted bed of dirt and stones. While rocks pelted the Packard's undercarriage, tree limbs swung out of the dark to swat the roof and windshield. "Jesus," Atticus said, but he was more relieved than not to have Bideford behind them.

The road curved sharply left and for a moment they could see the lights of King Street again, shining faintly through the tree branches. Then they turned right and went up, George hissing as the track got even rougher. But at the top of the rise, as though they'd passed a test, the road smoothed out significantly and the trees stopped pounding on the roof.

"Tell you what," George said. "After all this, Montrose had damn well better be there."

"Yeah," said Atticus. "Be funny if it turned out he was in Ardham, Minnesota, wouldn't it?"

They rounded another sharp bend and saw a barrier up ahead: a barred metal gate between stone posts with a sign reading PRIVATE. George eased to a stop in front of it. By the headlights they could see that the gate wasn't chained or padlocked. A simple lift-latch secured it.

They sat in the car, listening for grizzlies. And shoggoths.

"I'll flip you for it," George said finally.

"No, that's OK, I'll get it," said Atticus. He added, laughing, as he reached for the door handle: "You were right about the coffee."

A fury of light and sound engulfed them. The patrol car had been hiding in the trees back at the bend and had crept up from behind even as they sat listening. The sudden stab of its high beams served as a signal to the men in the bushes beside the gate; they ran up on the

Packard in a pincer movement, using the butts of their guns to smash in the side windows. Atticus recoiled from the spray of glass. George bent forward and was about to reach under the seat when a stronger instinct of self-preservation forced him back; he thrust his hands in the air even as a shotgun muzzle floated into view outside his shattered window.

The next few moments unfolded with a grim familiarity: They were ordered from the car; struck; screamed at; searched; struck again; and finally marched to the back of the Packard and made to sit on the rear bumper with their hands behind their heads and their feet crossed in front of them.

Sheriff Eustace Hunt stepped in front of the patrol car's headlights like a malevolent body eclipsing a sun. His two deputies, lesser satellites, orbited into view beside him. All three lawmen had shotguns, the sheriff's double-barreled, and Atticus noted they were careful to stand back, out of reach of any desperate lunges.

"What did I tell you, Eastchurch?" the sheriff said, addressing the deputy on his left. "Sometimes you can just feel it: someone who doesn't belong, trying to sneak in the back door when they think you aren't paying attention."

"Yeah, but you'd said they'd be gypsies, Sheriff," the deputy replied.

"We-e-ell, that was a little poetic license," the sheriff said. "Nothing wrong with that, as long as you're correct on the main point." Nodding at the license plate: "They are travelers, that's for sure."

"Unless the car's stolen," offered the second deputy.

"Well now, that's a fair point, Talbot . . . What about it, boys?" the sheriff asked George and Atticus. "You really from Illinois? Or are you just a couple of car thieves from Worcester?"

"Sheriff," George said, and then fell silent, eying the guns.

"Go on," the sheriff said. "We're all dying to hear it, really."

George shook his head slowly. "I don't know who you're lying in wait for here, Sheriff, but you're making— This is a misunderstanding."

The sheriff chuckled. "You hear that, Eastchurch?" he said. "The way he caught himself, there? He was going to say I was making a mistake, but if he says that, he's a Negro telling a good white Christian man that he's wrong, and you know that never ends well. Pointing out a misunderstanding, though, that's just being polite, like letting me know I dropped something . . . I think I like this one, Eastchurch. He's smart."

"Not that smart," opined the deputy.

"We do what we can within the limits God has set for us," the sheriff said. "I'm smart, too," he told George. "I'll prove it, by predicting what you're going to say next: You're going to tell me you don't know anything about a burglary in Bideford last night, or two other burglaries in Bucks Mill last week. And when I ask you about the campfire John Wakely saw burning in these woods on Friday, you're going to say, 'What campfire, Sheriff? Do we look like Boy Scouts?'" His good humor dissipating, he continued: "You got greedy. Your real mistake was coming to Devon County at all, but if you'd stopped with Bucks Mill, you might have got away with it. My other deputy, Coleman, he had me halfway convinced it was local kids who were doing the robberies—in fact he's over in Instow tonight, on his own stakeout. He's going to be sorry when he hears he missed out on the fun."

"Sheriff Hunt," Atticus said. All three shotguns were suddenly pointed at his head, but he took a breath and continued speaking in a calm voice: "My uncle George is right, Sheriff Hunt. This is a misunderstanding. We aren't burglars. You can go ahead and check the car for stolen goods, if—"

"Eastchurch," the sheriff said.

"Yeah, Sheriff?"

"Tell me I didn't just hear that. Did this nigger just give me *permission* to search his car?"

"I believe he might have, Sheriff."

The sheriff shook his head in disbelief. "This one," he said, "I don't like."

But Atticus went on, unwavering: "We aren't burglars, Sheriff. Or car thieves, either. We're guests."

"Guests?" The sheriff barked laughter. "In *my* woods? I don't think so."

"Guests of Ardham," Atticus said. "I'm sorry if we're trespassing on your territory, here, but we were invited, and we don't know any other way to go."

"Ardham!" More laughter. "Boy, you are a lousy liar. I've heard some odd things about that commune out there, but if you think they'd extend a welcome to the likes of *you* . . . Well, let's just say you should take that alibi back for a refund."

"It's the truth, Sheriff. We were invited to the manor house in Ardham. The big house, up on the hill. We're expected."

"Sure you are. And who is it that's expecting you, exactly?"

"Montrose Turner."

The sheriff clucked his tongue. "Now see that, right there, is a basic failure of research. You take the trouble to learn *my* name—which is telling—but if you'd really done your homework, you'd know the only Turners around here are Andrew and Grace Turner, over in Instow."

"Montrose Turner is my father," Atticus said. "He's staying at the manor house in Ardham. He asked us to meet him there."

"But he didn't tell you who you'd be guests of," the sheriff said. "That's funny. Where I come from, if you stay at a man's house, you know that man's name, even if someone else does the inviting. Maybe you do things differently in Illinois."

"Sheriff—"

"Or maybe, company you keep, you're used to even stupid lies being believed."

"You don't have to believe us, Sheriff," Atticus said. "Just take us to Ardham."

"Just take you there. Three in the morning, just go knocking on doors."

"The hour won't matter. We're expected."

"You're sure of that, are you?"

"Positive," said Atticus, actually managing to sound as if he was.

"All right then," the sheriff said nodding. "We'll go to Ardham."

Atticus and George both sat very still, waiting for the catch.

"Yeah, we'll go to Ardham," the sheriff continued. "The thing is, though, it can be a tricky drive. You've seen how the road twists and turns, and it gets worse past this gate. The good news is, I know a shortcut. Through there." The sheriff nodded at the darkness beside the road. "Talbot, get us a flashlight, would you? We're going for a stroll in the woods, and I wouldn't want anybody walking into a tree by accident."

"Sure, Sheriff." The deputy ducked back to the patrol car.

The sheriff gestured with his shotgun. "You boys stand up slowly now," he said. "Keep your hands behind your heads."

"Sheriff," said Atticus.

"Hold on a second," said George.

"Stand up," the sheriff repeated. "Or I'll take you to Ardham right here."

"**K**eep that light steady, Talbot," the sheriff said. "The young one's thinking about running, and I don't want to have to strain my eyes when I blow a hole through his back."

From the moment they'd left the road, Atticus had been watching for some sort of cover that he and George could dive behind and so survive the first volley that would accompany any attempt to escape. But either the sheriff really did know these woods or the Wood itself was conspiring against them: The ground they walked on was level, with only light undergrowth, and the trees, which earlier had crowded so close beside the road, were sparse enough here to offer only minimal protection. Even so, on his own he would already have made a break for it. Now, reckoning they had only a few more steps before being ordered to their knees and shot, he tried to catch George's eye without turning his head: If they broke and ran at the same time, one of them might make it.

"Don't try it, boy," the sheriff said. "I know what you're thinking, but I used to shoot skeet down at Camp Lejeune. The two of you could run opposite ways and I'd still hit you both without reloading. I—"

The sound came from up ahead, just beyond the range of the light: a sudden sharp *crack!* like a rifle shot or a thick branch breaking, followed by a heavy thump in the undergrowth. Atticus, George, and the three lawmen all stopped and the flashlight beam wavered.

"Keep that light *steady*, Talbot," the sheriff commanded. Out in the darkness, a big something slid or was dragged along the ground. They heard the snap of another branch, and another, and then the prolonged groan of an entire tree being shoved over. A crash.

BOOM!

The shotgun blast was louder than all of the sounds that had preceded it. George staggered and dropped to his knees. Atticus let out a strangled cry and dropped down beside him, throwing arms around him and feeling for the wound. But George shook his head: He wasn't shot, just rubber-legged with fear.

Atticus looked around. The sheriff had pivoted slightly to the left and was aiming his shotgun out into the woods, smoke curling from one of the barrels. Deputy Talbot pointed the flashlight in the same direction. But Eastchurch still held his gun steady on Atticus and George.

The sheriff called into the darkness: "These are *my* woods, understand? Man or beast, you'd better get your ass away from here!" He fired off his second barrel and George jolted in Atticus's arms.

A stillness fell. The sheriff broke his shotgun and reloaded, then stood listening. From the woods came only silence now: the tree-feller, man or beast, either dead or playing dead.

"All right," the sheriff said. "Where were we?"

Atticus spoke softly to his uncle: "Come on, George. Get up."

"No, that's OK, you boys stay down," said the sheriff. "I think we've walked far enough. Time to finish this up. Unless," he added, "you'd like to talk about those burglaries now."

The new sound came from the road behind them: a soft *whump!* of ignition accompanied by a blossom of flame. By the time the sheriff and his deputies turned to look, the blossom had become a blazing pyre with a car-shaped silhouette.

"The hell?" Deputy Talbot said.

Sheriff Hunt locked eyes with Atticus. "Boy," he said. "Did you neglect to mention something?"

A car horn sounded. The Packard's horn, Atticus thought. Which would make the sheriff's car the burnt offering.

"Eastchurch," the sheriff said, "you come with me. Talbot, you stay here. If they do *anything*, you put them down." The sheriff hesitated, as if debating whether to preemptively carry out the last part of that order himself. Then the Packard's horn sounded again, and he spun on his heel and ran back towards the road, with Eastchurch following a few steps behind.

Atticus turned his head to face George, who nodded meaningfully. He looked down: A thick tree branch lay on the ground just in front of George's knees.

Atticus turned his head again until he could see Deputy Talbot out of the corner of his eye. The deputy was standing about six feet away, with his shotgun in one hand and the flashlight in the other. The gun was pointed roughly in Atticus and George's direction, but the muzzle had dipped towards the ground. Meanwhile the flashlight beam, like the deputy's attention, was wandering: He shined it at the retreating figures of the sheriff and Eastchurch, then back at Atticus and George, then out into the woods where they'd heard the tree go down.

Atticus took his hand off George's chest and reached for the branch. He gripped it tightly and readied himself, waiting until the flashlight beam had begun to move away again. Pushing off George, he sprang up, stepped back, and spun around, swinging the branch in a vicious arc, putting everything he had into it.

The branch passed through empty air. Atticus stumbled and nearly fell down again. He stood teetering above the flashlight, which now lay on the ground. Holding the branch with both hands he looked around wildly for the deputy, expecting at any instant to be shot. But the deputy was gone.

The hell? Atticus thought.

Then he heard it. Out in the Wood, straight ahead and much closer than before: The beast. Definitely beast, he told himself, and big—big enough to knock down trees, or yank unwary deputies off their feet—but stealthy now, making just enough noise as it moved through the undergrowth to let Atticus know it was there.

It was moving away from him. He bent down and scooped up the flashlight, fumbling it; by the time he had it steady the beast was already beyond the range of the beam. Circling towards the road.

"Atticus," George said. "Help me up." Atticus went to him and slung an arm around his shoulders. As they were getting to their feet, the light from the fire dimmed, briefly, a big blur of shadow passing between them and it.

In the distance, Sheriff Hunt called out: "Eastchurch? . . . Where the hell are you?"

A long pause. Then a shotgun went off. Atticus and George both saw the muzzle flash. It looked like it was out on the road, the gun firing straight up into the air.

Then stillness, broken only by the crackle and hiss of the flames.

Atticus and George exchanged glances. George sighed and shrugged. Atticus turned off the flashlight and led the way back towards the road, trying to move silently.

They were almost there when Atticus's foot kicked something hard. A shotgun. Single-barreled. He crouched down and looked around for some other trace of Deputy Eastchurch, and wasn't really surprised when he didn't find one. He passed the flashlight to George and picked up the gun and continued to the road.

The patrol car was now an anonymous blackened hulk pushing flames and smoke into the air. The Packard's rear hatch and tailgate were open, and by the flickering firelight Atticus could see that the blankets on the mattress in back had been shoved to one side.

Sheriff Hunt lay belly-down on the ground directly behind the station wagon, bleeding from a gash on the back of his head. Lying beside him, bloodied and dented, was the emergency gas can with which he'd been cold-cocked.

"Letitia?" Atticus called softly, and she came out of the shadows on the far side of the road, holding the sheriff's shotgun.

"What happened to the other two?" she said.

"Grizzly bear ate them," Atticus replied, trying not to dwell on the next question: Why them and not us?

The patrol car coughed out a fresh ball of flame. "Hell," George said. The heat was intense, and it was something of a marvel that the Packard hadn't caught fire too. "We've got to get out of here."

While he ran to the front of the station wagon, Letitia and Atticus faced each other over the prone body of the sheriff. Letitia was smiling, self-satisfied. "I told you God sent me along for a reason," she said.

Atticus glanced back into the Wood, thinking: I don't think it's God that saved us.

George had the gate open and was standing by the driver's door. "Come on!" he called to them. "Let's go!"

Letitia put the sheriff's shotgun into the back of the Packard. Atticus picked up the gas can—still half full—and stowed it in back as well. Then, while Letitia ran around to the passenger's side and climbed in the front seat, he stood over the sheriff, holding Deputy Eastchurch's shotgun, and asked himself another question.

"Atticus!" George said. "Come on!"

"Hell with it," Atticus said. He slid the shotgun into the Packard beside the other one and climbed in after it. George started the engine.

Atticus had pulled the tailgate shut and was about to close the hatch when he saw the other car. It was back at the bend in the road, its engine and headlights off, only visible because of the flames from the burning wreck reflecting off its silver skin.

George stepped on the gas. Atticus lost his balance and nearly tumbled out over the tailgate. By the time he'd caught himself they'd already started around another curve and the only thing visible was the fading flicker of the fire. In another moment, that was gone too.

Atticus opened his eyes to gray light and morning mist. He sat up stiffly, feeling broken bits of glass on the seat beneath him. George was asleep behind the wheel, head tipped back and snoring, and Letitia lay in back wrapped in a blanket.

Atticus opened his door and got out. The Packard was parked beneath a circle of trees, screened from the road by a tall stand of bushes. Opposite the direction of the road he heard the sound of flowing water. He moved towards it carefully, and pushing through another screen of foliage found himself atop a steep embankment. The stream below was rocky and shallow by the bank but deepened swiftly to a dark central channel.

Across the water, still half-shrouded in mist, was the farm village described by the census taker. The Shadowbrook curved like a moat around Ardham's fields, which were divided into plots by low stone walls. The plot directly across from where Atticus stood lay fallow; a herd of goats was grazing on the wild grasses and shoots that grew there. Off to the right in the middle distance, Atticus could see a bridge connecting the Shadowbrook's two banks.

North beyond the fields the land rose up to another, higher tier of open ground that held white-walled cottages and, to the left, a group of larger buildings including a steepled church. Higher still, overlooking all else, was the looming pale shape of the manor. Its outline was hazy and indistinct in the mist, but Atticus could see lights shining in several windows.

There were lights in some of the cottages too, though not as bright. A man came out of one of them and walked down to the fallow field carrying a stool and two metal pails; the goats heard him coming and ran to meet him. Then came a splash off to the left and Atticus saw a woman dipping a wooden bucket into the stream. The woman was close enough that he could have called to her, but like the goatherd she was white, so instead he did a quiet fade back behind the bushes.

A hand came down on his shoulder. George. Atticus put a finger to his lips and said softly, "Looks like we found it." He spread the branches so that George could peer out.

"Looks like we did," George said, not sounding enthusiastic. He pulled back, frowning, turned towards the car, then finally looked at Atticus again. "Can I ask you something?"

"You want to know how we got here?" Atticus thought about it. He remembered driving away from the burning patrol car, remembered a seemingly endless and increasingly dreamlike journey through the dark Wood . . . And remembered waking, moments ago, to gray light and mist.

"I don't know," Atticus said, to George's frown. "I was going to ask you."

They all sat up front, George driving, Letitia in the middle, and Atticus on the passenger's side holding the revolver in his lap.

The bridge into Ardham was an arch of moss-covered stone. Iron posts topped with hooks had been set along the sides at intervals. Atticus assumed these were for hanging lights of some kind, though he couldn't help contemplating other potential uses, particularly for the posts at the center of the span that offered the longest drop. George, perhaps thinking along similar lines, drove quickly to the far side, then had to slam on the brakes when a white man stepped into the Packard's path.

The man, who carried a rudimentary fishing pole and a pail full of still-twitching trout, regarded them through the windshield. They waited to see whether he would curse, or yell for help, or reach for a stone, or just swing the pail. In the end he did none of those things, but instead bowed his head, as though in apology, and stepped back to give them the right of way. George was so surprised by this that at first he could only stare, but the fisherman waited patiently, eyes downcast, for him to get the car in gear.

They drove on. The road forked, one branch leading west among the cottages and the other continuing uphill. They went up. At the top of the incline the road, now graded with crushed gravel, became a curved drive in front of the manor house.

The manor, built of pale gray stone, consisted of a central flat-topped structure three stories high, flanked by two two-story wings under roofs of angled slate. Most of the windows in the wings were dark, but those in the center structure were alight, and Atticus glimpsed a figure on the third floor looking out.

George pulled up to the manor's front entrance. To their left on the grassy ellipse encircled by the drive, bracketed by a pair of iron benches, was an icon from Horace's maps: a sundial atop a pedestal. They spared it a brief glance, but their attention was drawn inevitably to the silver car parked farther along the drive in front of the west wing. Dew beaded its hood and the opaque curve of its windshield.

"Well," Atticus said. "I guess we'd better knock and see what's for breakfast." He put the revolver in the Packard's glove compartment and got out.

The space above the manor's double doors was decorated, in silver, with a half sun peeking over a horizon. Smaller half suns were fixed to the doors themselves, serving as back plates for the door knockers. Atticus mounted the front steps and reached for the knocker on the right, but before he could grab hold of it the door swung inward.

A ginger-haired man in a butler's uniform appeared on the threshold. He was extraordinarily pale—practically an albino—but his gaze was unflinching, and the smile he gave Atticus was immediate and unforced.

"Mr. Turner, I presume," the man said. "Welcome to the Ardham lodge, sir."

"**M**y name is William," the man told them. "I was asked to look out for you, Mr. Turner, and see that you and any companions you might have are made comfortable." He turned to George. "You'd be Mr. Berry, perhaps? The elder Mr. Turner's half-brother?"

"Yeah, I'm Montrose's brother," George said.

William nodded. "Mr. Turner thought you might come as well. And you, Miss . . . ?"

"Dandridge," Letitia said.

"She's a friend of the family," Atticus said. "A good friend."

"A welcome guest, then," William assured him.

"And who is it we're guests of, exactly?"

"Mr. Samuel Braithwhite." William spread his hands in a gesture that encompassed more than just the building in whose doorway he stood. "This is Mr. Braithwhite's vacation home."

"Mr. Braithwhite," Atticus said slowly, as if testing the feel of the name on his tongue. "And would that"—he pointed at the silver car—"happen to belong to Mr. Braithwhite as well?"

"The Daimler? Yes, sir. A custom model, specially commissioned by Mr. Braithwhite. It's a fierce machine, isn't it?"

"Very," said Atticus. Then: "I appreciate you welcoming us, William, but I'm anxious to see my father. Can you take us to him?"

"I'm sorry, sir, but I'm afraid he's not here. Mr. Turner and Mr. Braithwhite drove to Boston yesterday afternoon to meet with Mr. Braithwhite's lawyer."

"They drove to Boston? I thought you said that was Mr. Braithwhite's car."

"Mr. Braithwhite has many cars, sir," William replied. "Now, if you'd like to come inside, I can show you to the rooms where you'll be staying. Don't worry about your luggage, I'll have it brought up."

But Atticus, thinking of the sheriff behind them in the woods—or maybe back in Bideford by now, rounding up a lynch mob—made no move to enter.

"Is something wrong, sir?" William asked. Then he noticed the broken windows on the Packard. "Oh my . . . Did you run into some sort of trouble on the road?"

George laughed. "Yeah, you could say that."

"Bideford," William said. It wasn't a question. "I'm *terribly* sorry, Mr. Turner . . . Were any of you injured?"

"Not yet," Atticus said.

"Well, you needn't concern yourselves further. You're perfectly safe here."

Atticus pictured the patrol car blazing in the night. "I wouldn't be too quick to promise that."

"Oh no, Mr. Turner," William corrected him. "I *do* promise it. As Mr. Braithwhite's guests, you are under Mr. Braithwhite's protection. As long as you remain in Ardham, you needn't worry about anyone from

Bideford. The same guarantee of protection extends to your father, of course, while he's traveling with Mr. Braithwhite . . . Now please, come inside."

The entrance foyer of the lodge resembled the lobby of a rustic hotel unlikely to ever be listed in *The Safe Negro Travel Guide*. The dark-paneled walls were hung with dramatic nature scenes in which white people hunted, rode horses, or simply stood around looking awed by the landscape.

Corridors led off into the wings, and at the back of the foyer double doors opened onto a dining hall. To the left of these doors, a cubbyhole in the wall held ranks of keys on hooks; William stood before it tapping a finger against his chin.

While William debated room assignments, Atticus went to look at a painting hanging on the other side of the dining hall entrance. It was a portrait of a white man in robes, standing in an alchemist's laboratory. The man gripped a wooden staff with his right hand, and prominent on his right index finger was a silver signet ring engraved with a half-sun symbol. The man's left arm, outstretched, gestured towards a window with a view of a crowded harbor. The sky above the water was starry night, but there was a pink glow on the horizon.

"Titus Braithwhite," Atticus said, reading the brass tag on the frame.

"Ardham's founder," said William. Keys in hand, he joined Atticus in front of the portrait. "The Braithwhites made their fortune in shipping, but Titus Braithwhite had a keen interest in natural philosophy—science. Some of his more esoteric studies made his Boston neighbors uncomfortable, so he established Ardham and built the lodge as a retreat where he and his fellow philosophers could conduct their experiments in private."

"Seems like a strange choice of location," Atticus said. "Given how the people of Bideford felt about witches."

William chuckled politely. "Titus Braithwhite wasn't a witch, Mr. Turner."

"You don't need to be a witch to hang as one, though, do you?"

"No, that's true, sir. But Titus Braithwhite had an understanding with the community leaders in Bideford. Through his wealth and his political connections, he did certain favors for them, and in exchange they helped preserve his privacy. Kept away the curious. I suppose you could say he put their prejudices to good use."

"I wouldn't know about that," Atticus said. "I've never experienced prejudice as a positive thing."

"Of course, sir . . . Perhaps it was wrong of him," William conceded. "And perhaps he was punished for it. In 1795, there was a terrible fire here. The lodge was destroyed and Titus Braithwhite perished along with his associates and most of his family. The current Mr. Braithwhite is descended from a cousin who was living in Plymouth at the time of the tragedy."

"What does the current Mr. Braithwhite do? Is he still in shipping?"

"His interests are quite diversified."

"And what's his interest in me and my family, William? If you don't mind my asking."

"I don't know, sir. And it wouldn't be my place to say, in any event. I keep Mr. Braithwhite's house, not his business."

"You sure?" Atticus nodded towards the portrait. "You seem to know a lot about the family business."

"Just the history, Mr. Turner. Think of me as a tour guide—a humble one. May I show you to your rooms now?"

Stairs to the second floor were located just inside the west-wing corridor. A window on the half landing let in light from outdoors, but as in the foyer there were also electric wall sconces and ceiling lamps.

"How is it you have power out here?" Atticus asked.

"There's a generator shed out back, behind the car garage," William said. "When Mr. Braithwhite had the lodge rebuilt in the 1920s, he added a number of modern improvements. You'll have the full range of creature comforts during your stay, including hot running water."

At the top of the stairs they turned right. The center section of the lodge on this floor contained a gaming lounge, a library, and a smoking room. William gave them a brief tour of the amenities, stressing that they were welcome to use any and all of them—the one exception being that the smoking room was traditionally for men only.

"So much for no positive prejudice," Letitia muttered.

"What's on the third floor?" Atticus asked.

"That would be Mr. Braithwhite's private suite," William said. "I'm sure he'll be delighted to show it to you once he returns. In the meantime," he continued, leading them onward, "I'll be putting you in the east wing. It's quieter than the west wing, and you'll have it all to yourselves, so Mr. Braithwhite's other guests shouldn't disturb you."

"You have other people staying here?"

"Not yet, sir. But Mr. Braithwhite has called a gathering of the other lodge members. I expect them to begin arriving shortly."

"You expect them," Atticus said, "but you don't actually know what the gathering is about."

"You catch on quickly, Mr. Turner."

William led them down the east-wing corridor, stopping at the third door on the right. "This will be your room, Mr. Turner," he said, fitting a key in the lock. "It forms a double suite with the one next door, where we'll put Mr. Berry."

As he came through the door, Atticus's eye went first to the king-size bed, its massive headboard carved with yet another scene of white people doing things outdoors. Against the right-hand wall was a wardrobe, itself large enough to have contained a fold-down bed. The left side of the room was arranged as a sitting area, with wingback chairs, a fireplace, a minibar in a glass cabinet, and a writing desk that faced a wide and many-paned window.

"Cozy," Atticus said. Coming farther into the room and turning around, he discovered the bookcases that lined the walls beside the doorway.

William walked around the bed to another door, next to the wardrobe. "Your bathroom is in here, Mr. Turner. There's a full selection of toiletries, but should you need anything you don't see, please don't hesitate to ask. Also, I don't know what clothes you've brought, but if you'd like to dress for dinner, you'll find some spare suits in here." He indicated the wardrobe. "Dinner is served in the downstairs hall at eight p.m.," he continued, coming back around to the sitting area. "Lunch is at one, and breakfast is available from six to nine. But you can also have food brought to your room at any time, day or night." He touched the handset of an antique phone on the writing desk. "Just dial zero and you'll be connected with a member of the staff."

"What if I want to make an outgoing call?"

"I'm sorry, sir, I'm afraid it's an internal line only. Mr. Braithwhite had hoped to have real phone service at the lodge, but it proved impossible, for bureaucratic as well as technical reasons. Unfortunately, his relationship with the rest of Devon County isn't nearly as cordial as the original Mr. Braithwhite's."

"I sympathize," Atticus said. He paused to look out the window. "Speaking of community relations, who are those people living down in the cottages?"

"Simple folk," William replied.

"Simple? You mean like Amish?"

"After a fashion. The Ardhamites' sect is a good deal older than the Mennonites', however."

"And they live here year-round?"

"Yes, sir. Ardham is their refuge from the world. In lieu of rent, they provide services and upkeep for the lodge. Most of the food you'll be eating here comes from the village."

"So they keep Mr. Braithwhite fed, and in return he keeps them safe?"

"Exactly, sir."

"What about electricity and hot running water?" Atticus said. "They get those too?"

"As I say, they're simple folk. They aren't interested in such things." William turned to George. "Mr. Berry. Your room is right through here. Let me show you."

After William and George had gone through the connecting door, Letitia said: "Come take a look at this."

Atticus joined her by one of the bookcases. "What is it?"

"Just look."

"Huh," said Atticus. "Mr. Burroughs . . ." The top shelf was filled with Tarzan novels, and the one below it had the complete run of John Carter books along with Carson Napier of Venus and the Pellucidar series. The other shelves held more authors and titles he knew, some seeming wildly out of place in these surroundings.

"They got all your favorites, huh?" Letitia said.

"A lot of them, yeah. And a lot of books I always meant to read . . ."

"Don't get comfortable," Letitia suggested.

"I'm way ahead of you," Atticus said, crouching down. The lowest shelf was Lovecraft Country: Algernon Blackwood, Robert Bloch, August Derleth, William Hope Hodgson, Frank Belknap Long, Clark Ashton Smith, and the man himself. Finger-walking over the book spines, Atticus stopped at a red leather-bound volume that stuck out conspicuously from between *The House on the Borderland* and *Beyond the Wall of Sleep*.

The cover of the red book was embossed with the half-sun symbol and the words BY-LAWS AND PRECEPTS OF THE ADAMITE ORDER OF THE ANCIENT DAWN. Atticus showed it to Letitia and then, hearing William and George returning, slipped it back into the shelf and stood up.

"Miss Dandridge," William said. "Your room is across the hall. If you'll follow me . . ."

They went out.

Atticus looked at George. "You have your own library too?" he asked.

"Yeah," George said. "I get my meals brought up, I could stay in there for a month and not mind."

Atticus nodded. "I wonder if that's the idea. Nice of him to give us our own wing, isn't it?"

"Very . . . You see any other stairs besides the ones we came up?"

"No. Not in this hallway."

"Let's hope they don't have another fire," George said.

Across the hall, Letitia let out a shriek. Atticus and George bolted towards the sound.

They found Letitia and William in the suite's bathroom. Letitia was standing with her hands clasped in front of her at the edge of what Atticus thought, at first glance, was a hole in the floor: a sunken tub, done all in black marble, large enough that the four of them could have sat in it without touching.

"Would you look at that," George said over Atticus's shoulder. "'Titia's got her own pool."

A few moments later, in the hall: "I'll have your luggage brought up now, Mr. Turner. I don't know if our mechanic will be able to do anything about the broken windows on your car, but I'll see that it's parked out of the weather."

"Thank you," Atticus said. "William?"

"Yes, sir?"

"When did Mr. Braithwhite say he and my father would be back from Boston?"

"He wasn't sure. Perhaps this evening, though it could be as late as tomorrow." Smiling: "But I'm sure we can keep you occupied in the meantime. In addition to the diversions you've already seen, there are music and exercise rooms on the ground floor, and some other entertainments I can show you. Of course you're welcome to go for a walk around the grounds or down in the village. Or if you'd like to go farther afield—into the Wood, or up into the hills—I can arrange a guide so you don't lose your way."

"No, that's OK, I don't think we'll wander too far."

"Very good, sir. Then if there's nothing else at the moment—"

"Just one thing," Atticus said.

"Yes, sir?"

"When my father was here, which of these rooms did you put him in?"

The briefest hesitation. "That one, sir." William pointed to a door to the right of Letitia's room.

Atticus tried the knob. "Locked."

"Of course, sir. I could get the key from downstairs, if you'd like. But there's nothing to see. Your father took all his effects with him to Boston, and the room's been cleaned." A pause. "Would you like me to get the key, Mr. Turner?"

"No, that's all right," Atticus said. Turning from the door, he matched William's smile with his own. "I trust you."

Atticus and George sat out front of the lodge on one of the benches, watching a peacock strut around the base of the sundial.

"Titus Braithwhite," George said, after a long silence. "That name mean something to you? You had a look on your face when you were staring at his picture."

"Did I?" said Atticus. He leaned back against the bench. "Titus Braithwhite owned my mother's great-great-great-grandmother."

"I thought Dora didn't know where her people came from."

"She didn't know much. Just that her great-ancestor was a woman named Hannah who belonged to Titus Braithwhite, a slave trader from Boston. Hannah was a maid at Braithwhite's country estate until the night she ran away."

"Through those woods? Brave woman."

"Brave, yeah, but also scared out of her mind," Atticus said. "There was some kind of calamity at the house and Hannah barely escaped with her life."

"The fire?" George said.

"Probably. Although it was part of the story Mom told me that Hannah would never tell anyone exactly what happened, only that it was something so terrible she *had* to run . . . Anyway, she got away, and made a new life for herself as a free woman, but she went the rest of her days in fear that Braithwhite or his family would track her down."

George tried to put the next question delicately: "When she ran," he said, "was she with child?"

"I asked Mom that, one time. She said I was missing the point of the story."

"Which was?"

"Don't look back. And never trust anyone named Braithwhite."

"I take it she didn't tell Montrose."

"No, and she made me promise not to tell him either. But I guess he finally found a clue somewhere. Or maybe one found him."

Letitia came out of the lodge, fresh from the bath and dressed in a violet gown that would not have looked out of place at Cinderella's ball.

"Good Lord," George said.

"You like it?" Laughing with pleasure, Letitia did a twirl for them, sequins flaring in the morning sun that had broken through the mist.

"It's beautiful," Atticus said. "But you didn't pack that in your little suitcase, did you?"

"No, silly, I found it in my room. And a dozen more like it. Didn't you check your wardrobes?"

"You found it," George said. "And it fits?"

"Like it was made for me." She did another twirl.

Atticus stood up. "I think we should take a walk down to the village."

"Really?" said George. "I was just thinking we should barricade ourselves in our rooms until Montrose gets back."

"I wouldn't hold my breath on Pop coming back. I think we need to go look for him."

"You think he's in the village?"

"I don't think he's in Boston with Mr. Braithwhite, let's put it that way."

"If they're keeping him someplace, isn't it more likely it'd be up here?"

"Depends on your assumptions." Atticus glanced up at the lodge's third-floor windows, then back down at George, who was staring at him quizzically. "Call it a hunch," he said.

"All right," said George. "I'll play that. And if we do find him—"

"We get the hell out of here and don't look back."

George nodded. "Sounds like a plan."

"It's a plan, all right," Letitia said. "But you don't really think it's going to be *that* easy, do you?"

Their car had already been moved, so they followed the drive to the end of the lodge's west wing and around back to the garage, a long narrow shed with Dutch-doored stalls like a converted horse stable. Going down the line they found a panel truck, two dark-windowed Rolls-Royce sedans, and a vintage pearl-gray roadster.

The Packard was in stall number five. Atticus retrieved the revolver from the glove compartment and checked that it was still loaded. Then he realized he had no good way to carry it; it was too big to slip in a trouser pocket without being conspicuous. "I need to go back upstairs and get a jacket," he said.

But Letitia held out a hand. "Give it here." She made Atticus and George look away while she hid the gun, somehow, in the folds of her gown. When she was done she did another twirl for them, showing off.

"We get out of this," Atticus said to her, "you're going to have to tell me some of those stories."

They returned to the front of the lodge and found a footpath leading down to the Ardham church. Descending, they encountered a group of villagers coming up: a man Atticus recognized as the goatherd, carrying a freshly skinned and dressed carcass over his shoulders; a woman holding a pair of plucked chickens and a basket of eggs; and two more men lugging sacks of root vegetables and other produce. Despite their burdens, they gave Atticus, George, and Letitia the right of way, stepping off the path and bowing their heads as the fisherman had done. "Morning," said Atticus in passing, but none of the Ardhamites responded or even met his eye.

The church and the other village buildings were arranged in a rough square at the end of the cottage road. Across from the church was a workshop, in front of which a man sat using a foot-operated grindstone to sharpen the blade of a scythe. The workman glanced up as Atticus and the others reached the bottom of the path, but quickly refocused his attention on his task. The mastiff chained up beside him was less circumspect: Upon noticing the strangers it jumped down from the workshop porch and would have kept coming if not for the chain.

George eyed the dog warily. "So where do you want to look first?" he said. Before he finished asking the question, Letitia had the church door open.

"Guess we start right here," said Atticus.

The church's interior was one large room. An entry alcove, with a rope-pull hanging down from the steeple above, opened out into a nave whose rude wooden pews offered seating for about forty people. Tall narrow windows in the sides of the nave let in light through frosted glass, and an oil lamp with a rose glass vessel hung above the center aisle, its feeble flicker like the glow of a dying star. At the front of the nave the room narrowed again, the raised platform of the chancel holding neither altar nor pulpit, but only a wooden lectern on which a big book rested.

On the wall above the lectern, a stained-glass window that was the church's only real decoration showed a scene from the Garden of Eden. Atticus had started forward to get a better look when Letitia, a few steps ahead of him, let out a gasp and put a hand to her mouth—then laughed through her fingers.

In the window, Adam and Eve embraced beneath a pink half-sun—a rising sun of ancient dawn. The scene, though familiar, was missing a few elements. The devil serpent was absent, and though the Garden's trees and shrubs were brightly colored by the dawnlight, there was no forbidden fruit, Eve's hands being otherwise occupied.

And there were no fig leaves. Atticus stared, mouth open, never having encountered stained-glass pornography before.

"Well," said George, "they aren't Baptists."

"No," said Atticus. "They're Adamites . . . whatever that is." He went up to the lectern to see what kind of Bible it held, but his curiosity was frustrated: The big book was sealed with a hasp lock and chained to the lectern for good measure.

They went back outside. The workman had gone into the shop and was hammering away at something, but the mastiff was still straining at the end of its chain.

They continued to explore, their attention focusing next on a stone-and-mortar construction to the west of the church. The building was round, about ten feet high and thirty feet wide at its base, tapering slightly towards the top. High up on one side they could see the rusted remnants of an iron grille that at one time had covered a window; but the opening had been mortared shut. The iron-banded door was locked and so solid that when Atticus pounded his fist against it, it barely made a sound.

"What do you think?" he said, looking at George and Letitia. "Too obvious?"

"Can I help you folks?"

The woman had flowing red hair and pale skin, and Atticus's first thought was that she must be related to William. His second was that she looked a lot like the stained-glass Eve, only with clothes on: a long-sleeved cotton blouse, denim pants, and leather boots. A ring of keys in various sizes jangled against her hip as she came towards them.

"Morning," Atticus greeted her, smiling. "My name's Atticus. This is George and Letitia. We're staying up at the manor."

"Figured as much," the woman said. She smiled too, but there was a hint of mockery to it. "I'm Dell."

"You the law around here, Dell?" She cocked her head at the question. Atticus pointed to her key ring and nodded at the stone building. "This is the jail, right?"

"The *jail*?" Dell snorted. Stepping past him, she took the ring from her belt and used the largest of the keys to unlock the door. She hauled it open with both hands, then stood gesturing for Atticus to go in. "Mind the first step."

He had to duck his head to get through the doorway, and there was a drop, the stone floor a good eight inches below the threshold. The interior was cool and dry and full of smells savory and sweet. As his eyes adjusted, a severed limb appeared in front of him: a deer leg, dangling by a chain from a wooden beam. Other chains held other big pieces of meat, dried or smoked, some intact, some with large portions carved off.

Moving away from the door, Atticus examined the bins along the walls, his nose often revealing the contents before his eyes did. He heard a pattering behind him. Letitia and George had come inside too, and Letitia was stamping her feet, checking for a cellar. But the floor seemed solid and Atticus saw no trapdoors.

"Animals," Dell said from the doorway.

"What's that?" said Atticus.

"We get animals coming into the village, looking for food. Raccoons, foxes, bears now and then. Bears will come right through a cottage door if they're hungry enough, but they can't get in here."

"We heard there were grizzlies out in the woods," Atticus said.

"Grizzlies!" Dell snorted again. "No, no grizzlies, just black bears," she said, adding lightly: "But the blacks are bad enough. They're smart. Not *smart* smart—they're beasts—but clever enough to cause mischief. And they're persistent. We use dogs to drive them off, but sometimes they won't quit, even after they've been hurt. Those ones do end up in here . . . after a fashion." She nodded at one of the haunches of meat.

While Atticus and the others contemplated the fate of the bear, Dell stepped back from the threshold and put a hand on the door. For an instant it seemed that she meant to shut them in, but she was only giving them room to come out.

"Ready to move along?" she said.

Dell escorted them to the sloping apple orchard west of the village, where they collected another silent bow from the beekeeper who tended the hives there. Dell described her own job in Ardham as that of "village warden," a managerial role that included acting as liaison to the manor. She laughed at Atticus's suggestion that she and William were related. "I'm not high and mighty enough to be in *his* family," she said. Atticus wanted to ask about the church and Dell's role in that, but struck again by her resemblance to the stained-glass Eve, he found himself unable to broach the subject, and she didn't volunteer anything herself.

From the orchard they went down to the river, where they startled the fisherman, then circled back to the village square. Atticus wanted to investigate the cottages as well, but didn't want a chaperone, so he thanked Dell for the tour and made as if to go back up the footpath. Dell headed for the workshop, where the workman was still hammering noisily on something. As soon as she went inside, Atticus changed course, leading George and Letitia towards the cottage road.

They didn't get very far. The mastiff noticed their course correction and set up a furious barking. Atticus walked faster and didn't look back. But then a pack of other dogs appeared ahead of them, running out from behind the nearest of the cottages. There were four of them: two medium-sized mongrels, a rat terrier, and an extra-large beast that looked like a cross between a wolfhound and a Great Dane. They didn't attack. They moved into the middle of the road and waited there, panting, to see if Atticus and George and Letitia would come closer.

The mastiff stopped barking and Atticus looked over his shoulder. Dell had come back out on the workshop porch and was standing with her arms crossed, her lips curved in an openly contemptuous smile. Not *smart* smart, he heard her say. We use dogs to drive them off.

"Yeah," Atticus said. "OK."

They went back up the hill. The dogs lost interest in them as soon as they turned back to the footpath, but looking down from the crest they could see the wolfhound-Dane mix and one of the other mongrels wandering along the cottage road like sharks patrolling the shore of an island.

"So what do you think?" said Atticus.

"The workshop's got a stone foundation," Letitia noted. "It's the only building other than that storehouse that did."

"You think there's a cellar?"

She nodded. "And with that hammering, someone could be down there yelling and you wouldn't hear it."

Atticus looked at George, who shrugged a shoulder. "If Montrose doesn't show by tonight we could sneak back down after dinner," he suggested. "Maybe bring some chops for those dogs."

"Maybe," said Atticus, thinking of the two shotguns still in the Packard, but thinking, also, of a night patrol through a village outside Pyongyang, a supposedly straightforward search-and-rescue mission that had ended with four Negro soldiers dead. "Maybe we need to come at this another way."

"What do you have in mind?"

"Not sure yet. I'm still thinking it through."

"Well, if we go back inside," George suggested, "we can think it through over some room service."

"Sure," Atticus said. "Maybe I'll do some reading, too."

Braithwhite's other guests began arriving in mid-afternoon. Atticus, upstairs studying the by-laws of the Adamite Order of the Ancient Dawn, took a census of the lodge membership from his window: fourteen Caucasian men, ranging in age from fifty to at least seventy. They drove or were driven in expensive cars and limousines; half of the vehicles had Massachusetts license plates and the rest were from neighboring states, except for one late-arriving limo from the District of Columbia. All of the lodge members wore fat silver signet rings that marked them as initiates of the Order.

Initiates: The red book referred to them as Dawn Seekers, Sons of Adam, and Antenauts, "Sojourners to the time Before" (as in, "Before the Fall," though the Antenauts' Fall, like the Ardhamites' Eden, was different from the one Atticus had learned about in Sunday school). The book didn't use the word "wizards," but it was clear they were that too, or wished to be. Observing each man in turn, Atticus tried to deduce which if any of them had real magic powers; but evidently sorcerers, like Communists, were hard to identify by sight.

At quarter past seven, not long after the last of Adam's Sons had been ushered into the lodge, the phone rang. It was William, calling to see whether Atticus and his companions would be having dinner in the hall. "We planned to," Atticus told him. "Is there a problem?"

"Not at all, Mr. Turner," William said. "Why don't you make yourselves ready, and I'll be up to collect you at eight o'clock."

From his wardrobe, Atticus selected a finely tailored black suit. It fit him perfectly, as did the shoes. George opted for a tux, and Letitia answered the knock on her door wearing an elegant white evening dress. Earlier, Letitia had announced her intention to smuggle the purple Cinderella gown out to the Packard, along with some other choice items from her wardrobe. "If we do end up making a run for it," she'd said, "I don't see why some of these nice clothes can't come with us." But from the expression on her face now, Atticus guessed the plan had encountered a snag.

"What happened?" he asked. "William catch you sneaking out the back door?"

"No, I got the dresses out to the car just fine," Letitia said. "But there's a problem."

Before she could elaborate, William appeared at the end of the hallway. "Good evening, Mr. Turner, Mr. Berry," he said. "Miss Dandridge, you look lovely. I hope you're enjoying your stay so far."

"It's been an interesting day," Atticus said. "But you know, you didn't really have to come get us. We could have found our own way downstairs."

"I understand, sir. But if I may speak frankly, I'm afraid some of the lodge members can be a bit . . . *brusque* with strangers. Until you've been formally introduced, I thought it might be best if I escorted you."

"You don't want them mistaking us for staff, is that it?"

William smiled his smile. "Your table is waiting for you, Mr. Turner."

The Sons of Adam were all gathered downstairs in the foyer. Servants were circulating with trays of drinks and hors d'oeuvres, but some of the older lodge members were grumbling about the fact that they hadn't already been seated in the dining hall. The Antenaut from D.C.—a doddering senior whom Atticus had nicknamed Preston Brooks for the way he brandished his cane—was proclaiming loudly to the room that *he*, at least, should not be kept standing around like some houseboy.

Then Atticus entered the room and everyone got quiet. Unlike the villagers, the members of the lodge had no compunction about staring. Most of the stares were just curious—albeit to a degree that was rude—but Preston managed a triple take: his initial curiosity giving way, at the sight of George and Letitia, to confusion and then outraged bafflement. *"Three?"* he bellowed, hoisting his cane into the air. "Why are there *three?"*

"This way, Mr. Turner," William said, simultaneously pretending not to see Preston and moving to shield Atticus from him. Letitia gave Preston a little wave as they breezed by him into the dining hall.

William led them to a table beneath a red-and-silver banner bearing the half-sun symbol. The table's position at the center of the hall and the zone of separation around it suggested a place of honor—or, perhaps, that they were being put on display. Two waiting servants pulled out chairs for George and Letitia, while William seated Atticus himself. The servants poured water and wine, and more servants brought a soup course from the kitchen.

Meanwhile the Sons of Adam were led inside. They were seated in groups of two and three, except for Preston, who got a whole table to himself. A number of the lodge members continued staring at Atticus, until Letitia started making faces at them; after that they focused on the soup.

The young man showed up during the salad course. He was white, in his early twenties, with brown hair, and a sharp-looking suit almost identical to the one Atticus was wearing. He made his way discreetly to the only remaining empty table, over in the corner near the kitchen entrance. The Antenauts paid scant attention to him, but the servants were a different story; within moments of sitting down he had both food and drink in front of him.

The main course arrived. "If you're hungry," Atticus suggested, "you should eat up now."

"Why?" said George. "You planning on skipping out before dessert?"

"I was thinking I might make a nuisance of myself," Atticus told him. "We'll see what develops from there."

Most of the other diners were still finishing their salads. Atticus waited until a group of Antenauts, Preston among them, were about to be served their main courses. Then he stood up.

"Excuse me!" he called out, striking a spoon against his water glass. "Excuse me! Can I have everyone's attention?"

Instantly all eyes were upon him. Most of the Antenauts remained curious, but a few were visibly annoyed by the interruption of the meal service; Preston reached for his cane.

Atticus addressed the room:

"My name is Atticus Turner," he said. "Like you, I'm here as a guest of Mr. Braithwhite, but I'm afraid I'm still in the dark as to why. I came to Ardham looking for my father; I haven't found him yet, and I don't know what Mr. Braithwhite wanted with him, and I don't know what Mr. Braithwhite wants with me." He paused and looked around at their upturned faces, to see if anyone cared to volunteer the information; but they only went on staring and scowling.

"I don't know what Mr. Braithwhite wants with me," Atticus continued, "but I do have a theory. And I was hoping you gentlemen wouldn't mind helping me test that theory.

"I understand you all belong to a club called the Order of the Ancient Dawn. I happened across a copy of your by-laws this morning, and I've been looking through it." He drew out the red book from inside his suit jacket and held it up. "I hope that's not a breach of security," he added, acknowledging the looks of consternation this caused. "I know fraternal societies like to keep secrets. I've got some experience with that. My father and my uncle George, here, they're both members of the Prince Hall Freemasons, and there are certain things they just won't talk about.

"You gentlemen familiar with the Prince Hall Freemasons? I know you've heard of the Masons, but Prince Hall—this might interest you— Prince Hall was an abolitionist who lived in Boston at the time of the Revolution. He joined the Massachusetts militia to help fight for independence. And he wanted to join the local Freemasons, but because he was a colored man, they wouldn't let him in. So he and a group of other freedmen formed their own Masonic lodge.

"I have to say, I was disappointed to read in your rulebook that Prince Hall wouldn't have been welcome to join your club, either. Not surprised," he added, looking at Preston. "But disappointed.

"But then I kept reading, and I found out there's a loophole—a membership clause that supersedes all the others. Men who are related by blood to Titus Braithwhite are automatically considered members of the Order. Not just *eligible* for membership—they're members, period. Don't even need to apply.

"Of course, 'by blood' is a vexed phrase, and there's something like ten paragraphs in the by-laws spelling out who does and doesn't count as a blood relation. But the way I read it, a direct descendant of Titus Braithwhite would certainly qualify. Assuming there was such a person.

"And there's more! Braithwhite members of the Order are *special* members. How does the book put it? 'Not just Sons of Adam, but Sons Among Sons.'" Atticus glanced up at the banner over his head. "Sons Among Sons, that's a nice play on words . . . But what it means is, Braith-whites are club officers. They're empowered to call lodge meetings— and to give orders to other members. Orders that must be obeyed.

"Which brings me back to my theory," Atticus said. "I think the reason I'm here has something to do with the fact that I'm a direct descendant of Titus Braithwhite—and maybe not just *a* descendant, but the last one. I'm not a hundred percent sure that's the case. It's a hypothesis. But I think you gentlemen know the truth of it and I believe that's why you're here.

"Now if it is true, I could just order you to tell me, and by your own rules you'd be bound to. I could do that, but the fact is I've traveled a long way in the past few days, and I'm tired, and at this point I'd rather be talking direct to Mr. Braithwhite. So what I'm actually going to do is this: As a Son Among Sons, I'm going to have you all stand up, right now, and walk out of this room. Leave your glasses and your plates where they are; just take yourselves. Go out that door and through the foyer and outside, onto the front lawn. You can use the benches if you like. But you stay out there, until either I or Mr. Braithwhite tell you it's OK to come back inside.

"Gentlemen," Atticus concluded, "that is an order."

Silence as he finished. Preston had his cane in a death grip and looked as if he himself were being strangled; nor was he the only Antenaut exhibiting signs of abject fury. As the moment stretched out, Atticus had time to wonder whether he'd guessed wrong, and he felt George and Letitia tense, waiting for the mob to erupt.

Then a chair scraped, and Atticus turned to see a red-faced Son of Adam getting slowly to his feet. The man gave a curt bow and turned and started for the door. The other two lodge members at that table were the next to rise, and then two at a table next to them. And then they were all standing, even Preston, though he didn't bow.

As the Antenauts went out to the foyer, the servants began their own exodus through the kitchen. William lingered to close the doors behind the departing lodge members before following the rest of the staff. Which left Atticus, George, Letitia, and the young man at the back corner table, who alone among the white people had thoroughly enjoyed Atticus's performance. As Atticus walked over to him, he applauded, holding up his hands to display his silver ring.

"I know you already know this," the young Antenaut said, "but the by-laws actually state that the Son Among Sons is the *oldest* Braithwhite present. Which in this case happens to be me. I've got a year and ten days on you." He grinned. "Not that those other idiots know that. And not even that old fart Pendergast will risk breaking the rules . . . Just as well. He'd probably smash the jaw of any ordinary Negro who talked to him that way."

"He might try," said Atticus.

Braithwhite's grin broadened. "It's Caleb, by the way," he said. "Would you like to sit down, Atticus?" He gave a nod, and a chair on Atticus's side of the table slid out on its own. Atticus blinked but didn't flinch. He remained standing, placing a hand on the chair back.

"Caleb," Atticus said. "And Samuel Braithwhite, that'd be your father?"

"That's right."

"But it was you driving the Daimler, right? And you're the one who picked up my father in Chicago."

"That was me," Caleb agreed. "My father's not much for long road trips."

"Why bring my father into it?" Atticus asked. "I'm the one you really want, right? The one your father wants, for whatever . . . Why not just come get me?"

"Because there are rules," Caleb Braithwhite said. "You had to come of your own free will, and if I'd asked you, you might have said no. Would have said no, is my guess . . . But we can't refuse our fathers, can we?"

"Where is my father?"

"Safe. And he'll stay that way, as long as you do what you're told."

"I want to see him."

"I'm sure you do." Braithwhite paused, mouth open, as George and Letitia came and stood beside Atticus. "Now, now," said Braithwhite; George let out a grunt and dropped the steak knife he was holding. As the blade clattered to the floor, Braithwhite shifted his gaze to Letitia, who was poised with her hands open at her sides.

"I want to see my father," Atticus said. "Now."

Braithwhite continued to eyeball Letitia.

"Mine first," he said.

There was a service elevator in the kitchen. "Family only," Caleb Braithwhite said as he pulled open the gate.

"It's all right," Atticus told George and Letitia. "Wait down here for me."

"You two should finish dinner," Caleb said. He looked over at William, who was hovering in the background. "Take care of them, will you? And send someone down to the village to fetch Delilah."

"Yes, sir."

The elevator rose slowly. Caleb Braithwhite used the time to share another rule. "My father isn't a tactful man," he said. "He may say things that make you want to hit him. But I'd advise you not to waste the effort. He's immune."

"To being hit?" Atticus said.

"To a long list of things."

"Maybe I'll just hit you, then."

Caleb smiled. "You might try," he said.

On the third floor, the elevator opened into a small private dining room. A table with a single chair at its head held the remains of a meal.

There was a painting on the wall opposite the elevator. More abstract than the portrait downstairs, it showed a crowned figure in robes standing beneath a pink sky. This kingly figure had a hand outstretched towards a line of shadow shapes issuing from a stand of trees. Those closest to the trees were little more than dark blobs, but those nearer to the king had begun to sprout limbs and heads and tails, though even the one at the king's feet was not quite recognizable. A dog, maybe.

"Father?" Caleb Braithwhite called, standing by one of the room's two doorways. In the distance there was a loud slam and a rattle of something falling. Then silence for a bit, and finally, approaching footsteps.

Samuel Braithwhite didn't look like a wizard or a king. He looked like a banker after hours, or maybe an inventor in the Edison mold. He had his shirtsleeves rolled up and his collar unbuttoned and he was wiping his hands with a rag as he came in. He seemed neither surprised nor especially pleased to find Atticus in his dining room, but as though determined to make the best of the intrusion, he spent several moments looking Atticus up and down.

"He's darker than I expected," Samuel Braithwhite said finally. "Are you sure he's the right one?"

Caleb nodded. "It's him."

"My guests are all out on the lawn."

"Yes, sir. That—"

"William called up and told me what happened. How did he get a copy of the by-laws?"

"I don't know, sir," Caleb said. "He's had the run of the house all day. I suppose he just found it."

"Hmm." Braithwhite regarded his son through narrowed eyes. "And when you saw what was happening downstairs, why didn't you put a stop to it?"

"I—"

"Never mind. I know why." Braithwhite sighed. "So . . . It's Turner, is it?"

"Mr. Turner, to you," said Atticus.

"Do you have any idea the bother you've just caused me? The Sons of Adam are insufferable enough under the best of circumstances. Now I've got to meet with them when they haven't had their supper."

"Sorry to inconvenience you."

"You don't know the meaning of sorry. Yet." Braithwhite gave his hands a final wipe and tossed the rag on the table. "So, *Mister* Turner, you want to know what you're doing here?"

Atticus nodded. "I guess it's not to share in the family fortune."

"No," Samuel Braithwhite said. "You *are* the family fortune."

"Come again?"

Rather than repeat himself, Braithwhite gestured at the painting on the wall. "What do you think of this artwork, Mr. Turner?"

Atticus shrugged. "Not really my thing," he said.

"The artist's name was Josef Tannhauser. He was a contemporary of Titus Braithwhite's. Not a lodge member, but he had similar interests. He died in a Boston asylum in 1801. This painting, one of his last, is called *Genesis 2:19*. Are you familiar with the verse?"

Atticus shook his head.

Braithwhite quoted: "'And out of the ground the Lord God formed every beast of the field, and every fowl of the air; and brought them unto Adam to see what he would call them: and whatsoever Adam called every living creature, that was the name thereof.' In Tannhauser's conception, this act of naming is much more than a simple matter of picking labels. Adam is sharing in the creation, assigning each creature its final form and its station in the hierarchy of nature."

"Putting everything in its place," Atticus said.

"Exactly. At the dawn of time, just for a moment, everything is where and as it should be, from God to man to woman down to the lowliest wriggling creature." He looked at Atticus. "And then entropy sets to work, as it will. Paradise is lost; Babel and the Flood bring confusion and disorder; what was an elegant hierarchy becomes a mess of tribes and nations. Of course," Braithwhite added, "it didn't really happen that way. Biblical literalism is for the simple. But it's a useful parable."

"About entropy," Atticus said. Entropy and history and social evolution, or devolution: The red book had had a lot to say on those subjects. "And that's where you come in, right? You and your Order, you're going to turn things around, find a way back to the Garden. With magic."

Braithwhite pursed his lips. "That's a vulgar word," he said. Looking pointedly at Atticus: "A simple man's word. We're not magicians. We're scientists. Philosophers of nature. Nature," he repeated, rapping his knuckles on the dining table. "Nature is solid. Nature has rules. People who go on about magic believe that anything is possible. It isn't. You don't just wave a wand and turn lead into gold. It doesn't work that way."

"How does it work, then?"

"For the majority, it doesn't work at all. Nature holds itself impervious to the wishings of would-be sorcerers. But." He reached for the table again and ran his hand slowly over the wood grain. "There *are* cracks. Not exceptions to the rules, you understand—there's no such thing—but special cases, natural anomalies that can be discovered and exploited by men of sufficient vision. Even then there are strict limits on what's possible—a token wonder here and there is all most seekers can hope for. Only the most extraordinary of natural philosophers can move beyond that, to truly great works."

"Men such as yourself."

Braithwhite, sensing he was being mocked, grew testy. "My full potential has yet to be demonstrated," he said. "But I'm already more powerful than any other living initiate. You'd do well to keep that in mind."

"What about Titus Braithwhite?"

"He was one of a kind. A genius of the art."

"Yeah," said Atticus. "And how'd that work out for him, in the end?"

"Badly," Braithwhite acknowledged. "It's perilous work, to challenge entropy, and genius is no guarantee against accidents. Titus Braithwhite understood the risks. He chose to push on, regardless."

"And burned the house down."

"Fire was part of it," Samuel Braithwhite said. "We still don't know precisely what happened that night. An Ardhamite villager named Tobias Foote, who was long believed to be the only survivor of the catastrophe, said that before it imploded, the lodge blazed with every color in nature and some outside it. The sight drove Foote mad—he ended up in the same asylum as Josef Tannhauser and died within the year. I have the diary he kept before he passed. It's gibberish, for the most part, but among the ravings are hints of the existence of a second survivor—a 'dark woman' who fled into the Wood just as the house began to glow.

"But that discovery came much later. At the time, it was an unmitigated disaster. All the best minds in the Order perished. The handful of lodge members who weren't present for the ritual were all second-rate hangers-on, and in the wake of the catastrophe, they scattered. A huge body of esoteric knowledge was lost and the work the Order had been undertaking came to a dead stop.

"It wasn't until the beginning of this century that my father rediscovered some of that lost knowledge and began putting the pieces of the Order back together again. We've made great strides since then, had some extraordinary successes, and we're ready now, we think, to take up the great work that was interrupted in 1795. But the world hasn't stood still either. When the Order of the Ancient Dawn was first founded, the age of kings was only just giving way to the age of the common man—and Titus Braithwhite's horror at that prospect was part of what drove him to take the chances he did. I can only imagine his horror today, after a hundred and eighty years of the common man. And all of that is nothing compared to what's coming in the next few decades. So you see, we need to act quickly. We're running out of time."

"Well, that's all very important-sounding," Atticus said. "But I don't see what it has to do with me."

"Adam's Sons, Mr. Turner," Samuel Braithwhite said. "Adam's *Sons*: The power of the true philosopher is carried in the blood—and Titus Braithwhite, a Son Among Sons, was a very powerful man. You are a reservoir of that power. Diluted, no doubt, and also tainted somewhat, but still useful for the work we have to do. The Order of the Ancient Dawn requires you."

Atticus looked from Braithwhite to his son, searching their faces for some sign that this was all a big put-on, a rich man's elaborate joke.

The truly funny thing was, he wasn't the least surprised; while reading the red book, he'd imagined something very much like this. It was just that it sounded so much more ridiculous spoken aloud.

"You *require* me," Atticus said. "To be your magic Negro?"

But Braithwhite didn't see the humor of it. "I don't think you've grasped your situation," he said. "I can understand why you might be confused. The problem is you're two very different things at once. On the one hand, you're the avatar of Titus Braithwhite, the closest thing to him still walking on this earth. It's out of respect for that that I've treated you the way I have: inviting you to my house instead of having you dragged here; keeping you not just safe, but comfortable; welcoming you, feeding you, *clothing* you.

"All that, for Titus Braithwhite. But at the same time, yes, you're Turner, the Negro. And *that* I have no particular respect for. I'll tolerate it—in my house, even in my presence—for the sake of the other; but my tolerance isn't infinite, and you're already testing the limits."

Immune, Atticus thought, hands itching to turn into fists. Be interesting to test the limits of *that*. But he hadn't forgotten why he was here and didn't step to.

"I want to see my father."

"If I let you see him, will you stop bothering my other guests? Will you behave?"

"I'll leave your guests alone," Atticus said. "As long as they do the same for me."

Braithwhite pursed his lips again. But if the old man's exasperation was plain, so was his desire to end this conversation. "Take care of it," he told his son. "And see that he doesn't cause any more trouble."

"Yes, sir," Caleb Braithwhite said.

"Tell William I'm ready for the meeting. Have him fetch the others from the lawn and send them up here."

"Yes, sir."

"As for him," Braithwhite senior said, nodding at Atticus, "we'll need him for the ritual tomorrow. Until then I don't want to see him again, or get any more calls from William about his antics. Is that absolutely understood?"

"Yes, sir," Caleb said, for a third time. Then he bowed, like a villager, his face fixed in an expression of solemn respect. It wasn't until he and Atticus were back on the elevator, headed down, that he allowed his amusement to show.

"**D**ell will take you to see your father," Caleb Braithwhite said to Atticus. They were in the foyer with George, Letitia, Dell, William, and a couple of other house servants, large men whose presence seemed intended to insure that no one acted up. The Antenauts had already gone upstairs. Through the open dining hall doors, Atticus could see other servants clearing the tables.

"You'll stay here," Caleb told George and Letitia. "William's going to take you back up to your rooms." Smiling at Letitia: "Unless you'd like to have dessert with me."

"Thanks, I'll pass," Letitia replied. To Atticus she said: "We'll be waiting for you."

Atticus nodded, and Caleb Braithwhite said, "You do understand, if there is any more trouble, there'll be consequences."

"Yeah, I got the message," Atticus said. He turned to Dell. "Let's go."

They descended the hill in the summer twilight. The villagers had already retired for the evening; Atticus could see lamps and candles burning in the cottages and more lamps strung along the bridge to the east. The village square was deserted and dark, except for the workshop.

"It's me," Dell called as she stepped onto the workshop porch. The mastiff, unchained, met her at the door. She grabbed it roughly by the scruff and shoved it aside, and it backed up into the corner by the door and settled on its haunches—but it remained alert, tracking Atticus's every move and growling low in its throat.

The workman sat in the center of the shop on a stool tilted back against a post. On the worktable beside him was the newly sharpened scythe, a tall mug filled with something frothy, and a collection of small stones, like checkers, arranged on a grid incised into the table's surface. "Any problems?" Dell asked him, and he shook his head, allowing himself a long look at Atticus.

The trapdoor was concealed beneath a trunk in a back corner of the shop. Dell got it open, revealing a steep set of wooden stairs descending into darkness.

Atticus stood looking into the dark hole. "You put my father down there?" he said, turning his head to include the workman in the question.

Dell responded without shame or embarrassment: "I did what I was told." She took a lantern from a hook on the wall, lit it, and offered it to Atticus. "You'll need this."

"You aren't coming down?"

"He doesn't like me," she said. "And he throws things."

"Good for him," said Atticus.

He went down. The cellar like the storehouse was cool and dry, though there was a musty smell here. The lamplight reflected off long rows of jars in wooden shelves—preserves of some kind—and illuminated jumbles of workshop detritus: a broken-spoked wagon wheel, a wooden mallet with a splintered handle.

"Pop?" Atticus called, and heard a sound from the far end of the cellar. Moving towards it, he began to encounter a different kind of detritus: streaks of dried gruel or porridge, a smashed apple core, bits of broken glass. Atticus thought: He throws things.

A few more steps and the lamplight fell on a rough wooden cot. A figure sat hunched on the edge of the mattress with a blanket wrapped around its shoulders. On the floor, a gleam of metal: A chain was padlocked around the figure's left ankle and secured to a ring in the wall.

"Pop?" His father looked up red-eyed and raised a hand against the light, exposing a palm covered in old scars. Atticus drew the lamp back and held it up to illuminate his own face. "It's me, Pop."

He saw the recognition come into his father's eyes, followed almost immediately by another, all-too familiar expression: disappointment, laced with disgust. Despite everything, Atticus felt a disgust of his own rising in response, like bile at the back of his throat.

"Really?" said Atticus. "*Really*, Pop?"

"Twenty-two years," Montrose Turner said. "Twenty-two years, you fight me on everything. And now the one time I *don't* want you to mind me, what happens?"

"You want to talk about years, Pop? How many years was Mom telling you to let it go? Why couldn't you mind her?"

Montrose sprang to his feet, shrugging off the blanket. "You want to have a discussion about your mother?" he said. "Step a little closer."

But Atticus shook his head. "I'm not here to fight with you, Pop." He looked down at the chain, then back up at his father's face. "You all right?"

"Of course I'm all right!" Montrose said, still bristling. "Why'd you have to come here?"

"Because you asked me to," Atticus said. "Why didn't you wait for me? After you sent me that letter . . ."

"Ah!" Montrose put up his hand again to fend off the question and looked away. After a moment he said: "It was that boy. Caleb. He got in my head somehow."

"What, he hypnotized you?"

"No! It wasn't like that! It was like . . . I don't know what it was like. I knew he wasn't on the level, all right?—I'm not *stupid*—but what I kept telling myself, as long as I *know* he's not on the level, it's like I'm putting one over on him. I'll just play along, until I get at the truth . . .

And I needed to get at the truth. Not for me. For Dora. For *you* . . . So when he offered to let me ride back with him, I said sure, why not?" He frowned at the chain. "Why not?"

"So he brought you back with him. And put you down here?"

"No, that was the father," Montrose said. "They had me up at the big house at first. For a few hours. But the charade was starting to wear thin, and the old man's not nearly as good a liar as the boy. Or maybe he just didn't care to have me under his roof. As soon as I met him, it's like the spell, or whatever it was, was broken. I got unruly." He smiled, thinly, but the smile didn't last. "So they turned me over to the serfs," he concluded. "What day is it?"

Atticus had to think. "Monday. Night. You left home eight days ago."

"Eight days, that's all?"

"I came as soon as I got your letter."

Montrose shook his head. "I didn't expect to see you for a month, if that. Been praying I wouldn't see you at all." The disgust crept back into his voice: "Twenty-two years."

"Yeah, twenty-two years, Pop. You hold that thought." Setting the lantern on the ground, Atticus turned and stalked back to the stairs.

Dell was waiting above by the trapdoor. She opened her mouth to say something and Atticus hit her in the forehead with the mallet. Her eyes rolled up and she dropped like a stone. Even as she fell, Atticus stepped past her to meet the onrushing mastiff, dealing it a solid blow to the skull as it leapt.

The workman scrambled up next, spilling his drink as he grabbed for the scythe. Atticus dropped the mallet and got a shovel from the wall. He deflected the scythe blade with the shovel blade and caught the workman in the throat with the side of the shovel's handle. He seized the choking workman by the forelock, banged his head against the table, and half-dragged, half-wrestled him back to the trapdoor and pitched him down the stairs.

The mastiff was struggling to stand but couldn't get its legs to work together. Atticus hit it with the shovel until it stopped moving. Then he paused, listening to his own breathing and the sound of the village around him. Another dog was barking somewhere, over by the cottages, but the barking didn't come closer and soon quieted.

Atticus got Dell's key ring. He found a bolt cutter too.

The workman was lying motionless at the bottom of the stairs. Atticus stepped over him and went back to his father and gave him the keys and the bolt cutter. Then he dragged the workman away from the stairs and propped him against a shelf of preserves. He went up and got Dell in a fireman's carry and brought her down and put her next to the workman. By then Montrose was free. He came over and held up the lantern and looked at his jailers. "I get the next two," he said.

"You can get the next fifty," said Atticus. "And you might need to, if we don't get out of here soon."

"You have a car?" Montrose asked.

Atticus nodded. "Woody."

"Woody?" said Montrose. "George is here too?"

"Your family cares about you, Pop. Live with it."

They went up and dumped the mastiff down the hole and closed the trapdoor and slid the trunk back on top of it. They blew out all the lanterns and went to the front door and stood listening again in the dark.

"Where's George?" Montrose whispered.

"Bringing the car, I hope."

"You hope?"

"Just wait." Atticus held up a hand. "You hear that?"

A vehicle was approaching along the cottage road. Atticus leaned out onto the porch to see if it was the Packard coming, only to get caught in a sudden splash of high beams.

It wasn't the Packard. It was the Daimler. By the time Atticus fully registered that fact the silver car had already come to a stop in front of the workshop. Letitia poked her head out the driver's window and called Atticus's name.

"You brought a girl with you?" Montrose said.

"Let's talk about it on the road," Atticus suggested.

They got into the back of the car, Atticus sitting behind Letitia, Montrose behind his brother. "Montrose!" George said, turning to look at him. "You all right?"

"You brought a *girl* with you?" Montrose said.

"Hi, Mr. Turner!" Letitia said good-naturedly, smiling into the rearview as she got the car turned around. "They tried not bringing me, but the Lord Jesus and I had other ideas."

Atticus looked at George. "You got away all right?"

"I think so," George held up the revolver. "We put William in 'Titia's bathroom. Tipped the wardrobe in front of the door, yanked the phone, and locked the hall door, too. One of those big guys is in there with him, so it probably won't take them that long to bust out, but we got clear of the manor without anyone raising the alarm."

"And Woody?"

"Had to leave it," George said sadly. "It's blocked in by all those limos—'Titia noticed when she was outside earlier. But this was still parked out front."

"Had the keys right in it," Letitia added, her tone suggesting: a gift of Providence. And whether you believed that or not, Atticus supposed there were advantages to escaping in the Daimler. No villagers came out to challenge them as they drove past the cottages. The dogs didn't even bark.

"Yeah," said George, "but I'll miss that car. Maybe when we get home I can trade this in on a new one."

"How you going to do that?" Montrose said. "You got underworld contacts I don't know about?"

"I might be able to help," said Letitia. She swung the car to the right to go onto the bridge.

The engine died in the middle of the turn. It didn't sputter or stall; it just shut off. As the car slewed to a stop facing the bridge, Letitia reached for the ignition key, twisted it back and then forward again. Nothing happened.

"What the hell is that?" said Montrose. Looking down the length of the bridge, they could see the lanterns hanging in pairs from the iron hooks. Five pairs, now four, the furthermost pair having just winked out. A moment later the next pair were extinguished as well, creating the impression of a wave of darkness advancing out of the Wood.

By the time it swallowed up the third pair of lanterns it was clear that it was more than just an optical illusion. The Daimler's high beams still functioned, and they could see the glow of the headlights extending to the center of the bridge span and then vanishing abruptly into a void.

Letitia's hand dropped away from the ignition. The darkness had stopped advancing but seemed to gain substance as it settled onto the middle of the bridge, a blob of living shadow barring their escape. Genesis 2:19, Atticus thought numbly. Adam forgot one.

"Oh, *hell!*" exclaimed Montrose. He reached forward over the seat back, grabbed the revolver from George, and shoved his door open.

"Pop, wait!" said Atticus, thinking he meant to attack the thing on the bridge, but on exiting the car his father went the other way. Atticus turned around in his seat and looked out the back window.

Caleb Braithwhite was coming down the road from the manor. He walked slowly, not hurrying, and despite being some distance away Atticus could see his face clearly, as if a light were shining on it. He was smiling.

Atticus cursed. He got his door open and scrambled out, but as he stood his feet became rooted to the ground, as though he'd stepped onto quick-drying cement.

His father hadn't gotten much farther. Montrose was standing about five paces beyond the Daimler's back end. He was leaning forward, as into a stiff wind, and his right arm was fully extended before him. He had the revolver pointed, the hammer cocked and his finger curled around the trigger. But he didn't, or couldn't, shoot.

Caleb Braithwhite just kept coming straight on, making no attempt to move out of the line of fire. Atticus reached down with both hands and tried to lift one of his paralyzed legs. He couldn't budge it. Behind him he heard Letitia and George pounding at the inside of the Daimler's front doors.

Caleb came to a stop before Montrose, stood smiling down the barrel of the revolver. Atticus prayed he would pull the gun towards him and so snag the trigger, but when he did finally take it he was careful, slipping his thumb beneath the hammer to keep it from falling and twisting the gun sideways.

Then the gun was in his hand. He swung out the cylinder, checked that it was loaded. Snapped it closed. Recocked it.

"No," Atticus said. "No!"

Caleb spared him a glance. "I told you," he said. "Consequences."

He pointed the gun at Montrose's chest and pulled the trigger.

Morning again.

Atticus, sitting vigil at his father's bedside, was awakened from a doze by the crowing of a rooster down in the village. He leaned forward over the bed, confirmed that Montrose was still breathing, and then, drawing down the covers, stared at his father's chest as it rose and fell in the gray dawnlight.

There was no wound.

Even now he had trouble accepting it. He'd seen and heard the gun go off, had seen his father crumple. Servants had come running from the lodge; Atticus, half out of his mind with rage, had fought them as best he could with his legs frozen but was quickly overpowered. He and the others had been carried back up to the east wing and locked in the double suite. Able to move again, he'd shouted at George and Letitia to get water and towels. But when he'd torn open his father's shirt, what he had found was not the anatomical ruin he was expecting but unbroken skin and bone, beneath which his father's heart still beat strongly.

He hadn't believed it at first—he'd *seen* the gun go off, at point-blank range—and in desperation he'd rolled his father's body first one way and then the other, looking for the gunshot wound that wasn't there.

No wound. No bullet hole or powder burns on the shirt either. And the only blood came from Atticus's own raw knuckles.

In the midst of being manhandled, Montrose had opened his eyes and told Atticus to leave him be, he was fine—though he sounded as dismayed as his son that this should be so. He tried to sit up and a sudden spike of pain knocked him right back down. He steeled himself and tried again, this time getting all the way to his feet before the agony of the phantom bullet in his chest caused him to pass out. Atticus caught him as he fell, got him back into bed, and started coming to terms with the double-edged miracle: His father was alive. And couldn't be moved.

Now, as Atticus put the blanket back in place, his father stirred and blinked himself awake. "Hey, Pop," Atticus said, speaking gently but prepared to pin him down if he tried to rise.

But Montrose had learned his lesson: He shifted position on the mattress but remained horizontal. "I was dreaming about your mother," he said.

"Yeah? Good dream?"

"She didn't say 'I told you so,' at least." Montrose turned his head carefully, looking around the room. "Where's George and Letitia?"

"In George's room," Atticus said, pointing at the connecting door.

"They OK?"

"'Titia got a black eye fighting the guy who was carrying her and George is a little banged up too. Otherwise they're fine."

Montrose turned his head again. "You try breaking that window yet?"

"We're not leaving without you, Pop."

"You could at least get the girl out of here."

"If you think you can talk Letitia into running, I'll go wake her up right now."

"No," said Montrose. "I guess that's not my strong point, talking people into things." He frowned at his son. "You know what Braithwhite's planning to do with you?"

"Not the particulars," said Atticus. "But I can guess."

Montrose nodded. "He's going to summon up one of the Elder Klansmen. A host of shiggoths too, probably. And you're the sacrifice."

"I'm glad you're feeling good enough to joke about it, Pop."

"Well I'm not saying I'm happy, but I read enough of those stories of yours to know how it ends. The grand wizard and his minions get eaten too. Or driven mad."

"Usually," Atticus said. "But Braithwhite didn't seem too concerned when I talked to him. Maybe he knows what he's doing."

"The father is a fool," Montrose said. "It's the boy who's the dangerous one. You get a chance to push him into the pit, you don't hesitate."

Half an hour later, not long after Montrose had slipped once more into sleep, Atticus heard a key in the hallway door. It was Caleb Braithwhite. He was alone.

"You here to take me upstairs?" Atticus asked him, keeping his voice low.

"No." Braithwhite stood just inside the doorway, at ease but seemingly reluctant to intrude. "The ritual won't be for another few hours yet. My father and the other members are still debating exactly when to hold it."

"The timing matters?"

"My father doesn't think so, but Pendergast and some of the others have conflicting astronomical theories that they feel very strongly about. So they're hashing it out over breakfast. Assuming they don't kill each other, I'd expect them to come for you around noon."

"Them?" Atticus said. "You aren't going to be there?"

"No. I've been ordered off the premises until the ritual is complete."

"Is that to preserve the family bloodline, if things go wrong? Or do the grown-ups just not want you underfoot?"

"A little of both," Caleb Braithwhite said. "I came to say goodbye—and to apologize." He nodded at Montrose's sleeping figure. "I really am sorry about this."

"Yeah, I saw how unhappy you looked pulling the trigger last night."

"I did what I had to do. I told you—"

"Save your breath on that," Atticus said. "You want to do something right? Take Letitia with you. George too, if you can."

"I can't."

"You know there's no need to keep them here. I'm not going to make more trouble, not with Pop like this."

"You're *probably* not going to make more trouble," Braithwhite allowed. "But I'm certain that Letitia would, if I tried to take her out of here without you. And my father's orders are explicit: I leave. No one else."

"Then we've got nothing more to say to each other."

"All right." Nodding. "I'll go, then." But he hesitated, hand on the doorknob. "I'll have breakfast sent up."

"Don't bother."

"No, trust me, you want to eat something," Caleb Braithwhite said. "You want to keep your strength up, for the ritual. And you never know when a meal will be your last . . . None of us do."

Atticus was ready when they came for him. He'd shined his shoes, put on fresh trousers and a clean white shirt, and rolled up his sleeves as if preparing for hard labor.

William, who unlocked the door, smiled as if he'd come to escort Atticus to lunch. The servants in the hall behind him—a couple of them sported bruises from the night before—were less congenial.

Atticus took a last look at his father, and at George and Letitia standing beside the bed. "You all take care of each other," he said. "Pray for me."

The room where the ritual was to take place was a large rectangular space at the center of the third floor. Though windowless, it had a skylight, as well as half a dozen wall sconces fitted with bright bulbs. From scuff marks on the floor and various other signs Atticus surmised the room was a workshop that would ordinarily have been crammed with heavy furniture and equipment. But today it had been emptied of everything not crucial to the business at hand.

A freestanding door had been erected at the east end of the room. The timbers that made up the frame had been carved with letters from a strange alphabet, spelling out what Atticus assumed were words of power. The door itself was a glossy black, with silver hinges and a silver knob.

White chalk flecked with silver had been used to draw a circle on the floor around the door. Parallel lines extended from a gap in the circle's west arc, forming a foot-wide path that connected to another circle at the far end of the room. This second circle contained a curious device: a silver cylinder, waist-high, capped with a hunk of clear crystal.

Midway along the path between the door and the cylinder, directly beneath the skylight, was a third circle. More of the strange letters were inscribed around its circumference and at its center was a large symbol resembling a broken, five-pointed star formed from curved lines, as though, Atticus thought, an ordinary pentagram had been distorted by a magnetic field. The thought of magnetism wasn't random—the series of circles reminded him of a circuit diagram, and he could guess how the ritual was supposed to work. The door would open to admit some force or energy from Elsewhere. The cylinder, which must be a capacitor of some kind, would capture it. To complete the circuit, a conductor was needed: to coax the energy forth, to direct it where it was meant to go . . . and to blow, like a fuse, if it proved too powerful to contain.

"You want me to stand there," Atticus said.

"Yes," said Samuel Braithwhite. Dressed in ceremonial robes, he still looked more mundane than wizardly, like a Harvard professor who'd misplaced his mortarboard. The other Sons of Adam, similarly garbed, were gathered back behind the circle containing the cylinder, which also happened to be the part of the room closest to the exit. William and the servants had been dismissed and told to wait downstairs; Atticus wondered if any of them had the sense to run for the hills.

"We'll also need you to recite an invocation," Braithwhite said. He signaled to one of the more nervous-looking Antenauts; the man came forward holding a rolled-up parchment which he unfurled and showed to Atticus.

"I can't read that," Atticus said. "I don't even know what language that is."

"It's the language of Adam," said Braithwhite. "Everyone can read it. You just need to remember how."

"If you say so . . . What comes through that door?"

"Light. The first light of creation."

"The first light of creation," Atticus repeated. "And what's that do to me?"

Preston banged his cane on the floor. "Time!" he called.

"You'll find out soon enough," Braithwhite said to Atticus. "Now get in."

Galled by Braithwhite's tone, Atticus once more contemplated hauling off and decking the man. But his fists, he knew now, would not obey him if he tried that. And there was his father to consider, and George and Letitia too; their only chance was for him to go through with this.

So he stepped into the circle.

"Face the door," Braithwhite commanded, "and hold out your hands."

Atticus cupped his hands in front of him. Braithwhite produced a knife from within his robes and cut across both palms, the blade so sharp that blood was welling up before Atticus felt any pain.

"Time!" Preston called again, and one of the other Antenauts blew into a horn, a long buzzing note that rattled the base of Atticus's spine. Blood dripped from his hands onto the floor, the droplets skittering like blobs of mercury to the curved lines of the pentagram, which absorbed them. The noon sun's light shone down and the pentagram seemed to absorb that too. It began to glow.

Braithwhite, now holding a piece of silvered chalk, squatted beside the circle. He made a single stroke across one of the letters, changing it to another, and Atticus felt the paralysis grip his legs again. Braithwhite nodded to his assistant, who offered Atticus the parchment. Atticus took it but found he still could not make sense of the invocation.

Then Braithwhite stood up and walked quickly around behind the door and back to the other side of the circle that held Atticus. As the horn sounded a second time, he stooped and changed another letter. Understanding came over Atticus in a flood. Now he could read the words on the parchment and hear them in his head. But when he tried to utter them aloud his tongue was stopped; a weight like an invisible finger pressed against his lips.

"Time!" Preston called. "Time!" The horn sounded again and Braith-white made a third stroke with the chalk. Atticus opened his mouth.

When he began speaking he was aware of Braithwhite and his assistant, scurrying back to join the other Antenauts. But as Atticus went on reciting the words of power the room around him seemed to fade, until all that remained was the door in front of him and the shining pattern on the floor.

Light appeared around the edges of the doorway, light in a hue Atticus could not recall having seen before and which he could not have described, but which at the same time seemed intimately familiar. As the light grew brighter, Atticus found his own comprehension growing with it. Oh, he thought, as the doorknob began to jiggle and twitch. Oh, I see now.

Not long after he'd deployed to Korea, Atticus had attended a Sunday service in camp. The unit's regular chaplain was in the

stockade, having been accused, along with several other Negroes, of in-
stigating a brawl with some white soldiers who'd refused to share their
mess tent. The substitute chaplain took it upon himself to lecture the
black enlisted men of the 24th Infantry about the importance of racial
tolerance. They should strive to live on earth as they would in heaven,
he told them. In the Lord's house they would surrender their mortal
bodies; there would be no more races, no men and women either, only
pure souls, united in God.

The obvious complaint about this sermon was that it was being
preached to the wrong congregation. It wasn't the Negro soldiers who had
defied President Truman's integration order—and they hadn't started the
fight over the mess tent either, whatever the MPs claimed. But some of
Atticus's comrades took issue with the chaplain's theology as well: "No
men and women in heaven?" he heard a soldier behind him grumble. "If
I ain't a man anymore, how's that different from just being *dead*?"

Atticus knew the answer now, and the answer to his question to
Samuel Braithwhite. An experienced natural philosopher might hope
to survive exposure to the unfiltered light of creation, but Atticus would
be annihilated by it. Stripped of identity, of everything that made him
Atticus: not just unmanned, but un-named. It would be like dying, but
a positive oblivion rather than a negative one. A return to the infinite
possibility of the primordial state.

Positive oblivion. The prospect frightened him less than he would
have expected, and he could see how, to a certain type of person, it
wouldn't have been frightening at all, but rather a fate worth seeking.

To a certain type of person. Not Atticus, though. He liked who and
what he was. He always had. It was God's other creatures he occasionally had problems with.

And so, because he did not seek oblivion, and because he wasn't
ready to die, either, he reached into the rolled-up cuff of his left sleeve
and pulled out the slip of paper that was hidden there. The unsigned
note that had been delivered along with his breakfast.

"For Atticus," it said. "A twist in the tale. When you can read this, do so:" and then three words in the language of Adam.

Time, Atticus thought.

He spoke the words aloud, and the glowing pattern on the floor transformed. The circle around the door was broken and the connecting path melted away. The circle around Atticus closed up, and not a moment too soon: The door was opening.

A veil of protective darkness dropped over Atticus's eyes, shielding him from the light that otherwise would have burned him where he stood. His mind, seeing that the darkness was good, decided to drift off into it.

As he fell unconscious, he heard the Sons of Adam screaming.

When the darkness lifted he was curled up on the floor. The wounds on his hands had closed, leaving only faint scars, and he was otherwise unharmed.

The same could not be said for the rest of the room. The floorboards outside the protective circle were blackened and scorched, as were the walls and the ceiling. The magic doorway and the capacitor were burnt and melted wrecks, and the skylight had become an open hole in the roof.

As for the Sons of Adam, they were more Sons of Pompeii, now: ashen figures, caught in poses of terror. Then Atticus stood up and the vibration of his footfalls triggered a final dissolution. Surrendering to entropy, the Antenauts crumbled into piles of white dust.

Atticus tried not to get any on his shoes as he walked out.

He found George and Letitia and his father all waiting down in the foyer. With their bags beside them, they looked like unhappy tourists at checkout, clearly regretting their choice of accommodations but otherwise none the worse for wear.

"Pop!" exclaimed Atticus. "You OK?" To which Montrose responded with a sullen shrug.

"William called the room a few minutes ago and told us we were free to leave," George explained. "By the time the servants came to unlock the door, Montrose was up and about."

"What about Mr. Braithwhite and the Order?" Letitia asked. "Are they—"

"Gone," said Atticus. "All of them." He looked at his father. "Braithwhite junior staged a coup."

"Told you," Montrose said nodding.

"So where does that leave us?" George wondered.

They heard a car out front and went to look. It was William, bringing George's Packard from the garage. The broken windows had been replaced and the entire vehicle had been buffed and polished until it looked practically brand-new.

"Mr. Turner!" William said brightly as he got out of the car. "I'm so glad you survived your ordeal intact!"

"Yeah, me too," Atticus said. "Nice job on the repairs."

"Mr. Braithwhite's doing," William said. "He saw to it personally this morning before he left. He asked me to tell you that he's sorry he can't be here to see you off in person, and he apologizes, again, for all that you've been put through. He hopes you'll accept a few tokens of his sincere regret: some boxes of books for you and your uncle, and for you, Mr. Turner"—he looked at Montrose—"a copy of all the genealogical data Mr. Braithwhite managed to collect about your late wife's family. Miss Dandridge, I've taken the liberty of repacking your dresses. Also, Mr. Berry, in addition to repairing your car, Mr. Braithwhite made a small modification to it that he believes you'll find agreeable."

"What sort of modification?" George said.

"A dash of immunity. From now on, you should find you're much less likely to run into trouble on the road. Law enforcement officials, in particular, will tend to treat you as though you're invisible to them."

"So George can speed and get away with it?" Montrose said. "That's an option?"

"Yes, sir. I confess I'm ignorant of the mechanism, but Mr. Braithwhite has it on all his own cars as well. It's quite useful when he's in a hurry—or when he can't find legal parking."

"What about Sheriff Hunt?" Atticus asked. "Are we invisible to him too?"

"In a manner of speaking," William said. "My understanding is that the sheriff is preoccupied with hiring new deputies. He's entirely forgotten his encounter with you the other night—and he'll go on forgetting it, so long as you're careful not to cross his path again. To that end, as you leave here, you'll want to take the left-hand way whenever the road branches. After the third such branching, you'll find yourself exiting the Wood—and Devon County—without having passed through Bideford."

"And that's it?" Atticus said. "We just go home?"

"Unless you'd prefer some other destination, Mr. Turner." Looking past him, William raised a hand and snapped his fingers. Servants came out of the lodge, carrying the bags.

"What about Mr. Braithwhite?" George said, after the luggage had been put in the car.

"Mr. Braithwhite, sir? What about him?"

"I think my uncle George is asking what Mr. Braithwhite's plans are," Atticus said. "Now that he's lord of the manor."

"I'm sure I don't know, Mr. Turner," William said. "As I told you when we first met, I keep Mr. Braithwhite's house, not his business."

"And as I told you, I think you know a lot about his business. My 'ordeal,' for example—I wouldn't have survived it, if you hadn't passed me that note."

"That was entirely Mr. Braithwhite's doing, Mr. Turner. I was simply following his instructions." William paused to consider. "I suppose I could be credited with the wisdom of knowing *which* Mr. Braithwhite to follow . . . But the choice wasn't difficult." He smiled. "Well," he concluded, "I have a bit of cleaning up to do, so you'll have to excuse me. Do drive carefully." And with that, and a final nod, he went quickly into the lodge, shutting the doors behind him.

The four of them stood in the afternoon sunlight, thinking: Dismissed.

"It never fails," Montrose said. "No matter what they do to you, afterwards it's like nothing happened. You're supposed to just be grateful you're still breathing."

"Well, I am grateful for that," George admitted. He stepped up to the car and ran a hand along the wood trim. "Immunity. Huh."

"We'll have to give that a try on the way back to Marvin's," Letitia said. "I'd be happy to drive, if you want."

George laughed. "Not a chance," he said. "I got first dibs."

Letitia and Montrose rode up front with him. Atticus squeezed himself in between the luggage and Braithwhite's going-away presents, so he could look out the back as they drove.

He watched the lodge for as long as he could see it. When they'd crossed the bridge and entered the Wood, he watched the road, alert for any flash of silver on the twists and turns behind them. He saw no sign of Braithwhite's Daimler, but as they reached the third fork in the road, he glimpsed a big shadow moving back among the trees. Come to say goodbye? Atticus wondered. Or just farewell for now?

Another mile on they passed a sign that said LEAVING DEVON COUNTY. "Praise Jesus," said Letitia. George added his own "Hallelujah," and Montrose muttered, "Good riddance." Atticus said nothing, only faced forward, and tried to believe that the country into which they now traveled was different from the one they left behind.

DREAMS OF THE WHICH HOUSE

❧

No part of said premises shall in any manner be used or occupied directly or indirectly by any negro or negroes, provided that this restriction shall not prevent the occupation, during the period of their employment, of janitors' or chauffeurs' quarters in the basement or in a barn or garage in the rear, or of servants' quarters . . . No part of said premises shall be sold, given, conveyed or leased to any negro or negroes, and no permission or license to use or occupy any part thereof shall be given to any negro except house servants or janitors or chauffeurs employed thereon as aforesaid.

—"Standard Form, Restrictive Covenant,"
drafted for the Chicago Real Estate Board by
Nathan William MacChesney of the
Chicago Plan Commission, 1927

Summer was waning when Letitia got the blessing she'd been waiting for. By then, her ordeal in Ardham had come to feel like a distant memory, and there were times, as June became July and July became August, when she wondered if she'd been wrong about God having something special in store for her. Maybe the virtue of helping Atticus find his father was supposed to be its own reward—that, and getting to go home alive, afterwards.

If that *had* been the case, she'd have accepted it and been grateful. Though her brother, Marvin, might claim otherwise, Letitia knew better than to believe God owed her anything. But she also knew that the Lord moves at His own speed, and that patience is often part of the price He exacts for giving us what He wants us to have.

The blessing when it finally did come was everything she'd hoped for, and more. Letitia had been wrong about one thing, though: Her ordeal wasn't over.

She came by the Safe Negro Travel Company the same day she deposited the check. George was alone in the office, looking over the proofs for the autumn edition of the *Guide*. Letitia got straight to the point.

"Real estate," George said. "You win a sweepstakes?"

"Kind of," Letitia said. "I got a registered letter last week." Actually, the envelope had been addressed to "Miss Dandridge," and since Letitia was staying at Ruby's, it would have been fair to assume the letter was meant for her. But Letitia was home by herself that morning, and curiosity got the better of her. "The letter was from a lawyer. He said he had some money from one of Daddy's business partners, to pay off an old debt." "Business partner," in Warren Dandridge's case, meaning "gambler." Letitia's father had made his living at cards: poker and gin rummy, primarily, though he'd play any game he could win.

"I know what you're thinking," Letitia said.

"I'm not thinking anything, honey. I always respected your dad."

"I know you did. But you'd be a fool not to think it. Daddy wasn't a con man, but he ran with con men. Ruby wanted to burn the letter."

"But not you, huh?"

"I had to go see." Thinking even if it was a con, she might be able to turn it to her advantage somehow. "The lawyer's office was in this fancy building on LaSalle Street. The security guards didn't even want to let me in the lobby." They'd made her use the service elevator, which she'd found reassuring. Playing hard to get was an old con man's trick, but a white lawyer in a white building was a lot of trouble to go to to fool someone, and she didn't think her father's friends respected women's intelligence that much.

"Did the lawyer tell you who this business partner was?" George asked.

"No. That was the whole point of the lawyer—he wanted to be anonymous."

"Hmm."

"I know," she said. "As soon as he told me that, I was sure he was going to ask me for money up front, some kind of fee. But he didn't want anything, not even a signature. All I had to do was show him my driver's license and he gave me a check."

"How much was the check for?"

"This stays between us?"

"Of course."

She told him the amount.

"Well now," George said. "With that, you really could buy an apartment—a small one, anyway. If—"

"If the money's real, yeah. I'll know soon enough. But meantime, the reason I'm here, I want something more than just an apartment."

"A house?"

She hesitated, unsure what name to give her desire. "A *place*," she said finally. "With space for me and Ruby so we're not always on top of each other, and a room for Marvin to stay in when he visits, and some extra rooms to let out . . ."

George smiled. "You want to be a landlady?"

"I know it's not glamorous," she said, "but yeah, I think I'd like that." Letitia cast an appraising glance around the office. "Maybe space to run my own business, too . . ."

"Well I admire your ambition," George said, "but even if you can afford the down payment on the kind of place you're talking about, you know no bank is going to give you a mortgage."

Letitia nodded. Because banks didn't like to invest in colored neighborhoods, or neighborhoods likely to become colored, mortgage loans were almost impossible for Negroes to obtain; for home financing, most were forced to rely on installment contracts. The payment structure was similar to a mortgage, but you didn't own the property until the contract was paid off—and if you defaulted, even on the very last payment, you lost everything you'd put into it. The upside was, anyone could get one: Sellers were often eager to offer contracts to buyers they thought would default, because it allowed them to collect multiple down payments on the same property.

"The other problem," George added, "is finding a place. I don't have to tell you what the housing situation's like."

"Well, about that," Letitia said. "I was thinking I might try pioneering."

"You want to buy property in a white neighborhood?"

"I know you know people who've done it. Like Mr. and Mrs. Powell—didn't you help get them into East Woodlawn, back when there were practically no Negroes living there?"

"Yeah," George acknowledged reluctantly. "But what happened with Albert and Thea is as much a cautionary tale as a success story . . ."

"So tell it to me," Letitia said. "How did it work?"

"Well," George said, "this was six years ago, right after the Supreme Court ruled that racist housing covenants were unconstitutional. Albert and Thea had plenty of money saved up and they'd been wanting to buy a house for the longest time, so they took the ruling as a go signal. That's when Albert came to me and asked if I knew a real-estate broker he could trust.

"See, what the justices actually said is that race-restrictive covenants aren't enforceable in court. Property owners can still abide by them voluntarily, though, and most white folks, unless they're desperate, aren't going to sell to colored people if it costs them all their friends. So Albert needed a broker who'd play along with a shell game, and he also needed to find a white person who'd act as a front man."

"To buy the house for him, you mean? He had to pay someone for that?"

"That's usually how it works," George said. "Albert had a bit of luck there. His sister is married to a white man. Jewish," he clarified, "but German enough to pass for Lutheran. So Albert got his brother-in-law to buy the house, using Albert and Thea's money, and with the understanding that they'd get title once the deal closed.

"The next step was taking possession. Even with the Supreme Court on their side, Albert and Thea were worried their new neighbors might try to stop them moving in. So they did it on the sneak: went to a Saturday-night mass, asked St. Jude to look out for them, and made the move the next morning while the neighbors were all at their own churches. Once they got the van unloaded, Albert put in a call to the local police and let them know they had a new Negro couple living in their precinct who were probably going to need protection.

"Of course the cops turned right around and told the neighbors. And so by Monday morning, when Albert and Thea left to go to work, every other house on the block had a sign up saying WE ARE A WHITE COMMUNITY—UNDESIRABLES MUST GO.

"That was Monday. Tuesday night, someone threw a brick through Albert and Thea's front window. Albert called the police again, and when they didn't do anything, he called the NAACP and the city Commission on Human Relations. I made some calls too. Eventually the cops stationed a patrol car in front of the house. For what good it did: That first year, there were thirty-nine instances of vandalism, including two arson attempts. Albert's dog was poisoned. And of course he and Thea couldn't even walk down the block without people hurling abuse at them . . ."

Letitia nodded, understanding the point George was trying to make here, but eager to make her own: "In the end, though, they kept the house. Right?"

"Oh, yeah," George said. "Albert went prematurely gray from not sleeping for a year and Thea had a heart attack, but they kept the house . . ." He shook his head. "You're serious about this, huh?"

"Well, George," Letitia said, "I can't imagine the Lord giving me this opportunity if He didn't intend me to use it."

"And Marvin and Ruby, they're on board too?"

One thing the lawyer had been clear about: The check was intended to go to Warren Dandridge's *daughters*. So Marvin and his skepticism weren't a part of it. As for Ruby . . .

"Yeah," she said. "They're on board."

The words on the frosted-glass pane read HAROLD BAILEY, REALTIST. Realtist: a Negro real-estate broker. Not to be confused with a white Real*tor*, whose national association Negroes could not join. A pair of decals indicated Mr. Bailey was also a member of the Prince Hall Freemasons and the Improved Order of Elks.

The lights in Mr. Bailey's office were out and the door was locked. Letitia, standing in the third-floor hallway with Ruby, tried to control her impatience.

A bystander might not have guessed they were sisters. Letitia, slender and light-skinned, favored her father. Ruby, curvy and dark, suggested a youthful Momma—but a Momma who could be pushed around. Her pliability wasn't limitless, though, and there was a core of genuine Momma within her that could emerge, given time, like a mountain rising from the sea. The trick was getting what you wanted from her before you ran aground. So far Ruby seemed willing to play along with Letitia's scheme, but if this morning's meeting had to be rescheduled, she might start having other ideas.

"He *said* nine o'clock . . ."

"Well I promised Mrs. Parker that I'd be over to watch Clarice by eleven thirty," Ruby said. "And I *was* hoping to stop into Mandel

Brothers' basement to look for shoes for that new catering job I told you about."

"I don't see what you want to start another job for," Letitia said. "Now that we got this—"

"Of course you don't see. You need to know how to hold down *one* steady job before you can talk about *another*."

"I *am* going to have a steady job now, Ruby. That's what this is all about. Security!"

"Yeah, big landlady on Easy Street." Ruby sighed. "We could still give the money to the church."

"Ruby!" Letitia was horrified. "You didn't *tell* anyone from church, did you?"

"No, don't worry, Uncle Pennybags, I didn't give away your secret."

"You better not have. Daddy wanted *us* to have this money."

Ruby snorted. "Like you care what Daddy wanted."

"I do care! And I care about *you*." Which brought another snort. "You want to spend the rest of your life living in one tiny room?"

"Of course I don't. But—"

"And hard as you work? When's the last time you came into a fortune like this?"

"Never," Ruby said. "That's how I know not to trust it."

A door opened at the far end of the hall. The sisters turned to look at the white man who'd come out to look at them.

"Miss Dandridge?" the man said.

"I'm Miss Dandridge," said Letitia. Feeling Ruby bristle beside her: "We both are."

"I'm John Archibald. I'm a friend of Mr. Bailey's. He asked me to tell you that he won't be able to meet with you today—"

"Oh."

"He also told me what it is you're here for. I'd be happy to help you myself, if you'd like." He stepped farther into the hall as he said this, and Letitia looking past him at the open door saw the word REALTOR painted in reverse on the glass. "Of course," he added, noting her hesitation, "if you'd rather wait for Mr. Bailey . . ."

Ruby's hand was on Letitia's arm, tugging: *Let's go.* But it might be another week before Ruby had free time again. Too long. "You and Mr. Bailey," Letitia said. "Are you just friends, or . . ."

"Partners," Mr. Archibald said. "Silent partners."

"These are all white neighborhoods."

"Yes," said Mr. Archibald. "That's what Hal told me you were interested in."

"Nobody told *me* anything about white neighborhoods." Ruby looked pointedly at Letitia, who went right on turning pages in the three-ring binder Mr. Archibald had offered them.

"There's something I don't understand about these prices," Letitia said. "Like these two buildings here: They look almost the same, in terms of square footage and lot size. But the first one's so much cheaper." She showed him the listings.

"It's a matter of location," Mr. Archibald explained.

"But they're on the same street."

"Different blocks, though. With that first property, the block is still entirely white-owned. As I'm sure I don't have to tell you, it can be difficult to be the first Negro to break into a block—"

"We don't want difficult," said Ruby. "Definitely not."

"—so in this case the seller, an investor Hal and I both know, has agreed to offer what we call a first-in discount. Once that first sale goes through, subsequent sales become much easier. Eventually, as in the case of that second property, things reach a tipping point where ownership of the whole block can turn over in only a year or two."

"Lots of commissions for you," Letitia said.

"Lots of commissions for me *and* Mr. Bailey," he corrected her. "And lots of new homes for deserving Negro families."

Letitia nodded. "Fair enough." It wasn't, but she couldn't be too outraged by a practice she hoped to benefit from. The real problem was, even with the first-in discount, she wasn't sure she could afford what she wanted—and however much of a straight shooter he made himself out to be, she didn't doubt Mr. Archibald would gladly take her money for a property she'd end up defaulting on.

She turned another page in the binder.

"This can't be right," she said, reading over the listing. "This price can't be right, can it?"

Mr. Archibald leaned forward to see what property she was looking at. "Oh," he said. "The Winthrop House."

"The which house?" Letitia said.

"It's ugly," said Ruby.

"It'll be prettier once it's ours," Letitia replied. "Like a baby."

Noon of the following Sunday, and the sisters in their church clothes stood before a boxy edifice whose brick exterior exhibited all the charm of a public school building. But it was the inside Letitia cared about. Looking up, she could see the glass tent of the skylight that, according to the property listing, capped a two-story atrium surrounded by fourteen other rooms. Fourteen rooms: The apartment Letitia and her siblings had grown up in had had just two, plus a shared bathroom on a different floor.

The Winthrop House shared its narrow block with a defunct tavern and an overgrown lot that had at one time been a park. The block was on the west side of a two-lane street. The east side was lined with small single-family homes, all white-owned; a woman sitting on the porch of the cottage directly opposite the Winthrop House had watched with trepidation as Letitia and Ruby approached and was now glaring openly at them.

"It's a lot longer trip to work from here, too," Ruby said.

"Yeah, but when you come home you'll be able to stretch out and be comfortable."

"I'm comfortable where I am."

"This'll be more comfortable," Letitia insisted. She looked up again, at a rust-eaten chair perched incongruously at the roof's northeast corner. "Must be a nice view. I wonder if you can see the lake from here." She turned around smiling and was met by the white woman's hostile stare.

"Yeah, nice view," said Ruby, casting her own glance across the street. "I'm sure we'll be *real* comfortable."

Mr. Archibald arrived a few minutes later. He tipped his hat to the glowering white woman and hustled Letitia and Ruby inside.

Dust motes floated in the sunlight streaming down onto the atrium's chessboard floor. Archways to the left and right of the front door gave access to what Mr. Archibald identified as a dining room and a parlor, though given the absence of furniture they had to take his word for it. Stairs ran up the atrium's right wall to a gallery in back, with more doorways visible above and below.

Letitia approached the atrium's centerpiece, a sheet-draped figure standing inside a raised marble ring. The property listing had mentioned a fountain, but it hadn't occurred to her that it might be indoors.

"May I?" she asked.

"Please," said Mr. Archibald.

Letitia grabbed a fold of the sheet and pulled, unveiling a naked divinity cast in bronze.

"Lord," said Ruby. The bronze idol, her hair pinned up with a crescent-moon tiara, gripped two massive torches, one in each hand, their flames rising past the level of her shoulders. A skeleton key dangled between her bare breasts. At her feet was a basket of hissing snakes, copper tubing in their coils feeding down into the guts of the fountain.

"Hecate," Mr. Archibald said helpfully. "Goddess of the moon."

"I see the moon all right," said Letitia, circling around to the fountain's rear. Two additional faces sprouted from the back of Hecate's head, like something out of a carnival freak show; a chorus of toads, spigot-mouthed like the snakes, formed an unsightly mound behind her heels. "This is going to have to go."

"I can certainly speak to the seller about it," Mr. Archibald said. "But as I explained yesterday, under the terms of the purchase contract—"

"Yeah, I was paying attention." Because she wouldn't own the house until it was paid off, any "significant alterations" to the property had to be approved by the seller. "You sure I can't talk to them directly?"

"No, I'm afraid not." The property listing said the Winthrop House was owned by Penumbra Real Estate, which Letitia assumed was run by Mr. Archibald's investor friend—or perhaps by Mr. Archibald himself. All communication with Penumbra was to go through him. "I'll convey your concern."

"Be sure you do." Letitia sniffed. "The kind of tenants we're hoping to rent to—families, churchgoing folk—they're not going to like this. At all." Reflecting as she said it that South Side Negroes would put up with a lot worse than pagan statuary to get a roof over their heads. But they shouldn't have to put up with it, she thought—and for sure *she* didn't want to look at Hecate's moon every day.

She shifted her attention to a pair of dark doorways, one up on the gallery, one directly beneath it, both screened by iron accordion gates. "That's the elevator?"

"Yes," Mr. Archibald said. "The builder of the house, Hiram Winthrop, had it installed for his wife. She'd had polio," he explained.

"You hear that, Ruby?" Letitia said. "Polio. Like Marvin."

"Marvin climbs stairs just fine," Ruby replied.

"Well, not everyone does. That could be a selling point, for tenants." Old people, she thought. Quiet. Easy to get along with. Paid their rent on time.

"The elevator *does* need to be repaired," Mr. Archibald noted, the delicacy with which he said this making it plain whose responsibility that would be.

Ruby snorted. "Of course it does. What else is wrong with the house?"

"The wiring needs to be looked at. The power is off right now, but the last occupant reported that fuses were blowing constantly. Also—"

"No," Ruby said, "what's *wrong* with it?" She fixed him with a narrow-eyed stare: Momma, peering up from the depths. "A house this size, with a price this low, and you're willing to let *us* have it? That's about more than a fuse box. What aren't you telling us?"

Mr. Archibald hesitated. It was plain from his expression that he'd been waiting for this question and was even relieved that the subject had been broached; yet still he wasn't sure how to answer.

Letitia saved him the trouble: "It's haunted."

"What?" said Ruby.

"It's a haunted house. What else could it be?" She looked at Mr. Archibald, who confirmed her guess by not saying no. "So who's the ghost? Mrs. Winthrop? She ride her wheelchair up and down the halls at night?"

"I honestly don't know," Mr. Archibald said. "I—"

"Wait a minute," said Ruby. "This is *true*?"

"All I've heard are stories." Mr. Archibald raised a hand, Scout's honor. "I haven't experienced any phenomena myself, nor do I expect to. But it's true that some prior occupants have reported . . . incidents. Bumps in the night. And the last several attempts to sell the house have all ended with the buyers backing out."

"And when were you planning on mentioning this, exactly?"

"Miss Dandridge, please. I wasn't trying to withhold information from you. But I consider myself a rational man. I don't believe in—"

"It's OK," Letitia said. "We're not afraid of dead people."

"Letitia!"

"One thing, though—now that the cat's out of the bag, you think the seller might come down on the price even more?"

"Le*titi*a!"

"*Ruby*!" Matching her tone for tone. "It's got an elevator!"

The first to arrive for the moving-in-day party was George's wife, Hippolyta. She drove up in her Buick Roadmaster, with Horace beside her and a secondhand bedstead tied to the car's roof.

The elevator wasn't working yet, so they wrestled the bedstead up the stairs—Letitia and Horace holding one end, six-foot Hippolyta the other—and into the room Letitia had chosen for herself, where a box spring, mattress, and sheets were already waiting. After making up the bed, Letitia stepped back and took a deep breath, half-expecting to wake and find herself under the covers at Ruby's old place. But the dream house stayed solid around her, so she took another breath and laughed, and turned to Hippolyta. "Come on," she said. "I'll give you the tour."

They came out on the gallery and caught Horace downstairs, peeking under Hecate's sheet. "Careful!" Letitia warned, making Horace jump. "You'll go blind!" She laughed again. "Come on back up, there's something you and your mom will both like."

She led them to a room in the southwest corner of the second floor. With its built-in bookcase, it had probably been intended as a study, and Letitia had plans to turn it into a rentable bedroom. But at the moment it housed an oversized rich man's toy.

Mr. Archibald had called the device an orrery: a model solar system, though the system it modeled wasn't Sol's, but rather that of a double star. The twin suns were gold and silver spheres mounted on a central pivot. Ranged around them on brass arms of varying length were eleven planets, some with satellites of their own, and a comet carved from a hunk of milky quartz. All of this was supported by a squat metal table whose windowed top offered glimpses of complex gearwork.

"Whoah," said Horace. Hippolyta stayed silent, but her eyes were as wide as her son's as she leaned in to examine one of the larger planets, a glass ball filled with fluid that formed bands and swirls like the atmosphere of Jupiter.

"Told you you'd like it. And it moves, too. Horace, duck down and flip that little lever on the base, there." Eagerly he did as she asked. The orrery came to life, suns dancing around on their pivot, brass arms turning. The exposed gearwork emitted a noisy *tick-tick-clack*, but the motion of the planets was smooth, and if you squinted the right way you could make the arms disappear so that they seemed to float free.

Letitia looked sideways at Hippolyta, who in that moment resembled the world's tallest child on Christmas morning. "It's yours if you want it."

"Mom!" Horace said. "Yes!"

"Oh, no . . ." Hippolyta's face saying *If only*.

"I can't sell it to an antique store," Letitia explained, "because it's not mine to sell. But my contract doesn't say anything about loans. And I know you'd appreciate it."

"Mom . . ."

"Where would we put it, though?"

"My room!" cried Horace.

"Uh-huh. And after we moved out your bed to make room for it, where would you sleep?"

"On the floor!" He demonstrated, lying faceup on the hardwood while the planets wheeled above him.

"You're welcome to the pictures, too," Letitia said. The wall opposite the bookcase was decorated with heavy glass photographic plates showing clusters of stars.

Hippolyta went to take a closer look. "It's funny, I don't recognize any of these constellations," she said after a moment. She peered curiously at an image of a spiral galaxy that had been labeled THE

DROWNING OCTOPUS. "Do you know where these were taken?" Letitia shook her head.

Horace, on his feet again, opened a narrow door beside the bookcase. "What's in here?"

"Stairs to the roof," Letitia told him. "Don't go up." To Hippolyta, she said: "I'm serious about giving this thing to you. You could put it on your own roof, maybe."

"That'd be a feat, getting it up to our roof," Hippolyta said laughing. "You'd have to take it apart just to get it out of this room."

"I could take it apart!" Horace volunteered. "I could put it back together for you too! We can—"

The hall door banged shut. Horace jumped and his mother started as well. Only Letitia kept calm, outwardly at least, not even batting an eye.

"Drafty old house," she said.

More guests arrived. Some brought furniture, others food and drink for the party. Tree Hawkins, the bouncer from Denmark Vesey's, brought himself and three friends as large as he was. They came in a rust-bucket Cadillac with a broken muffler, their arrival noted by everyone within earshot, the plan being they'd sneak out the back at the end of the night and leave the car behind as a caution to the neighbors: Make trouble and find yourself tangling with giants.

By nightfall there were upwards of fifty people in the house—more warm bodies than the Winthrop House had known in years, maybe ever. Letitia, checking on the buffet that had been set up in the dining room, stopped to chat with Atticus's father, whose housewarming gift had been a shotgun and a box of shells.

"Three," Montrose said, nodding at the family portrait above the dining room fireplace: Hiram Winthrop, his wife, and a boy about Horace's age. "All this space, for three people."

"Two, actually," Letitia said. "I did some homework. Turns out Mrs. Winthrop died, right before they were supposed to move in. So it was just him and the boy. And the servants, of course." The servants' quarters were in the basement, underneath the kitchen and the laundry room.

"You know how he made his money?"

"The family fortune came from a string of textile mills back east. But I gather old Hiram, here, was more about spending it than making it."

"Textile mills." Montrose grunted. "Cotton money."

"Yeah, it's funny how things come back around, isn't it?"

In the atrium, Tree and the other bouncers had brought out instruments, and some of the guests were dancing—or trying to. The band kept going off tempo, eliciting mostly good-natured groans from the crowd.

Letitia went up to Charlie Boyd, who was sitting on the edge of the fountain. Hecate's sheet was now swaddled around her like a toga, and someone had stuck a Howard University Bison pennant on one of her torches. "What's wrong with Tree?" Letitia asked. "They're usually better than this."

Charlie shrugged. "You ask me, this isn't their first party of the day. But Tree claims it's bad vibrations."

"Vibrations?"

"Through the floor." Charlie mimed banging a broomstick on the ceiling. "You don't have somebody living downstairs already, do you?"

"Not yet. But there's some nice bunk beds down there, if you're interested."

"Thanks, I already live in a basement. You want to rent me one of those upstairs bedrooms, though . . ."

"We'll talk," Letitia promised. "You seen Atticus around?"

"He said something about going up to the roof."

The wall switch in the orrery room clicked uselessly, but by the light from the hall Letitia could see the roof door standing open. She stepped carefully around the orrery, glimpsing as she did so some-thing small and many-legged swimming in the fluid of the model gas giant. A trick of the shadows, that vanished when she looked straight at it.

On the roof, the chimneys were arranged like standing stones around the tent of the skylight. Atticus was over on the far side, sitting in the chair with his back to her. Letitia was about to call his name when she was seized by sudden doubt, another trick of perception making it seem as though the figure in the chair had a head of straight, fine hair combed back above a pale neck.

Then Atticus turned around smiling.

"Hey," he said. "I tell you you look nice tonight?"

She did a perfunctory twirl beside the skylight, the act reminding her where she'd gotten this particular dress. Reminding him too: His smile faltered.

She came and stood next to him. Across the street, the neigh-bors were having their own party. *Worse music, worse drinking,* Letitia thought, recalling an observation her father had once made about how white people celebrated.

"They've been pretty well behaved," Atticus volunteered. "Some boys were out on the lawn before, trying to blow up Tree's Cadillac with their eyeballs, but they lost heart and went back inside. I don't think you'll have any trouble tonight. Tomorrow . . ." He shrugged.

"I'm not worried," Letitia said automatically.

"Ruby is. Can't say I blame her, either."

"Ruby said something to you? When, just now?"

"I ran into her on the street a few days ago. Look, Letitia, I know it's not my business—"

"You got that right," she said. "And if you're so concerned about us, how come Ruby has to run into you? What's it been, three months now since we got back? In all that time, how often have you called or come by to see how I am?"

"I know," he said, nodding. "I know, and I'm sorry. But after what happened, I thought it might be safer for you if I kept my distance. In case it's not over."

"Yeah, I figured. But you could have done me the courtesy of asking if I *wanted* to be kept safe that way. Haven't I earned that much?"

Atticus didn't have an answer for that. He looked off into the night, pretending to be interested in the navigation lights of a passing airplane.

After a moment Letitia said: "I heard you're working for George now."

"That's a matter of opinion," said Atticus. "I've been doing odd jobs for him, research for the *Guide* mostly. He sends me out on scouting trips."

"Like Hippolyta?"

"Aunt Hippolyta chooses her own destinations. I get a list, and George covers my gas and expenses."

"Sounds like work to me."

"Pop calls it make-work. He's been on me to stop fooling around and use my G.I. benefit to go to college. He's not wrong," Atticus said. "But I don't know . . . Something's not settled yet."

"Well, if you're looking for more make-work," Letitia said, "I could use a hand around here. You know anything about fixing elevators?"

"That sounds like a job for Pop. You should ask him."

"I'm asking you. I can't pay you a salary, but I can give you free room and board when you're not out on the road for George. Let you get a little distance from your father, if you want it."

Atticus thought about it. "So I'd be your handyman on call? And someone to help keep the neighbors at bay, maybe?"

"Couldn't hurt," Letitia acknowledged. "Maybe you could wear your uniform now and then, let them know I've got a soldier living here."

"All right." He nodded. "Only thing, I'm headed to Colorado tomorrow, to check out this new motel chain and talk to some gas station owners about carrying the *Guide*. I should be back by Friday, though. You and Ruby be OK alone till then?"

"Of course we will. And we won't be alone." Letitia smiled. "We got the Holy Spirit looking out for us."

$\mathbf{M}$omma was coming to see the house. The visit had slipped Letitia's mind somehow, until she woke with a start late Monday morning, realizing she had only moments to get ready.

She dashed out to the gallery and discovered to her dismay that she'd also forgotten to clean up after Saturday night's party: The atrium's black and white tile was buried beneath mounds of colored confetti, and there were paper streamers everywhere. And when she looked into the dining room (having descended to the ground floor without taking a step) she saw more mess: plates and cups spilling off the table, and stains on the walls that would have to be scrubbed.

And Hecate! The goddess was naked again, but grown even more obscene, her breasts bigger, her behind bigger too, the corner of her mouth turned up in a cruel smirk as if anticipating Momma's reaction. Letitia pressed a hand to her own mouth, horrified: *I'm going to get the belt for sure!*

She turned, meaning to run back to the kitchen, find a push broom, sweep everything up—confetti, tableware, Hecate, all of it—but the goddess clapped a heavy bronze hand on her shoulder and held her fast. Outside, a taxi door slammed, and Letitia heard Momma telling the driver to be careful with her suitcase.

Light flared beneath the gallery. The elevator was rising out of the basement, its gleaming white interior bright as a beacon. Hiram Winthrop rode inside, glaring at Letitia out of the glass helmet of the spacesuit he was wearing. Then Letitia blinked and Winthrop's head was replaced by a swirling darkness in which many-legged creatures swam.

As the elevator continued to ascend, Hecate tightened her grip, crushing Letitia's shoulder. Momma pounded at the front door. "Letitia!" she called. "I know you're in there! Le—"

"—*titia.*"

She sat up in her bed, in the dark, her sister's hand on her shoulder. "What?" she said. "What?"

"There's someone in the house," Ruby whispered.

Letitia listened, hearing nothing at first, then detecting a faint rhythmic sound in the distance. "What is that?" Without waiting for an answer, she shrugged off Ruby's hand and swung her legs out of the bed, the shock of the cold floor against her bare feet bringing her fully awake. She retrieved the shotgun from under the bed, broke it open, ran her thumb over the brass casings of the shells already loaded in the barrels, snapped it shut again, and went out onto the gallery.

The moon was shining through the skylight, illuminating the atrium floor—the spotlessly clean floor, Letitia noted—and Hecate, the goddess in her element. Turning right, Letitia saw that, as in her dream, the elevator was now on the second floor, the gate standing open. "That's what woke me up," Ruby told her. "I heard it moving."

Letitia stuck her head into the empty elevator car, smelling musty wood and leather. She paused, listening again. The rhythmic sound was louder now: *Tick-tick-clack, tick-tick-clack.*

The door to the orrery room stood ajar, letting a wedge of warm electric light into the hall. Letitia counted to three, invoked the Savior's name, and stepped into the doorway. *Tick-tick-clack, tick-tick-clack:* The stars and planets pivoted and whirled, and Letitia did too, sweeping the gun from side to side, corner to corner. But the room was, visibly at least, unoccupied.

"What is it, Letitia?" Ruby said from ten paces back in the hallway.

"Nothing," said Letitia. She stepped back, lowering the gun, and the door slammed in her face, making Ruby shriek. The elevator was next, the gate crashing shut, and then, one after the other, what sounded like every other door in the house: Crash, crash, crash, *crash*.

"Oh my God, oh my God," Ruby said, her panic pushing Letitia the other way, from fear towards anger.

"Damn it, Ruby," she said, "stop wailing! It's just noise!"

And then the greatest crash of all, a tremendous jolt as though the whole house had been lifted off its foundation and dropped. Letitia fought to keep her balance while Ruby collapsed against the wall. "Letitia!" she cried, only terror of falling keeping her from headlong flight. "I want to go home!"

"You are home," Letitia said. When the Winthrop House bucked a second time, she was ready for it, feet braced like a captain on the deck of a rolling ship. Her ship.

"We're not leaving," she said. "This is our house now." Leaning into the storm: "We're at a tipping point."

But Ruby wouldn't stay.

Not long after daybreak, in what felt like an inversion of her dream, Letitia watched Ruby lift a hastily packed suitcase into the back of a cab. "Where are you going to go?" Letitia said, and her sister replied, "Away from here."

As the taxi drove off, Letitia felt eyes on her and looked across the street to find the white woman on her porch, the smugness of her expression making Letitia wonder whether she knew about the ghost. Then she noticed Tree's Cadillac, still parked at the curb, but sitting now on four flats with "NIGGER" scratched crudely across the front hood. So that's it, Letitia thought. You think *that's* what Ruby's running from? She stared contemptuously across the street until her neighbor's grin deflated like a punctured tire and she remembered something urgent she had to tend to indoors.

"*I'm* not leaving," Letitia announced to the empty street.

Back inside the Winthrop House all was quiet, for now. The bucking and banging had continued for a quarter of an hour before abruptly ceasing, leaving a dissipated feel in its wake, as though the house were a spent battery. How long to recharge? Letitia wondered, gazing quizzically at Hecate. Is this going to be an everyday affair? Twice weekly? I'll take whatever you throw at me, but I need tenants, too, and even South Siders might draw the line at nightly earthquakes. Then again, people rent apartments next to the L tracks all the time.

She decided to worry about it after breakfast and made her way to the kitchen, where she noted that the dishes, pots, and pans—most of which had come with the house—had been left undisturbed by the shaking. Come to think of it, none of the photographic plates in the orrery room had been knocked down either. So the ghost didn't like to damage its own property. Interesting.

Letitia got out a bowl and a box of pancake mix. She was getting a measuring cup when she heard a soft creak of hinges behind her. She went into the corridor that connected the kitchen to the laundry room and found the basement door open. She stared at the steps leading down into darkness. Leaning forward carefully, she flipped the light switch. Nothing happened. She thought about the fuse box at the base of the stairs and thought, Maybe later. She closed the basement door and went back to the kitchen.

Letitia picked up the pancake mix again, registering the strange scrabbling inside the box a half-second too late. She tipped the box over the mixing bowl, releasing a cascade of roaches, maggots, spiders, and other squirming and crawling things. A fat millipede scuttled out of the measuring cup across the back of her hand and she jumped back screaming and waving her arm. The box hit the floor shuddering, its sides beginning to swell. Letitia glimpsed a mass of red worms erupting from a split in the cardboard and then her backpedaling feet carried her through a swinging door into the atrium.

She stood beneath the gallery, watching the crack under the

swinging door. As the hammering in her chest subsided, she heard the sound of running water. She looked over at Hecate but the fountain was dry. She came out from under the gallery and looked up.

Warily she climbed the stairs. Steam was wafting from the master bath beside her bedroom. Inside, the tub was near to overflowing, and floating in the water was what Letitia took at first glance to be a body, bloated and purple. Then she caught a glitter of sequins. She dropped to her knees beside the tub, turned off the faucet, and reached into the scalding water to clutch the sodden gown. Purple seeped between her fingers, mingling with the dye from a half dozen other dresses, all ruined.

She knelt there, close to tears, until something made her turn her head and look at the mirror above the sink. Traced into the condensation on the glass was the same word that had been scratched on Tree's Cadillac. Beneath it was a second, shorter obscenity. Letitia blinked as though she'd been slapped. For a moment, all feeling left her body.

Then rage filled her, and she was up on her feet and moving.

She grabbed the shotgun and headed for the orrery room. The door slammed shut as she approached, but she walked straight up and fired one barrel at close range, blasting away the doorknob and a six-inch circle of wood around it. She shoved through the doorway and took aim at the orrery.

As she squeezed the trigger an invisible force shoved the gun muzzle upwards. The shot punched a hole in the ceiling. Letitia swiped plaster dust from her eyes and gripped the shotgun like a baseball bat. But the ghost tore the weapon from her grasp, and then she felt hands on her shoulders, pushing her backwards into the hall. The door, what was left of it, slammed shut again.

"You can't keep me out forever!" Letitia yelled. She kicked at the door, then ducked her head and stared balefully through the hole. "And when I do get inside, I'm going to take your little toy apart piece by piece. You just try and stop me!"

With a rattle and a crash, the elevator gate slammed open. Letitia straightened and turned towards the sound, feeling a sudden dash of fear. The phantom hands fell on her shoulders again; she tried to fight, but there was nothing solid to land a blow against, and she was dragged, kicking and flailing, out onto the gallery.

The elevator car was no longer on the second floor, or the first floor either. The ghost shoved Letitia to the brink of the open shaft; she caught the edge of the gate with one outflung hand and clung to it fiercely as she was tipped forward over the abyss.

"What you going to do?" she cried. "You break my neck, and then what? You think I won't come back and haunt *you*? Go ahead! Make me a ghost! See what that gets you."

The force pushing against her slackened. The air around her seethed with malice but she sensed uncertainty, too.

"I know you were here first," Letitia said. "I know you think it's your place. But you don't get to keep it all to yourself, not anymore. I'm *staying*. Dead or alive, at war or in peace—that's up to you."

A sudden jolt broke her hold on the gate. Letitia gasped and shut her eyes and committed her soul to the Lord.

But the ghost flung her away from the shaft, not into it; and as she collapsed against the gallery banister, she heard the gate rattle shut.

Wednesday evening.

There had been a fire in an apartment house on State Street. The building's tenants were gathered on the sidewalk, waiting for the firemen to depart so they could go back inside—either to salvage their possessions or, lacking other options, to reclaim their flooded and burned-out apartments.

Letitia observed the crowd from a nearby bus stop, her mind mostly elsewhere. It had taken a little more than twenty-four hours to track Ruby back to her old one-room flat—the lease to which, it turned out, she had never surrendered. Letitia had intended to sweet-talk her sister, get her to give the Winthrop House another chance, but the discovery that Ruby had had an escape route planned all along struck Letitia as a betrayal, as though Ruby had made a promise with her fingers crossed.

Ruby would have none of it. "You're mad at *me*?" she said. "You drag me to live in a haunted house and it's *my* fault when it doesn't work out?"

"Well how's it supposed to work out when you don't even commit to it?"

"You commit to it," Ruby told her. "You keep the house and the money too, I don't care—it's all yours now. That's what you wanted anyway."

"That is *not* what I wanted! The house is for us, Ruby! For *us*."

"Yeah, you go on and commit to that, too. Whatever helps you sleep at night."

That wasn't fair, Letitia thought petulantly. Of course she wanted the house for herself—of *course* she did—but it was never *just* about her. Why couldn't Ruby see that?

She noticed a tall and light-skinned Negro man standing among the tenants displaced by the fire. He was holding his cap in his hands, wringing it like a dishrag as he stared at a row of soot-stained windows on the apartment house's upper floor. Seeing the bewilderment on the man's face, Letitia felt a redeeming impulse to good Samaritanism. But before she could act on it, a little girl at the man's side rounded on her in suspicion. "What are *you* looking at?" the girl demanded.

"Celia!" the man said sharply. He threw Letitia a quick look of apology. Then the bus came and Letitia, feeling rebuked, boarded without saying a word.

It was after dark by the time she reached her stop. From there she had another mile to walk, and though the blocks she passed were mostly colored, she stayed alert and kept a hand on the straight razor in the pocket of her skirt.

She was almost home when a mint-green Oldsmobile sedan cruised up alongside her. Letitia recognized it as belonging to one of her neighbors from across the street. The driver, a blond boy in his late teens, began calling to her: "Hey . . . Hey . . . Hey."

Momma hadn't given birth to any Heys. Letitia ignored him and kept walking.

Up ahead on her left was the defunct tavern. An alleyway ran behind it to the back of the Winthrop House. Letitia had sworn never to use the servants' entrance, but the blond boy didn't know that; as she approached the mouth of the alley, the Oldsmobile sped up and swerved onto the sidewalk in front of her, cutting her off.

"Hey," said the blond boy. He leaned smiling out the driver's window. "How you doing tonight? You need a ride somewhere?"

Letitia looked him in the eye. "I need you to get out of my damn way," she said.

The blond boy reared back in exaggerated surprise. "Wow . . . Listen to you." The doors opened on the far side of the sedan and two other boys got out. The blond boy got out too. They surrounded her. They were all taller than she was, but Letitia stood straight and clutched the razor in her pocket, thinking, First one to touch me gets a scar.

"You should learn to be more polite," the blond boy was saying. "I mean, we're just trying to be friendly. And here you are, walking around alone, at night, in someone else's neighborhood."

"It's my neighborhood too."

"No, it isn't." He raised a hand as though to strike her and then held it, inches from her face. "You don't belong here. You—"

A low growl interrupted him. He stepped back and half-turned, hand still raised, as a dog emerged from the shadows of the alleyway. It was a German shepherd, a big one, with its fangs bared and its ears flat back against its skull.

"This is Charlie Boyd, Jr.," Letitia said. "He's staying with me, helping me keep an eye on my house . . . Charlie, this boy says we don't belong here. What do you think of that?"

The shepherd lunged forward barking and snapping, and the blond boy danced back, saying, "Hey . . . Hey . . . *Hey!*" this time in a higher register. Letitia waited until the dog had the blond boy pinned against the side of the Oldsmobile and then did a slow count to ten. At the end of the count she snapped her fingers and the dog quieted and came to heel instantly.

Keeping his eyes on the shepherd, the blond boy fumbled for his door handle. Letitia looked around at the other two boys, who beat a hasty retreat to the far side of the Oldsmobile. All three got back into the car. From the driver's seat, the blond boy looked at Letitia and started to say, "This isn't over," but Charlie Boyd, Jr., put his front paws up on the driver's door and leaned in the window barking furiously, and the blond boy threw the car into reverse and stepped on the gas. The sedan backed all the way across the street and into the light pole on the far sidewalk, smashing a taillight and putting a good-sized dent in the fender. The blond boy gritted his teeth and shifted into drive and peeled out, leaving fat streaks of rubber on the asphalt. *"This isn't over!"* he shouted, and as the Oldsmobile roared off into the night, the other boys screamed threats of their own.

Letitia just smiled. The taillight and the fender didn't make up for Tree's Cadillac, but they were a start.

She looked at Charlie Boyd, Jr., who looked back at her expectantly. "Yeah, OK," she said. "Your daddy goes to the top of the tenants' list."

Barking happily now, Charlie Boyd, Jr., escorted her the rest of the way to her front door. But he wouldn't come inside with her. As she fitted her key in the lock, the shepherd's ears pricked up, and by the time she got the door open he'd turned tail and was trotting around the side of the house to his makeshift kennel in the garage, leaving Letitia to face Hecate alone.

Thursday.

Mr. Wilkins, an old friend of Momma's who managed a Salvation Army store, was coming by to see what furniture Letitia still needed.

He'd offered to deliver whatever she required in exchange for Letitia giving his mother a room with the first six months rent-free. Letitia was confident she could bargain that down to three months, but even so, she had to be careful. She was running out of rooms to trade for favors.

While she waited for Mr. Wilkins, she sat in the dining room dealing out practice poker hands, a peculiar form of devotion her father had taught her. Warren Dandridge had insisted that poker was a Christian game: Players who practiced virtue—learning and respecting the odds, keeping their emotions in check, managing their bankrolls intelligently—tended to prosper, while those who succumbed to vice—chasing long shots, letting passion rule reason—went the way of all unrepentant sinners.

The Baptists he'd grown up with hadn't much cared for this way of thinking, especially after he took five hundred dollars off a minister's son who'd tried to bluff a busted straight draw. By the time he met Momma he'd learned never to play against anyone he might share a pew with. Instead, like an itinerant preacher, he made his living on the road, traveling a circuit of back rooms and illegal gambling clubs. He played virtuously and strove against the unholy trinity of cheats, thieves, and police; he came home bloody and bruised sometimes, but he came home with cash in pocket. He provided for his family.

One day in 1944 he was playing in a basement casino in Detroit when the place was raided. The casino had a back exit that the cops had somehow missed, and in the confusion he and a friend managed to slip out and escape. They were a block away, still running, when they passed an off-duty patrolman coming out of a bar. The patrolman knew nothing about the raid but he went for his gun anyway and shot Warren Dandridge in the back, killing him.

Letitia still missed her father terribly, but she knew he was looking down on her, and with a deck of cards she could call him back to earth anytime she wanted. As she dealt the cards onto the table, she heard his voice in her ear, laying out the parameters of each hand—the game, the stakes, the size of the pot, her position relative to the other players—and then asking the question: What would a good Christian do here? And Letitia would answer, smiling, sensing him beside her nodding his approval.

She'd gathered up the cards and was reshuffling them when she felt another presence behind her. She didn't turn around.

"Hello, Mr. Winthrop," she said. "You play poker?"

No answer, but the goosebumps on her neck told her he was standing very close. She'd feel his breath if he still drew it.

Letitia gave the deck one more shuffle and dealt a hand: Three of diamonds. Three of clubs. Six of clubs. Six of hearts. Seven of spades. "Straight draw, two-four limit with one- and two-dollar blinds," she said. "Pot's opened in front of you and there's four other players behind. You stay in or fold?"

A tingle of electricity in the air. The seven of spades twitched on the table, separating itself from the two pairs.

"Uh-uh," Letitia said. "You're only going to make the full house one time out of twelve. And when you don't—"

The seven of spades twitched again.

"OK. If you want to go broke . . ." She dealt another card. The six of diamonds. "Hmm." Letitia picked the card up, checked the back for marks. There were none, but maybe he didn't need any. "Interesting . . . I *was* going to invite you to sit down, but maybe we need to find a game where peeking won't help . . . How about checkers? You ever play that with your boy? My daddy—"

An invisible fist pounded the tabletop. The deck was wrenched violently from her hands, cards flying into the air.

"What!?" Letitia cried. "What'd I say?"

THUD!

It sounded like a bird flying into the front window. Letitia turned to see a clump of what looked like mud splattered across the panes and dripping down onto the sill. A second, larger clod burst against the upper sash, making the glass shudder. As Letitia pushed her chair back and stood up, she heard clods striking other windows as well, splatting against the brickwork. By the time she got out into the atrium the noise had become continuous, a storm of brown hail bombarding the front of the Winthrop House.

She opened the front door and was assaulted by the reek of manure. Two farm trucks idled in the street. Hooded figures stood in the open back of each, reaching into big buckets of fresh cow shit. One of them pointed at Letitia and they concentrated their fire, Letitia ducking back only just in time, cow patties exploding against the shutting door.

Charlie Boyd, Jr., came tearing around the side of the house and was met by a barrage of shit clods. A lucky throw caught him between the eyes, turning his barks to yelps of anguish.

The bombardment continued. Letitia ran up the stairs. She had her hand on the shotgun when she heard glass breaking in one of the front bedrooms; she prayed it wasn't the one with a bed already in it. Then she heard the trucks' motors revving up. "No!" she shouted, dashing back down to the atrium. She yanked the front door open and went out, feet skidding in the manure now mounded on the doorstep. "Come back here!" she called. "You come back here!" She ran into the street after the trucks and raised the gun to her shoulder.

Most of the vandals saw her coming and ducked down, but one of them was facing the wrong way and for a moment she had a clear shot, the gun's twin barrels aligning perfectly with the space between the hooded figure's shoulder blades. Then time seemed to stop and Letitia heard her father's voice again, reminding her of the rules of this particular game: who could be shot in the back with impunity, and who couldn't, and what lay at stake if you confused the two.

The moment passed. Letitia lowered the gun without firing, and the figure whose life she'd just spared laughed at her and waved as the trucks rolled away down the street.

Inside the Winthrop House, the telephone began to ring. It rang a dozen times before Letitia heard it over the pounding of blood in her ears and a dozen times more before she walked, stiff-legged, to pick it up.

Heavy breathing on the line. "Who is this?" Letitia said.

A male voice answered: "This is the only warning you're going to get. Next time, we're coming inside."

He hung up. Letitia put the phone down and walked in blind circles of rage, her legs finally carrying her back to the dining room.

On the dining room table, the scattered playing cards had been gathered and stacked neatly to one side. A chessboard Letitia had never seen before had been set up with the black pieces on her side of the table. The white king's pawn was already advanced two squares from its starting position.

Letitia stared unblinking at the board for a long time. Then she leaned the shotgun carefully against the wall and sat down and put her elbows on the table and propped her chin in her hands. "All right," she said nodding. "All right."

And then she said: "What do you want to play for?"

Friday, dusk.

They came in through the kitchen. The silence that had lain on the house since just before sunset was broken by the smash and tinkle of glass as a crowbar knocked out the windowpane above the sink. A boy wearing a grain sack for a hood and work gloves that still stank faintly of manure pulled himself up into the window. Crouching unsteadily with one foot on the sill and the other on the back edge of the sink, he pulled a snub-nosed revolver from beneath his belt. The .38, which had seemed so potent when he'd taken it from his father's dresser, now felt small and ineffectual, and his hand shook as he extended it in front of him, expecting the German shepherd to come leaping from the shadows.

The shepherd did not come leaping. Worried that the grain sack was interfering with his hearing, the boy pulled it off, exposing a head of blond hair. Behind him in the alley a voice whispered hoarsely: "Jesus, Dougie!"

"Shut up," he said. He listened to the house. Nothing. With his finger on the trigger of the revolver he climbed down clumsily from the sink, in the process nearly shooting himself in the thigh.

The back door was locked and bolted. The bolt was stuck and he had to hammer it open, making a godawful racket and chipping the revolver's grip. He opened the door and two other boys came in, one carrying a gasoline can and the other the crowbar.

"Where's that fucking dog?" the boy with the gas can said.

"I don't know," said the blond boy. "I thought it'd be out back. Maybe she took it with her."

"She didn't take it with her," said the boy with the crowbar. "I told you. She drove off with some other nigger an hour ago. The dog wasn't in the car."

"Well it's not in here." Relaxing, eyes adjusted to the dimness, the blond boy surveyed the kitchen, so much larger than the one in his own house. "You believe this place?" Trailing his hand along a countertop, he went over to the dining room door.

"Dougie, where are you going?" said the boy with the gas can. "Let's get this over with."

"I want to look around first."

"Dougie . . ." But the blond boy went into the dining room, and after a moment the boy with the gas can followed him. The boy with the crowbar started to follow as well, but as he crossed the kitchen he felt a sudden draft.

The blond boy continued through the dining room into the atrium. At his first glimpse of Hecate he started and swung the revolver up, but then he laughed.

"What is that?" said the boy with the gas can. He pulled off his hood and squinted at the goddess. "Is that . . . some kind of voodoo thing?"

Together they walked forward until they were standing directly in front of Hecate, the blond boy grinning, the other boy frowning.

"Come on, Dougie. Let's torch the place and get out of here."

"Relax," said the blond boy. "Where's Darren?"

"I don't know. He was right behind me."

"Go get him."

The other boy sighed with exasperation, but then he set the gas can on the floor and turned and walked back to the kitchen. The blond boy stepped into the dry fountain pool. He looked up smiling into Hecate's face and reached out a hand to cup one of her breasts. "Hey babe," he said.

He heard a sharp hiss and something nipped him in the shin. He yelped more in surprise than pain and stumbled back, tripping over the marble ring. He fell hard and sprang up again, scrambling for the gun, which he had dropped, thinking, the dog. But there was no dog, only Hecate, motionless on her pedestal.

"Ronnie!" he called. "Darren! Where the hell are you guys?"

Beneath the gallery, the elevator gate rattled open. The boy ducked sideways to get a clear view of it, but the elevator was a well of darkness among shadows. "Who's there?" he said. "Darren? Don't screw around, I'll blow your damn head off!"

Something was there. Not Darren. Not Ronnie. Not the dog. Suddenly he wanted very badly to run, but he looked down and saw to his horror that his feet were sliding forward, gliding over the tile as though the floor were greased. "No," he said, "no way," and he raised his arm to fire but the .38 flew from his grasp and then hands were on him, a grip of iron, dragging him screaming into the darkness.

They came home late, and laughing. Atticus's Colorado trip had gone well enough for George to slip him a little extra cash, and he'd decided to spend the bonus taking Letitia out on the town. They'd had dinner and gone dancing. Letitia was flying high as they rounded the corner, but the sight of the fire truck in front of the Winthrop House sobered her instantly. Atticus barely had a chance to slow down before she was out of the car and running for the front door.

Inside the house all the lights were on and men in uniform were nosing around. A policeman turned from ogling the fountain to challenge her: "Who the hell are you?"

"I live here," Letitia said. "What's going on?"

"You work here? You the maid?"

"I *live* here."

Both the first- and second-floor elevator gates were open and a pair of firemen were up on the gallery looking down into the shaft. The elevator itself was between the two floors, with the bottom of the car suspended just below the top of the ground-floor doorway. A blond head stuck out through the narrow gap, on the verge of being guillotined. Letitia, who'd seen a similar gruesome accident in a housing project once, thought the blond boy might already be dead, his throat crushed. But then one of the firemen jumped down, none too delicately, onto the roof of the elevator car, and the jostling brought the boy to life, screaming hysterically.

Atticus entered as the screams were trailing off into whimpers. "What happened?"

"Kid broke in to vandalize the place," the policeman said, indicating the gas can on the floor. "Not sure how he got himself stuck, but one of the neighbors heard him howling and called us."

"I want him arrested," Letitia said. "And charged."

"Don't worry, we'll charge him." The policeman looked at Atticus. "Is this really your house?"

"Her house," said Atticus.

"And you just moved in, right?" The policeman eyed the gas can and nodded to himself. "You mind my asking how you managed to afford a place like this?"

"Yeah," said Letitia, "I mind."

Another policeman emerged from the dining room. "We found two more in the basement," he announced.

"In the basement?" said the first policeman. "Are they . . ."

"No, they're alive. More or less." The second policeman grinned. "White as sheets and covered in bug bites, but still breathing." He paused to flick something from his sleeve, then jerked a thumb at Letitia and Atticus. "Who's this, the help?"

"**R**ent's due the first of the month," Letitia said. "You have use of the kitchen, laundry room, and up and downstairs bathrooms. The basement's off limits, and so's the corner room upstairs marked 'Private.'"

The new tenant, Mr. Fox, stood nodding in the dining room doorway. From behind him came a stamp of hard-soled shoes hopscotching on the atrium tile. "Celia," he said.

"It's all right," said Letitia. "Your room is next to Mrs. Wilkins's. She's hard of hearing, so noise doesn't bother her, and she loves children. If you need someone to watch your daughter while you're at work, I'm sure she'll be glad to."

Mr. Fox nodded again. He gestured at the chess set on the table. "That your game?"

"Yeah."

"Black has checkmate in three."

"I know," Letitia said. "I'm just waiting for my opponent to figure that out. You play?"

"Now and then," Mr. Fox said. "A little gin rummy, too."

Letitia smiled. "You've come to the right house, then. Why don't you and your daughter go take a look at your room? Just turn right off the top of the stairs and follow the hall. It's the room with the green curtains. I'll be up in a minute."

Mr. Fox nodded once more and turned away, calling his daughter's name.

Letitia stood up and went to the window. A moving van was parked in front of the cottage across the street, and two of the other houses had FOR SALE signs on their lawns. "Bye-bye," Letitia said waving, and behind her on the chessboard the white king tottered and fell.

"**M**r. Archibald?"

The Realtor, leaving his office for the night, found Atticus standing out in the hall. "Yes?"

"Atticus Turner," Atticus said. "I'm a friend of Letitia Dandridge's. She bought the Winthrop House?"

Mr. Archibald locked his office door and slipped the key in his pocket. "I'm afraid I don't have any other properties like that one," he said. "But if you'd like to come back during business hours—"

"I'm not in the market."

"No? Then I'm not sure how I can help you."

"It's about the Winthrop House. I have a question."

"I'm sorry," said Mr. Archibald. "If Miss Dandridge has a concern, she knows how to contact me. But I don't know you. Now, if you'll excuse me . . ."

Rather than step aside, Atticus widened his stance. "There's a picture of the Winthrops on the dining-room wall," he said. "Something about it's been nagging at me, but I couldn't put my finger on what. Then yesterday I found this box of other photographs down in the basement, and I figured out what the problem is. In the dining-room photo, you can't see Mr. Winthrop's right hand." As he said this he looked at Mr. Archibald's hands, which were small and pale and unadorned by even a wedding band. "In some of the other pictures, though, you can. You can see the big silver ring he wore. And then there's this . . ." He brought out a picture showing two men in front of a shiny black roadster. "Assuming that's a new-model Ford, I'd say this was taken about twenty years ago. And the man with Mr. Winthrop looks an awful lot like Samuel Braithwhite. You familiar with that name?"

The Realtor didn't even glance at the photo. "Get out of my way, Mr. Turner."

"Penumbra Real Estate," Atticus said. "Is that a Braithwhite family company, or is it owned by the Order? And which do you work for?"

"I'll ask you to move one more time. Then I'm going into my office and calling the police."

Atticus sidestepped just enough for Mr. Archibald to squeeze past him. The Realtor moved swiftly down the hall and had reached the elevator when Atticus said: "I spoke to Mr. Bailey, too."

The Realtor paused, his finger on the call button.

"He does know you," Atticus continued, "and he admitted to doing the occasional deal with you, but he was real surprised to hear you described him as a partner. That day Letitia and Ruby were supposed to meet with him? He says he never called you. Turns out the cops grabbed him on his way over here and kept him handcuffed in the back of a patrol car for two hours, asking him about some liquor store robbery. Meantime, you stepped in and stole his customers. He's still pretty upset about that."

"Not too upset to take his share of the commission," Mr. Archibald said.

"Yeah, he said you cut him in to keep him quiet. But he's still thinking about reporting you to the Realtor's Association. Trouble is, he thinks they'd be less concerned about you cheating Negroes than doing business with them in the first place."

"The way of the world," said Mr. Archibald, pressing the elevator button. "Still, what does it matter? Hal and I both have our money, and your friend has a very nice house. Everyone's happy."

"For now," said Atticus. "But you need to tell Caleb Braithwhite that whatever he's up to, his business is with me. Letitia's not a part of it."

"I don't know what you're talking about, Mr. Turner."

"Yeah, you do. And there's something else you should know: I looked up your home address in the phone book. Can't say I've been to the neighborhood before. But if anything were to happen to Letitia, I'm sure I could find my way."

The elevator arrived. Mr. Archibald remained in the hallway a moment more, mouth open, groping vainly for a retort.

Then, like a ghost, he was gone.

ABDULLAH'S BOOK

~⧉~

As to my freedom, which you say I can have, there is nothing to be gained on that score, as I got my free papers in 1864 from the Provost-Marshal-General of the Department of Nashville. Mandy says she would be afraid to go back without some proof that you are sincerely disposed to treat us justly and kindly; and we have concluded to test your sincerity by asking you to send us our wages for the time we served you . . . At $25 a month for me, and $2 a week for Mandy, our earnings would amount to $11,680. Add to this the interest for the time our wages has been kept back and deduct what you paid for our clothing and three doctor's visits to me, and pulling a tooth for Mandy, and the balance will show what we are in justice entitled to. Please send the money by Adams Express, in care of V. Winters, Esq., Dayton, Ohio.

—*letter from Jourdon Anderson to his former owner, August 7, 1865*

The Monday before Thanksgiving, George and Montrose went to the bank to retrieve the Book of Days. The Book was a ledger that contained a full accounting of their great-grandmother Adah's servitude: the labors she'd performed, the indignities she'd suffered, and the wages and penalties she was owed. Adah had died in 1902, but the family continued to keep the Book, meeting annually to calculate and record the interest on the still unpaid debt.

Every year, after adding a new line to the ledger, they'd tell the story of how the Book had come to be: how Adah had been born into slavery on a Georgia plantation in 1840; how at the age of seven she'd been set to work in the fields; how she had toiled there until November 22, 1864, when Union soldiers with torches had arrived at the plantation gate; how she had then become one of the thousands of ex-slaves following in the wake of Sherman's army; how in February of 1865, sick with typhoid, she'd been consigned to a hospital camp set up in an old sanitarium outside Savannah; how, through the haze of her fever, she'd gradually come to realize that the sanitarium was not a place of healing but a death trap meant to reduce the population of freed Negroes; how, still ill, she and another former slave named Noah Pridewell had contrived to escape; how they'd made their way west, coming, after many more trials, to Kansas, where they settled and married; and how finally in 1878, on the fourteenth anniversary of her emancipation, she'd begun working on the Book.

Adah's daughter, Ruth, did most of the actual writing; though Adah had learned to read, she had no penmanship. What she did have was perfect recall. By concentrating on a given date, she could summon a memory of everything she had done, and everything done to her, from the moment she woke up until the moment she fell asleep.

Ruth recorded each day's labors on a separate line in the ledger. Where appropriate, Adah added, in her own hand, symbols representing insults she'd suffered: Whippings. Beatings. Other.

In the matter of wages Adah deferred to the wisdom of her old master, Gilchrist Burns. Burns was in the habit of renting out his slaves when they weren't needed on the plantation, and he made no secret of what he charged, so the slaves all knew exactly how much he valued their labor. As a child, Adah "earned" twenty cents for a full day's work. By age sixteen, she was up to a dollar a day—the same as a male field hand, Master Burns being remarkably egalitarian when it came to money destined for his own pocket.

For the penalties, Adah consulted her Bible. She charged twenty-seven dollars and twenty-six cents for each whipping, 27:26 being the verse in Matthew's Gospel where the Savior was flogged. Her price for the most common of the "other" insults, twenty-two dollars and a quarter, was based in Deuteronomy.

Ruth entered the figures in neat columns, subtotaled and summed them. The final tally, after the subtraction of living expenses but before interest, came to $8,817.29—a small fortune at the time.

But for Adah it was the count of days that carried the greater significance. Holding the completed Book in her hand, she realized that she'd performed a kind of exorcism. Though her memories of slavery remained as sharp as ever, their weight had been transferred to the ledger's pages. Now doubly and truly freed, she set about living the remainder of her life with a peace she hadn't known before.

The Book itself went to Ruth, who spent the next quarter century trying unsuccessfully to collect the money. The surviving members of the white Burns clan felt that their responsibility had ended with the destruction of the plantation, and they ignored Ruth's letters—as did eleven governors of Georgia and six U.S. presidents.

Eventually Ruth passed the Book on to her eldest daughter, Lucy, who passed it, in turn, to George. Horace would be the Book's next steward, unless Montrose, who had appointed himself deputy bookkeeper at the age of five, pried it from George's dead hands first. As for George and Montrose's sister, Ophelia, the middle child, she'd long ago removed herself from the line of succession. She'd be there for Thanksgiving, with a pen—out of the three of them, she'd always had the cleanest hand—but the safekeeping of the Book she left to her brothers.

She knew they would never let anything happen to it.

George and Montrose met outside the bank at noon, having come by separate routes. This had been standard procedure since 1946, when, driving together to pick up the Book the day before Thanksgiving, they'd been stopped by police and, one thing leading to another, had been hauled to the precinct house, where only a hefty bribe had sufficed to get them out before the bank closed for the holiday.

Today both their journeys had been uneventful, but as they entered the bank they could tell that something was amiss. The lobby was packed, unusually so even for a lunch hour, with lines snaking from the teller windows all the way to the door. And where ordinarily the bank's manager, Ben Rosenfeld, would have been out on the floor to greet them, today they were met by a security guard, Whitey Dunlap.

"What's going on, Whitey?" George asked. Looking across the lobby, he could see the blinds were drawn on both the manager's and assistant manager's offices.

"Cops were in earlier," Whitey explained, keeping his voice low. "Detectives from the organized crime squad."

"What'd they want?" said Montrose.

Whitey shrugged. "They had me posted out on the sidewalk, so I don't really know, but we were an hour late opening and a rumor got started there was a run on the bank. Mr. Rosenfeld's been on the phone with depositors all morning, trying to calm things down. He said to say he's sorry he can't serve you personally, but I can take care of you."

The safe deposit vault was in the basement. Whitey unlocked the vault door and ushered them inside, then stooped to pick a cigar butt off the floor. Frowning, he checked the corners of the vault as if the litterbug might still be present.

George got his deposit box key out. "You mind, Whitey?"

"Sure . . ." Holding the cigar butt pinched between two fingers, Whitey fished out his own key.

As George withdrew the box from its slot in the wall, Montrose stood close, ready to leap in if George suffered a sudden stroke or got raptured away. He saw George's expression change as George realized the box was light.

"What?" said Montrose. George lifted the box lid. Inside was the leather folder that contained the Berry family's 1833 emancipation papers, along with other, more recent documents like Horace's birth certificate. But the Book of Days, which should have been lying on top of it, was missing, and in its place was a terse handwritten note:

THE WITCH'S HAMMER
750 W. Berwick Street
At your earliest convenience.

"Son of a *bitch*," said Montrose.

The note was signed with the half-sun symbol of the Order of the Ancient Dawn.

They went together, in George's Packard.

"Tell me you brought the gun," Montrose said as George was getting the car started.

"Under my seat," George replied, but when Montrose tried to reach for it, George checked him. "I'll handle it."

"*You're* going to shoot him?"

"I'm going to get Adah's book back." He resisted the urge to point out that Montrose had already had his chance to shoot Caleb Braithwhite and it hadn't gone so well. "You want to help, get my city map from the glove box and find that address." Grumbling, Montrose complied.

George tried to be patient with his brother. And that was how he thought of Montrose, how he always introduced him to people: as his brother, not his half-brother. Kinship being, to George's way of thinking, an in-or-out proposition. Still, the fact of their different fathers was inescapable at times, and never so much as in the matter of Adah's book.

The Berrys had been blessed, their last owner, Lucius Berry, being one of the rare true Christians salted among the ranks of the so-called faithful. Lucius's parents and siblings had died in the 1832 cholera epidemic, leaving him sole ownership of the family tobacco farm and the seven human beings who worked it. Interpreting the epidemic as divine confirmation of what his conscience already knew, Lucius set out to atone for his family's sin: He sold off the rest of his inheritance, put his slaves into wagons, and escorted them safely out west, where he gave them not just their freedom but money and land to make a new start. Proving that such an act was indeed possible.

"Blessed" didn't, of course, mean free of all suffering. The emancipated Berrys still had their share of tribulations. One of the original seven was murdered by white settlers who objected to sharing a property line with a colored man, and out of the first generation of freeborn Berrys, three sons and a daughter were lost to the Civil War. And then there was George's father, Jacob Berry, a successful businessman, dead at age twenty-four, his prosperity no shield against the asthma that plagued him all his short life. George had been only three, and Ophelia still a baby, when a cloud of dust stirred up by a passing horse cart sent Jacob Berry's lungs into their final, fatal spasm.

After her first husband's death, Lucy Berry married Ulysses Turner, a man with a very different family history. The Turners, George's stepfather never tired of saying, had been given nothing: not freedom, not even their name. Ulysses's grandfather had been born Simon Swincegood on the Swincegood plantation in North Carolina. In 1857 he'd escaped into the Great Dismal Swamp, where he lived as a maroon for six years before emerging to join the Union Army. It was while in the swamp that he'd taken the name Nat Turner—a popular sobriquet among the maroons, and one that had to be earned through feats of prowess, like killing slave catchers and raiding white settlements.

Or so the story, as told by Ulysses, went. In hindsight, George recognized these tales of Great-grandpa Turner's exploits as his first exposure to pulp fiction—which was not to say they were fantasy, only that they were more "inspired by actual events" than gospel truth. But Montrose believed every word, and it was no surprise that he grew up thinking a Turner, not a Berry, ought to be the guardian of Adah's book.

George knew his stepfather shared Montrose's opinion. The man made no secret of his disdain for how "easy" the Berrys had had it, or of his belief that George had been born soft. But as a Turner, he was bound to respect certain traditions. And so it transpired that on the last night of May 1921—the night white Tulsa declared war on black Tulsa—Ulysses allowed George, against his mother's wishes, to go and rescue Adah's book from the safe in Ulysses's shop on Archer Street, even as the first wave of white arsonists were crossing the railroad tracks. Because of the other events of that awful night, George never bragged about what he'd done, never tried to hold it over Montrose's head, but he knew he'd proved himself, and he knew Montrose knew it too.

"Berwick Street," Montrose said now, showing him on the map. "It's up in Lake View."

"All right," George said. "Hang on." He sped north, driving in a way no colored man should drive when headed into white Chicago. But the enchantment laid on the Packard in Ardham still held, causing traffic cops and patrolmen to either avert their eyes from the car or stare straight through it. Which would have been gratifying, George reflected, if not for the knowledge that he was using Caleb Braithwhite's magic to do Caleb Braithwhite's bidding.

The sign outside the Witch's Hammer showed a tall-hatted Puritan burning a woman at the stake. The building would have been easy to overlook, otherwise: Blank brickface with a high-set row of glass blocks in lieu of a front window. Steel door painted to match the brick. The kind of place that would have, and maybe had, made a good location for a Prohibition speakeasy.

George got out of the car holding the pistol at his side. Montrose opened the back of the Packard and armed himself with a tire iron.

A handwritten note taped above the door handle said the Witch's Hammer was CLOSED FOR PRIVATE FUNCTION, but the door wasn't locked. With Montrose at his heel, George went inside, into a long low-ceilinged barroom.

Caleb Braithwhite was seated at a table in the middle of the room with another white man, who was in the process of lighting a cigar. The cigar man was a big, thickset bruiser, with graying brown hair styled in a flattop. His nose looked like it had been broken more than once in the past and the burst capillaries in his cheeks spoke of decades of heavy drinking, but the blue eyes that regarded George and Montrose through a haze of smoke were alert and intelligent.

Two more white men stood leaning against the bar. They'd removed their jackets, exposing matching shoulder holsters, and police stars pinned to their vests. Sandwiched between them was a Negro man with his head bowed, hands cuffed in front of him. George almost didn't recognize his nephew, who was supposed to be in Iowa today on a research trip for the *Guide*.

Atticus looked up, embarrassed.

"Hi, Uncle George," he said.

"George Berry and Montrose Turner," Caleb Braithwhite said, "these are Detectives Burke and Noble"—he nodded at the men bracketing Atticus—"and Captain Lancaster of the mayor's commission on organized crime. Captain Lancaster also heads the local chapter of the Order. We've been negotiating a merger of the Ardham and Chicago lodges, and as part of that, we've decided to pool our resources on a research project—one that I'd like you to help us with."

George barely heard the words. Atticus's presence had caught him off guard, as it was no doubt intended to. In his confusion he let his thumb stray to the hammer of the pistol he was holding. It was the tiniest of gestures, but the detectives reacted by reaching for their own guns and Captain Lancaster slipped a beefy hand into his jacket.

"Gentlemen," Braithwhite said softly, making everyone pause. "Let's not be hasty . . . Captain Lancaster, I think I saw a bottle of forty-year-old Dalmore in the back room. Why don't you and your men go help yourselves while I explain matters to Mr. Berry and Mr. Turner?"

"You sure?" the captain said.

"We'll be fine." Smiling: "We're all friends here."

Captain Lancaster stood up and pointed a warning finger at George. Then he nodded to the detectives and the three of them left the room.

"So," Caleb Braithwhite said. "Let's get the ground rules out of the way. Violence won't work. I have immunity." He looked George in the eye. "You can't shoot me. Or hit me." He shifted his gaze to Montrose, who was straining fruitlessly to raise the tire iron above the level of his waist. "And even if you could, it wouldn't get Adah's book back. Now, if all that's clear, let's see if we can deal with one another like civilized people." Turning finally to Atticus, Braithwhite unlocked the cuffs with a wave of his hand.

"What is it you want?" George said.

"A trade," said Caleb Braithwhite. "A book for a book. What I was saying just now, about merging the two lodges? This isn't the first time that's been attempted. In the 1930s, my father tried to reach a similar arrangement with a former lodgemaster of Chicago."

"Hiram Winthrop," Atticus guessed.

Braithwhite nodded. "It didn't work out. And it ended the way things usually do, when powerful men can't come to terms."

"What's that got to do with a book?" said George.

"Winthrop was an explorer. He traveled to some very interesting places and brought things back with him. One of the most valuable was a book, written in the language of Adam."

"A magic book?"

"A treatise on natural philosophy. A rough English translation of the title would be *The Book of Naming,* or *The Book of Names.*"

Atticus raised an eyebrow. "The *Necronomicon?*"

Braithwhite smiled. "That would be a book of *dead* names. *The Book of Names* is just the opposite. Its subject is life. Transformation. Genesis."

"So what happened to it?" George asked.

"After Hiram Winthrop's death, my father managed to acquire a number of his former possessions. But the book wasn't among them. My father assumed Winthrop had hidden it somewhere. Unfortunately, Chicago had become unsafe for him by that point, so he wasn't able to conduct a thorough search."

"But your new friends, they know where it is?"

"According to Captain Lancaster, the book is in the Museum of Natural History. Hiram Winthrop was on the board, and he apparently had a secret room installed."

"So why not just go get it, then?"

Braithwhite glanced over his shoulder at the door to the back room. Then he said in a low voice: "The captain's being cagey about it, but I know he hasn't been lodgemaster for very long. And nobody wants to talk about what happened to the previous lodgemaster . . . Anyway, the deal is, he shows me the entrance to the secret room, and I go in and get the book . . ."

". . . or find someone to get it for you," George concluded. "And if we say no—"

"Then you've got till Thursday," Braithwhite said shrugging, "to decide how to break the bad news to the rest of the family."

That night was the scheduled monthly meeting of the Prince Hall Freemasons. With the holiday coming up, attendance was expected to be light, but the lodge secretary, Abdullah Muhammad, was required to be there. And Abdullah—his given name was Percy Jones—had a cousin who worked as a night watchman at the natural history museum.

George and Montrose showed up early, hoping to talk to Abdullah before the meeting. But Abdullah arrived only just on time, having stopped to pick up the lodgemaster, Joe Bartholomew, who everyone called Pirate Joe for the eyepatch he wore.

One member who did show up early was Mortimer Dupree. Mortimer was a dentist who had, in the words of Montrose, got hypnotized by the pyramid on the back of the dollar bill. Of course there were a lot of people with romantic misconceptions about Freemasonry; those who joined learned to embrace it as the social club, charity, and mutual-aid organization that it actually was, or quit in disillusionment when they found out they weren't going to become secret masters of the universe. Mortimer had chosen the former course, but still clung to the hope that there was a Masonic inner circle that ordinary Masons weren't told about, and that one day he'd get a tap on the shoulder. Meanwhile, he did what he could to demonstrate himself worthy.

Lodge meetings typically included a lecture for the edification of the membership. In the past, George had spoken about the practicalities of growing and expanding a business, and Montrose had given a talk on genealogical research. Mortimer's lectures tended to more occult subject matter, like the mysterious moving coffins of Barbados, or the Nazca lines of Peru. Tonight when George and Montrose arrived, he was setting up a scale model of King Tut's tomb, complete with figurines of Howard Carter and Lord Carnarvon.

Ordinarily George would have been happy to hear a story about the mummy's curse, but tonight he had other priorities, so as soon as the meeting got under way, he moved to suspend regular business so he could make a special appeal for aid. The motion was granted, but soon enough George realized his error: For though he spoke of Caleb Braithwhite in as mundane a way as possible, he could see Mortimer getting more and more excited. And when he got to *The Book of Names*, Mortimer immediately drew the same connection Atticus had, and blurted it out, to the confusion of those present who were unfamiliar with the works of H. P. Lovecraft.

"The *Necronomicon*?" said Pirate Joe. "What's that?"

"A book of black magic," Mortimer said enthusiastically. "Written by the mad Arab Abdul Alhazred . . ."

"The stuttering Arab, more like," said Abdullah. "It's 'Abd al,' not 'Ab-*dool.*' Abd means 'servant' and al is 'the,' so Abd al al-Hazred would be 'servant of the-the Hazred.'"

Pirate Joe blinked his eye. "What's a hazred?"

"A white guy from Rhode Island trying to be funny," said Montrose.

"Forget the *Necronomicon*," George said impatiently. "This is about a real book."

"A real magic book," said Abdullah.

"Well . . . Supposedly."

"Meaning what? You don't believe it's magic?"

"It doesn't matter."

"It does to me." Abdullah pressed a hand to his chest. "Abd Allah. Servant of God. There's a lot I'll do for a lodge brother, George, but one thing I won't be party to is making an evil man more powerful. It sounds like this Caleb Braithwhite is bad enough already."

"He is," George said. "Which is why we're not actually going to give him the book. The way it's supposed to go, Montrose, my nephew, and I meet Braithwhite and his friends on Wednesday, after the museum closes. They take us inside, show us where the secret room is, and we go in and get this *Book of Names*. But what I want to do is go in early—tomorrow night—and find the room and *The Book of Names* ahead of time. And then—"

"And then," said Mortimer, "you swap in a decoy—a fake *Book of Names*, which you 'find' on Wednesday and give to Braithwhite in exchange for your great-grandma Adah's book!"

George looked at him crossly. "Yeah," he acknowledged.

"But where do you get a fake *Book of Names* from?" Pirate Joe wanted to know.

"I'm still working on that," George said. "The thing is, we know that Winthrop, the guy who hid the book, was serious about keeping Braithwhite's father from getting his hands on it. So who's to say this whole secret room isn't a decoy? The way I figure it, it's OK if Braithwhite realizes the book we give him is fake, as long as he believes the fake came from Winthrop."

"You hope," said Abdullah. "What if he sees through you? Or what if he buys it, but decides to hang on to your great-grandma's book until you find the *real* secret room?"

"That's like six bridges ahead," George said. "I'll cross it when I come to it."

"Better to resist temptation by avoiding it altogether," Abdullah suggested. "Let's play it this way: I'll get my cousin to let you into the museum tomorrow, but I'm coming with you. If we find *The Book of Names*, you give it to me."

"What are you going to do with it?"

"That building on Calumet where we just opened the new prayer room? It's got an incinerator in the basement . . . Worse comes to worst, you can tell Braithwhite that Abdul Alhazred went back to memorizing the Koran."

George didn't like it, but he could see Abdullah was prepared to stand firm on this—and maybe he was right to. "OK," George said. "The book's yours, *if* we find it. But—"

Mortimer interrupted again: "This is great!" he said, rubbing his hands together. "What time do we meet up at the museum?"

"You couldn't just tell him no?" Atticus said.

"He's a brother of the lodge," George replied.

"Not the steadiest brick in the pile, maybe," added Montrose.

Quarter to midnight, and the three of them huddled by the staff entrance on the museum's east side, watching Mortimer Dupree make his way towards them. Rather than follow the sidewalk, Mortimer opted to use the landscaping as cover, darting from tree to tree in a manner that would surely have raised the suspicions of any passersby. Fortunately between the late hour and the near-freezing temperatures, the area was deserted.

"Nice outfit," Montrose said when Mortimer finally reached them. The dentist had on black shoes and trousers, a black pullover sweater and black wool cap, and black suede gloves. Slung over his shoulder on a strap was a bulging black bag, which rattled. "Those your burglar tools?"

"Be prepared," Mortimer said. He pointed at the more modest bag George was holding. "Did you get the decoy?"

"Yeah," George said. "It's a Hebrew encyclopedia of kabbalah, in a nice old binding." He pulled the book out so Mortimer could see. "We got it at Thurber Lang's shop. Closest thing to a real magic book he had."

"It doesn't matter how nice the binding is," Montrose noted, not for the first time. "Braithwhite's going to know it's not right."

"Of course he is," said George, "but that's OK as long as he doesn't figure out we made the switch."

"Yeah, so you keep saying."

"We just have to sell it right, when we give it to him."

"You should have let me booby-trap it," Montrose said. "Have it blow up in his face when he opens it, see if he's immune to that."

Abdullah and Pirate Joe arrived just before midnight. Abdullah led the group down a flight of steps to a basement door marked EMPLOY-EES ONLY. At 12:01 the door opened and Abdullah's cousin looked out frowning.

"What the hell, Percy," he said. "You brought the whole club with you?"

"Hey Bradley," said Abdullah. "Remember that time you got evicted and the sheriff gave you an hour to move all your stuff out? I don't recall you complaining when I came by with a big crew then."

"Well, that was that and this is this," Bradley said. But he stepped back from the doorway and waved them inside. "Quiet as the grave until we get upstairs," he said.

He ushered them through a locker room and down a hallway, past a half-open door marked SECURITY. A radio was playing inside the security office; they heard a rustle of newspaper pages and then a white man's voice said, "Fucking Irish cunts." Bradley put a finger to his lips. They continued on, on tiptoe, to the end of the hall and up a flight of stairs, emerging in the museum gift shop.

"My supervisor, Mr. Miller," Bradley said, judging they were safely out of earshot. "Most nights he doesn't leave the office except to use the toilet, but every now and then he likes to check I'm not goofing off on my rounds. He thinks it's real funny to jump out and go 'boo,' too, so I don't always hear him coming."

"Don't worry, we won't let him sneak up on us," Abdullah said.

"Uh-huh," said Bradley. "Tell me about this secret room you're look-ing for. You even know what part of the museum it's supposed to be in?"

Abdullah turned to George. "Montrose and I went through the mu-seum's annual reports at the library this morning," George said. "There were a few different renovation projects during the years Hiram Win-throp was on the board, but we think the one we're interested in was in 1925. Winthrop sponsored and led an expedition to the Sudan that year, and when he got back he oversaw the installation of a new exhibi-tion hall. Assuming that's when he put in the secret room, we want to look in the northwest corner of the building, on the second floor."

"Second floor, northwest corner." Bradley nodded. "That's good. Mr. Miller doesn't like to walk that far."

They crossed the museum's central concourse and went up to the second-floor gallery. The hall that had once housed Winthrop's Sudan exhibition was now home to a collection of zoological specimens from the Amazon. Bradley left them at the entrance, beside a display case filled with hand-sized tarantulas. "I'm going back downstairs to do my rounds," he said. "I'll check on you in half an hour. Try not to make too much noise." Eying Mortimer in his burglar's outfit: "And don't mess with any of the exhibits."

"Don't worry about it," Mortimer said.

They spread out, searching for secret panels and trapdoors. They found nothing in the exhibition hall itself, but at the hall's west end was an L-shaped passage that connected to another room. A tile mosaic on the passage wall depicted a pink stone archway in the middle of a desert. Blue sky and sand surrounded the arch, while the door-sized space within it was a dull and featureless black.

"That's got to be it," Atticus said. The sides of the arch were decorated with hieroglyphs, but the symbols on the keystone were individual letters, and he recognized the alphabet. "That's the language of Adam."

"Must have to press one of the tiles to open it," said Mortimer. He stepped forward and went up on tiptoe to reach the keystone, but the tile was firmly fixed and wouldn't push in.

Pirate Joe pointed at another tile on the right side of the arch whose hieroglyph showed a man holding an ankh like a key. "Try that one."

The ankh tile didn't work either. Abdullah and George offered additional suggestions, until Montrose grew frustrated. "Stop poking at it!" he said. "We got to be systematic about this."

"What if it's more than one tile?" Pirate Joe said. "What if you've got to press two at once? Or three, even?"

"Then we're going to be here all night," George said. "But if that's what it takes—"

The snick of a knife blade got everyone's attention. The Freemasons turned to find Atticus slitting his thumb.

"What are you doing?" said Abdullah.

"Trying a little natural philosophy," Atticus said. "It's a long story." He moved to the front of the group and drew a line in blood across the keystone, taking care to touch every one of the letters. The tile soaked up the blood almost instantly, and as the stain faded, the hue of the keystone brightened. The brightness spread to the other tiles in the arch, while the dark tiles began to blur and flow together. The darkness grew vivid, acquired depth, until, in a moment of seamless transition, what had been just a suggestion of an opening became an actual hole in the wall.

When the process was complete, Abdullah was the first to speak. "Northwest corner of the building," he said. "And this should be an outer wall, right?"

"Or close to it," George said nodding. The dim light did not penetrate far past the opening, but peering into the darkness they all sensed that the passage within extended for some distance—beyond the perimeter of the building into what should have been open air.

Mortimer got excited again. "It's an alternate dimension!" he said. "Another universe, maybe."

"Yeah," said Pirate Joe. "So who wants to go first?"

George went first. Then Montrose. Then the others.

Past the narrow entrance was a straight, level passageway, about ten feet wide, with dark stone walls rising to a vaulted ceiling. The air was chilly and dry and unpleasantly stale.

George and Montrose had each brought a flashlight; Mortimer had brought three. The passageway continued beyond the range of the beams.

"Should we leave somebody here to mind the exit and let Bradley know where we've gone?" Pirate Joe said. Atticus looked sideways at Mortimer, who clutched his bag defensively. "No way!" Mortimer said. "I want to come!"

"Let's just do this," said Montrose, impatient. So they all set off together, with George, Montrose, and Abdullah in front, and Mortimer, despite his professed eagerness, keeping carefully to the rear.

The passage ran on straight and unbranching and quickly grew monotonous. "Anybody counting steps?" Abdullah said.

"If we weren't in Dimension X we'd be crossing the railroad tracks by now," Montrose guessed.

"There's an all-night coffee joint right outside the station on the other side," Pirate Joe noted. "Maxie's Depot. They got good doughnuts."

"I could go for a doughnut," said Atticus. "Mortimer, you bring a jackhammer?"

"What?" Mortimer sounded startled. "No, I—"

"I see something up ahead," George said. Everyone got quiet and looked. A glimmer in the darkness. They continued forward slowly, the object emerging in the focused beams of the flashlights: A chest. A silver chest, resting on a dark waist-high pedestal. A change in the feel of the air and the echoes of their footfalls hinted at a large open space.

"Looks like we found the treasure room," Montrose said. "Get your burglar tools ready, Mortimer."

"Wait," said George. He put out an arm to stop his brother and lowered the beam of his flashlight. Less than five feet in front of them, the dark stone floor dropped away.

George raised the light to the chest again and studied it more carefully. There was no pedestal; the chest was just hanging there in the darkness.

He sensed another object hovering nearby. He swung his light up and to the right. "Oh, Jesus," he said.

The dead man had been white, in life; in death, his desiccated flesh had taken on a grayish cast. His suit hung loosely on his withered frame, and the hands jutting from his sleeves were hooked to display blackened fingertips and broken nails. His eyes were mercifully shut, but his lips stretching back from his teeth had opened his mouth up wide, and visible within was the pale tip of his shriveled tongue.

George's hand holding the flash trembled slightly, and in the wavering light the tongue-tip seemed to wag, as though the former lodge-master of Chicago were trying to speak. Or scream.

-ᗺᘓᗷ-

"It's a sphere," said Abdullah, shining his light over the smooth stone walls curving away from around the end of the passageway. "I'd say about fifty yards across." The chest was at the sphere's center, and the passageway opening halfway up the side. The dead lodgemaster floated in the upper hemisphere, somewhere around the horse latitudes, turning slowly like a piece of ocean debris caught in a sluggish current.

"What's keeping him up there?" Montrose wondered. "And that." He nodded at the chest, which unlike the corpse hung motionless, a fixed point in space.

George stepped to the brink and stuck out an arm experimentally. "Grab my belt."

"What?" said Montrose.

"You and Atticus, grab the back of my belt."

Montrose and Atticus stood behind George, each grabbing a section of his belt with one hand and hooking the fingers of the other under the waistband of his trousers. "All right," George said, "hold tight," and he leaned forward.

He hadn't leaned far—just enough to get the majority of his body mass inside the spherical room—when gravity abruptly loosed its grip on him. His feet left the floor, and carried by momentum he tilted forward, going fully horizontal, arms flailing, while Montrose and Atticus fought to steady him.

"Holy God," Mortimer said.

"Uncle George?" said Atticus.

"I'm all right," George told them, laughing nervously. "Feels like I might lose my dinner, but it's kind of fun, too. Just don't let go, OK?"

The blast of air came without warning, striking George broadside. Like a parade balloon caught in a crosswind, he yawed and lurched violently to the right, dragging his handlers with him. Montrose, on the windward side, was shoved to the brink by George's pivoting body. He leaned too far over the edge and suddenly he was floating too, leaving Atticus the sole anchor point.

Pirate Joe darted forward and grabbed one of Montrose's ankles. Abdullah caught the other. Another blast of wind struck, but Pirate Joe and Abdullah and Atticus hung on and dragged Montrose and George to safety. As soon as they were back inside the passageway, gravity reasserted itself, and all five men ended up in a heap on the floor, with Mortimer standing behind them saying "Holy God!" over and over again.

George rolled clear of Atticus, on whom he had landed, and gave his heart rate a moment to settle. Then he pushed himself up and helped the others to their feet. He picked up his flashlight and shone it on the dead lodgemaster, who was still turning lazily in the upper latitudes.

"So that's what happened to him," George said. "Stuck his neck out too far with no one to hold on to and got blown into orbit."

"And then what?" said Atticus, brushing dust from his sleeves. "You think he died of thirst?"

"That, or hypothermia," George guessed. "Or maybe he just cracked his head against the wall while he was tumbling."

"He's not tumbling now," Montrose observed. "You suppose that wind only blows right here at the entrance?"

"Could be." George saw where his brother was going. "Mortimer," he said, "you got any rope in that bag?"

"Yeah, sure. Plenty."

"We need enough to tie me a harness, with a good hundred feet left over."

"No," said Montrose. "Not you."

"Yes me," George said.

But Montrose shook his head. "You're too big. So am I, for that matter. We want somebody small, somebody who won't drag the rest of us into the void if we're wrong about that wind." He looked around, eyes settling on five-foot-four Mortimer Dupree. "Somebody we can toss."

"**O**n three," George said. He and Montrose stood a few steps back from the end of the passageway, holding Mortimer suspended between them like a human battering ram. Behind them, Pirate Joe and Abdullah each had charge of one of two ropes, the first bound in a makeshift harness around Mortimer's chest, the second tied to his right ankle as a backup line. Atticus stood to his father's right, holding their most powerful flashlight.

"OK," Mortimer said, reaching up to switch on the headlamp strapped to his forehead. "I'm ready. I'm ready." He shut his eyes. "Jesus."

"Don't worry, Dupree," said Montrose. "After this, the Illuminati will pledge you for sure."

"OK," George said. "One . . . two . . . *three!*"

As he was lobbed headlong into space, Mortimer opened his eyes again. The transition to weightlessness was instantaneous, but his brain clung stubbornly to the notion that a man hurled from a precipice must fall *down*, and hard. *"Oh sh-i-i-i-i-i-i-i—"*

A blast of air drowned out his exclamation. But he had cleared the edge of the sphere and the wind didn't touch him. Pitching up slightly, he coasted towards the chest with his arms spread like improbably effective wings. Abdullah and Pirate Joe played out the ropes, trying to keep them from tangling. "OK," George said. "Start putting the brakes on."

By now Mortimer had recovered enough to call out his own directions: "Almost there . . . slow . . . slow . . ." Applying light friction to the ropes, Abdullah and Pirate Joe eased him to a stop within a few feet of the chest. From their perspective, he appeared to float just above and to the left of it.

"You OK, Mortimer?" George called.

"I could use a new pair of undershorts," Mortimer replied. "But at least now I know how Superman feels."

"Try using your X-ray vision on the box," Montrose suggested. "What do you see?"

"Lots of decoration on the outside," Mortimer said. "Stars and planets and like that. I can see more of those funny letters, too . . ." A pause. "I don't have to bleed on it, do I?"

"Not yet," George said. "Can you tell how it opens?"

"There's no lock or latch that I can see. There's a seam running around the top that might be the edge of a lid. If I drift a little closer, I could try . . . Whoah!" Mortimer twisted suddenly in midair. "I see a chain! A big one, stretching out the back, towards the far wall . . . It looks like cast iron, and it's pulled taut, almost like the chest is hanging from it, except, you know, sideways."

George turned to Montrose. "Could there be some kind of magnetic field?" he said. "Pushing the chest this way?"

"I suppose," Montrose said. "But if there is, it ought to affect everything in the room . . . Hey Mortimer!" he called. "You feel anything tugging on your belt buckle? Or your fillings?"

"No," Mortimer said. Then, concerned: "Why?"

"Tell us more about the chain," George said. "You think we could cut it?"

"Not without a big blowtorch . . . Why'd you ask about my fillings?"

"Don't worry about it. Can you see how the chain is attached to the chest? Could we unhook it, maybe?"

"Hold on . . ." Twisting again, and using the ropes for leverage, Mortimer inverted himself. He reached for the chest and managed to snag a bit of decorative filigree with the tip of one finger—the most tenuous of grips, but enough to impart a little momentum. A few more seconds and he was able to grab the chest firmly and pull himself to it.

The chest bobbed at the end of its tether as Mortimer collided with it. From the far side of the sphere came the sharp metal bang of a door or gate slamming open, followed by a noise like something sliding down a chute. Mortimer, who was now straddling the chest, turned his head towards the sound. "Huh," he said.

The sliding had stopped. Now they could hear a soft whir of rotor blades.

"Huh," said Mortimer Dupree.

"Mortimer?" George said. "What are you 'huh'-ing at?"

"I don't know exactly," Mortimer said. "It's like a little submarine."

Atticus aimed the flashlight at the black torpedo that came cruising out of the shadows of the far hemisphere. The thing was a couple of feet long, with an oversized propeller and stubby wings that let it steer itself through the air; its nose was ringed with faceted crystal knobs like dragonfly eyes that glittered in the light. It circled the room in a counterclockwise direction. As it neared the mouth of the passageway they could hear the click of internal gearwork.

"I think we better get Mortimer out of there," Atticus said when the thing had gone by.

"Yeah," George concurred. "Mortimer!" he called. "We're going to pull you back!"

"Why?" Mortimer said. "You think that thing's dangerous?"

"Just let go of the damn chest, Dupree," Montrose said.

But instead of letting go, Mortimer tightened his hold and hunkered down, swiveling his head to track the torpedo. As it swung around the far side of the chest, the sound of the propeller changed pitch. When Atticus picked it up in his flashlight beam a moment later, it was moving faster—and then, as it came nearer, its nose opened up and deployed a nasty-looking cluster of chopping blades. The blades spun up into a blur with a high-pitched whine like a dentist's drill.

"Hey!" Mortimer scolded the torpedo as he would an unruly stray. "Hey! No!"

The torpedo went for the harness rope. The spinning blades chopped through it effortlessly. The frayed, severed ends floated apart while the torpedo flew on, circling back around the chest for another pass.

George grabbed the ankle rope which was now the sole remaining lifeline and gave it a sharp tug. "Mortimer," he said, "you need to let us pull you back." But Mortimer continued to hug the chest and stare wide-eyed at the torpedo.

George let go of the rope and reached into his jacket for his pistol. "Atticus, I'm going to need that light steady."

"Got it," Atticus said.

The torpedo flew back into view from behind the chest. George took careful aim and pulled the trigger. The noise of the gunshot was deafening but the bullet missed—he could see it strike the wall. Quickly he took aim again and fired. And missed.

"God damn it," Montrose said. "Let *me* . . ." He started to reach for the gun, but before he could wrestle it from George's grasp, Abdullah stepped up between the two brothers, gripping the ankle rope in both hands. As the torpedo homed in, he gave the rope some slack and then flicked it sharply, sending a tall wave down its length. The torpedo tried to adjust course but instead of severing the rope completely it only nicked it.

"Shoot it!" Mortimer shouted. "Shoot it!"

George fired another shot at the retreating torpedo. And missed.

"God damn it!" Montrose said.

Then Pirate Joe spoke up in a commanding voice: "Brother Dupree," he said, "I give you my oath as a fellow Mason we are not going to let you die, but you need to get your ass off that chest *right now.*"

Trembling, Mortimer raised himself up into a crouch on the lid of the chest—and froze.

"Do it or you're out of the club, Mortimer," Pirate Joe said.

With a cry, Mortimer launched himself into space. Montrose and Abdullah commenced hauling on the rope—which, as it went taut, began to pop and fray along the portion that the torpedo had nicked. "*Gently,*" George cautioned.

Meanwhile Mortimer, flying up at an angle, found himself careening towards the dead lodgemaster. "Get away!" Mortimer shouted at the corpse, but the dead man didn't move and they collided and spun around in a tangle of arms and legs. Another strand of the rope parted. The torpedo, now on its return trajectory, angled up towards the entwined bodies and put on a final burst of speed.

Mortimer heard the whine of the approaching blades. He twisted, using the lodgemaster's corpse as a shield. The torpedo plunged into the dead man's back. The blades chewed through his spine and what remained of his heart and lungs before getting stuck partway through his breastbone, the overheated drill motor screaming in protest. "Get aw-a-a-ay!" cried Mortimer, placing his hands on the dead man's shoulders and shoving.

Abdullah and Montrose cleared the frayed section of rope. Tugging firmly once more, they dragged screaming Mortimer down to the passageway and grabbed him.

The torpedo executed a sluggish turn and headed towards the passageway itself, pushing the dead lodgemaster before it. The grinning corpse spread its arms as if for an embrace. George raised his pistol again, aimed for the bloody bulge on the dead man's chest, and squeezed off three more shots, one of which finally struck home. There was a small explosion, a jangle of breaking gearwork, and the propeller stopped dead. Carried by momentum, the corpse continued to drift forward.

Then the wind came again and sent the lodgemaster tumbling away into the shadows, the dead torpedo sticking out of his back like a grotesque wind-up key.

"Maybe we're thinking about this the wrong way," Montrose said, a few minutes later.

"Well, if you know the right way," said George, "I'm all ears."

"Instead of asking how we're going to get that chest," Montrose said, "we should be asking how Winthrop would get it. This is his *secret* treasure room, right, so he's not going to come down here with a bunch of other guys, he's going to come alone. But then what does he do?"

George shrugged. "Man's a sorcerer. Maybe he flies out to the chest."

"That dead guy was a sorcerer, too," Montrose pointed out. "He couldn't fly. If they could fly, the booby traps wouldn't make sense."

"OK." George nodded. "So what's the answer, then?"

"The room's a machine," Montrose said. "There's a reason it's set up so you can't see the chain from here. If you don't know about the chain, you assume the chest is just floating free and you got no choice but to go in and try to snag it. And then you've got problems . . . Mortimer." He turned to the dentist, who was sitting far back in the passageway with his chin in his hands. "Did you see where the other end of that chain went?"

"Where?" Mortimer raised his head. "I told you, it goes to the far wall."

"Just to it? Like it's bolted to the wall? Or into it?"

Mortimer considered. "I'm not sure," he said. "I couldn't really see how it was attached. I know there was a hole in the wall that that flying thing came out of. Could be the chain went into another hole."

Montrose turned back to George. "That chain's on a reel. I guarantee it."

"So the chest comes to us," George said. "But how do we get it to do that?"

"That's the tricky part. If it's a magic word, we're stuck."

"What else could it be?" George scanned the walls and ceiling near the end of the passageway, looking for a switch they'd somehow failed to notice.

"It won't be in here," Montrose said. "If it were me, I'd put it just outside, so you can't see it without sticking your head out, but you can reach it without looking."

George knelt by the end of the passageway, and being careful not to lean too far forward, slipped his fingers over the edge and began feeling along the lip. Montrose joined him, the two of them working in opposite directions.

George was a third of the way up the left-side wall when he found a shallow depression with a button inside it. "Think I got it," he said.

He pressed the button and the chest, driven by whatever invisible force held sway over it, began gliding towards them, the chain unwinding from the hidden reel in the wall with a steady ratcheting sound. The chest reached the mouth of the passageway and stopped, still floating, just shy of halfway inside it. The top swung up and back on motorized hinges.

In contrast to its ornate, shiny exterior, the inside of the chest was gray and industrial. A fluorescent bulb set inside the lid flickered on, casting a harsh light over the contents.

The Book of Names rested on a thick leather pad and was held in place by a pair of buckled straps. The book's size suggested an encyclopedia volume or an unholy scripture. It was bound in the hide of some large-pored animal, and the Adamite letters on its cover had the look of scars, as though the creature in question had been cut and allowed to heal before it was skinned.

"What do you think?" said George, looking at the straps and the pad. "Any more booby traps?"

"Don't know," Montrose said. "Maybe." But then he shrugged. "Hell with it . . ."

They reached into the chest together and undid the straps. George grabbed one end of the book and Montrose grabbed the other and they lifted it out. There were no booby traps, but *The Book of Names* was heavy and the sudden tug of gravity as they got it clear of the chest and fully into the passageway caused them both to tighten their grips.

"It's OK," Montrose said, "I got it."

"No," George replied, "*I* got it."

"Excuse me, brothers," said Abdullah.

It was after one o'clock when they returned to the museum. George was last out of the passageway, and when he looked over his shoulder he saw that the opening had closed up silently behind him.

"Bradley?" Abdullah called softly, walking out into the exhibition hall. He was holding *The Book of Names* away from his body as though it were unclean, and his arms had begun to tremble from the effort. "Bradley, you here?"

No answer. They started across the exhibition hall, but had only gone a few steps when a match flared in the shadows up ahead. In the same instant they heard guns cocking off to their right, and Detectives Burke and Noble stepped out from behind a display case with their pistols leveled.

"You see?" Caleb Braithwhite said. "I told you they'd pull it off."

"Yeah," Captain Lancaster replied, "and I told you they'd try to fuck us." Cigar alight, he shook out the match and tossed it away. "All right, let's get this over with . . . You're trespassing," he said to George and his companions. "I could book you all for B and E right now, or I could just have my men shoot you and save the paperwork. And *you*." He pointed a finger at Abdullah. "Percival Avery Jones, of 5713 South Wabash, apartment 2C. You want to think about your wife, Rashida, and your son, Omar, and what happens to them if you don't come home. And your cousin Bradley? As of right now he doesn't work here anymore, but if you make me pry that fucking book out of your hands, I can see to it he gets a new job, folding laundry down in Joliet."

Abdullah was hugging *The Book of Names* to his chest now, but his arms were still trembling.

"Rashida," Lancaster said. "Omar."

Abdullah bowed his head. "I'm sorry, George," he said, his voice thick with shame. He took a step forward, but George put out a hand to stop him.

"We had a deal," George said to Braithwhite.

"We did," Braithwhite agreed good-naturedly, "and I'm ready to honor it." He nudged a bag on the floor by his feet. "Assuming that's the real *Book of Names*, of course." He smiled. "I'm not interested in kabbalah."

Six bridges ahead, George thought. He tried to think of some alternative, but the only play here was the obvious one: Survive the night and hope for some future opportunity to make things right.

He withdrew his hand and waved Abdullah forward. Braithwhite took the book from him and leafed through it.

"Well?" said Captain Lancaster.

Braithwhite nodded. "It's right," he said.

"Then we're done," said the captain. He glanced wordlessly at the detectives, who relaxed and put their guns away. "Museum's closed," Lancaster announced. "Find a fire exit and get the fuck out." He put the cigar into his mouth, turned on his heel, and walked off, the detectives following behind him.

"All yours," Caleb Braithwhite told George, giving the bag another nudge with his toe. "There's a little something extra for your troubles . . . Until next time." He left, too.

"'Next time,'" Montrose grumbled.

George went over and looked inside the bag. Adah's book was on top, wrapped in clean white cloth. George made sure the ledger was unharmed, then checked to see what the "something extra" was. His jaw dropped open.

Montrose, standing over him, saw it too. "Son of a bitch," he said.

"What is it?" said Atticus.

"Money," George told him, gazing in disbelief at the banded stacks of hundred-dollar bills. "It's the Burnses' debt, I think. He's paying it off."

"The debt to Great-grandma Adah? You're talking about the principal, right? The original eighty-eight hundred?"

"No," George said, "I'm talking about all of it: the original eighty-eight hundred, plus ninety years' interest." As he groped inside the bag, counting up the stacks, he felt the ledger in his other hand grow lighter, and then his whole body with it, as if gravity were once more letting go. "Three hundred thousand," he said. "Three hundred thousand dollars."

"Son of a *bitch*," said Montrose.

HIPPOLYTA DISTURBS
THE UNIVERSE

⊰⊱

Right there's your problem. This teleporter isn't plugged in!
—*Orithyia Blue*

Jupiter was up. Hippolyta squatted in a snow-covered pasture, distracting herself from the cold by picking out the bright dot between the constellations of Cancer and Gemini. Mars was up too, she knew, in Aquarius near the western horizon, though hidden from her by the wooded hillside at her back. Just as well: She wouldn't want the Martians to see her like this.

Back in the car, she sat with the heater running and flipped through issue #11 of *The Interplanetary Adventures of Orithyia Blue*. Horace had created the comic after Hippolyta suggested that it might be nice to read a science-fiction story about a woman for a change. Orithyia Blue, graduate of the Howard Astrotechnical College class of 2001 and the solar system's best troubleshooter, zipped from planet to planet in her trusty Buick Spacewagon. Called in to repair faulty telescopes or malfunctioning computers, she inevitably found bigger problems: unrest between the fire and shadow tribes of Mercury; political intrigue on the moons of Saturn; a cousin of the Loch Ness monster rampaging in Mars's Grand Canal.

In this latest issue Orithyia, headed home to Earth for the holidays, decided to stop at the Marshall Field's on Ceres to do some last-minute Christmas shopping for her son. But Megajoule, the Robot Overlord of

Titan, still smarting from the defeat Orithyia had dealt him in issue #7, sent his minions to ambush her. A wild chase through the asteroid belt ensued, in which the question was not "Will Orithyia survive?" (she was a crack space pilot skilled at thinking in three dimensions, while Megajoule's robots could scarcely tell left from right) but "Will she get to the store before the toy department closes?" Hippolyta had a good chuckle over one page devoted entirely to a close-up of Orithyia's shopping list. Whatever else might change in the future, the tastes of twelve-year-old boys were seemingly immutable. Who'd have guessed they'd still have Matchbox cars in the twenty-first century?

Well, she thought, Horace had been good this year, and she still had a few days to make his Christmas wishes come true.

Hers first, though. Setting the comic aside, she picked up the other book from the passenger seat, this one titled *A Survey of Astronomical Observatories of North America*. Hippolyta had found it during her last visit to the Winthrop House. She'd been in the orrery room, about to flip the switch that started the planets turning, when a hidden drawer in the orrery's base had sprung open.

Most of the observatories in the *Survey* were familiar to her. But at the back of the book Hippolyta discovered a handwritten addendum:

HIRAM WINTHROP OBSERVATORY
WARLOCK HILL, WISCONSIN

Underneath this was a set of sixty-four three-digit numbers, neatly arrayed in eight rows of eight. Beneath that was the legend "T. Hiram."

In addition to the *Survey*, the hidden drawer contained a pair of keys. One looked like a typical house key, but the other was rod-shaped, about six inches long with a loop at one end—coincidentally, a lot like the key Orithyia Blue used in the ignition of her Spacewagon.

Hippolyta showed the book and the keys to Letitia and asked if she could take them.

"You planning on driving out to Wisconsin?" Letitia said.

"I'm going to Minneapolis next week," said Hippolyta. "But I could make a detour on my way back."

Letitia cocked her head to one side and appeared to think it over. Hippolyta heard a knock under the floor.

"Yeah, OK," Letitia said. "But you be careful," she added. "It might have been Mr. Winthrop's observatory when they built it, but God knows who they've got running it now."

"I'll be careful," Hippolyta promised.

Her father had introduced her to astronomy. He hadn't meant to. When he'd brought home the telescope in December of 1928, a Christmas present to himself, he'd justified the expense by claiming it was really for Hippolyta's brother, Apollo, to get him excited about science and boost his poor grades. But Apollo's only interest in the sky was that balls sometimes fell out of it.

Nine-year-old Hippolyta stepped up. She started following her father to the roof of their Harlem apartment building and accompanying him on longer expeditions to the countryside. The latter took place about once a month: He'd borrow a car from a friend and they'd drive fifty miles upstate to a small farm owned by another friend, Mr. Hill, a Negro so light-skinned he was practically white. Arriving at the farmhouse after dark, they'd say hello to Mr. Hill and his wife, Gretchen, and then after a brief chat and maybe some pie, the Hills would go to bed and Hippolyta and her father would go out into the fields.

There, away from the city's lights, she got her first look at the true night sky. Her father would aim the telescope while Hippolyta consulted an ephemeris, calling out directions to whatever celestial object they had chosen as their quarry.

Mars was her father's favorite. He told her about Percival Lowell, a white man from Boston who'd become convinced that the lines he saw on Mars's surface were canals. Lowell's fellow astronomers had been skeptical, but he'd inspired more than a few science-fiction writers, and Hippolyta's father's sympathies lay with the writers. Unfortunately their little two-inch-aperture telescope wasn't powerful enough for him to see the canals for himself. He'd stare at the featureless red disk it showed him and try to make lines appear through sheer force of will (which was maybe not so different from what Lowell had done), all the while speculating aloud about Martian stargazers who might be looking back at him.

Hippolyta was more intrigued by Lowell's other astronomical obsession. Mysterious disturbances in the orbits of Uranus and Neptune had led astronomers to posit the existence of a "trans-Neptunian body." Lowell had searched for the so-called Planet X until his death, but it remained undiscovered.

Hippolyta decided that *she* would find Planet X. Her father indulged her, letting her aim the telescope at random patches of sky like a fisherman casting for a minnow in a vast ocean. It was hopeless, of course. As she learned at the library, planet-hunting required specialized equipment: To track down Planet X, she'd need not just a bigger telescope, but one that could take photographs; and another device, called a blink comparator, that could flip between photos of the same star field taken on different nights, to reveal whether anything moved. Lacking the money to buy these things or the wherewithal to build them, Hippolyta's only recourse was to become a professional astronomer, which she assumed was a reasonable goal. Compared to her brother's intention to be the first Negro pitcher for the Yankees, it wasn't even all that ambitious.

In October the stock market crashed; by December her father's friend had lost his job and sold his car, ending their trips upstate. Hippolyta continued to stargaze from the roof, but she often did so alone. Her father was having his own job troubles and had to hustle extra hours to make ends meet.

And then, on March 14, 1930, the morning paper brought word that Clyde Tombaugh, a junior astronomer at the Lowell Observatory in Arizona, had found Planet X. Hippolyta was torn between excitement and disappointment, but as the news sank in, the latter emotion predominated.

Her father did what he could to console her. "Paper says they don't have a name for it yet," he pointed out. "I bet they'd be open to suggestions."

Hippolyta's mother, making oatmeal at the stove, perked up at this. Never much given to flights of fancy, since the stock-market crash she'd been trying extra hard to inculcate a more practical outlook in her children. "Bernard," she warned.

Her husband ignored her. "You could write a letter to the observatory," he told Hippolyta.

Like any would-be discoverer, Hippolyta had of course given plenty of thought to what her planet's name should be. In keeping with convention, it should be drawn from classical mythology; and it should connote darkness, and cold, and remoteness. After much consideration, she'd narrowed it down to two possibilities: Pluto, god of the underworld, and Persephone, his queen. She wanted to choose Persephone, because it seemed unfair that Venus should be the only girl planet. But the name was less suitable, otherwise. Persephone, born a nature goddess, had lived in warmth and light until Pluto raptured her down into Hades, and even then she spent only part of each year in the underworld. Whereas Pluto, like Planet X, resided always in darkness, and always had.

Pluto, then. Pluto was the name.

Hippolyta wanted to stay home from school to write her letter, but her mother wouldn't hear of it. Instead she wrote it in class that day: three hundred words on why Planet X should be called Pluto. She begged an envelope from the school office and addressed it to MR. CLYDE TOMBAUGH, C/O THE LOWELL OBSERVATORY, FLAGSTAFF, ARIZONA.

Her father was waiting for her outside the school after last bell. Before Hippolyta could ask why he wasn't at work, he said: "Have you got it?" She nodded and showed him the letter. "We won't tell your mother about this, all right?" She nodded again and took his hand, and they walked together to the post office.

Two more months passed. Her father got a new job across the river in Hoboken, from which he returned home only on the weekends and sometimes not even then. Her mother remained in Harlem but started leaving the apartment earlier and coming home later. Apollo made Hippolyta's breakfast and saw her off to school.

They no longer got the morning paper, so Hippolyta was at the library when she first read the news that Planet X had been given its official name. When she saw what the name was, she let out a whoop that got her shushed by two librarians. But her elation was short-lived. The newspaper article gave credit for the name not to Hippolyta Green of Harlem, but to Venetia Burney of Oxford, England.

Hippolyta was puzzled. She'd known other people would be writing to the observatory, and because Pluto was a logical name, it wasn't surprising that someone else had thought of it too. But England? How had a letter sent from across the Atlantic Ocean reached Arizona before one mailed from New York City?

Then, reading on, she understood. Venetia Burney wasn't just any girl. Her great-uncle Henry Madan was the Eton College professor who'd named the moons of Mars, and her grandfather Falconer Madan was the former head of Oxford's Bodleian Library. It was Falconer who'd arranged to have Venetia's suggestion forwarded to the Lowell Observatory, by telegram.

By telegram! So Hippolyta's effort had been for nothing. Despite her haste, her letter had probably still been sitting in the Harlem post office when Venetia's telegram—*which she hadn't even written herself!*—had jumped to the head of the line.

Hippolyta tried to focus on the one bit of good news: According to astronomers' preliminary calculations, the existence of Pluto still did not fully account for the irregularities in the orbits of Uranus and Neptune. Which meant there could be other trans-Neptunian bodies waiting to be discovered. Waiting to be named.

She maintained her composure until late that evening, when her mother returned home from work. Hippolyta's mother had forgotten all about Planet X, but Hippolyta still remembered her skepticism about the letter-writing idea, and the sudden thought of that, and of what her mother might say now—"What did you *expect* to happen?"—opened the floodgates. Hippolyta started bawling.

Her mother, barely through the apartment door and not having spoken a word yet, looked over in alarm. "What?" she said. "What's wrong?" For several minutes Hippolyta didn't answer, only wept, while her mother held her and stroked her hair. Finally Hippolyta choked out a few words, between sobs: "I'm going. To find. The next one. I'm *going to.*"

"All right, baby," her mother said, still mystified. "You'll find the next one. Of course you will."

Warlock Hill was located in the rugged expanse of forest and farm-land between La Crosse and Madison, outside the village of Amesboro. Hippolyta passed through Amesboro around ten o'clock and found most of the villagers asleep. The only building with lights still on was one that, from the sign above the door, she took to be a white Freemasons' temple.

The turnoff for Warlock Hill was marked PRIVATE, the point under-scored by a chain stretched across the access road. Beyond the chain the road was unplowed, but a walking path had been shoveled out of the snow.

Hippolyta pulled her Roadmaster in beside the Chevrolet truck already parked there. She took the *Survey* and the keys, and reached into the glove box for a flashlight and the .38 George insisted she bring with her on her cross-country expeditions. She left Orithyia Blue on the passenger seat to mind the car.

Outside, she stood looking up, savoring the moonless night. Rather than turn on the flashlight, she let her eyes adjust and then stepped over the chain and began to follow the path by the glow of the Milky Way.

The road curved and she saw a wooden shack up ahead, spilling lamplight onto the snow. She kept walking, the crunch of her bootsteps masked by the sound of a nearby stream, until she could see in through the shack's front window.

There were two white men inside, sitting in chairs drawn up to a pot-bellied stove, while a kerosene lantern and an empty gin bottle shared the table in the corner behind them. The men didn't look like astronomers. Farmers, maybe, recruited in this off-season to serve as night watchmen. Poor ones: both asleep, one with his head tilted so far back she could see nothing but beard stubble, the other hunched forward, chin on chest and eyes closed, on the verge of toppling face-first into the stove.

Hippolyta decided not to disturb them. Just a quick look around, she told herself, fingering the keys in her pocket. In and out, while the country folk were abed, and then home to the city with no one the wiser.

She started walking again before she could lose her nerve.

The first time Hippolyta visited an observatory uninvited in the middle of the night was at Swarthmore College in 1938.

She wasn't a student. Even if there had been money for college, majoring in astronomy would not have been a practical option. For a while she tended a fantasy of becoming an astronomer without a college degree. Clyde Tombaugh had done that, winning his job at the Lowell Observatory on the strength of his amateur observations of Mars and Jupiter. But when she confided her ambition to a guide at the Hayden Planetarium, he dismissed it with four simple words: "You are a Negress," he said.

Hippolyta's nine-year-old self wouldn't have taken no for an answer, but with adolescence she'd undergone a drastic change. She'd sprouted up seemingly overnight, becoming a giantess as well as a Negress, and the increase in mass had brought a corresponding increase in inertia, a willingness to accept, often without protest, the limits placed upon her. Visiting relatives commented on how withdrawn Hippolyta had become, though they guessed wrong about the cause, her grandmothers and aunts muttering worriedly about boy trouble. Hippolyta in those days might have been game for some boy trouble—might have done something very stupid—but the boys she knew were intimidated by her size and either mocked or ignored her.

One other side effect of her growth spurt was that she learned how to sew. What mechanical talent she had—talent that in another life might have been applied to grinding telescope lenses—was directed, in this one, to making clothes that would fit her. After Hippolyta finished high school, her mother sent her to Washington, D.C., to work in her uncle Jasper's tailor shop.

Jasper had a Ford Phaeton that he insisted Hippolyta learn to drive, so that she could run errands for him. At first she went along with this as she did with everything else, but once she got out on the open road, she realized driving was something she actually enjoyed, something she might even develop a passion for. In short order Hippolyta had her license, and after proving she could be trusted behind the wheel alone, she began prevailing on her uncle to lend her the car for personal use as well—which he agreed to do, provided she paid for her own gas. Hippolyta ended up spending a lot of money on gasoline.

One February weekend she drove up to see her parents. Hippolyta's father was still in Hoboken, working as a chauffeur for a man named Arnold Silberstein. Mr. Silberstein's daughter Myrna had just started her second semester at Swarthmore, and there was a box of books she'd forgotten to take with her. Mr. Silberstein had been planning to have Mr. Green drive the box down, but on hearing that Hippolyta would soon be headed back south, he asked if she wouldn't mind making the delivery instead.

Hippolyta arrived at the campus well after dark. She'd left the books with the matron at Myrna's dormitory and was walking back to the car when she spied the dome of Swarthmore's Sproul Observatory. She changed course. At first she just meant to get a closer look at the outside of the building, but upon finding the entryway open and unguarded, she went inside. She climbed the stairs to the second floor and went down a hall to a door marked STELLAR OBSERVATION. From within came the sound of a motor and the rumble of the dome rotating.

She was trying to work up the courage to knock when the door opened on its own. A gangly white boy in horn-rimmed glasses looked out, seeming bemused to find her there. "Delbert Shaughnessy?" he said.

"Excuse me?"

"Delbert Shaughnessy," the boy said. "Our new lab partner. You're not him?"

Hippolyta just stared, until the boy stopped grinning and blushed with embarrassment.

"Sorry," he said. "That was rude. I'm Tom. Tom Appleton."

"Hippolyta Green," Hippolyta said.

"Hello, Hippolyta. Are you here to see the telescope?"

"I'd like to," she said cautiously, not convinced he was done teasing her. "If . . . if it's not against the rules."

"It probably is," Tom Appleton said. "But I won't tell if you won't. You picked a good night for it," he added, confiding: "We're looking at Pluto."

In a heartbeat, she was nine years old again. "Pluto? Really?"

"Looking *for* it, I should say. We're having trouble finding it. That's why I was hoping you were Delbert."

"Cancer," Hippolyta told him. "Pluto is in Cancer."

"It's supposed to be," he agreed, and stepped back smiling. "Come in, please." Looking over his shoulder at two other boys, he called out: "Arthur! Eugene! Good news! The cavalry is here!"

Hippolyta would never forget that night, sifting the heavens for Pluto. The great difficulty in finding it lay in knowing that you had done so—knowing which of the faint points of light in the target star field was not a star but a world, a frozen orb reflecting the sun's rays. It took multiple sessions with the blink comparator and some confused discussion with her new colleagues—"I'm pretty sure it's that one." "That one?" "No, *that* one."—but in the end Hippolyta was able to look through the telescope and say, with confidence: "Hello, Planet X. Nice to finally meet you."

It was a magical moment, and in the comic-book version of Hippolyta's life, it changed everything. Reality was different, of course: When, a month later, she contrived to return to Swarthmore, she found the doors of the observatory building locked, and before she could track down Tom Appleton (whose phone number she'd been too shy to ask for) she was stopped by a campus security guard, who threatened to have her arrested for trespassing.

So that was that. Hippolyta went back to her uncle's tailor shop, where she would work for several more years. And then came George, and Horace, and the rest of her life. She continued to look at the stars, most often through the windshield of a car, but it would be a long time before she saw Pluto again.

Then, just a couple of years ago, she'd gone out to California on a research trip for *The Safe Negro Travel Guide* and found herself adrift in the foothills of the Palomar. The check-in clerk at the motel where she'd planned to spend the night said he had no room for her—he'd left the VACANCY light on by mistake. The clerk at the motel across the road professed a similar oversight. Hippolyta was debating whether to sleep in her car or just push on to San Diego when she saw a sign for the Palomar Observatory. Remembering Tom Appleton for the first time in ages, she got the crazy idea to drive up and see whether Palomar's astronomers needed any help—and surprised herself by acting on it.

Halfway up the mountain she encountered a stranded astrophysicist, Yervant Azarian, whose own car had developed carburetor trouble. He accepted Hippolyta's offer of a ride and proceeded to test her bona fides, asking if she could name the eleven moons of Jupiter in the order they'd been discovered. Hippolyta replied that it was a trick question: A twelfth Jovian moon, still unnamed, had been discovered just months before by the Mount Wilson Observatory. Azarian was satisfied. He escorted Hippolyta into the dome where the world's largest telescope was kept and allowed her a glimpse of that night's quarry, Bode's Nebula.

Since then, Hippolyta had made a hobby, during her travels, of staging impromptu visits to other observatories she happened to be in the vicinity of. She wasn't always welcomed—the guards at Mount Wilson had turned her away twice—but she hadn't been arrested, and none of the astronomers she'd met had called her a Negress.

She hadn't been to the Lowell Observatory yet. She told herself she was saving it for a special occasion; really, she was building up her courage. And in the meantime, she'd begun cultivating another fantasy: That these observatory visits weren't just whimsical sidetrips, but steps on a path, leading towards . . . well, she wasn't sure, exactly. But something.

A wanderer in darkness, she followed an eccentric orbit, each new disturbance angling her closer to some long-awaited rendezvous. She could only hope that when the moment came, she'd be wise enough to know it, and brave enough to act.

⊰⊱

A footbridge took her across the stream, and then she was climbing Warlock Hill. She had to use her flashlight here: Trees blocked the stars, and the fieldstones set into the hillside to serve as steps were slick and uneven. She counted sixty-four stones before emerging onto the hilltop, a flat round clearing with a dome at its center.

A concrete dome. Hippolyta's brow furrowed as the flashlight beam played over the structure. She could see no opening through which a telescope might be aimed, nor any means by which the dome could be rotated.

Finding the way in was easy enough, as here too a path had been shoveled through the snow. She followed it clockwise around the dome to where a door was set into the concrete.

Hippolyta used the first of her keys. She shone her flashlight inside and saw a short flight of concrete steps leading up to a metal walkway with handrails. A power switch was mounted just inside the doorway.

The walkway was raised above a pool of shiny black liquid that filled the base of the dome. Lights ringed the pool, illuminating the dome's interior surface, which was as smooth and blank as its exterior. The walkway led to a central platform with some sort of control console. Beyond the platform the walkway continued, extending about three-quarters of the way across; fixed to the end of it was a vertical rectangular frame that seemed to have been coated with the same dark shiny fluid that was in the pool.

Hippolyta stepped carefully along the walkway. She didn't know what the substance in the pool was—her frozen nose could detect no odor, chemical or otherwise—but she guessed it would not be good for swimming in.

She examined the console. Arrayed on its face in eight rows of eight were sixty-four windows, each displaying the number 001, the individual digits stamped onto separate metal reels. To the right of the number array were a small round hole and a single large button.

Hippolyta tried pressing the button first. The console emitted a loud sterile click but nothing else happened. She got out the rod-shaped key and inserted it into the hole. It fit perfectly. She slotted it all the way home.

The lights flickered. From beneath the platform came a whir of machinery starting up, the sound broadening and deepening to a bass hum that produced a standing wave on the surface of the pool. Gradually the hum faded, settling into a barely audible register. The lights flickered again, and dimmed, and then the whole dome just disappeared, leaving Hippolyta exposed on the open hilltop.

No. The dome was still there. What she was seeing was a projection, a live panorama from outside: There was Jupiter, and there was the path she'd trod through the snow.

She turned her attention back to the console. A red glow emanated from around and between the metal reels, illuminating the numbers. Hippolyta focused on the lower-rightmost window in the array. She touched a finger to the 1, giving it a light downward nudge; the reel ticked over to 2. She looked up. The view was unchanged. She thought: Now try the button.

This time when she pressed it there was a deep *thrum* of vibration from beneath the pool. The dome went black and for a moment she could see nothing but the red glow from the console. Then the projection came back up and she found herself in a starry void. The hilltop had vanished.

Hippolyta craned her head around, looking for familiar constellations and not finding any. Two stars did stand out, not because she recognized them but because they were close enough to appear to her as tiny disks, one blue, one orange, set like mismatched eyes just a few degrees apart. Twin stars!

Near the base of the dome was a third object: a small, irregularly shaped asteroid, tumbling slowly but visibly, each moment's rotation exposing a new portion of its surface to the light of the twin stars.

Hippolyta laughed and clapped her hands. If only her father could see this!

She turned again to the console, calculating: If each of the sixty-four number settings went from 000 to 999, that would put the sum total of possible combinations at ten to the 192nd power. Hippolyta tried to think what word, ending in -*illion*, you'd use to describe that figure, came up with "sixty-thrillion," and burst out laughing again.

Sixty-thrillion celestial panoramas. But they couldn't really all be different, could they?

Hippolyta reached out and ticked the 2 in the lower right window over to 3. Then, seized by a giddy abandon, she began changing numbers at random.

She pressed the button again, and—

Thrum.

—she was skimming an ocean of blue clouds, mountainous azure thunderheads rising all around her, while above through a thinner haze she glimpsed another unfamiliar sun and the broad bands of a ring encircling the planet.

It was beautiful. It was also frightening—especially the view straight ahead and down, the frame at the walkway's end now looking very much like a doorway through which she might dive, or fall, into a turbulent sea whose depths were lit by titanic lightning flashes. In a sudden terror of vertigo, Hippolyta reached for the console array, changed a single number, and hit the button again.

Thrum.

Bright light! A scorched landscape of black rock was tinged red by an enormous sun cresting the horizon in front of her. Hippolyta put up a hand to shield her eyes—then spread her fingers to peer at an optical illusion. The edge of the sun intersected the doorframe at the end of the walkway, highlighting a discontinuity in the image. The portion of the projection that fell within the frame appeared to be *closer*, somehow.

Hippolyta shivered, the winter air inside the dome conflicting with the hellish vision that surrounded her. She thought about the snow lying on the ground outside and asked herself what would happen if she were to toss a snowball through that open frame. Would it splatter against the wall of the dome, spoiling the illusion? Or would it flash into steam as it encountered the heat of an alien star?

Interesting experiment. Hippolyta might even have tried it, if the next thought hadn't occurred to her: You don't open a doorway just to chuck out snowballs. Doors are for walking through. Which implied a place to walk *to*, a destination where a human being could stand without asphyxiating or being turned into a charcoal briquette.

Of course, with sixty-thrillion destinations to choose from, it could take an eternity of trial and error to find one that wouldn't kill you. Hippolyta would have liked nothing better than to stay here and sample those myriad worlds, but she didn't have much time, so she decided to cheat and look up the answer in the back of the book.

Working quickly, she set the dials. She took a last look at the scorched planet of the red sun (about to be lost to her forever, she realized, since she had not copied its address down). Then she pressed the button.

Thrum.

Out of the momentary blackness, a great spiral galaxy appeared. It hung in a night sky before her and was reflected, like a brilliant, many-armed moon, in the surface of a dark ocean whose waters lapped the shore of a white sand beach.

Hippolyta went to the end of the walkway and stood staring through the open frame. Then she leaned sideways, steadying herself against the handrail.

No simple illusion, this: When she looked *around* the doorframe, she could see the unbroken panorama projected against the curve of the dome a few feet away; but when she looked *through* the frame, the beach was *right there*, and no mere projection but a seemingly three-dimensional space into which a single step would carry her.

Right there, and yet also, obviously, elsewhere. She could see the night surf breaking on the beach, but she couldn't hear it. And the air she drew in and expelled visibly from her mouth was still Wisconsin air, *winter* air. The air on the beach—she couldn't say how she knew this, but felt certain it was so—the air on the beach would be warmer.

She stretched out a hand. As it passed within the frame she felt a tingling against her palm that quickly became unpleasant. She reached further, encountering increasing resistance and pain, and finally drew back, having meanwhile intuited a new piece of information: This doorway didn't allow half measures. You couldn't just stick a finger or a toe through; you had to commit, step boldly.

Sure, Hippolyta thought, glancing at the dark pool beneath the walkway. And the next thing that happens is you fall in the muck, and probably break a leg in the bargain. Because it's a trick; it has to be.

"But I won't tell if you won't," she said, and stepped through the doorway.

The air on the beach *was* warmer.

The salt breeze blowing in over the gently plashing surf felt like late spring or early fall. The shoulder season, Hippolyta thought: Tourist cabins would be a bargain, provided you could find someone to rent to you. She breathed deeply, the sea air differently scented than that of her native Atlantic but containing sufficient oxygen—she didn't grow dizzy or faint.

The sand felt strangely springy. Hippolyta looked down and bounced experimentally on the balls of her feet. It wasn't the sand, she realized: It was her. She was lighter. Not much—unlike Orithyia Blue on Mars or Ganymede, she did not go bounding into the air—just enough to feel it in the tendons of her ankles as they flexed: gravity turned down a notch.

Smiling, Hippolyta stretched out her arms, went up on tiptoe, and executed a graceful half-pirouette. To face, behind her, a seven-by-three-foot rectangle cut out of the fabric of reality, through which could be seen the chilly interior of the dome on Warlock Hill. The doorway on this end was framed by thin bars of light that cast a faint glow on the sand.

She walked around it, curious to see what it looked like from the backside. Not like much: Though the glowing frame was visible from every angle, when viewed from behind it was an empty frame, the same beach inside and outside the lines. She circled around to the front again, watched Wisconsin rotate back into view out of nowhere. "OK," she said nodding.

Next she surveyed her wider surroundings. The beach fronted on a high rocky cliff, atop which Hippolyta could make out a line of trees, their leaves shining silver in the light from the galaxy. To her left the cliff ran straight as far as she could see, the strip of beach in front of it unbroken save for a single boulder, a dark lump on the sand in the middle distance. But to her right, just a couple of hundred yards away, a ridge of rock extended fingerlike from the cliff, forming a high promontory that cut down across the sand to the water. The side of the ridge was marked by a gray zigzag that registered instantly as a staircase, and up top she could see two buildings. One, set back near where the ridge joined the cliff, appeared to be a single-story flat-roofed structure; the other, located at the very end of the promontory overlooking the water, was dome-shaped, and while it was difficult to make out details, Hippolyta would have sworn she detected the bulge of a telescope hatch.

Just a quick look around, she thought. In and out. But what happens—looking back through the doorway to Earth, she made herself ask the question—what happens if, while you're up there, somebody comes and turns the machine off?

You wake up, she answered. Because this is a dream. Obviously.

The warm sea breeze, caressing her cheek, begged to differ on that point.

She ignored it.

The staircase bolted to the side of the ridge was enclosed in metal bars, and there was a gate at the bottom. The gate wasn't locked, but the latch was a complicated affair requiring two more-or-less human hands to operate. Wondering what sort of intruders this was meant to keep out, she recalled the ocean-dwelling squid men of Europa from *Orithyia Blue #5*. If it *was* squid men, Hippolyta thought, she should be OK; they respected pistol fire.

A buzzer sounded on the ridge above her as she pulled the gate open. She stepped through quickly, shut the gate, and listened. Nothing now but the surf.

Despite the reduced gravity, the steps rattled disconcertingly beneath her feet as she ascended. She sprinted up the last flight and stopped to catch her breath on the top landing. Now she could see the dome clearly: It *was* an observatory. She guessed the other building was a residence, a guesthouse for planet-hopping astrophysicists. There was no sign of life in either structure.

To exit the top of the staircase she had to pass through two more gates, set in opposite sides of a ten-foot-wide cage. This reminded Hippolyta of the booby-trapped airlock the corsairs of Neptune had used to knock out Orithyia Blue in issue #4, but she was well past the point of no return now, so she said a quick prayer and entered the cage.

The inner gate wouldn't open. She'd bent to get a closer look at the latch when she heard crackling and felt invisible fingers teasing her hair. She looked up. Blue sparks were dancing around a series of coils suspended from the top of the cage.

That can't be good, Hippolyta thought, and then her head filled up, appropriately enough, with stars.

When Hippolyta came to she was lying on a cot in a small lamplit room. Her first thought was that she was back in Wisconsin, in the guard shack. But the ceiling and walls that surrounded her were metal, not wood, and the figure sitting watch on her was a Negro woman with iron-gray hair and a face deeply seamed with wrinkles. The old woman had the *Survey* in her lap, open to the page with the numbers, and she was holding Hippolyta's .38.

Eyes on the gun, Hippolyta sat up. She felt light-headed, but there was no pain and no obvious bumps or bruises from the fall she must have taken. She swung her legs over the side of the cot.

The old woman spoke: "Stand up before I give you leave, and your brains will be all over that wall behind you." She said it calmly, not threatening but as though making a simple observation about how the universe—this corner of it, anyway—worked.

"All right," said Hippolyta, and folded her hands in front of her.

"Who are you?"

"My name's Hippolyta Berry."

"You work for him?"

"Who?" Hippolyta said.

"Winthrop! Hiram Winthrop."

"No. I—"

"Don't you lie to me!" The old woman snatched up the open book, presenting it face-out like a warrant. "This writing is in his hand!"

"I don't know whose hand that is. I found the book in the Winthrop House, but—"

"So you were in his house. So you work for him!"

"No," Hippolyta said. "It's called the Winthrop House, but Hiram Winthrop is dead. My friend Letitia Dandridge lives there now. It's her house."

"You're friends with a white woman named Letitia Dandridge?"

"She's not a white woman."

"A *colored* woman owns the Winthrop House? And she sent you here?"

"No one sent me. I came out to see the observatory on my own."

"Why? What would possess you to do that?" She dropped the *Survey* back into her lap and thrust the gun forward. "I told you not to lie to me!"

"Wait," said Hippolyta. "Just wait. I can explain. Years ago, when I was a little girl, my father brought home a telescope . . ."

"**W**ell," the old woman said when Hippolyta had finished. "I don't suppose anyone would make up a tale like that. You got one thing wrong, though: Mr. Winthrop did send you."

"No. I told you, he's—"

"Dead, yeah, I got that. But I'm talking about his spirit." Hippolyta must have looked skeptical, for the old woman suddenly narrowed her eyes. "Oh, what? You're too smart to believe in ghosts? Flying across the universe, though, *that's* logical . . . I'll tell you something else, too: You're too late again. This planet? Mr. Winthrop already named it."

Hippolyta glanced at the book, feeling a sudden, absurd pang of disappointment. "T. Hiram," she guessed. "*Terra* Hiram: Hiram's world."

The old woman nodded. Then she said: "You can get up now. My name's Ida."

"**Y**ou hungry?" Ida asked her.

"No, thank you."

"*I'm* hungry," Ida said.

They'd come out to a larger room with a dining table and chairs, a counter and sink along one wall, and windows that looked out towards the dome at the end of the promontory and down at the beach. The room and pretty much everything in it was fashioned out of the same grayish metal; studying the wall behind the chair she sat in, Hippolyta could see seams where big metal plates had been fitted together like jigsaw pieces.

"This house was built from a kit," Ida explained. "Portable explorer's cottage, or somesuch. It's got an instruction manual. What I'd really like to see, though, is the box the parts came in."

She turned to an appliance resembling a miniature oven that rested on the counter beside the sink. It had a swing-down door on the front and a control panel featuring an eight-digit number window, a green light, and a button, which Ida pushed. There was a *chunk* of a lock engaging and the green light turned red. A bass note sounded. After about half a minute the noise ceased, the red light turned yellow, and the door unlocked. Ida opened it and lifted out a gray metal pan, its top sealed with foil. She carried the pan to the table and peeled the foil off, releasing a puff of steam. Hippolyta leaned forward: The pan was filled with some sort of sweet-smelling white sponge cake. "Angel food?" she guessed.

"Manna," said Ida, sitting down. "That's what the manual calls it. Supposed to have all your daily requirements. It's kept me alive, anyway." She reached in and tore off a hunk of the cake and popped it in her mouth.

Hippolyta picked up the foil sheet that had sealed the pan. Impressed on it was a series of eight digits: 00000001.

"Every number's something different," Ida told her. "It's all food, but the manual doesn't have any menu description beyond number one, so you don't know what you're going to get until you get it. And the box has a regulator that only lets you run it once every four hours"—she indicated the yellow light—"so if you conjure up something nasty, you either have to choke it down or wait. Mary, she liked to stay up nights and play the food lottery. I kept hoping she'd hit the number for hot chocolate."

Hippolyta looked over at the food maker. "Do you know how it works?"

"There's a big round tank in the utility room with pipes running in and out of it," Ida said. "The manual calls it 'the prime matter vessel,' and stresses how you must never, ever, ever try to break it open. The prime matter, I gather that's something like the dirt God made Adam out of, right before He breathed life into it." She tore off another hunk of manna. "Tasty dirt."

"Who's Mary?" Hippolyta asked.

"We worked together at the Winthrop House," Ida said. "There were six of us: James Storm, who was Mr. Winthrop's chauffeur; Gordon Lee, the cook; Mr. Slade, the handyman; and me, Mary, and Pearl, the maids.

"It was Pearl who ran off with Mr. Winthrop's son. Mr. Winthrop knew they'd been getting together and didn't care, but the thought of them living as man and wife, that was a horse of another color. He gathered up the rest of us and demanded to know where they'd gone off to. He promised Pearl wouldn't be harmed, but we all knew that was a lie and no one spoke up. So Mr. Winthrop called in some men from his lodge and they bundled us into cars and drove us out of the city.

"I thought they were taking us into the woods to torture us. That's how my brother Roy died, in Kentucky. But Mr. Winthrop had something else in mind. He brought us to the hilltop and took us into that bunker or waystation or whatever you call it, and opened a portal to this world. Herded us through it and set us on this rock. Then he made us go there." She pointed out the window at the observatory. "Made us look through the telescope at this smudge of light on the edge of infinity. 'That's the Milky Way,' he said. 'Earth is there, along with everyone and everything you've ever known or loved. It's so far away, if you tried to walk back from here, the stars would all burn out before you even made a start. God Himself would die of old age before you made it home.'

"Well, we were all good and scared by that point. I could see Mr. Slade, in particular, was anxious to share what little he knew about Pearl and Mr. Winthrop's son. But Mr. Winthrop had laid some sort of enchantment on us, to keep us from acting up while he frightened us. Mr. Slade *wanted* to talk, but he couldn't. None of us could. Not without Mr. Winthrop's leave. 'I know you're ready to cooperate now,' Mr. Winthrop said. 'But I think some of you might still have it in mind to mislead me. And since you've already wasted enough of my time, I'm going to leave you here to stew for a few days first.'

"I wondered about that. For a man who didn't want his time wasted, it seemed like a complicated way of going about things. He *could* have just tortured us. But I suppose a planet is like any other vanity: not worth having if you don't take every chance to show it off.

"So he left us here. To stew. But meanwhile something must have happened in Chicago, because he never came back to finish questioning us. Nobody else came, either."

"When was this?" Hippolyta asked.

"Nineteen thirty-five," said Ida. "July the eighteenth, that's the day Mr. Winthrop brought us here . . . You happen to know what date he died?"

Hippolyta shook her head. "I know it was a long time ago. But I don't know exactly when, or how."

"I can guess at the how. If it happened the way I think it did, Mr. Braithwhite must have done him in." Ida watched Hippolyta carefully as she said this, but Hippolyta had never heard the name Braithwhite before. "Samuel Braithwhite," Ida continued after a moment. "He and Mr. Winthrop were partners, in what business I couldn't say exactly. But then something soured between them, and by that summer they were feuding. I suppose it was the distraction of the feud that let Pearl and Mr. Winthrop's son slip away like they did. I remember, about a week before they ran off, I overheard Mr. Winthrop on the phone, talking about banishing Mr. Braithwhite. 'Banish,' that's the word he used . . . Thinking about that later, it occurred to me that maybe he meant to bring Mr. Braithwhite here, to trap him, and that maybe that was the real reason he'd brought *us* here." She smiled grimly. "White man's exile, complete with servants . . . But if that was Mr. Winthrop's plan, Mr. Braithwhite must have gotten the better of him. I suppose Pearl got the better of him too, you want to think of it that way." She looked down at the table, her smile fading until only grimness remained. "I hope it was worth it. I truly do." Then she shrugged away the thought and looked up again. "What year is it now? Nineteen fifty-four?"

"Yes," Hippolyta said.

"November?"

"December. The twenty-first."

"December twenty-first!" Ida said. "I'll have to redo my figures . . . We kept a careful count of the days," she explained. "But this world doesn't turn as fast as Mother Earth. High noon to high noon is closer to twenty-five hours here. And I'm pretty good at math, but fractions always trip me up." She shook her head and sighed, then broke out in a smile—a happy one, this time—as another thought struck her. "December twenty-first, almost Christmas. Mary would've liked that." Hippolyta said nothing to this, but Ida saw the question in her eyes. "It's all right. You can ask me."

So Hippolyta did: "What happened to Mary? And the others?"

A stout twelve-foot-high double fence stretched across the width of the promontory where it joined the cliff. This barrier, Hippolyta guessed, was not so much booby-trapped as flat-out lethal, the red light on the control box just inside the gates a cyclopean eye vowing doom to would-be trespassers.

In the open space between the fence and the cottage four crosses had been erected. They were made from branches bound with lengths

of some fibrous stuff like palm fronds or strips of sawgrass. Three of
the crosses had been driven directly into the thin layer of sandy soil
that covered the ridge; the fourth was set on a cairn of stones that was
large enough to contain an actual body.

"That's Mary," Ida said of the cairn. "Gordon we buried at sea, and
none of us could bring ourselves to handle what was left of James.

"James was the first to go. Mr. Winthrop warned us that the beach
was dangerous, but James thought that was just to scare us. He said
there had to be a way to open the portal from this side. Our second day
here, he was down on the sand looking, when Scylla got him."

"Scylla?" said Hippolyta.

"Gordon was next," Ida went on. "On day 34. After the shock of
what happened to James wore off, he got fidgety. He wanted to explore,
out there." She gestured at the pale trees lining the cliff. "He'd go out
each morning for an hour or three. At first he brought back souvenirs:
stones, bits of wood, these strange flowers one time. Mr. Slade put an
end to the souvenirs—he said we couldn't know what might be deadly
to pick up—but he couldn't get Gordon to stay put.

"Then one day Gordon didn't come back. It was getting late afternoon and I decided we'd better go look for him. Mr. Slade refused to
go. Mary didn't want to go either, but she was afraid to be left alone
with Mr. Slade, so she came with me. We picked up Gordon's trail and
tracked him a couple miles down that way, to a part of the cliff that juts
out right over the water.

"We found him lying on his back, next to this . . . nest, I guess. He
was dead for sure, but the critter that killed him looked like it might
still be alive, and it was wrapped around his head like a caul.

"We didn't want to leave him like that, but even if we'd found the
strength to carry him back here, we knew Mr. Slade wouldn't let us
through the fence with him. So Mary and I said a prayer, and then I
grabbed Gordon's wrists and she grabbed his ankles and we tossed him
off the cliff into the ocean.

"We came back and told Mr. Slade that Gordon was dead. Mr. Slade got hysterical, screaming about how he didn't deserve to be in this fix and enough was enough. 'From now on,' he said, 'we're just going to sit tight and wait for Mr. Winthrop. And when he gets back, you're going to tell him where his son and that bitch went. If I have to help him beat it out of you, I will.'

"Well, he didn't scare me. He was a little man—even Mary could have whipped him in a fair fight. But I knew we'd have to take care just the same. We'd all begun to suspect that Mr. Winthrop might not be coming back, and I could see if Mr. Slade ever completely lost hope, he'd be in to murder us in our sleep. So I watched Mary's back and she watched mine, and we went on like that through day 87.

"Day 88 a storm blew in. We'd had showers and squalls before, but this was different: *black* cloud, sheets of rain, booming thunder. The manual said the house was proof against lightning despite being metal, but we were all on edge.

"For dinner that night, Mary decided to play the lottery. She got Mr. Slade to pick the number. I guess she was hoping if it was something nice, he'd take it as God's grace and be a bit less unpleasant.

"But it wasn't nice." Ida shuddered at the memory. "Mary had dialed up some foul dishes before, but this was the first one that was still moving." She clenched the fingers of one hand as though gripping an object the size of a plum. "They were grubs. Fat, white, hairy things. Killed *my* appetite. Mary's, too—she'd try a bite of almost anything, but not that.

"Mr. Slade, though . . . He started laughing. He laughed the way a man laughs when he finally grasps that hell is a real place—the way my brother laughed, the night he died. He picked up one of those grubs, and bit into it, and chewed with his mouth open, laughing all the while . . .

"Then he stood up, so quick he knocked his chair over, and picked up the pan to throw it. I think he meant to dump it on one of us, but he couldn't decide whether he hated me or Mary more, so he threw it between us and scattered those vile things all over the floor. That got me mad—I knew who was going to get stuck with the cleanup—so I jumped up too, ready to wrestle Mr. Slade to the ground. But he didn't come at me. He went over to the window and stood there with his back to us.

"Lightning flashed. Mr. Slade started laughing again. 'Thank God,' he said. 'My God, thank God, there's a light on the beach!' Mary and I went over to look but you couldn't see two feet in that storm. 'Just wait,' Mr. Slade said, and the lightning came again, and still there was nothing. But Mr. Slade was out of his mind by then. 'I'm going home,' he said. 'You can stay here and die, I'm going home *now*.'

"He went out into the storm. We didn't try to stop him. It wasn't Christian, but all I could think in that moment was good riddance. Lightning came again and I caught one last glimpse of him, starting down the stairs to the beach. Then he was gone.

"Mary helped me clean up and went to bed. I sat up all night, watching to see if Mr. Slade would come back. But morning came and there was no more sign of him.

"And then it was just the two of us. Enduring." Ida leaned forward to place a hand on the cairn. "We got on OK. We always had. And it's not so bad here, if you're careful not to get killed. I used to tease Mary—she's originally from Savannah, and she always wanted a house by the ocean. 'Got your wish,' I'd say. She'd get so mad: 'It's just like home. The beach is *right there* and I'm not allowed to go swimming.'" Ida laughed and patted the cairn again. "She had chest pains, though. All that weird food, it wasn't good for her heart, and she was nervous a lot of the time, worried that Jesus wouldn't be able to find her here.

"But He did, finally. Day 4,932, that's the morning Mary didn't wake up." Ida looked at Hippolyta. "Nineteen forty-nine, I want to say June twenty-sixth though I guess that's wrong."

"Five years ago," Hippolyta said. "And you've been alone since then?"

"Better me than her," Ida said. "Alone never bothered me much. I can still talk to Mary all I want to; Jesus and my brother, too. And I've got Mr. Winthrop's observatory to keep myself occupied." She grinned. "I'm sure he didn't intend that. But it's got its own manual and a book for recording observations, and I've made good use of both of them over the years."

She looked at Hippolyta again, her expression both assessing and conspiratorial.

"So," she said. "Would you like to see my telescope?"

The galaxy had begun to set, the lowest of its arms dipping like an oar beneath the ocean horizon.

"The Drowning Octopus," Ida said, as they walked towards the end of the promontory. "That's what Mr. Winthrop called it in his notes. Said it was 'blue-shifted,' which means it's coming this way. I didn't tell Mary that, though. I knew she'd only worry."

"What about this star system?" Hippolyta asked. "Is it one star, or more? Does this planet have any moons? How many other planets are there?"

"There's one sun," Ida told her. "It's brighter than Earth's. One moon, too, but smaller and farther away. As for planets, there's four others Mr. Winthrop knew about. Six, now."

"You discovered two planets?"

"Winthrop was on the trail of the fifth one," Ida said. "I used his notes to find it. Named it Ida, to spite him. The sixth one, though—Pearl—she was all mine. She's up now," Ida added, pointing back at the sky above the cliff. "She's got her own little moon you can spy through the telescope. Should be able to see it tonight."

They reached the dome. Ida had her hand on the observatory door when she suddenly turned and looked down at the beach, and cursed.

"What's wrong?" said Hippolyta, but even as she spoke she saw it too: Down on the sand beside the glowing portal, another light had appeared, a kerosene lamp carried by one of a pair of white men dressed for Wisconsin winter. The lantern-bearer was looking in their direction, but with the lamp flame shining in his eyes, Hippolyta doubted he could see more than a vague silhouette of the promontory. Meanwhile his companion, armed with a rifle, was gazing at Winthrop's Octopus as if he meant to shoot it down.

Hippolyta met Ida's accusing stare. "They aren't with me," she said.

"Just be still and keep your voice down," Ida told her.

"What if they come up the stairs?" Hippolyta whispered. "Do you need to—"

"They aren't going to make it to the stairs. Scylla's on to them."

Scylla: The boulder, Hippolyta realized. While she and Ida had been visiting, the boulder had moved down the beach and now rested no more than twenty feet from the portal. Closer up, it looked more like a giant cannonball than a rock.

The man with the rifle had noticed it too. He approached it, switching his gun to one hand and making a fist of the other, as though intending to rap on the side of the black sphere, which was as tall as he was. But he was still more than an arm's length away when the sphere suddenly burst open like an orange turning inside out, dark rind splitting to reveal a wriggling white pulp. Dozens of pale tentacles shot out, wrapping around the man's limbs, torso, neck, and head, and yanking him forward to be swallowed whole before he could cry out. By the time his companion realized something was wrong and turned around, the sphere had closed up again.

The lantern-bearer held his lamp up high and called out a name. Thinking his friend had gone home to Wisconsin, he stepped to the portal and peered at the control room. Hippolyta almost shouted a warning but Ida grabbed her wrist and hissed, *"Be still."* Then the man hoisted his lamp again and started for the sphere.

Scylla was slower on the draw this time. The man actually had time to turn and run. The tentacles that reached for him were thick ropy things that squirmed over the sand and seized his ankles, slamming him facedown on the beach.

He screamed as Scylla reeled him in—a desperate, plaintive cry that echoed off the cliff. Then the sphere snapped shut, cutting off the sound and sending an object like a mossy stone tumbling down to the water. The oil from the lamp, which had been smashed by a pinwheeling arm, continued to burn for another moment.

Then all was peaceful once more, the beach's dark stillness disturbed only by surf, starlight, and the soft glow of the portal back to Earth.

"You need to leave," Ida said.

Back inside the cottage, Ida slid the leftover manna, pan, foil, and all, into a slot beneath the counter marked MATTER RECYCLE. "I expect there'll be other men coming after those first two," she said. "Before they get here you have to go back and shut the door. Throw away the key." She fed the *Survey*—and T. Hiram's celestial address—into the slot as well.

"I'm not going back down on that beach," Hippolyta said, and then blinked, stunned by her own words, what it would mean if she really couldn't go back. Horace, she thought.

"Scylla's had her supper," Ida said. "If it goes the way it did with James, she'll wander off now and be sick awhile. We don't digest well." She rinsed her hands in the sink and held them up to a wall-mounted blower to dry them. "I'll walk you down, make sure you get through the portal OK."

"You're not coming back with me?"

The blower shut off, but Ida remained facing the wall. "You have a child?" she said.

"Yes."

"You love her?"

"Him," Hippolyta said. "Yes."

"Then you should understand. I'd like to see Pearl again, find out what's become of her. If Hiram Winthrop were *dead* dead, I might risk it. But if he's still looking for his son from beyond the grave, I need to keep my distance."

"But Winthrop knows where you are."

"He knows where he left me," Ida said, turning around. "He won't know I'm still here unless you tell him. He might send someone else, I suppose, but if you're the best he could manage in nineteen years, I should be fine for whatever time I've got left. It's my planet, now.

"Or it will be," she added, giving Hippolyta a look she didn't care for, "once you're gone."

Ida vanished for several minutes into the back of the cottage, returning with Hippolyta's coat and a worn canvas shoulder bag. "I'm going to keep your revolver," she said. "In case I get other visitors." Hippolyta made no objection but felt a tingle of unease settle between her shoulder blades when Ida indicated she should lead the way.

They descended the stairs. As predicted, Scylla had moved off, becoming a barely discernible speck in the distance. Still Hippolyta was wary, stepping onto the beach as she would onto a minefield.

They made it to the portal without being eaten. Ida reached into the bag and brought out a parting gift for Hippolyta: a gray metal box about five inches on a side, its hinged lid secured with strips of sawgrass. "For your silence," Ida said.

Hippolyta felt that uneasy tingle again. She thought: You didn't know Christmas was coming, but you just happened to have a present lying around? Who for? "It's all right," she told Ida. "You don't need to bribe me."

"Take it," Ida insisted, shoving the box into her hands. It was heavy for its size, and whatever was inside must have been snugly packed—as Hippolyta fumbled to hold on to it, she could feel no telltale shifting of contents. "Don't open it now," Ida said. "After. Once you've shut the portal and got rid of the key and are safe away . . . You'll understand."

"Ida," Hippolyta said. "You don't have to stay here. You can—"

"No!" Ida dipped her hand into the bag again, came out with the .38. "You go back . . . You go, and when that door's shut, you're just a dream I had." Gesturing with the gun: "Now *get.*"

And still Hippolyta might have tried to convince her, but just then Scylla made a ghastly retching noise up the beach. The sound galvanized Hippolyta into motion. She pivoted on the sand and half-stepped, half-leapt through the doorway.

Sudden shock of winter cold. The increase in gravity staggered her, and if not for the railing to lean against she would have fallen.

She steadied herself and turned around, to find Ida staring at her from several feet and thrillions of miles away. The old woman was waving. Not saying goodbye; urging her to get on with it.

Hippolyta stumbled back to the control console. But with her hand on the key, she hesitated. Mouthing the words broadly so that her lips could be read from across the universe, she said: "Ida, are you sure? Are you absolutely—"

Ida brought the gun up. Despite the sound barrier between them, Hippolyta would have sworn she could hear the hammer cocking.

She yanked the key from its slot. The dome went dark and the almost imperceptible background hum ceased. Then, as the lights came up, there was a new sound: the *tick-tick-tick* of tiny metal reels as each number window reset itself to 001.

Hippolyta looked at the key in one hand and the box in the other and thought about tossing them both into the black pool. Instead she pocketed the key and, holding the box to her chest, turned and started for home.

Clouds had covered the sky above Warlock Hill in her absence. She emerged from the dome into pitch darkness and made her way carefully down the hillside. She'd crossed the footbridge and was passing the empty guard shack when her flashlight gave out. She continued blindly following the path, ducking her head against the falling snow that blew into her eyes.

She came to the chain sooner than she expected to and would have tripped over it in the dark. But suddenly she could see again. She looked up into the glow of headlights: A second Chevy truck had pulled up behind the first and three more white men had gotten out. One of them, by looks another moonlighting farmer, had the front passenger door of Hippolyta's Roadmaster open and was leaning in to check the glove box. The other two, who stood idly by while the car was searched, were more refined sorts: silver-haired patricians in long dark coats.

It was one of the dark coats who first noticed Hippolyta. "You there!" he shouted, brandishing a pistol. The other dark coat drew a gun as well, while the farmer popped his head up out of the car.

"Don't shoot!" Hippolyta dropped the dead flashlight and Ida's gift box and put her hands up.

"Who are you?" the first dark coat demanded. "What are you doing here?"

"Don't shoot!" Hippolyta repeated. Keeping her hands raised, she stepped over the chain.

Gripping her collar like a leash, the dark coat shoved her up against the Roadmaster and stuck his gun in her face. "Who the hell are you?"

"I'm just trying to get home!" Hippolyta told him. "Please, mister . . . I took a wrong turn, and I'm just trying to get directions back to the highway!"

She could see he didn't believe her. At the same time he was

obviously having trouble conceiving why else she would be here. Whatever sorts of trespassers these people were worried about, she didn't fit
the description.

The farmer hopped the chain and picked up the box that Hippolyta
had dropped. He held it by his ear and shook it, then used a buck knife
to cut away the sawgrass binding the lid shut.

"Wait a minute," Hippolyta said.

"Shut up," said the man with the gun in her face.

The farmer lifted the lid of the box and squinted at the little black
sphere stuffed inside it. *For your silence,* Hippolyta heard Ida say, and
she thought: Oh Ida, you didn't have to do that—I wouldn't have told
anyone. And yet she did understand: not only the lengths to which a
mother might go to protect her child; but the impulsive acts to which a
heart, disturbed by years of longing, might be prone.

The farmer, who understood nothing, stuck his face up close to the
sphere and sniffed it. "What is that?" said the second dark coat. The
farmer shrugged and prodded the sphere with the tip of his knife.

The sphere exploded out of the box, turning itself inside out as it
flew up, little tentacles reaching towards startled blue eyes. The farmer's feet shot out from under him and he flipped onto his back, clawing
at the creature, which had flattened and stretched itself over his face
in an attempt to devour his head.

"Jesus Christ." The dark coat loosened his grip on Hippolyta and
pivoted towards the stricken farmer, in the process aiming the gun
away. Hippolyta braced herself against the car and shoved him, hard.
He lost his grip on her entirely and stumbled headlong into the other
dark coat, the two of them coming together with a loud double *pop!* and
falling entangled in a heap. They rolled apart; their jaws went slack and
they looked up, unblinking, as though transfixed by some astronomical
wonder.

Meanwhile the farmer, smothering, went into convulsions, beating
his arms and legs frantically against the snow.

He was still doing it, but slower, when Hippolyta got in her car and drove away.

"**H**orace," she said, three days later, "have you seen that comic book you gave me?"

Horace, sitting contented among his spoils at the foot of the Christmas tree, looked up at her. "Which one?"

"The new *Orithyia Blue*. Number eleven."

"No. You took it on your trip, remember?"

"And you didn't take it out of the car since I got back?"

Horace shook his head. "What's wrong, Mom?"

"I'm worried I might have lost it," Hippolyta said.

"You read it though, right?" Horace took a quick inventory of his presents: the Matchbox cars, the big box of art supplies, the remote-control Robert the Robot. "You *must* have."

"I did," she said. "I liked it." Hippolyta forced a smile, telling herself: registration papers still in the glove box, nothing else missing from the car, maybe it's not what you're thinking. "I just feel bad, that's all."

"It's OK." He picked up the Matchbox London bus and swooped it through the air like a double-decker spaceship. "I can draw you another copy if you like."

"That'd be nice," Hippolyta said. "Tell me something, though: That first copy you gave me. What name did you use on it?" Since learning that Dr. Seuss had been born Theodor Geisel, Horace had been experimenting with professional pseudonyms. George didn't care for the practice, pointing out that Berry was a good name that deserved to be honored, but Hippolyta had supported Horace's right to sign his work as he wished. Thank God.

"H.G.," Horace told her. Short for "Horace Green," the initials a nod to both his mother's maiden name and the author of *War of the Worlds*. "The same as on all the *Orithyia Blue*s."

"Right." Hippolyta exhaled softly in relief. "Right, of course . . . And you're sure?"

"I think so." Horace looked at her curiously. "Why does it matter?"

"It doesn't." She smiled again, reassuringly, but Horace continued to stare at her until George came in from the kitchen, bearing three steaming mugs on a tray.

"So," George said. "Who wants hot chocolate?"

JEKYLL IN HYDE PARK

⊰⊱

I knew myself, at the first breath of this new life, to be more wicked,
tenfold more wicked, sold a slave to my original evil; and the thought,
in that moment, braced and delighted me like wine.
—*Robert Louis Stevenson,*
The Strange Case of Dr. Jekyll and Mr. Hyde

New Year's Day, Ruby woke up white.

Her luck had been running bad since Christmas, and she'd figured
she still had a blow or two coming. But she certainly hadn't expected
this. Not that she had any right to complain: She *did* ask for it.

The trouble started on Christmas Eve. Ruby was working for Demarski Catering, serving drinks at a party at a big house up in Ravens-
wood. The manager that night was Katherine Demarski, Ruby's least
favorite; the youngest of the five Demarski siblings, Katherine loved
having the chance to boss other people around, and she never used a
kind word where a mean one would do. Worse, in Ruby's estimation,
she was lazy, always disappearing when things were busiest.

It was during one of Katherine's absences that the owner of the
house approached Ruby with a special assignment: A guest had gotten
sick in one of the second-floor bathrooms, and he wanted it cleaned up.
Wiping up vomit wasn't part of Ruby's job description, but neither was
saying no to the host, so she went and found a rag and a bucket.

She was searching for the bathroom when she startled Katherine Demarski in an upstairs hallway. "What are *you* doing up here?"

Katherine demanded. Ruby showed her the bucket and explained her mission. "Well, get to it," Katherine said. "And then get your ass back downstairs." Ruby's eyes went flinty at the word "ass," but she held her tongue and did as she was told.

The next morning she attended Christmas services and went out to eat with some of her friends from church. That afternoon she was supposed to work another catering function, but when she came home to get ready, the police were in her apartment. They told her that a pair of pearl earrings had been stolen from the master bedroom during the party last night and they had it "on good authority" that Ruby had taken them.

They handcuffed her and made her wait in the hall while they tore her room apart. Then they took her to the station, where she was interrogated by a Detective Moretti. He was very unhappy to be working on Christmas and made sure Ruby knew it. Ruby kept her own feelings to herself and focused on keeping her answers short and consistent. She only lied once, when the detective asked her, if *she* didn't take the earrings, who did? Ruby said she had no idea.

Around six p.m. the detective locked Ruby in a holding cell, told her to reflect on her sins, and left. A couple of hours later, a good Samaritan let her out to use the toilet and offered her a chance to make a phone call. But she didn't see the use in calling anybody, and despite being innocent, she was embarrassed. She didn't want anyone to know she was in custody.

She spent Christmas night in the holding cell. Detective Moretti never came back. In the morning a different detective came up to the bars and asked Ruby if she was ready to confess yet. She repeated that she hadn't done anything. The detective shrugged, opened the cell door, and told her she was free to go—for now. "But don't disappear," he added.

Ruby went home to clean up her apartment. At first she was nervous, wondering if Detective Moretti was going to burst in and haul her back to the station for more questions, but by the time she got everything back in order, she was just angry at the way she'd been treated.

The next morning she was outside Demarski Catering when Katherine's brother Leo drove up. He wasn't pleased to see her.

"What the hell are you doing here, Ruby?" he said. "You know you're fired, right?"

"I want my paycheck," Ruby said.

"Well, you're not getting it. My dad signs the paychecks, and he's not going to sign one for you. The cops were at his house on Christmas morning."

"Yeah, they were at mine, too," Ruby said.

"I know. He offered to go with them, to knock a confession out of you. And if he catches you here . . ."

"He should thank me for keeping my mouth shut. I didn't say a word about your sister."

"What about my sister?"

"You figure it out."

"No," Leo said. "That's bullshit."

"I didn't take the earrings," Ruby said. "But she's the one who said I did, right? And you were there. Think about how she sounded when she said it."

He did. She watched him push the thought away. "Kathy's a good girl."

"I don't care what kind of girl she is. I just want my money. Bad enough I lose my job without being robbed in the bargain."

Leo got out his wallet and took some cash from the billfold. "Here."

Ruby counted it. "You owe me another twelve dollars," she said.

"Jesus, Ruby. Just take it and be grateful."

"Grateful!"

"That's all you're going to get, OK?"

"This isn't right, Leo."

"It is what it is," he told her. "Now will you please get out of here before my dad comes and beats the shit out of you?"

It is what it is. Life isn't fair, Ruby. You need to understand, Ruby. Lord, how she tired of hearing that! Life *wasn't* fair, but still it would be nice if, just once in a while, someone else had to do the understanding.

Self-pity wouldn't pay the rent. That same day she was out looking for work. A housecleaning service in Kenwood was hiring, and a number of downtown hotels were looking for maids and dining-room staff. But they all wanted references, and the manager at one of the hotels said that because of a recent rash of thefts, they'd also need to run her name by the police.

In the evening she called around to see if anyone needed a sitter. No one did, not even the Berrys, who usually liked to go out on the holidays. "We were going to that New Year's party at your sister's place," George told her, "but now Hippolyta's not feeling up to it."

"I hope she's not too sick," Ruby said.

"Not sick at all, just moody," George said. "She and Letitia didn't have a fight, did they?"

"Not that I heard. But Letitia and I haven't talked much lately."

After another long and frustrating day answering help-wanted ads, she came home to find an invitation to the Winthrop House New Year's Eve party on her door. "Ruby," Letitia had written, "I know you're probably working but we'll be going till dawn so you should come by. Charlie Boyd's cousin (the good-looking one) will be there & he asked about you. P.S., I spoke to Mr. Winthrop and he promised not to make the house jump while you're here." Ruby stood shaking her head at this: Letitia now exacting promises from the ghost who'd tried to evict her.

Letitia in her mansion, bought with money she hadn't lifted a finger to earn.

It is what it is.

Come New Year's Eve, Ruby was still unemployed, so after dinner she made herself up and put on her good dress. She had the cab drop her at the corner of Letitia's block, in front of the closed-up tavern. Rather than proceed directly to the party, she lit a cigarette and stood smoking and shivering in the cold, thinking about the last night she'd spent in this neighborhood.

Tonight the Winthrop House was all lit up, its brilliance accentuated by the darkness of the houses across the street. One house still had a FOR SALE sign on its lawn; the new owners of the others were presumably at the party. Ruby knew she ought to join them before she froze, but instead she took shelter in the tavern doorway and finished her smoke.

She was reaching into her purse for another cigarette when the door opened behind her and a white man emerged from the pitch-dark interior. Ruby stepped away quickly, but the man was untroubled by her presence. After locking the door behind him, he turned to her smiling and touched a finger to the brim of his hat. He was young, Ruby saw, well-groomed and a sharp dresser. And cute.

"Evening," he greeted her. He glanced down the block at the Winthrop House, from which the sounds of a dance band could be heard. "On your way to the party?"

"I'm invited," Ruby said. "Still not a hundred percent sure I'm going. What about you?"

"Not invited, unfortunately. Just passing through the neighborhood."

She nodded at the tavern. "This your bar?"

"It is now. My father owned the property," he explained. "He died last summer. I've been meaning to come and take a look at the place."

Definitely cute, Ruby thought. And it had been a while. "So where you going now?"

He shook his head. "I don't have any plans."

"You want to come to the party with me?"

"I'd love to," he said, smiling. "But only if you want to go."

"Well," Ruby said. "There is that."

"Can I make a suggestion? There's a club I know in Uptown, called Widdershins. We could go there."

She thought it over. Going to the North Side with a white man she'd just met was probably a terrible idea. But when the alternative was the Winthrop House . . . "This Widdershins. It's not a *haunted* club, is it?"

He laughed. "Alcoholic spirits only, I promise."

"All right then," she said. "I'm Ruby. Ruby Dandridge."

"Caleb Braithwhite," he replied, offering her his arm. "It's nice to meet you, Ruby."

"A Sherpa?"

"Yeah, you know," Ruby said. "Like on Mount Everest?"

"I know what a Sherpa *is*," Braithwhite said laughing. "I've just never heard anyone say they'd like to be one before."

"Well, you said *dream* job . . . When that man made it to the top of the mountain last year, the paper had a picture of the Sherpas carrying his gear for him, and you could see all these other mountains in the background where they were climbing. I thought that'd be something, to get up every day and go to work with a view like that." She shrugged. "I know it's silly, but—"

"I don't think it's silly. A little hard on the ankles, maybe."

"I've never had a job that wasn't *that*," Ruby replied. "But for that view, it'd be worth it."

They'd taken a break from dancing, retiring to a private table on the balcony; below, other couples still on the floor moved slowly to "Cabin in the Sky" while a big clock set up behind the bandstand ticked away the last minutes of 1954. Ruby was on her third cocktail, pleasantly buzzed and having fun. She liked Caleb Braithwhite. Under other circumstances she'd have been suspicious of a man who spoke so little of himself while asking so many questions about her, but tonight she'd decided to enjoy being the center of attention; if his show of interest had an ulterior motive, she could guess what that was, and didn't mind.

"What about you?" she said. "You have a dream job?"

"I'm working on it."

Ruby waited for him to say more. When he didn't, she adopted a teasing tone: "Is it a *secret*?"

"It's a new situation," he told her. "Being able to choose my own destiny, I mean. Most of my life, that wasn't the case."

"This got something to do with your daddy?"

"Everything to do with him," Braithwhite said nodding. "He was a very powerful man who didn't like to be contradicted, even when he was wrong—and of course as his son, I was expected to obey without question. I had my own feelings about that, but for years there wasn't anything I could do. He was stronger than I was." He shrugged, frowning, and then, as he had several times already, turned the conversation back to her: "Do you get along with your father?"

"I did, when he was home," Ruby said. "I was closer to Momma, though. She passed last year. Emphysema."

"I'm sorry."

Ruby looked down at her drink. "I do miss her, some days," she said. "She could be hard too, though. Especially when she wanted something from you."

"What did she do for a living?"

"Talked to dead people." Ruby smiled, knowing how much Momma would be irked by that description. "You know, a spiritualist? She worked out of a beauty salon, the Two El's. Momma was the second El, Eloise. Her best friend, Ella Price, she put up the money to open the business, so she got to be the first El.

"It was a package deal," Ruby explained. "The storefront was an old photographer's studio. Ladies would come in, get their hair and nails done, and then after, they got to go in the darkroom for a session with Momma. And the more they spent on beauty treatments, the longer the session."

"That sounds like a great business plan."

"Yeah, they did all right for a while. Then after she got sick, Momma tried to get me to come in and take over for her, but I wouldn't. We were fighting about that up to the day she died."

"Why didn't you want to do it? Because you're afraid of ghosts?"

"Because I don't like lying to people," Ruby said. "Momma *did* have powers. She could read your mind, but not like a psychic; more like the way my daddy did at the poker table. Not that she even had to read minds at the Two El's. A woman sits down to get her hair done, all you need to do is listen, and by the time she gets out of the chair, you know exactly what she's worried about and who she wants to hear from on the other side. The rest is just parlor tricks."

Momma would have taken exception to this description too, Ruby knew. Had done, many times, furiously insisting that she didn't *trick* people, she *helped* them: Godly work, and true.

But Ruby had seen more than one version of Momma's act. Before the Two El's opened, she'd used to conduct séances at home. Most of her clientele were neighborhood people, but now and then she'd get a white customer who'd heard about her from an employee. For these folks, she'd put on a show. She would alter and throw her voice, and crack her toe and ankle joints to simulate ghostly rapping; a ruler hidden up her sleeve gave her leverage to make the table jump even as her hands rested innocently atop it. Afterwards, Momma would laugh and joke about how gullible these people were. White folks' belief that Negroes were magically gifted struck her as the most absurd form of superstition. Sorcery was in the Bible, which meant it was real, but to Momma it was self-evident that like every other kind of power it would be concentrated in the hands of the mighty. A *real* magician would almost surely be a white man, most likely the sort whose ancestors went around in powdered wigs.

Fair logic, but Ruby had to ask: Weren't Momma's colored clients equally gullible? Maybe Momma could make a distinction between strangers she took advantage of and friends and acquaintances she helped, but Ruby didn't know how to draw that line, and refused to learn, no matter how angry Momma got. And Momma got very angry towards the end, calling Ruby an ungrateful child, a foolish child, too, passing up the chance to assume her mother's vocation; she'd come to nothing in this life, being such a fool. Fine, Ruby said, throwing it back at her, let me come to nothing: At least when *I* go to meet Jesus I won't have to explain why I cheated people in His name.

A change in the music woke Ruby to the fact that she'd been staring at the table, not speaking. "Sorry," she said, but Braithwhite shook his head and said, "Don't apologize." Again she waited for him to say more, maybe offer some smooth assurance that he understood what she was feeling, but he only looked at her, his expression of concern making her think that maybe he *did* understand, a little.

Ruby finished her drink and stood up. "Come on," she said, reaching for him. "Dance me into the new year."

Walking back to the car at two in the morning, they stopped to kiss on a deserted street corner, then continued on, Ruby laughing and leaning drunkenly on Caleb Braithwhite.

Braithwhite's Daimler was parked under a streetlamp in front of a line of dark storefronts. There were two white men there, one on each side of the car, bent down trying to see in the windows. The men straightened up as Braithwhite and Ruby approached, Ruby stiffening as she realized the man on the curbside was holding a pistol.

The gunman tilted his chin at Braithwhite. "This your car, chief?"

"Yes," Caleb Braithwhite said. "It's *mine*." Ruby clutched his arm, silently begging him not to play the hero, but he detached himself from her and stepped forward, a cold grin on his face, as if the threat of deadly violence were a source of amusement to him. Ruby thought about running, then, that notion joined by another, uglier one: That if the men shot Braithwhite, they might be too distracted to chase after her. But even as she was thinking this, her hand was in her purse, groping for the knife she carried to defend herself.

The gunman raised the pistol as Braithwhite came towards him. "Keys," he said. "Wallet. I won't ask twice."

"That's right," Braithwhite said. "You won't."

A look of surprise stole over the gunman's face, and Ruby thought the pistol must have jammed in the cold. "What are you waiting for?" the thug standing out in the street said. "Shoot the fucker!" But the gunman didn't fire, so the thug started coming around the car to deal with Braithwhite himself. Braithwhite put up a hand, palm out, and an invisible wrecking ball struck the thug in the gut, flinging him up and across the street to land in a boneless heap on the far curb.

The gunman had both hands on the pistol now. "Let me go!" he pleaded, as if Braithwhite were the one with the weapon. Braithwhite carefully extracted the gun from the man's grasp, then stood weighing it in his hand for a moment. He nodded his head and the gunman stumbled backwards. "Run," Braithwhite said.

The man turned and fled. Holding the gun at his side, Braithwhite raised his other hand, balled into a fist, and made a throwing motion with his arm. Halfway down the block already, the running man pitched forward, slamming facedown into the sidewalk and sliding on the icy pavement. He scrambled up again and dashed off howling into the night.

Ruby, who'd been holding her breath since the thug went flying, now let out a ragged gasp. Braithwhite turned to face her. "It's all right," he said, tossing the pistol in the gutter. "It's over." He smiled and took a step towards her, but she shied back, brandishing the knife from her purse, the gesture feeling even more futile than if she'd done it while the gunman was still there.

"**W**hat just happened?" Ruby said, in the car.

"Nothing remarkable," Caleb Braithwhite said. "Those men underestimated us. Nature took its course."

"Us? I didn't do anything."

"You kept your head. I know you wanted to run, but if you had, that man might have shot you before I could stop him."

She sensed he was trying to flatter her and got annoyed, which was better than being scared. "What are you?"

"I think you know what I am. Though we probably have different names for it."

They were cruising down Lake Shore Drive. Ruby looked out the window at the passing lights of downtown. "I want to go home now," she said.

"Let me ask you something, first. Are you happy with the way your life is going?"

Turning back to stare at him: "What?"

"I wasn't just pretending to be interested in you, tonight. I like you, Ruby. I think we're very similar, in some ways."

"Yeah, sure," Ruby said. "Two peas in a pod."

"I know how it feels to always have your own desires come in second to someone else's," Braithwhite said. "Believe me, I know."

"So what if you do? What's that to me?"

"You asked about my dream job," he said. "I told you I was working on it. I am. But I'm at a point right now where I could really use some help. A very particular sort of help, from a very particular sort of person."

"You want to *hire* me?"

"You are looking for work, right?"

Ruby eyed him suspiciously. "What kind of job?"

"An interesting one," Braithwhite said. "I can't promise you mountain views, but it shouldn't be too hard on the ankles."

Her expression turned cross. "That's not an answer."

"Sorry. I don't mean to be coy. But it's an odd job, and there's secrecy involved, so before I get into details, I'd like to show you what I'd be offering in exchange."

"Which is what?"

"The freedom to choose your own destiny."

"Freedom?" Ruby snorted. "You're going to pay me in freedom?"

"There's a cash salary, too, but yes."

"How?"

"If I told you, you wouldn't believe me. But I can show you. You'll need to trust me and take a small leap of faith, but I think you'll be very glad you did—and if you don't like it, or if you decide the job's not for you, you can still say no afterwards."

They'd left the lake shore and were passing through the Hyde Park neighborhood now. Braithwhite turned down an alley into a courtyard ringed by townhouses.

"What's this?" Ruby said.

"Another of my father's properties," said Braithwhite. He parked behind one of the townhouses but left the motor running. "What I want to show you is inside. Or," he added, one hand on the gearshift, "I could just take you home."

Home: the sane choice. Saner still, perhaps: Get out of the car right now, run screaming into the night as the gunman had. But with that thought came the thought of what she'd be running back to.

"I can walk away if I don't like it?" Ruby heard herself say.

"You can walk away anytime," Braithwhite promised.

"What do I have to do?"

"Just say yes."

"OK," Ruby said. "Show me."

⊰⊟⊱

She woke, head pounding, on blood-slick sheets.

The late morning sun roused her, creeping up the side of the bed to stab her in the eyes. Ruby pressed her eyelids shut and tried to retreat back into unconsciousness, but the sun kept at her, hot rays burning the skin of her face and neck made sensitive by a monster hangover.

With a groan she rolled onto her back and tried to sit up. She had difficulty getting traction, the bedsheets warm and slippery beneath her. At first this was merely irritating, but as she woke up a little more, a scary thought struck her. She opened her eyes; the sun's glare snapped them closed again, but not before she glimpsed the arterial red of the bedclothes.

Oh Lord Jesus. Ruby rolled off the side of the bed in a panic, landing facedown and thrashing, kicking away the bloody top sheet that had trailed her to the floor. She pushed herself up, felt her heart beating fast but strong in her chest. Not my blood, she thought, praying it was so. Not my blood. Whose, then? Had she killed someone?

Her attempt to recall the previous night's events yielded up a single clear memory, of sitting at a table across from Caleb Braith-white, watching as he set a small glass vial filled with red liquid in front of her. She sensed that this offering was part of a larger bargain and that it had everything to do with her current situation, but when she tried to dredge up more details she got nothing, only an echo of her mother's injunction to never let a man you'd just met mix your drinks for you.

She stood up, eyes still shut tight. Groping blindly forward she found an open doorway and stepped through into cool darkness, cold tile beneath her feet. She bumped up against a sink, spun the taps, and splashed water on her face and chest. The water cleared her head, but the panic came surging back. "Please God, please God," Ruby said, head bowed over the sink. Then she opened her eyes and looked up and saw a crazed white woman's face hovering in the dark just inches from her own.

Ruby screamed.

Her mind must have gone blank for a few seconds, because the next thing she knew, she was back in the bedroom, fallen on her backside. There was no respite from the madness, though: She'd struck the bathroom door in passing, and rebounding from the wall it swung shut, revealing another, full-length mirror, the glass reflecting the same wild-eyed white woman, now sprawled on the hardwood floor.

Ruby screamed again; the white woman in the mirror screamed with her. Ruby clapped her hands over her mouth; the white woman aped the gesture. The white woman: her.

There wasn't any blood. Just bright red hair, long and gently waved, and freckles, dense on her shoulders and upper arms, more sparse on her breasts and her flat white belly. Between her legs was another thatch of red: Viewed in the mirror from this undignified angle, it looked like some weird ginger-furred animal had crawled up in her lap. When Ruby looked down and saw that it was *her* lap, right *there*, she let out a yelp and went scooting backwards, as if by moving fast enough she could leave it behind.

She banged her head against the radiator on the wall behind her. Wincing, she pressed one hand to her scalp and slapped herself with the other, saying, "Wake up, wake up, wake *up*!" But it was no use: When she checked the mirror again, her cheek had reddened, but she was still a white girl.

Ruby saw then she had a choice to make: She could give up and go completely mad, or she could just deal with the situation. Being Eloise Dandridge's daughter, she decided to deal.

With an effort she turned her attention from the mirror. She lifted a hand to the bed, touched the shiny crimson sheets. Satin. Ruby had never slept on satin sheets before, though she'd once cleaned the house of a woman who did. She scanned the rest of the room. To the right of the bathroom door was a dresser, and laid out on top of it were a pair of red shoes and a set of undergarments. A green dress hung from the back of another door in the far corner.

She rose to a crouch and peeked out the window. She was on an upper floor, overlooking a courtyard ringed by two- and three-story townhouses. A silver sedan with dark tinted windows was parked directly below; the sight of it triggered a flood of additional memories from the night before, coupled with an overwhelming desire to escape.

She stood up and went to the dresser. In her haste, she decided to skip the stockings and the flimsy lace garter belt and just put on the panties, averting her eyes as she did so. She wrestled with the bra, the unfamiliar breasts smaller and differently shaped than her own. The dress went on smoothly. Finally, she grabbed the red shoes, which were shiny like the bedsheets but had sensible flat heels; she tried them to make sure they fit but then carried them in her hand, not wanting to make any more noise than she already had.

The door opened on a dim hallway with stairs immediately to her left. She listened a moment and then started down, holding tight to the banister, not trusting the balance of this body. She made it safely to the bottom of the stairs. There, directly in front of her, she saw a door with a mail slot. Hanging on a rack just inside the door was her very own coat. Her purse was on the floor.

Ruby had put on the coat and was bending to pick up the purse when she heard footsteps coming up from below. She looked over her shoulder. At the end of a corridor beside the stairs she'd just descended was a sunlit kitchen that seemed familiar. Was that wooden table the one at which Caleb Braithwhite had offered her a drink?

No time to check; the footsteps had reached the top of the basement stairs and now a door creaked open just out of view. Ruby tucked the purse under her arm and slipped out the front door, taking care not to slam it behind her. She danced a moment on the frozen stoop, getting the shoes on, then dashed down the walk and out the low iron gate. From the sidewalk she glanced back; the townhouse, rough gray stone half-smothered in ivy, suggested a wizard's castle squeezed to fit onto a city lot.

Down the block, a cab had stopped in front of another house to let out a passenger. "Taxi!" Ruby shouted, but the driver had already seen her and was waiting by the open back door with a smile on his face. "Cab, miss?"

She banged her head again sliding into the backseat—even without heels, she was taller than she was used to. The driver shut the door for her and walked with agonizing slowness around to the other side. When he got behind the wheel, Ruby was twisted around, watching for signs of pursuit.

"Where to, miss?" the cabbie said. Ruby blurted out her home address. After a moment, when the taxi hadn't moved, she faced forward and saw the driver staring at her quizzically over the seat rest. "Are you sure about that address, miss?"

"Of course I'm—" But then she stopped and thought about it.

"Miss?"

"Downtown," Ruby said. "Take me downtown."

"Somewhere in particular, or—"

"Just *drive*."

Twenty minutes later she was standing outside Marshall Field's on State Street, taking stock. After paying her cab fare, Ruby had enough cash left in her purse to get by for a couple of days, if she were frugal. Add in her Oh Jesus money—the emergency fund stashed in the lining of her coat—and she might last a week. Her identification was useless now, though, which meant bank withdrawals were going to be a problem.

She studied her reflection in a department store window. She hadn't been in the right frame of mind to appreciate it earlier, but she was a good-looking white woman, and there was an archness to her features that suggested she was a take-charge girl, used to giving orders. Maybe, if she picked the right bank teller, she wouldn't need identification. Though her name might be an issue: Red hair notwithstanding, she didn't think she looked like a Ruby anymore.

What did she look like, then? Her gaze shifted to the display inside the window: mannequins in winter clothes, posed in front of a painted mountain range. The mountains were probably meant to be the Rockies, but to Ruby they evoked the Himalayas, and once again she imagined herself on Everest, this time in a new capacity: not a Sherpa, but a commander of Sherpas. The name, Ruby thought, what was the name of that white man, the one who reached the summit?

"Hillary." She spoke the name aloud, like an incantation: "Hillary." What do you think? she asked her reflection. Are you a Hillary? Her reflection smiled and nodded assent.

While she gazed at the window, other people were passing her on the busy sidewalk, stepping carefully around her. Now, even as she rechristened herself, someone walked right into her, shoving her roughly aside and continuing on without a breath of apology. Ruby opened her mouth to say "Excuse *you*," only to be dumbstruck by the realization that the person who'd shoved her was Katherine Demarski.

This flash of recognition was followed instantly by doubt. But it was her: Ten paces farther on, Katherine collided with a little Negro girl who was walking beside her mother. The girl fell down, crying out as she was nearly trampled, and the mother shouted "Hey!" Katherine, without breaking stride, looked over her shoulder and said, "Watch where you're fucking going."

The words stunned the mother into silence and drew nasty looks from some other passersby. No one did anything, though, and Katherine

plowed onward, like a human juggernaut against whom ordinary pedestrians were powerless.

But Hillary wasn't powerless.

Katherine had gone into Marshall Field's. When Ruby entered the
department store, she heard raised voices and quickly spotted Katherine at a cosmetics counter, going nose to nose with the girl on duty
there. Ruby walked up to the adjacent counter and pretended to browse
a rack of silk scarves while she eavesdropped.

They were fighting about someone named Roman, who was, or was
supposed to be, Katherine's fiancé. The countergirl—her name, for pur-
poses of this conversation, was You Fucking Bitch, which Ruby short-
ened to Effie—had been seen making time with Roman, and Katherine
wanted to make clear the many ways in which that wasn't going to fly.
Effie for her part denied having anything to do with Roman, but she also,
in what struck Ruby as a tactical error, tried to argue that Katherine and
Roman weren't as engaged as Katherine seemed to think.

The volume and level of profanity increased until a store manager
came over. "What exactly is the problem here, ladies?" he said. Fifteen
feet away, Ruby selected one of the silk scarves. Hillary looked out
from the mirror beside the display rack, nodding encouragement.

Ignoring the manager, Katherine spat a last warning at Effie and
stalked away. Ruby stepped deliberately into her path; as they collided,
she slipped the scarf into Katherine's coat pocket, leaving the corner
with the price tag sticking out. Then she ducked back, hands raised,
feigning mortification at Katherine's curses. In fact Ruby barely heard
the words, for in that same moment she saw the pearl studs in Katherine's ears.

Back out on the sidewalk, Ruby approached a policeman who was
getting lunch from a hot dog vendor. "Excuse me, officer," she said,
Hillary's voice brisk and no-nonsense. "I'm a manager in the store,
here? And that woman there just shoplifted a scarf from our boutique
department."

The policeman regarded her unenthusiastically, his eyes saying, What do you want from *me*?, and Ruby had no doubt that if he were dealing with a colored woman, his mouth would be saying it too. But Hillary looked right back at him, lips tight and eyebrows arched, sending her own message: You *will* do your job.

The policeman sighed. "Keep an eye on this for me," he said, handing his hot dog back to the vendor. Then he hitched up his trousers and asked, "That woman there? Brown coat and dark hair?"

"Yes," Hillary said, adding: "She was in our jewelry department, too. You should ask where she got the earrings she's wearing."

The policeman nodded dutifully and set off at a lumbering trot. He caught up to Katherine near the end of the block; when he grabbed her elbow, she jerked her arm away, her reflexive anger diminishing only slightly when she saw it was a cop who'd accosted her. The policeman, out of breath from the brief pursuit, pointed at the scarf peeping from her pocket. Katherine pulled it out and stared at it in confusion, then looked accusingly at the policeman as if he were the one who'd planted it on her. Then the policeman said something that made Katherine raise a hand to her earlobe and for an instant her composure broke and she got very nervous. But her anger came back, redoubled, and she shook her head firmly.

But the policeman was nodding; he'd made up his mind. He reached out to grab Katherine's arm again. Katherine batted his hand away and slammed her palms into his chest. The policeman's face turned red and he slammed Katherine in *her* chest, using just one hand but exerting considerably more force—knocking her clean off her feet. Katherine hit the sidewalk and bounced back up and launched herself at the policeman, arms flailing. Then two more cops came around the corner, goggling at the melee in progress, and in the space of five seconds Katherine went from fighting one policeman to fighting three.

Up to now, Ruby had been enjoying watching the tables get turned, but this sudden escalation in violence made her queasy. The cops were trying to wrestle Katherine to the ground. She clawed at the first po-liceman's neck, drawing blood, and he hauled off and punched her in the face, eliciting a cry of *"Damn"* from the hot dog vendor. As Kather-ine went down, all three cops on top of her, Ruby's stomach gave a sick lurch. She turned away as if to throw up and instead broke into a run.

"I didn't do that," she said, whipsawing between horror and a wild exaltation as her feet pounded the sidewalk. "I didn't do that, that wasn't me . . ." She ran on, all the way to the other end of the block, and rounding the corner dashed headlong into yet another policeman.

"Oh my God!" she cried, staggering backwards, fully expecting to get beaten down too now. But this new cop—young, rosy-cheeked, and smelling like he'd just come from an all-night New Year's Eve bash—reacted in good humor. "Watch yourself there, miss!" he said laughing. He caught Ruby's arm, not to arrest her but to steady her, his amuse-ment turning to concern when she didn't smile back at him. "Are you all right, miss? Somebody bothering you?" He looked past her, blood-shot eyes narrowing. "Was it them?"

Something about the way he said "them" . . . Ruby turned around and saw four Negro boys, teenagers, standing on the corner waiting for the light. Minding their own business.

"Was it them?" the cop repeated. "They say something to you? Do something?" Ruby felt her stomach give another lurch, and she thought: I could tell him anything at all right now and he'd believe me. I could get those boys killed, if I wanted to. *I could . . .*

The cop read her silence as affirmation. "Don't worry," he said, stepping around her. "I'll take care of it."

But Ruby stayed him with a light touch of Hillary's hand on his wrist. "No," she said. "They didn't do anything." The cop eyed her uncertainly. "Really," Hillary said. "They didn't do anything. Nobody did." The light changed and the boys started to cross the street. The cop looked like he might chase after them anyway, just on general principles.

So Hillary touched his wrist again and said: "Would you like to buy me lunch?"

"**R**oman, huh?" the cop, whose name was Mike, said. "Sounds like a real asshole. Excuse my language."

"No, Roman's a nice boy," she said. "At least I thought he was."

"If he cheated on *you*, he's an idiot."

Maybe she had gone crazy, after all. She hadn't really intended to have lunch with him, but when they got to the restaurant, a diner tucked under the Lake Street L tracks, the queasiness in her stomach evaporated and she realized she was starving, so instead of making an excuse to get away, she went in and sat down. And talked.

She told him she was Hillary Everest, a tourist in town for the holidays. Hillary Everest: Mike the cop didn't even bat an eye at that, and the thought came to her again that she could say anything to him, anything at all, and he'd believe her. Entranced by the novelty of a policeman taking her words at face value, she kept going, making up a whole story about her holiday adventures in Chicago, complete with a supporting cast of characters: her fool nephew Leo; her spoiled cousin Katherine; and dear old Aunt Effie, with whom she'd been staying. And when she got the inevitable question about whether she had a boyfriend, she conjured up Roman, her steady back home, who she'd just this morning learned had been stepping out in her absence. Watching Mike get aggrieved on her behalf, exactly as she'd predicted he would, gave her a weird thrill. This must be how it had felt for Momma holding her séances. And though it was wrong, hearing the lies come out in Hillary's voice, with Hillary's reflection faint but visible in the window beside the booth, made it feel *less* wrong, somehow—less Ruby's sin, anyway.

"So you're headed home tonight?" Mike said. "To . . ."

"Springfield, Massachusetts." She nodded. "I've got to be at work on Monday."

"It's a shame you're not staying longer."

"Oh, I'll be back," she said. Making him light up.

"Yeah? When?"

"This summer, maybe." Improvising: "I was talking to Aunt Effie about maybe taking some courses at the university here."

"What kind of courses?"

"Journalism."

"You want to be a reporter?" For the first time, he sounded skeptical—though of the idea, not of her.

"My brother Marvin's a reporter," she said, a touch defensive. "No reason I couldn't be, too."

"Hey." He put up a hand. "If that's what you want . . . If you do come back, you should give me a call. I'll show you the town for real."

"Maybe," she said.

The radio on his belt crackled. "Well, listen," he told her, "I should get back out there . . . No, you stay. Sit, have some dessert. And don't worry about the check, it's taken care of." He jotted his phone number on a napkin and gave it to her. "You have a safe trip home—and tell that Roman guy that Mike says he's a jerk."

She watched him walk out, waved to him as he passed on the side-walk, then focused on Hillary's reflection in the glass. Bad girl, Ruby told her, but Hillary just smiled, shameless, and Ruby felt herself smil-ing too. She thought: Revenge, free lunch, my own police escort if I want . . . What else comes with being you?

"Dessert, miss?" the waitress said.

With no particular place to go after lunch, she decided to just walk, some vague homing instinct causing her to set off north. As she crossed the river, the wind did its best to remind her she was bare-legged, but Hillary, fortified by a thick slice of chocolate cake, seemed impervious to the cold.

As she walked, she thought about the story she'd told Mike, marveling anew at the pleasure she'd taken in telling it. In crafting it—making up a life, the only limit her imagination. Her one regret was using her brother's name. That seemed truly wrong, involving Marvin in Hillary's business. Stick to Aunt Effie next time, she told herself.

Then she thought, journalism classes. What was that about? She caught Hillary's eye in a passing shop window, asked her the question Mike had asked: You want to be a reporter? Hillary shrugged and turned it back on her: Do you?

When she'd gone the better part of a mile the cold finally began to get to her, so she found a store that was open—a little antique shop on Wells Street—and went inside to warm up, telling the man at the front that she was just looking. "Just looking" was a phrase that had never worked particularly well for Ruby, but Hillary got a much better response, the proprietor inviting her to make herself at home. Back on the street, she began to notice a similar improvement in the reactions of the pedestrians she passed. Many white people, men especially, smiled at Hillary as they went by her, but what was really noteworthy was that the ones who ignored her, ignored her in a different way than they would have ignored Ruby. There was no side-eying, no pretending not to see her while wondering what she was up to; she didn't *require* attention. She was free to browse, not just individual establishments, but the world.

What else comes with being you?

On the edge of Lincoln Park she chanced upon a white hair salon, Donna's. The salon's sole occupant, a blond girl filing her own nails, looked up and smiled as Hillary entered. "Hi there, I'm Amy," she said. "What can I do for you today?"

"Just looking," Ruby almost replied, but she caught herself and said, "I'm not sure, exactly . . ."

Amy gave Hillary's hair a professional once-over. "A nice perm, maybe?" she suggested. "Put some curl into it?"

"No, no curls," Ruby said. She told herself she should just leave, but curiosity got the better of her: "Can you just . . . cut it?"

"Sure," Amy said. "How would you like it?" She gestured at a line of sample hairstyle photographs culled from magazines, taped up above the long wall mirror.

Ruby zeroed in on a photo of a famous aviatrix with a tousled bob cut. She was standing in the open cockpit of a small plane, a shadow of mountains visible behind her. "What about that one?"

"Amelia Earhart?" Amy nodded. "I can do that. If you think your boyfriend won't mind." She explained: "Some men don't like hair that short."

"I'll risk it," Ruby said.

While Amy busied herself with Hillary's hair, Ruby tried on a new life story for her. This time she was a Chicago native, born and raised in Hyde Park. Up until last year she had worked in her mother's beauty parlor, but then Momma had passed away, and Hillary had sold her share of the business to finance a trip overseas, a dream adventure. ("Did you go to Paris?" Amy asked. "Nepal," Ruby replied, just to hear how it sounded. "Is that near Paris?" Amy asked.) Now, having spent more time abroad than she could really afford, Hillary was back, staying at her sister's and looking for a new job before the last of her money ran out.

"Donna's hiring, if you're interested," Amy said.

"No, thank you," Ruby said. "I'm looking for something different."

"Like what?"

"I don't know." Eying Hillary in the mirror: "It's a new situation."

"If you like flying, you should do what my cousin Holly did. She's an airline stewardess. Goes all over the country," Amy said. "She wanted to fly international, too, but the airline people said she wasn't pretty enough. I bet you'd be, though . . . Maybe you could get paid to go to Nepal."

In the mirror, Hillary raised an eyebrow. "How do you get a job like that?" Ruby asked.

"I'm not sure how Holly did it, but you could always try that Light-bridge Agency. You know, the one with the billboard?"

A miraculously short time later Ruby was back on the street. The entire process—shampoo, cut, dry, *and* a manicure—had taken less than an hour. Ruby had known white women had it easier, but my God, this was like getting extra years on her life. And Amelia Earhart's haircut looked good on her, too.

She walked west with a new bounce in her step. At the first big intersection she looked up, and there atop a small office building was the billboard Amy had told her about:

JOANNA LIGHTBRIDGE CAREER & EMPLOYMENT AGENCY
WHO DO YOU WANT TO BE?

The billboard was illustrated with a lineup of white women, model-ing professions rather than hairstyles. The stewardess was second from the left, her uniform with its little winged badge making her look like an officer in some obscure branch of the air force that served marti-nis. Right next to her was a woman with a steno pad who might have been a reporter but was more likely a secretary—but high-class, Ruby thought, the kind who'd have her own office in a tower somewhere, and the power to admit or refuse people. As she scanned the rest of the lineup she felt that weird thrill again, her excitement having less to do with any specific option than with the overall sense of possibility and choice.

WHO DO YOU WANT TO BE?

According to the building directory, the Lightbridge Agency was on the sixth floor. "But I don't think they're open today," the lobby guard told her.

"Would you mind if I just went up and took a look?" Ruby said.

"Be my guest." He smiled and nodded at the visitor's log, which she signed "Hillary Earhart" in a bold hand.

On the way up, she checked herself over in the polished elevator doors. Should've stopped to buy stockings, she thought, though the dress was long enough that that might go unnoticed. The real problem was the coat—Ruby Dandridge's coat—which, as Amy had noted as politely as possible, didn't suit Hillary at all. ("It was my mother's," Ruby had told her.) She slipped the coat off, draped it over her arm, and smoothed the dress down carefully. Better.

The elevator doors opened on a wall of glass with a reception area behind it. The lights were dimmed and a CLOSED sign hung on the double glass doors.

Ruby went up to the glass and peered in at the portrait hanging behind the empty reception desk. It showed an impeccably professional-looking white woman in a blouse and jacket, arms crossed in front of her, her brown hair cut short in a style very much like Hillary's. Miss Lightbridge, I presume. Sidestepping a little, Ruby looked down the hall to the left of the reception desk and saw there was a light on in one of the offices back there. She glimpsed a shadow on the wall, a silhouette of a woman with short hair.

Ruby smiled, already grown accustomed to Hillary's good fortune. A private audience with the head of the employment agency: Why not? Just don't let her see your ankles.

She was reaching for the buzzer beside the glass doors when she noticed a bead of blood on the tip of her finger. She frowned, thinking Amy must have nicked her during the manicure, but when she turned her hand over, it wasn't just her index finger that was bleeding: Red liquid was welling up from under all of her nails.

The same panic that had seized her on waking now gripped her again. She felt her heart flutter and skip—only it wasn't her heart, it was her breastbone, expanding in her chest, as if a clamp that held the two halves of her rib cage together had suddenly sprung loose. "Oh, no," Ruby said.

Behind her, the elevator began to close its doors. She turned and lunged for it, smearing blood on the polished metal as she clawed her way back inside.

By the time the doors slid shut again, the transformation back to her old self was fully under way. As her torso thickened, the bra began to constrict her. She dropped the coat and purse, and groped down the back of her dress with both hands. The red shoes bit cruelly into her swelling feet. Reflected in the doors, she saw Hillary's beautiful hair coarsen, darken, and twist, while the white of her skin drained away.

With a ferocious tug, Ruby snapped the clasp of the bra. She gasped and bent forward, wiping more blood down the front of her dress, and watched as the last of the whiteness vanished from her hands and forearms.

The elevator, which had been moving, jolted to a halt. Quickly Ruby snatched up her coat—it was *hers* again—and buttoned it closed over the worst of the mess. The elevator doors opened. She tried to pat her hair into place, realized it was hopeless, and stumbled out into the lobby.

"Who the fuck are *you*?" the guard said.

"Just leaving," Ruby replied, flashing him a smile that was more like a grimace. She started limping for the exit, the shoes making each step absolute agony. The guard said something else to her, but Ruby kept on going, praying she could withstand the pain long enough to hail a taxi.

Three days later, she returned to the house in Hyde Park.

She resisted as long as she could, knowing it was madness to go back there, and that the only sane course was to treat the entire incident as if it had never happened. For the first twenty-four hours after she got home, she almost had herself convinced she was going to be sensible. But on the second day, when the swelling in her feet had gone down and she could walk again, she realized she had no interest in resuming her job search—not as Ruby Dandridge, anyway.

And so on the morning of the third day she rose early and dressed warm. She thought she might have to hunt around to find the townhouse again, but when the cabbie asked her "Where to?" the address just came to her.

On second viewing, the place seemed less like a castle; it was just a big old house in need of maintenance. But there was still an aura of enchantment about it, and Ruby stood for a long time on the sidewalk outside the gate. Last chance, she told herself. You go back in there, you might not escape a second time.

But she hadn't even escaped the first time.

She clutched her purse and stepped through the gate. She was halfway up the walk when the front door opened and Caleb Braithwhite looked out smiling.

"Hello, Ruby," he said.

"**D**o you remember taking the elixir?"

They sat on opposite sides of a little parlor just off the entryway. Ruby had her knife out, and she'd made Braithwhite leave the front door open, so she could hear street noises behind her and feel the frigid outside air snaking under her chair and around her ankles.

"I remember you offering me some kind of potion," Ruby said. "I don't remember drinking it."

Braithwhite nodded as if he'd been expecting this answer. "That's my fault, I'm afraid. I knew the transformation would be a shock to you, but I should have thought more about what else you'd had to drink that night."

Her eyes narrowed. "You put something in my drinks?"

"No. You were tipsy, but—"

"I was more than *tipsy*," Ruby said.

"You were still in your right mind when you made the choice," Braithwhite said. "But the shock of the transformation, on top of the effects of the alcohol, set off a panic attack. Perfectly understandable—the change really is quite startling."

"Startling," Ruby said, recalling the switch back in the elevator.

"You ended up passing out from the shock. I thought you'd just fainted, but you were out cold, so I carried you upstairs and put you into bed. I figured you'd be fine in a few hours."

Remembering the slick feel of the satin against her skin: "You took my clothes off?"

"They were falling off you. You'd torn your dress during the panic attack."

"So you decided to finish the job? Just took the liberty?"

"No liberties. I put you into bed, that's all. And then waited up to see if you'd wake. But you slept through the night . . . In the morning I had some work to do, down in the basement, and when I came back up to check on you, you'd gone. I decided not to chase after you. I didn't want to upset you any more than I already had, and I expected you'd come back on your own. I've made some adjustments to the elixir formula," he added. "The next time you take it, the change should be less jarring."

"Who said there's going to be a next time?"

"That is why you're here, isn't it?" He gave her a long look. "But before we go any farther," he continued, "there's something I need to come clean about: It wasn't an accident, the two of us meeting up the way we did."

"What do you mean?" Ruby said.

"I have a powerful intuition," Braithwhite told her. "A talent for sensing opportunities. I'm very good at finding ways to get what I want. I needed to be, to have any chance at satisfaction while my father was alive."

"You're saying your intuition told you to come find me on that corner?"

"Yes." He hesitated. "But there's more to it than that. There are some things I haven't told you about what I'm doing in Chicago that may upset you. And I do want to come clean, but I need you to understand—"

"Oh, I *understand*," Ruby interrupted. "You're telling me you're a liar, and New Year's Eve was just a setup." She shrugged, like this was no big thing to her, but in fact she felt betrayed, and furious that she'd allowed herself to be taken in. "You're a smooth operator, I'll grant you that."

"No!" Braithwhite said. "No, Ruby, it wasn't like that. I *did* have an agenda that night, it's true. But I also enjoyed myself. It was fun, being out with you. The conversation, the dancing. The kissing." He smiled.

"Yeah, you can just go on and forget about *that*," Ruby said, wagging the knife.

"All right." Braithwhite put his hands up, but his smile said: We'll see.

"What about those two men by the car?" she asked. "Was that—"

"A coincidence. A happy accident."

"*Happy?*"

"It's not that I wasn't pleased with the way the night was already going." Another smile. "But at some point I did need to come around to making my offer, and if we'd gotten any more intimate, that might have been . . . awkward. Running into those men provided a useful change in mood."

"What if they'd killed us?" Ruby said. "What would the mood have been like then?"

"There's no way they could have hurt me. And you were never in any real danger, either."

Ruby shook her head. "You're just a piece of work, aren't you?"

"I'm a man who knows what he wants—and how to get it," Braithwhite said. "I understand you're angry, and you have reason to be, but be honest, Ruby: I *was* right. You want this."

"Even if I do," Ruby said, "that doesn't mean I'm not out of my damn mind."

But then she shook her head again, and said: "Tell me about the job."

It had gotten very cold, so with Ruby's permission, Braithwhite shut the front door. They went back into the kitchen. Braithwhite set a teakettle on the stove, and then he and Ruby sat at the table, in the sun.

He told her a story. It began in Massachusetts in 1795, with a coven of white men led by Titus Braithwhite, a cousin to one of Caleb's paternal ancestors. The coven had sought to harness the power of creation, but had gotten something wrong—said "open sesame" when they should have said "abracadabra"—and called down Armageddon instead.

The story then jumped ahead a hundred years, to Caleb's grandfather, Addison, who'd formed a coven of his own, and Caleb's father, Samuel, who'd expanded the coven and built a new manor house on the ruin of Titus Braithwhite's old estate. In the course of their researches, they learned about a slave girl, Hannah, who'd escaped Titus Braithwhite's apocalypse, bearing her old master's unborn child. They spent years trying to find out what had become of her, but it was Caleb and his intuition that finally solved the puzzle and tracked down the last surviving member of that particular bloodline.

As Braithwhite described the plot his father had hatched to lure Atticus out to Massachusetts, Ruby remembered a phone call she'd gotten from George Berry last June, asking if she could watch Horace while George and Atticus went east to deal with some sort of family business. And she recalled who else had tagged along on that road trip.

"When Atticus and George came to your daddy's house," Ruby asked, "were they alone, or—"

"They were supposed to be," Braithwhite said. "But your sister decided to come with them." Making it sound like a compliment, he added: "Letitia's a difficult girl."

You don't know the half of it, Ruby thought, but then she thought, Or maybe you do.

This chapter of the story ended with Braithwhite betraying his father and saving the lives of Atticus and the others. Then, after a brief time out to collect his inheritance, Braithwhite had come to Chicago and made contact with another white men's coven. There was more backstory here, but at the first mention of the name Hiram Winthrop, Ruby interrupted: "Winthrop? As in the Winthrop House?"

"Yes. And to answer your next few questions in advance, yes, I'm the one responsible for Letitia getting the house. The lawyer who gave her the money and the Realtor were both working for me. Penumbra Real Estate is a company my father set up. I'm the real owner of the property."

Ruby was shaking her head before he'd finished. "I *knew* it!" she said. "I *knew* it was too good to be true!" She glared at him. "Why? Why *her*?"

"Intuition," Braithwhite said calmly. "I had thought about moving into the Winthrop House myself. I believe the house is hiding some valuable secrets—but uncovering them meant dealing with Winthrop's ghost. And not that I don't love a good contest of wills, but it occurred to me there might be a better candidate for this one."

"Letitia? But why would you think—"

"Your sister is very tenacious. I had a feeling that if she were properly motivated—if it meant she got to keep the house—she'd find a way to tame Winthrop. Obviously, I was right."

"Yeah, you were right," Ruby said. "But you were wrong, too. 'Titia doesn't know it was you who gave her the house, does she?"

"No, and I hope you won't tell her. It wouldn't make her happy."

"Like you care if she's happy."

"I do care, actually," Braithwhite said. "I like Letitia."

"But she doesn't like you, does she? So even now she's living in the Winthrop House, it doesn't get you what you want. You can't go ask her if she's found anything."

"No," Braithwhite agreed. "But you can."

"And that's the job? You want me to spy on my sister?"

"As a small part of the job," he said delicately, "I'd like you to spend some time with your sister. Don't interrogate her; just ask how she's been, see if she volunteers anything. Strike up a conversation with Atticus too, and whatever other tenants you can. Maybe do a little poking around the house yourself."

"What, on my own?" Ruby said. "Not a chance."

"All right. Just talk to the tenants, then. See if anyone's stumbled across anything interesting: Books, maps, keys, strange devices. Secret rooms. I'd also like to know if anyone else has come around asking questions, or if anyone seems to be watching the house."

"Anyone like who?"

"White men," Braithwhite said. "Police, especially."

She regarded him coldly. "What have you got my sister mixed up in?"

"That's another long story. And I'll tell it to you, but first, there's a gathering I'd like you to attend, tomorrow night. It'll answer a lot of your questions—and afterwards, we can talk about the rest of the job."

"What kind of gathering? You talking about a party?"

"Don't worry, you won't be serving canapés. You'll be a guest."

"Yeah, well," Ruby said, "my party dress got torn."

Braithwhite placed a small glass vial on the table, the red liquid inside it seeming to glow in the sunlight.

"I've got something that'll fit you," he said.

Practical divination," the old woman said. "Not gypsy mumbo-jumbo, but rational forecasting, based on math. It's been the main focus of our research since October of '29, and we've made solid progress, notwithstanding the odd bobble now and then. More recently, I've also developed a personal interest in the restorative arts." She looked down at the sclerotic hand that gripped the cane she leaned on. "Would that I'd begun a bit sooner, but one always assumes one will have more time . . . So what about you, dearie? What's your field?"

"I talk to dead people," Hillary said.

"By what method? Spirit radio? Barton's teletype? Not planchette, surely?"

"No, I just talk to them. It's a gift. My mother could do it, too."

The woman drew back slightly, lips pursed, as if Hillary had said something distasteful. But then she grinned wolfishly, and chuckled. "A *gift!* Careful who you say that to in here, dearie. They're liable to burn you for a witch."

"Small-minded people don't scare me," Hillary said, which earned another chuckle.

"No," said the old woman, "I can see they don't . . . Nantucket, you said?"

Hillary nodded. "We're a small lodge. Smaller than we used to be. Our lodgemaster defected to Ardham last spring. We're still reorganizing."

"Ardham." The old woman pursed her lips again. "I lost one of mine to them, too. But I understand he came to a bad end. As did his seducer, Mr. Braithwhite." Another chuckle. "Let's have some champagne, shall we, dearie? Where's that waiter?"

As the old woman turned, slowly, in search of a drinks tray, Ruby surfaced and made her own scan of the ballroom, looking for Caleb Braithwhite.

Earlier she'd sat with him in his car in the parking lot of this country club, watching through tinted glass as the other guests arrived, Braithwhite identifying each one by the city whose sorcerers' coven they represented: Baltimore. Atlanta. New Orleans. Las Vegas. Los Angeles. Some two dozen more. The old woman was New York.

In between limousine arrivals, Braithwhite gave Ruby her cover story. "You shouldn't have to say much. You'll be the only good-looking woman there. Most of them will want to flirt with you. Let them. Smile and look fascinated, and let them talk. See what they give away."

The plan was for the two of them to arrive separately, so when the time came, Braithwhite drove several miles to a garage where Ruby's own limousine waited. "Don't worry," he told her. "You'll be fine. Just mingle and observe."

Ruby was worried, though, and so nervous that by the time the limo had brought her back, she wasn't sure she'd be able to go through with it. In desperation she sought Hillary's eyes in the rearview; Hillary looked back in that arch way she had, ready to take charge. So Ruby let her: It was Hillary who stepped confidently from the limo to the curb, Hillary who strode into the club as if she owned the place, barely pausing to show her invitation to the dark-suited men at the door.

In the lobby she stopped to check herself in a mirror. The physical transformation, though no less strange, had been painless this time. Her red hair had come back full-length; rather than cut it again, she'd decided to wear it natural. Brushed out and lightly tousled by the winter wind, it had a wildness that contrasted nicely with her dress: red huntress in a black evening gown.

She proceeded to the ballroom. The buzz of conversation dipped as she entered and heads turned her way. Hillary assessed the crowd, deciding where to start, settling on an elderly trio—San Francisco, St. Louis, and Des Moines—giving her dirty-old-man looks from a nearby table.

She went over and introduced herself. Upon learning Hillary was from Nantucket, San Francisco quipped, "I think I know a limerick about you," to which St. Louis replied, "No, no—you mean her *brother*!" while Des Moines wet his lips and counted the freckles in her cleavage. Two fools and a toad, Ruby thought, but Hillary didn't even bother to be bothered.

She sat and took their measures. San Francisco, despite his jocu-
larity, was in considerable pain. He kept palming his abdomen and
grimacing, and each time he did so, he looked over at the table where
Los Angeles was sitting. Des Moines was insecure and self-conscious,
and glad to meet someone whose lodge, he thought, must be even more
insignificant than his own. Yet even as he judged Hillary to be beneath him, he also felt a need to impress her. He bragged about his
lodge's library and its most recent acquisition, something called the
Codex Phantasmagoria. "The Ziegler transcription, with all seven com-
mentaries. You know how *rare* that is?" She didn't, but she sensed that
St. Louis wanted the *Codex* for himself, and was making nice to Des
Moines in hopes of getting a chance to steal it.

After a few moments, she excused herself—cutting off Des Moines
in the middle of a monologue—and moved on to another table. As
Hillary continued to work the room, Ruby relaxed, realizing that these
folk too were inclined to take her at face value. Nor did they seem
especially alien to her, the main difference between them and other
rich, self-important white people she had encountered being their willingness to converse with her. About necromancy. But even the talk of
magic wasn't that peculiar, for most of them spoke of it as they would
of money, or politics, or any other means of bending the world to their
will.

She found she didn't like them much, and she had no compunction
at all about lying to them. Among the general run of fools and cranks
were some truly awful human beings.

While pretending to be spellbound by Denver's ruminations on
mind control, Hillary leaned back to eavesdrop on Los Angeles and Las
Vegas at the table behind her. Vegas, puzzled over having been snubbed
by San Francisco earlier, said, "I don't know what the hell's eating him,"
and Los Angeles laughed and said, "I do." Then he said that you could
fuck someone on a deal or you could trust their restaurant recommendation, but only a moron did both.

A little while later, she joined a table full of Southerners. Dallas was a middle-aged cowgirl with a husky voice and a bawdy sense of humor, and Richmond, Atlanta, and New Orleans were cultured gents who grasped the distinction between charming and repulsive. It was the most pleasant encounter Hillary had had so far, until the topic of conversation swung without warning to what the men all referred to as "the nigras." Dallas used a more familiar pronunciation.

It was nothing Ruby hadn't heard, or overheard, a million times before. But there was a difference between having people talk about you, or at you, and having them talk *to* you, believing you were one of them and expecting you to think as they did. It took a significant effort on Hillary's part not to give herself away, and to extricate herself from the conversation without telling the one sort of lie Ruby considered unpardonable—silence, in the face of some things, being damning enough.

And then there was Coeur d'Alene, a blond skeleton with crazy eyes and an expression so perpetually hate-filled that if he'd stood up and begun firing a rifle into the crowd, it would have come as no particular surprise. He had a whole corner of the ballroom to himself, as none of the other guests would come near him—and in this, Hillary followed the general wisdom. But as she made her escape from the Southerners' table, she happened to glance his way, and a certainty came over her that the rage blasting from his eyes was of the same species as the vileness on Dallas's lips.

Awful people. After nearly an hour among them she'd had enough, and started looking around the room for Caleb Braithwhite, wanting him to come so this could be over. But whatever grand entrance he was planning, it wasn't time yet. She did spot his partner, Chicago, having what looked like an intense conversation with the lodge representative from Amesboro, Wisconsin. And then she saw Des Moines, on his feet and headed her way. That was when, seeking shelter, she went over and said hello to New York.

New York had managed to flag down one of the circulating waiters, a tall, dark-skinned Negro in his twenties. As she selected a glass of champagne from the tray he offered her, she gave him a long look and said, "My, you're a strapping one, aren't you, dearie?" The waiter, his true self almost as well hidden here as Ruby's, only smiled politely, as if New York had complimented him on his choice of bow tie, and turned quickly to offer the tray to Hillary. "Miss?"

"No, thank you," Hillary said.

"You're not drinking?" New York said, watching the waiter walk away.

"I can't. I have a condition."

"Pity." She drained her own glass in a few gulps. "Well, come on, dearie. Let's have a look at Lancaster's prize before another line forms."

On the wall at one end of the ballroom hung a painting of a gray-bearded frontiersman riding a horse along a riverbank; visible behind him was a hilltop fort flying the Stars and Stripes. Ruby surmised that this was Morgan Glastonbury, who according to Caleb Braithwhite had founded the Chicago chapter of the Order in 1847. In his youth, Glastonbury had been a member of Titus Braithwhite's coven—one of the lucky ones, who'd been deemed too inexperienced or too untalented to participate in the apocalyptic ritual.

A display case had been installed under Glastonbury's portrait and was being guarded by six of the dark-suited security men. Inside the case, a large and ancient-looking book lay open, its exposed pages covered in strange letters. "*The Book of Names,*" New York said, gazing even more lustfully at the pages than she had at the waiter. Ruby peered out from behind Hillary's eyes, curious, that title evoking for her the book in which the Heavenly Father records the names of the saved. But this *Book of Names* didn't look like it was in God's hand.

"Pardon me." New York addressed the man in charge of the book's guard detail. "Mister . . ."

"Burke."

"Mr. Burke, this is the Winthrop copy?"

"Yes." A mean little grin appeared on his face as he anticipated her next question and his own answer to it.

"There's a page in the second appendix I'd very much like a look at. Could you—"

"Sorry," Burke said, not sorry at all. "The case stays locked."

"I understand you don't want me handling it. But perhaps *you* could—"

"If I opened the case for you, I'd have to open it for everyone. And then we'd have problems."

New York pursed her lips. "In my invitation to this event, I was given to understand—"

"I don't care what you were given to understand," Burke said, enjoying himself. "My orders are, the case stays locked."

"I don't care for your *tone*, young man."

Hillary backed up, not wanting to get caught in the crossfire if New York started casting lightning bolts with her cane. She felt someone behind her and turned.

It was Chicago. He had the face of a retired boxer who'd given up the ring for a barstool, but behind that brutish mask was a perceptive intelligence that, just now, he let show. "You must be the delegate from Nantucket," he said, offering his hand.

"Rose Endecott," Hillary said, taking it. His grip was firm and communicated a strength that could easily have crushed her fingers.

"John Lancaster," he said. "I'm glad you could come. A little surprised, too. When Braithwhite told me he'd invited you I didn't think you'd accept, given the history between your lodges."

"Our dispute was with Braithwhite's father," Hillary said.

"All water under the bridge, huh?" He studied her, his face not a boxer's now but a cop's.

"Lancaster!" New York elbowed her way in between them. "Lancaster, a word . . ."

"Sorry, Madeleine," Lancaster said. "I've got to get the show started. We'll talk later." A last glance at Hillary and he walked away, faster than New York with her cane could follow.

Lancaster headed for the open space beneath the chandelier at the center of the ballroom. "Attention!" he called. "Everybody, give me your attention!" The room fell silent. "At this time, I need everyone who isn't security or an invited guest to clear out!" The Negro waiters made their way (not unhappily, Ruby thought) towards the exit, a few guests jumping up to grab more champagne as they went by. When the staff had left and the doors were shut, Lancaster signaled to one of his men, who dimmed all the lights except those on the chandelier.

"Welcome to Chicago," Lancaster said. "Thanks for coming. I know it's a long way, for some of you, not just in terms of miles but in terms of trust. I appreciate your restraint, agreeing to treat this as neutral ground." He smiled paternally, as at a group of exceptionally well-behaved children. "I'm not much of a speech-maker," he continued. "My predecessor, Bill Warwick, he could give a hell of a speech. I've always been more of a doer than a talker. But I know how to listen, and I know good sense when I hear it.

"Late last summer I got a call from the new lodgemaster of Ardham, saying he had a proposal. I was skeptical. If you know the history between Chicago and Ardham, you know it's not exactly hearts and flowers. And here's this kid, Samuel Braithwhite's kid, calling me on the phone saying he wants to sit down. Well, I could have hung up on him. Or I could have lured him in and taken his head for old times' sake. But I decided to hear him out . . . and what I heard made good sense.

"Now, he is young," Lancaster cautioned. "And because of that, I know some of you are going to have trouble taking him seriously. This is the Order of the *Ancient* Dawn, after all. Most of us prefer to take our cues from those with a little more life experience." He brushed a hand over his graying flattop. "So I'm going to ask you to listen to him as if he were speaking for me. Because he is. And if you give our proposal a fair hearing, I think you'll find it makes good sense for you, too.

"Mr. Braithwhite, the floor is yours." Lancaster raised a hand towards a table at the edge of the open space, clearly expecting Braithwhite to be there; but his gesture was directed at an empty chair. He looked left and right, trying to see where Braithwhite had got to. The moment grew awkward, then comical. "Braithwhite?" he said. There were chuckles in the crowd, and a louder laugh Ruby recognized as belonging to Dallas. Lancaster went over to one of his men, whispering, *"Where the hell is he?"*

And then suddenly Braithwhite was there, stepping forward, seemingly out of thin air, to occupy the central space that Lancaster had just abandoned. Nice trick, Ruby thought, and around her she sensed the other guests thinking the same thing. Only Lancaster missed it, continuing to scowl at his man for a few more seconds until Braithwhite said, his voice soft but carrying: "Thank you, Lodgemaster." Lancaster spun around, startled and angry, but Braithwhite acted as if nothing unusual had happened and only bowed his head respectfully. Lancaster got control of himself; he nodded back and ceded the floor, going to sit in the chair where Braithwhite hadn't been.

Then Braithwhite raised his head and looked around at the assembled guests. The lights on the chandelier seemed to brighten, flattering him in a way they hadn't done for Lancaster, revealing him to be not just more attractive but more present, somehow. More vital. Lancaster had called him young, and he was, but young, in this light, didn't seem like a bad thing at all.

"Thank you all for coming," Caleb Braithwhite said. "I'd like to start by clearing up a misconception. You all know my father died last June, and by now I'm sure you've all heard the rumor of how it happened. He was trying to complete the ritual first attempted by Titus

Braithwhite in 1795. The ritual failed, less spectacularly this time—the house and the servants were spared—but all of the members of the lodge perished, except one." He pressed a hand to his chest.

Los Angeles spoke mockingly from the crowd: "So, then. No survivors of note."

Braithwhite took the barb gracefully. "Some people might feel that way," he acknowledged. "But again, I'm here to clear up a misconception. Not spread more ignorance.

"As I was saying: You've heard the rumor of how my father died. But what you've heard is false. The ritual didn't fail.

"It probably would have. My father himself put the odds of success at no more than fifty-fifty. My own calculations were more pessimistic. I estimated the likelihood of failure was closer to eighty percent, with a significant chance of catastrophe.

"Eighty percent," Caleb Braithwhite said. "Four out of five. For a long time I thought about playing those odds, but in the end I decided it just wasn't good enough. I needed to be sure. And I wanted them all dead."

There was a slow stirring among the listeners as they grasped the import of his words. Ruby saw Lancaster frown, this particular revelation apparently not part of the speech he'd sanctioned.

"That's right," Braithwhite went on. "I sabotaged the ritual. I killed them all, the whole damn lodge. You know why? Because I was tired of the bullshit.

"Understand, I admired my father. I respected him—up to a point. He had a first-rate intelligence and a virtuoso's grasp of the art. His defect lay elsewhere. It was the same flaw that Titus Braithwhite suffered from, the same flaw that afflicts all too many of you. He had a scientist's mind, a modern mind, but his heart was old. It was an alchemist's heart. A wizard's heart."

Another, louder stir. Ruby had spent enough of her life in church to recognize the cause: blasphemy. Lancaster was on his feet now, looking like he might call a halt before the crowd could become a mob. But Braithwhite was just getting warmed up.

"'The Adamite Order of the Ancient Dawn,'" he said, his tone sneering. "Does that sound like a scientific organization to you? Because I'll tell you what it sounds like to me: a joke.

"Alchemists!" he shouted. "Alchemists, all toiling away in your little claques. Jealous of each other. Keeping secrets from each other. When you're not busy plotting, you waste most of your time reinventing the wheel, rediscovering esoteric wisdom that ought to be common knowledge by now. And if you do learn something new? You hoard it. Lock it away, up here." He tapped his forehead. "Or write it down in *one* book, and then hide that book. And when the odds catch up to you? When the ritual goes wrong, when the book is lost, when the mind that wrote it is destroyed . . . Then it's back to square one, for the next generation.

"I could have waited my turn. Could have waited for my father to blow up the house, just like Titus Braithwhite did a century and a half ago; or for one of his associates to stab him in the back, or curse him, or cast him into an alternate dimension. But I value my time, and I don't see the point of running an experiment whose outcome is a foregone conclusion. I'm sick of belonging to an Order that wants to change the world but can't even change itself. I'm tired of the bullshit.

"So I decided to hurry my father along, get him to the end of the road he was traveling, so I could get started forging a new path. A modern path. A no-bullshit path.

"And the reason I'm here talking to you tonight is that I believe—I hope—that some of you might be ready to forge a new path too. Might be ready to come together and start acting like scientists. Not alchemists."

He paused, and the silence that met him was respectful, or at least attentive.

Richmond spoke up: "What is it you have in mind, Mr. Braithwhite? Union?"

"Union," Braithwhite agreed. Smiling: "Or confederacy, if you prefer."

"That's been tried before," said Las Vegas.

"On a small scale, yes," said Braithwhite. "Two or three lodges talking about a merger, with plans for further expansion. But it never goes beyond the first step, because somebody always gets greedy, or decides the other party is about to betray them. And then it ends in tears."

"So what's going to be different this time?" asked Baltimore. "You think you can merge all of us at once? You think that'll be easier?"

"Not easier, no," Caleb Braithwhite said. "But absolutely worth trying . . . One lodge, spanning the entire country, so big and powerful that any natural philosopher worth the name will *want* to be part of it. Your individual chapters will still control their own affairs, but you'll operate under one set of by-laws, administered by a board of directors empowered to settle disputes. There'll be no more hoarding or needless duplication of effort—like the scientists we claim to be, we'll *share* information. We'll share resources and risk, as well. If you have a particularly urgent research project"—here he looked at some of the older and frailer guests—"you'll be able to apply for help with it. And we'll decide, together, how to exploit the discoveries we make. How to change the world, once we can."

"And who's going to run this fantasy organization?" Los Angeles said. "If you've got a board of directors, you're going to need a chairman, right?"

"Or a chairwoman," put in Dallas.

"I have an idea for that," Braithwhite said. "I—"

"I'll just bet you do," said Los Angeles. "You know, Braithwhite, there's more than one story going around about your father. *I* heard a rumor that right before he died, he found a living descendant of Titus Braithwhite. A direct bloodline descendant." Ruby saw a few other guests nod, but it appeared that this was news to much of the crowd. "Now what occurs to me," L.A. continued, "you must know there's no way in hell we'd accept a squirt like you as our leader. But maybe you and Lancaster are cooking up a scheme to put this long-lost cousin of yours in charge." Braithwhite didn't react, but Lancaster laughed, louder than he probably intended to. "I'm sorry, did I say something funny?"

"I don't think you're funny," Braithwhite said. "But you're right, we are going to need a leader. I won't insult you by pretending I don't have an idea who that leader should be. And if there *were* a living descendant of Titus Braithwhite, and if I thought by trotting him out I could sway some of you to my point of view, well, I'd be tempted. But the problem with appeals to authority is that they're ultimately subjective. One man's honored tradition is another's superstition—and that's where the knives come out.

"Fortunately, as natural philosophers, we have a more objective standard to rely on: merit. We're students of nature, and nature has rules, rules that can't be bent or broken or bargained with, only understood—and through that understanding comes power, power that can be demonstrated. Objectively.

"So I propose we do that," Caleb Braithwhite said. "Chicago has been the site of two World's Fairs—two exhibitions of scientific progress. I say we hold an exhibition of our own. I say we meet back here, a few months from now, on Midsummer's Day. Each lodge will bring an example of its best work, its truest and most advanced expression of the art. We'll all show what we can do, and then we'll see. We'll see who really is the best among us. Who *deserves* to lead."

New Orleans laughed. "Like Moses and the wise men of Pharaoh, Mr. Braithwhite? One snake gobbles up all the others? Is that what you have in mind?"

"I'm hoping for something less confrontational," Braithwhite said. "But why not? If you think your snake is the biggest."

"It'll be a goddamned bloodbath." This from Coeur d'Alene, which caused heads to swivel in surprise, for he sounded almost happy.

"Snakes! More like wild dogs. We'll rip each other to fucking pieces before we agree on who's best."

"We might," Braithwhite conceded. "I agree the chance of failure is high. But when I think of what we might accomplish as a unified lodge, I consider that a long shot worth playing."

"It'll never work," said Los Angeles.

"You don't have to come, then," Braithwhite said. "But for those of you who are willing, there'll be an additional incentive. By now you've all had a chance to see *The Book of Names*. There are other versions of the *Book* extant, but the Winthrop copy is unique—it's by far the oldest, and it includes material not found in any other known edition.

"The book was recently recovered after being missing for nearly twenty years. It properly belongs to the Chicago lodge, but Lodgemaster Lancaster has graciously allowed me access to it, and at my own considerable expense, I'm having copies made. One for each of you. They'll be ready by Midsummer's Day."

"World's Fair door prizes, Mr. Braithwhite?" New York said, unable to conceal the tremble of excitement in her voice.

"It's not quite that simple," he told her. "You'll need to do a little more than just show up."

"What?" said Des Moines. "What do we have to do?"

"Try," Braithwhite said. He looked around the room, gathering them all in, and once again the light shining on him seemed to brighten. "Maybe we won't be able to agree on a leader or a new set of by-laws. And a merger can't work without real agreement, so to require success would be unreasonable. But a good-faith effort, that's not too much to ask. And that's what it's going to take, if you want a copy of the book: a good-faith effort."

"And who decides—" Los Angeles began, but Braithwhite overrode him.

"But if you can't be bothered to even try? If you come in bad faith? If there *is* a bloodbath? Then you get nothing," Braithwhite said.

"And you deserve nothing. Because then you really are just a pack of alchemists.

"So that's the deal," he concluded, "and I thank you for listening. Before we bring the waiters back in, I'll give you one more thing to think about.

"My father liked to say that history doesn't stand still. The world has changed a great deal since Titus Braithwhite's day, and it's about to change a whole lot more. What remains to be decided is what say, if any, you'll have in those changes. Do you want to choose your own future, or are you content to have it chosen for you? And if it's the former, what are you willing to risk? Who, and what, are you willing to become?

"These are the questions you need to consider. But think quickly. Because history *doesn't* stand still—and we're running out of time."

Once more Ruby lay on satin sheets, but in a bigger bed this time. Beyond the bed's foot she could see Caleb Braithwhite, shirtless, seated on a stool at a vanity table, shaving.

She had Hillary to blame for this. Driving back from the country club, Ruby had found herself strangely spellbound by the way the headlights of passing cars illuminated the planes of Braithwhite's face, and by the motion of his arms and shoulders as he steered an evasive course through the city streets. She'd recognized that what she was experiencing was an effect of the same glamour Braithwhite had used to sway the crowd during his speech, but knowing the feeling was artificial didn't make her feel it any less, and while she could have resisted, she decided not to. Instead, as they returned to the house in Hyde Park, Ruby told herself that while *she* was too smart to be seduced by magic, if Hillary did it, it didn't count.

Now, by the sober light of dawn, she could see red fingermarks streaking Braithwhite's bare back. They'd been in the middle of the act when the potion started to wear off. Ruby had felt the blood well up under her nails, but they were too far gone to quit and so she'd just hung on, shuddering and crying out, while her flesh snapped back into its original shape.

Reflected in the vanity's mirror she could see another set of red marks: a circle of letters tattooed on Braithwhite's chest, letters from the same strange alphabet used to compose *The Book of Names*. My mark of Cain, he'd told her. It keeps me safe.

It keeps me safe. So he knew his Bible, at least. Ruby recalled another white boy she'd been with briefly, Danny Young, who one day had begun expounding on a theory he had, that the mark God put on Cain was actually dark skin and that everything bad that had befallen the Negroes—slavery, lynching, Jim Crow—was a result of their being Cain's descendants. You'd be a better Christian if you learned how to read, Ruby had told him. Cain's mark was a *protection*; if the mark was his skin color, then God must have turned him white, not black.

Braithwhite was watching her in the mirror now. "Having second thoughts?"

More like seventh or eighth. "You were going to tell me about the job, after," Ruby reminded him, her tone saying: You'd better not expect this here to be a regular part of it.

"Playtime's over, huh?" He put down the razor, wiped his face, and turned around smiling. "I admire your work ethic, Miss Dandridge."

"Never mind what you admire," Ruby said. "Get to the point."

"All right. I assume you understand what I'm about, now."

"You want to be the Al Capone of warlocks."

"More like the Frank Costello, if we're going with a Mafia analogy," Braithwhite said.

"Abbott or Costello, I don't care," said Ruby. "But your friend Lancaster, he thinks *he* should be the big boss. And maybe you promised you'd back him on that?"

"'Promised' is a strong word. Let's say he takes it for granted that he ought to be the man in charge, and I try not to contradict him."

"You need to try harder, then. After your speech last night, even a stupid man would know you want the crown for yourself. And Lancaster's not stupid."

"No," Braithwhite said, "but he believes he can slap me down whenever he chooses, so he'll keep me around as long as I'm useful. He's got his men watching me. I know they're there, and I can slip away from them when I need to, but it's not always convenient—and if I do it too often, he'll start worrying. So what would be very helpful to me, over the next few months, would be to have someone I can call on to run errands for me."

"Someone who can be white or colored," Ruby guessed, "as the need arises."

"As the need arises. Does that sound like something you could do?"

"Depends on the errands. But supposing I say yes, how would it work?"

"Lancaster knows more about me than I'd like," Braithwhite told her, "but he doesn't know about this house. And if for some reason he were to investigate the property, he'd find that it belongs to a Miss Francine Chase. Miss Chase is a shut-in whose neighbors never see her, but recently she's been advertising for a new live-in maid."

"Hmm," said Ruby. "So I move in here, and then what? Just wait around in case you need something?"

"We'll prearrange times for you to be available in case I call or come by. Generally no more than two or three hours on any given day. The rest of your time will be your own, to do with as you like—and as *who* you like. The only other rule concerns how you come and go from the house. As Ruby, you'll always use the front door. But as—"

"Hillary."

"As Hillary, you'll go up to the roof. There's another empty townhouse around the corner from here that you can reach by walking along the rooftops. Hillary will come and go through there."

"And how long is this arrangement supposed to last? Until you get your crown?"

Braithwhite nodded. "I'd say six months to a year, depending on how Midsummer's Day goes and what happens after."

"And then?"

"Then, unless you decide you want a continuing relationship, we go our separate ways. And you get this, as severance." He opened a drawer in the vanity and handed her a copy of the deed to the townhouse. "It's not as grand as the Winthrop House, but at least it's not haunted. And it comes with a supply of the elixir. So what do you say, Ruby?"

She stared at the deed, feeling scared and trying not to show it. She thought: I know what I'd say if somebody else told me they'd been offered a deal like this. "Tell me something. What you said in your speech, about changing the world—what is it you're going to do, exactly, if you get the kind of power you want?"

"Nothing you have to worry about. You and your people will be protected."

"My people?"

"The people you care about," Braithwhite said. "Your family. Your friends. They'll all be looked after, I promise . . . So what do you say, Ruby?"

"**W**as it Jekyll or Hyde who was the bad one?" Ruby asked.

Noon of a Sunday, and she was eating lunch at the Winthrop House with her sister and Atticus, having invited herself over after church. Letitia's obvious pleasure at the visit had Ruby feeling guilty.

"Mr. Hyde was the alter ego," Atticus said. "The one who went out and did all the things that Dr. Jekyll was too respectable to do."

"Yeah, but they were both bad." This from Mr. Fox, one of Letitia's tenants, playing chess with his daughter at the other end of the dining table. "They were the same man."

"But didn't . . ." Ruby struggled to remember the story, which she'd read a long time ago in school. "Didn't the two of them end up fighting, or something? Mr. Hyde killed someone, right? And then Dr. Jekyll tried to get rid of him."

"Hyde got out of hand," Atticus said. "Hyde *was* Jekyll, but Jekyll with all the good bleached out of him, and most of the self-control. That's how come he beat Sir Carew to death. Jekyll stopped taking the potion and tried to go straight, but it was too late—Hyde started coming out on his own."

"The thing people overlook, though," Mr. Fox added, "is that that whole part of the story describing the relationship between Jekyll and Hyde, that's all Dr. Jekyll talking. And you can't trust Jekyll." As Mr. Fox spoke he looked away from the chessboard, and his daughter took the opportunity to sneak her queen onto a different square.

"So what are you saying?" asked Ruby. "You think Dr. Jekyll was lying about what Mr. Hyde was really like?"

"I'm saying people can be real creative when it comes to ducking responsibility. You got this guy who confesses to a murder, plus a whole bunch of other bad stuff he won't even describe, but he's got this complicated explanation for why it technically wasn't him. And he says he's remorseful, but right up to the end he's trying to escape being held to account for what he did." Mr. Fox shrugged. "Maybe Mr. Hyde was pure evil. But Dr. Jekyll would want to believe that even if Hyde was just Jekyll with a different face." He turned back to the board, and with a firm gesture moved his daughter's queen back where it belonged.

"What do you want to know about Mr. Hyde for?" Letitia asked.

"No reason," Ruby said.

Two days later, Ruby sat alone in the kitchen of the house in Hyde Park, waiting on Braithwhite's call.

Since taking the job, she'd run four "errands" for him. Twice, as herself, she'd gone downtown on shopping trips for the nonexistent Miss Chase, each time making her way to a second-floor window in

Carson's department store. The window overlooked one of Lancaster's favorite lunch spots, and her mission was to see who, if anyone, he left the restaurant with. (On the first occasion he'd been alone, but on the second, he was with that lodgemaster from the village in Wisconsin.)

For her third errand she'd gone, as Hillary, to a downtown parking garage, exited a certain stairwell at quarter past two, found Braithwhite's Daimler, and driven to a service garage in Oak Park that specialized in exotic foreign cars. The mechanics were expecting her, so she didn't even have to crack a window; she just sat tight in the Daimler while they changed the oil and checked the tires and performed several other time-consuming maintenance procedures. Then she drove back to the Loop. She did have one bad moment when the unmarked police car that had tailed her to and from Oak Park looked as though it might follow her into the parking garage, but that proved to be a false alarm.

Up until yesterday, the worst part of the job wasn't the errands themselves, or the waiting, but the uncertainty of the scheduling. It was true, as Braithwhite said, that much of her time was her own, but never being sure when she'd be free placed limits on what she could do when she was, even as a white woman. She'd quickly realized that a second job was out of the question, let alone a career. She consoled herself with the thought that this was a temporary situation—just a few months, a year at most. And at least she wasn't doing anything bad.

Then yesterday she'd had a new errand. Once again she'd gone as Hillary, but Hillary-in-disguise: Before setting out, she'd pinned her hair up under a kerchief, donned sunglasses, and put on Ruby's coat over a drab tan dress.

At noon she entered the central police station and asked the front desk sergeant where she could find the burglary division. She climbed the stairs to the third floor, turning left rather than right as she'd been directed, and came to a door marked SPECIAL INVESTIGATIONS, ORGANIZED CRIME UNIT. The room inside was unoccupied just then, as

Braithwhite had intuited it would be, but she didn't have much time. As she moved to an interior office whose door said CAPT. JOHN LAN- CASTER, she felt in her coat pocket for the charm Braithwhite had given her.

It was a disk of polished bone, about the size of a half dollar. En- graved on one side was the image of an owl with eyes so large and round they seemed more like binoculars. The obverse was marked with more of those strange letters, stained with what Ruby pretended was red ink.

Braithwhite hadn't said what this token was for, only that she was to hide it somewhere in or near Lancaster's desk. Finding one of the lower drawers unlocked, she stuck the charm at the very back, behind a rack of hanging files.

She'd made it back out to the stairs and had just started down when she saw two men coming up. One of them was Burke, the mean- spirited security man from the party. Hillary stayed cool and didn't react, trusting to her disguise, and Burke, who was talking to the other man, didn't even glance at her as he went by. But as she reached the half-landing, she heard Burke fall silent and sensed him looking back, and it took all her self-control not to look back as well. She continued down the stairs and across the lobby, hearing footsteps behind her the whole way and expecting any second to feel a hand on her shoulder. She went out onto the street and hailed a cab, still not looking back, not until the cab was several blocks from the station—and then, recogniz- ing that she had gotten away, she proceeded to go into shock, shaking uncontrollably and nearly passing out.

In the evening Braithwhite came by the townhouse in person to congratulate her on a job well done. He took Hillary out to dinner, and afterwards he made a point of restocking Ruby's supply of elixir, bring- ing up seven fresh vials from his workshop in the basement. Then, with the lights in the kitchen shining on him just so, he asked whether, perhaps, she might like him to stay the night.

No thank you, Mr. Braithwhite, she'd said, I think I'll sleep better on my own. She hustled him out, taking a fleeting satisfaction from his look of disappointment. Once he was gone, though, she started wondering whether he'd made the offer precisely so she could have the pleasure of refusing him. So she'd feel more in control. She thought: Six months to a year of mind games and nervous breakdowns, what's that going to do to you? Assuming you don't just get caught.

This morning she felt better about it. She told herself that if she didn't have another errand today, maybe Hillary would drop by the Lightbridge Agency, just to browse. In the meantime, she sat at the kitchen table in the sun, reading from the book that Atticus had lent her.

Now the hand of Henry Jekyll (as you have often remarked) was professional in shape and size: It was large, firm, white, and comely. But the hand which I now saw, clearly enough, in the yellow light of a mid-London morning, lying half shut on the bed-clothes, was lean, corded, knuckly, of a dusky pallor and thickly shaded with a swart growth of hair. It was the hand of Edward Hyde.

Of a dusky pallor, hmm. Ruby studied the backs of her own hands: straight-up dusky, hold the pallor, and thankfully hairless.

The teakettle began to whistle. She got up and turned off the flame and went into the pantry to get a box of tea bags. When she came back out and shut the pantry door, the basement door popped open on the other side of the kitchen.

Ruby hadn't been down to the basement yet. It wasn't off-limits—Braithwhite had told her to think of the house as if it were already hers—but the one time she'd been in a mood to go exploring, she'd found that door locked.

She set down the tea bags next to the stove and crossed to the basement door. There were two light switches on the wall inside; she flipped them both. A yellow bulb flickered to life directly overhead. Below, around a corner at the foot of the stairs, harsher, brighter white lights came on.

The basement was very cold, and there was a low hum of machinery that made it seem not just unheated but refrigerated. As Ruby came around the corner at the bottom of the stairs, she saw faint wisps of vapor eddying across the bare concrete floor, and her eye followed them back to their source at the center of the room: a gray, oblong pedestal, wrapped in metal pipes fuzzed with frost.

Resting on top of the pedestal was a glass coffin. A woman lay inside it: a white woman, with flowing red hair. She lay on her back, head resting on a red satin pillow, a red satin sheet covering her body.

Ruby stood with her hand still on the banister. She thought about the hot teakettle upstairs, thought about going back to it, forgetting she'd seen this. As if she could.

She walked forward into the cold basement. She stood beside the coffin and looked down at the pale freckled face both familiar and strange: for though she'd come to know it well, she was used to seeing it in a mirror.

The woman's eyes were closed, her lips slightly parted. She didn't appear to be breathing—or if she was, the breaths were so shallow that her chest didn't seem to move at all.

Her left arm was covered by the satin sheet, but her right lay on top of it, palm up. A silver cuff encircled her forearm, and ascending from it was a slender glass tube with a ruby red thread at its core. The tube coiled up and around and fed into the back of a spigot that jutted from the coffin's side.

A spigot. Like the kind a bartender might use to tap a keg.

Another one of those moments, then, when Ruby had to choose whether to go crazy or just deal. A close call this time.

She took a step back and tried to figure out how the coffin opened. There was no lid; the glass panels that made up its top and sides were joined to a gray metal frame that seemed all one piece. Maybe the whole thing lifted up. She scanned the top edge of the pedestal, looking for a lever or a catch.

"I wouldn't touch it barehanded unless you like frostbite."

Braithwhite was standing at the foot of the stairs, still in his coat, his cheeks flushed as though he'd been running. He was smiling though, an indulgent smile, as if it were Ruby who'd committed a transgression here—but one of the mildest sort, which he'd be happy to overlook.

"What," Ruby said. "What is this?"

"Her name is Delilah," Braithwhite told her. "She used to work for my father."

"Your father put her in this?"

"No, I did. Dell suffered a blow to the head, the night before my father died. She fell into a coma. I got her medical attention, but months later she hadn't woken up and she was starting to deteriorate. She would have slipped away before much longer. So I decided to see what I could do with her."

Don't you even act surprised, Ruby thought. You knew there was something more to this deal. You *knew* it. "You use her blood to make the potion? I've been drinking—"

"Blood is an ingredient in the process," Braithwhite said. "I know it sounds disgusting, but the final elixir is a distillation. Not blood, only its essence. The essence of Delilah.

"It doesn't hurt her," he continued. "Just the opposite, in fact. Right now, she's unconscious. She's not dead, but she might as well be. But when you wear her shape? She dreams. Your experiences and adventures, everything you do, she dreams. You're all the life she has now, Ruby."

Ruby shook her head in disbelief. "You trying to make this out like it's a *favor* to her?"

"A dream life is better than nothing. It's what I'd want."

"You're a liar. You want to help her, why not use your magic to cure her?"

"Healing is a different branch of the art. A complicated branch, and one I'm not well-schooled in. The elixir is low-risk. To revive Delilah from her coma would require what's called a ritual of regeneration, and if that went wrong it might kill her, or worse. It's not out of the question, sometime in the future when I've had more time to study, but for now this really is the best thing for her."

"For you, you mean."

"For us, if you want to think of it that way. But Ruby—"

"No," Ruby said. "This isn't what I bargained for. I— Stay back!" she shouted, as he stepped forward.

But he didn't approach her. He crossed the basement to a tall refrigerator cabinet clad in stainless steel. He paused in front of it, looking back at her as he spoke.

"I'm sorry I didn't tell you about this sooner," he said. "I knew you'd be upset by it, and I didn't want that, but I should have found a way . . . Well. You're free to go, if you choose to. I won't stop you. But before you walk away, you should understand what you're leaving behind."

He opened the cabinet door and stepped back to let her see what was inside: a dozen closely packed shelves holding what must have been hundreds of glass vials, all full.

"I made this elixir for you," Caleb Braithwhite said. "It's no use to me on my own, and I doubt I'll find anyone else to take it. I'll still look after Delilah, of course. Even if I can't wake her up, she'll survive a long time, in there. But that's what she'll be doing: surviving. Not living." He reached into the cabinet, selected a single vial, and closed the door on the rest. "It seems like an awful waste."

Ruby was shaking her head again, but she didn't speak or run out, even when Braithwhite came towards her.

"You should think it over, Ruby. Go for a walk. Take the day." He took gentle hold of her wrist and pressed the vial of elixir into her open palm, holding it there until her fingers closed around it. "I'll understand if you feel like you have to say no. But think about the reason. If you pass up this chance, which will never come again, is it because that's the right thing to do? Or because it's safe? Because not getting what you want is what you're used to . . . And do you really want to go on living that way?"

"You're the devil," Ruby said.

"I'm a man who knows what he wants—and how to get it," Braithwhite said. "But this isn't about who I am, it's about who you want to be. That's what you need to decide, Ruby. So take the day, and ask yourself: Who do you want to be?"

THE NARROW HOUSE

❧⚜❧

When I looked out in the morning I saw a mob of about 400 or 500
people coming over the hill and I saw them shoot a Colored man . . .
About 8 o'clock they came into the residential district and began
ransacking the Colored homes. I went up in the loft when I saw them
coming. After setting fire to several homes around, they came into
our house and after turning on the gas they piled furniture on top
and lighted a match. As soon as they left I went down and turned off
the gas and managed to put out the fire and went back into the loft.
About an hour later another bunch came along and when they saw
this house was not burning they came in and started a fire. I went
down again and succeeded in putting it out and returned to the loft
a second time. By this time the smoke was so bad that I decided to
go out and started across the street toward the iron foundry when
four fellows caught me. They said, "Where have you been, Nigger?"
and I told them I had just come from work. Then they said, "Well, we
are going to kill you."

—*G. D. Butler, survivor of the 1921 Tulsa riot,*
as quoted in The Chicago Defender, *June 11, 1921*

Quarter past dawn of a Sunday in late January and Montrose stood
beside his son's Cadillac, smoking to keep warm and watching an alien
invader emerge from the gloom across the road.

The invader was cherry red, about five feet tall, and emblazoned
with the words DRINK COCA-COLA IN BOTTLES. Beneath that familiar
slogan was another, executed in a cruder freehand style: WHITE CUS-
TOMERS ONLY!

Montrose knew that many of the white residents of this southern Illinois county would regard him rather than Jim Crow as the
true interloper. He regretted that none were present to debate the
matter; in particular, he would have loved to engage in a frank exchange of views with the owner of the store, John Perch's Gas &
Go, whose property the Coke machine occupied. But the store's
lights were out and the sign on the gas pump read CLOSED FOR THE
LORD'S DAY.

Two Negro boys came walking up the road. They were about ten
years old and dressed in bright winter coats, one yellow, one orange.
Montrose exchanged nods with the boy in yellow, then looked with
fresh concern at the Coke machine, regarding it as he would a Confederate soldier lying in ambush.

The boys walked heedlessly up to it, groping in their pockets for
nickels.

Montrose threw down his cigarette. "Hey!" he shouted. "What
are you doing? Don't put your money in that!" He crossed the road in
quick long strides, the boys looking around startled. "What are you
doing?"

The boy in orange, clearly not the brains of the pair, took the question literally: "Getting a Coke."

"It's all right, mister," added the boy in yellow, smarter but no wiser.
"Mr. Perch gave us permission."

"He did, did he?" said Montrose. "And why would that matter?"

"It's his store," the boy in orange said with a note of disdain, as
if Montrose were the dummy here. He reached for the coin slot, but
Montrose caught his wrist and yanked him away, and when the boy
opened his mouth to protest, backhanded him across the face. The boy
stumbled and fell, squawking.

"How's that feel?" Montrose said, looming over him. "You like getting hit in the face?"

"Mister, please—" said the boy in yellow.

"Be still or you'll get the same," Montrose warned. He stared hard at the boy on the ground. "I asked you a question."

The boy stared back, angry but frightened. "No," he murmured.

"What's that? I can't hear you."

"No, I don't like it."

"I didn't think so. And how about if I were to open a store across the way? You think you'd want to come in and buy a Coke from me?"

"No!"

"That's the first intelligent thing out of your mouth." Montrose pointed at the vending machine. "This here? This is a slap in the face. Every time you put in a nickel, you're telling Mr. Perch, 'Thank you, sir, may I have another?' A man who respects himself will never do that. You understand me?"

"We understand, mister," the boy in yellow said.

"Shut up. I want to hear it from him."

The boy in orange gritted his teeth and contemplated the cost of refusal. Finally he forced the words out: "I understand. Mister."

"All right, then. You get on out of here now. And don't let me catch you doubling back or I'll beat you for real."

The boys went on their way, the boy in yellow hurrying, the boy in orange making an effort to appear as though he wasn't. "Yeah," Montrose called after them. "And next time, get a Pepsi."

"I don't *like* Pepsi," the boy in orange called back. "Old fool!" He broke into a run and his friend ran with him. Montrose watched them go. I'm no fool, boy, he thought. As for old, well . . . I'm forty-one. But forty-one, in Jim Crow years, *is* old. Ancient, even.

Across the road, Atticus had come down off the snowy embankment carrying a roll of toilet paper.

"Don't say it," Montrose cautioned as he walked back towards the car.

"I'm not saying a word, Pop."

"Yeah, and get over to the other side. I'm driving."

Two days earlier, Caleb Braithwhite had been sitting in a booth in Denmark Vesey's when Montrose came in after work. Montrose hadn't seen Braithwhite since that night in the museum, but he'd known it was only a matter of time.

"What now?" he said.

"Hello, Mr. Turner," said Caleb Braithwhite. "Please, sit. Can I get you something?"

"I can buy my own damn drink." Montrose sat down in the booth. "What do you want?"

"I have another project I'd like your help with."

"Yeah? And what are you going to threaten me with this time?"

"Nothing," Braithwhite said. "I was hoping we could move beyond threats."

"To what, me being your nigger?"

Braithwhite looked affronted. "Have you ever even heard me use that word?"

"When you put me in a cellar with a chain around my ankle," Montrose said, "it's assumed."

"That was my father's doing."

"How about when I got shot, whose doing was that?"

"My father would have shot you for real," Braithwhite said. "He'd have killed your son. Instead, thanks to me, you and Atticus are alive, and my father can't bother you ever again."

"Yeah, but that story's got a sequel. More than one, it seems."

"I'm sorry about stealing Adah's book," Braithwhite told him, "but I needed to make a certain impression on the captain and his men."

"Uh-huh. Me and my family aren't your niggers, but you want the captain to think we are."

"I'd have handled it differently if I could. Still, nobody got hurt, and you have to admit you made out very well on the deal. Even if you could have convinced the Burns family to take Adah's claim seriously, they'd have nitpicked her accounting to death. I just gave you the money."

"No." Montrose shook his head sternly. "You do *not* get to do that. You do not get to count paying off a debt ninety years past due as a good deed."

"But it wasn't my debt."

"No, *your* debt is still outstanding. And don't think I've forgotten that, either."

"You mean Hannah? You want back wages for her too?"

"It's got nothing to do with *wanting*."

"Because I could arrange that," Braithwhite said. "Of course, with a century and a half of interest to cover, it might take some time to get the funds together. But if it'll help make up for the way I've treated you—"

"You don't get it," Montrose said. "You can't buy goodwill with money that ain't yours. It's not a favor to pay what's owed."

"Let's talk about real favors, then. There must be something you want, Mr. Turner. Name it."

Montrose hissed in frustration. "No, Mr. Braithwhite, let's talk about what *you* want. That's what this conversation is really about, and I can see you're not leaving until you speak your piece. So spit it out, and then I can tell you to go to hell."

"All right," Caleb Braithwhite said. "I want you to find Hiram Winthrop's son, Henry. He ran away from home not long before my father killed his father. He was sixteen at the time, and the story is he ran off with one of the housemaids. He also stole a number of his father's books."

"Books! So that's what this is about, more magic books?"

Braithwhite nodded. "My father thought Henry might have taken *The Book of Names*, so he was eager to find him. But Henry did a surprisingly good job of covering his tracks. The thing is, as far as my father knew, Henry wasn't a practitioner of the art. In fact, he apparently loathed natural philosophy. So he wouldn't have taken the books to use them—he'd have taken them to deny their use to Hiram Winthrop. But the books were also very valuable, and my father assumed Henry would eventually sell them.

"The market for that sort of literature is small; my father kept feelers out. It took longer than he expected, but a few years ago, a book called *The Atlas of Untrod Paths* that was known to have belonged to Hiram Winthrop went on auction in Manhattan. My father contacted the auctioneers and eventually traced the chain of provenance to a man calling himself Henry Narrow, who'd sold the book in Philadelphia in 1944. Narrow matched Henry Winthrop's description—he was the right age, and he'd been living with a Negro woman who was probably the missing housemaid. But by the time my father's people came looking for him, he'd vanished again."

"And this is where I come in?" Montrose said. "You want me to go to Philadelphia and pick up the trail with my special Negro powers?"

Braithwhite smiled. "No," he said. "Detectives Burke and Noble are going to Philadelphia. They're flying out tomorrow afternoon. While they're preoccupied with what they think is a new lead, I'd like you to go to Aken, Illinois.

"You see, I've had my own detective out looking for leads. Recently he discovered that a man named Henry Narrow bought a house in Aken in the summer of 1945. He bought it for cash, for a sum slightly less than what Narrow was paid for the *Atlas*."

"If you know where Narrow's house is, what do you need me for?" Montrose said. "Why not just send your detective?"

"I did," said Braithwhite. "He's disappeared, along with the fifty thousand dollars I gave him for book-shopping."

"So now you want to trust me with fifty thousand?"

"I trust you not to run off with it. I know you don't need the money."

"That still doesn't make sense, though," Montrose said. "You could go see Narrow yourself."

"I could. But he might not want to deal with me, especially if he knows how his father died."

"I don't want to deal with you, either. But here you are anyway. How's Henry Narrow any different?"

"He isn't. But those 'special Negro powers' you joked about? They might actually exist in this case. He's been living with a Negro woman—and he'll know you're not a member of the Order. I think he's more likely to deal squarely with you than he would with any white man I could send."

"Maybe," Montrose said. "But that ain't the real reason . . ." And then it came to him: "You're worried. You say this guy isn't a 'practitioner,' but that was when he was sixteen. How old would he be now?"

"About thirty-five."

"So for twenty years, he's been hauling around his daddy's magic books. Is there a particular one you're looking for?"

"I'll take whatever he still has," Braithwhite said, "but I'm especially interested in a set of handwritten notebooks containing his father's research."

"His father's research notebooks. And you're not concerned he might have looked into those at some point, maybe learned a trick or two?"

"It's not that easy."

"I'm sure. But over twenty years . . . Maybe your detective didn't run away with the money. Maybe Henry Winthrop turned him into a toad."

"That would be a good trick," Caleb Braithwhite said. "I'd like to learn that one myself."

"I bet you would."

"Is this the part where you tell me to go to hell?"

"No," said Montrose. "If you're scared of this guy, maybe I do want to meet him. But assuming I get him to sell me the notebooks, what's to stop me from throwing them into the nearest bonfire?"

"Nothing," Braithwhite said. "That wouldn't be the worst outcome, for me. Don't misunderstand, I want the notebooks, but it's more important to me that no one else gets them."

"Like Lancaster?"

"Especially him. Look, Mr. Turner, when I asked you before what you wanted, I already knew the answer. You want me gone: out of Chicago, out of your family's lives."

"You got that right."

"The thing is, if I left town now, you'd be at the mercy of Captain Lancaster and the rest of the Order. They don't care about you. But Atticus, because of his relationship to Titus Braithwhite, has a certain value to them. Not as a person, you understand, but as a sort of living fetish object. Now that they know he exists, they won't forget about him. Ever."

"Yeah, and I got you to thank for that."

"You have my father to thank for it. But that's spilled milk. My point is, if things go the way I hope they will, very soon I'll be in charge of the Order. Not just one lodge but all of them, all across the country. Captain Lancaster will be out of the picture and I'll make sure your family is left alone. You have my word on that."

"Uh-huh," Montrose said, not believing it for a second. "And you having these notebooks will hasten the day?"

"It couldn't hurt."

"Whereas if I don't give them to you, I might be slitting my own son's throat."

"I wouldn't put it that way," Braithwhite said, "but you wouldn't be helping Atticus."

"And of course if I burned the notebooks and you won through anyway, then you'd be a king who didn't owe me any favors."

"I suppose that's true."

Montrose smiled. "You see?" he said. "I knew there'd be a threat in there somewhere."

Aken, Illinois was a small city on the Ohio River midway between Cairo and Metropolis. The sun was just above the rooftops as they drove through the central business and municipal district, which felt like a ghost town at that hour. They paused for a red light in front of the Aken city hall, and Atticus was reminded uncomfortably of a three a.m. traffic stop in Bideford, Massachusetts. But Montrose, still heated from the encounter with the boys, glared furiously at the empty sidewalks, daring someone—anyone—to come out and look at him cross-eyed.

The light changed. They turned right and drove west along Elm Street, looking for number 213.

It would have been hard to miss. The house itself was unremarkable, but the owner of the property next door had erected a marquee sign on his garage roof with a flashing neon arrow that pointed at 213 Elm. The letters on the marquee read NIG ER LOVER. Father and son both looked up dumbfounded, Montrose saying to himself: Just when you think you've seen it all . . .

The front door of 213 Elm flew open and a short, burly white man came out brandishing a fireplace poker. He charged down the front walk but stopped abruptly a few feet from the Cadillac, lowering his weapon in sudden embarrassment.

Atticus rolled down his window. "Henry Narrow?" he said.

"David Landsdowne," the man replied. "Esquire."

"You're a lawyer?" Atticus glanced up at the marquee. "Affiliated with the NAACP, by any chance?"

Landsdowne nodded. "Two years ago, I was lead counsel on a lawsuit to integrate our county school system. Clark, my neighbor, wanted to make sure everyone knew which house to throw stones at . . . I'm sorry about this," he said, holding up the fireplace poker, "but when a car I don't recognize stops in front of the property it usually means trouble."

"No need to apologize," said Montrose, leaning across from the driver's side.

"Would you gentlemen like to come inside for some coffee?"

"Yes, sir," Montrose said. "We'd be honored."

They took their coffee in David Landsdowne's living room. As he passed around the cream and sugar, Landsdowne explained that his wife, Judith, had already left for church in Mt. Vernon, an hour and a half drive to the north. "After the lawsuit, our local pastor asked us to stop coming on Sundays. He was afraid someone would take a shot at me and send him to heaven by mistake. Judy found a new congregation and started attending again last year, but I guess I've lost the habit."

"You ever think about moving?" Atticus asked.

"Every time I replace a window. But I'm stubborn. If Judy were here, she'd tell you how stubborn I can be." Landsdowne settled in a chair by the fireplace; the poker was back in its stand. "So, Henry Narrow . . . Would he be an old friend of yours?"

"No, sir," Montrose said. "We've never met the man. We're here to see about buying some books from him."

"In that case, I hope you didn't come a long way. The reason I asked if you were friends is that Henry Narrow is dead—has been, for some time. He and his family were murdered in 1945, right after the war ended."

"Murdered?" said Atticus. "In this house?"

"No, the Narrows never lived here. The address you're looking for, 213 Elm Street, is on the other side of town, near the cemetery. This is 213 West Elm. It's common for visitors to get the two streets confused.

It's how I met Henry Narrow: He saw a Realtor's listing for the old widow Metzger's house, came to Aken to take a look at it, and ended up on my doorstep.

"He had a woman and a boy with him. He acknowledged the boy, Henry junior, as his son, but he introduced the woman, Pearl, as the boy's nanny. She was a Negro. Light-skinned. The boy was lighter still—light enough to pass, at least when he was standing by his father. But he resembled both his parents in different ways, and seeing the three of them together, it was obvious they were a family, in fact if not in law.

"It wasn't my business," Landsdowne said, "but they seemed like nice people, and there was the welfare of the woman and the child to consider. So while Judy was getting a cookie for Henry junior, I took Narrow aside. I told him that while there was no anti-miscegenation statute in this state, a family of mixed race, if recognized as such, would probably not find Aken very welcoming. I also told him I thought he had the right to live where he wanted, so if he was determined to make a home here, I'd help him find a place. The house next door, where Clark lives now, was about to go on the market, and I thought my neighbor at the time could be convinced to sell to the Narrows. Maybe with a bit of arm-twisting.

"But the widow Metzger's house, that was another matter. That part of town, I said, would be not just inhospitable but dangerous. The mayor and the chief of police lived in that neighborhood, and they were old-school Democrats—the kind who liked to wear sheets after dark."

"How'd Narrow react?" Montrose asked.

"He thanked me for the warning," said Landsdowne. "The way men do, when they don't intend to heed it. He told me that he and his family preferred to keep to themselves, so it was OK if the neighbors didn't want to be friends. 'Mr. Narrow, perhaps I wasn't clear,' I said. 'If these men don't like you, they won't just shun you.' But he insisted he'd dealt with such people before, had grown up around them in fact.

Then he said something odd. He asked me if any of the men I was talking about had a reputation for studying philosophy. I said no, that was part of the problem—they weren't students of anything, least of all that. 'That's all right, then,' he said. 'We'll stay out of their way and they'll stay out of ours.'

"I could see there was no point in arguing with him. And I assumed it didn't matter: I thought whoever was representing the widow Metzger's heirs would take one look at the Narrows, see what I had seen, and refuse to sell to them. But I was wrong about that. You wouldn't have guessed it from the car he drove, but Narrow had a lot of money. I heard later that he bought the house with cash, and the Realtor, Frank Barrington, made an unusually large commission on the deal. As for the widow's heirs, the nearest of them lives in Bloomington, so they didn't care what the neighbors thought.

"It must have been July when they moved into the house. The fire happened in August. It was the same week the Japanese surrendered, so the story was buried inside the newspaper. The paper claimed Narrow forgot to screen his downstairs fireplace before going up to bed, and a coal ignited the rug. The three of them were trapped upstairs and supposedly died of smoke inhalation. What the story didn't explain is why Narrow would have been using his fireplace on a warm summer night.

"About a week later I spoke to a friend of mine, Lewis Peters, who was a clerk in the coroner's office. I asked him if he knew anything that hadn't made the paper. He didn't want to talk about it, but I pressed him, and finally he told me that he'd gone into the morgue the morning after the fire to pick up some paperwork and he'd seen Henry Narrow's body. He said Narrow's skin had been blackened by smoke but he also had what looked like a bullet hole in his temple.

"I told Lewis if that was true, he needed to report it. 'There's no one to report it to,' he said. 'And there's no evidence even if I did. The bodies have been disposed of.'"

"You figure it was the mayor and the police chief?" Montrose said.

"I do," Landsdowne said. "Not that I could ever prove it. But if it was them, I suppose there was a measure of justice in the end.

"The house was damaged but not destroyed, and since the Narrows had no next of kin that anyone could find, the mayor contrived to have the city take possession of the property and put it up for auction. The auction was so poorly advertised that there was only one bidder: the police chief's son-in-law, who got the house at a bargain price.

"The son-in-law, the police chief, and the mayor went to a restaurant over in Cairo to celebrate. They drank a great deal, and drove back to Aken at one in the morning. The son-in-law was at the wheel. He came down Elm Street going much too fast and plowed into a tree right in front of the Narrow house. The car burst into flame and all three men died.

"After the funerals, a rumor started going around that it wasn't alcohol that had caused the crash. The story was that the son-in-law had swerved to avoid a little boy and a Negro woman who had darted out into the street. Since there were no witnesses to the accident I don't know how anyone could know that, but that was the story . . . and soon enough, other people started claiming they'd seen the woman and the boy as well."

"You believe it?" Atticus said.

Landsdowne shook his head. "I think there were some guilty consciences at work, there. The rumors did have a salutary effect—a number of Elm Street's other residents decided they no longer liked the neighborhood so much, and a few of the worst individuals left Aken entirely. Not enough of them, in my opinion. But our current mayor is a Republican, so maybe there's hope for the future."

"What about the Narrow house?" Montrose asked. "Is it still standing?"

"It's a ruin, now," Landsdowne told him. "It was never repaired after the fire. Ghosts or no, I imagine anything of value has long since been taken out of it."

"Might be worth a drive-by, anyway. As long as we're here."

"All right. Let me get a map and show you how to go. I'd offer to take you over myself, but at this point, you'll probably be more welcome in that neighborhood without me."

"Hill Street," Montrose said, annoyed, staring at the sign for the cross street in front of them.

"Should that last turn have been a right, maybe?" Atticus suggested.

"I know how to read a map."

"I didn't say you didn't, Pop. But I thought I heard Mr. Landsdowne say to turn right off Locust."

"That's what you heard, is it?" Montrose looked over at the house on the corner lot beside them. "We're in the right vicinity at least." Poking up out of the snow in the yard was a blackfaced lawn jockey.

Atticus looked at it too. "Maybe we should just go home."

"Nah. We've come this far, we'll find it." Montrose swung a right onto Hill Street, thinking he might circle around the block. But after a short incline the street dead-ended at the entrance to the Aken cemetery.

Montrose shifted into reverse and the car sputtered and stalled out cold. Cursing under his breath, he reached for the ignition.

"Hold on a second, Pop," Atticus said. Inside the cemetery, a Korean man was pushing a wheelbarrow along a line of graves, gathering up old flower wreaths and using a whisk broom to brush snow from the tops of the headstones. "Let me go ask this guy if he knows which way Elm Street is."

"Nah, stay in the car." Montrose turned the ignition key. The Cadillac's engine wheezed but wouldn't catch. Atticus opened his door and got out. "Atticus!"

"I'll be right back, Pop." He trotted off through the cemetery gates, his father calling after him.

Montrose tried the ignition again. The engine continued to wheeze. He sat back, cursing aloud this time, and stabbed at the button on the dashboard lighter.

He was fishing in his shirt pocket for a cigarette when the Cadillac bounced as though someone had jumped on the back fender. When Montrose looked behind him there was no one there. But he could hear somebody giggling.

He got out of the car. "Who's there?" he called. A snowball landed on the roof of the Cadillac and then he saw the boy, standing about fifteen feet away on the far side of the car. He was seven or eight years old and he was light-skinned, with big brown eyes and dark curly hair.

"Hey!" Montrose said sharply. He started around the car, concern tempering his anger as he realized how the boy was dressed, in a denim jumper and nothing else. No winter coat. No shoes or socks. Not even a shirt underneath the jumper. "Hey," Montrose said, in a different tone. "What are you doing out here? Where's your mother?"

The boy laughed and dashed away barefoot through the snow. Montrose went after him. They ran along the outside of the cemetery wall, Montrose's feet plunging deep into the snow drifted up against the stone, while the boy bounded lightly on ahead, stopping now and then to look back. They came to the corner of the cemetery property and the boy, still laughing, vanished into a thicket of snow-covered branches. Montrose plunged after him and found himself tumbling down a slope. He fetched up hard at the bottom, half-buried in snow.

Half-buried: His left arm was planted up to the elbow in a snow-mound, but his right hand rested on warm green grass. Summer grass.

Montrose lifted his head and looked over the grass at the back of a big yellow house standing bright beneath a hot noon sun. A Negro woman in a checked apron waited on the back porch steps for the boy, who came running towards her.

Montrose got to his feet, straddling winter and summer. He pivoted clockwise and stood firmly on the grass, the snow on his left shoe and pants leg melting away instantly in the heat. "Ma'am?" he called to the woman, who had taken the boy by the hand and was leading him inside. But she didn't respond and neither did the boy.

Montrose looked over his shoulder at winter, still just a hand's breadth away. Then he started towards the house. Halfway across the yard he looked back again and the snow had disappeared; the slope up to the cemetery was all green shrubbery and flowers.

He climbed the steps to the porch. The back door of the house was ajar. Montrose stood at the threshold, his attention drawn to a line of letters from Adam's alphabet carved into the right post of the door-frame. Looking farther to the right, he saw an identical inscription cut into the sill of a window.

"Ma'am?" Montrose knocked on the half-open door. No one answered, but the door swung wide, and he stepped inside, into a kitchen.

The woman was at the sink, scrubbing out a pot, though Montrose sensed that the majority of her effort was devoted to ignoring his presence. Meanwhile the boy, seated at a table with a sandwich and a glass of milk, looked up smiling, as though he and Montrose shared a private joke.

"Ma'am?" Montrose said again. And then, when she still didn't answer: "Mrs. Narrow?"

At last she met his eye. But the words she spoke weren't addressed to him. "Henry," she said. "There's someone here."

A white man appeared in an open doorway behind the boy. He regarded Montrose with curiosity, as though visitors to the house were rare. "Can I help you?" he said.

Recalling the family portrait from the Winthrop House, Montrose had no doubt that this was Hiram Winthrop's son. But you ain't thirty-five, he thought. Then again, you wouldn't be—you were only in your twenties when you died.

What name to address him by? Montrose chose to be direct: "Mr. Winthrop," he said.

The woman, who had returned her attention to the sink, looked up startled. The boy lost his smile, and the man's expression grew severe. "State your business, sir," he said, and Montrose felt the chill of winter at his back, icy tendrils curling down inside his collar and threatening to freeze him where he stood.

"It's about my son, Mr. Winthrop," Montrose said, his voice steady despite the cold. "My name is Montrose Turner, and I was sent here by a man named Braithwhite, who wants something that belonged to your father. But I didn't come for that; I came on behalf of my boy, Atticus. Braithwhite has designs on him, and I don't know how to stop him. But I think you might. So I've come to ask for your help, and I'm prepared to make a deal. If I can. If you will."

The cold receded. Summer returned. But the woman and the boy continued to watch and wait, until Henry senior nodded.

"All right, Mr. Turner. Come into the parlor. We'll talk."

They sat at a table by a front window. While Winthrop poured tea, Montrose looked out at the lawn. At the edge of the grass by the street was a big-boled oak with a tire swing. Montrose guessed this must be the tree the police chief's son-in-law had swerved into, though the tree showed no evidence of having been involved in a fiery crash.

Maybe the crash hadn't happened yet. The calendar above the mantel of the parlor fireplace said AUGUST 1945, and among the cars parked on the street, Montrose could not identify a single one of post-war make. Even as he considered the possibility, some more stubbornly rational part of his brain kept trying to protest. This was all wrong, it warned him; he did not belong here, sitting in a summer yesteryear with a dead man. He should get up and go back the way he had come, without delay. And definitely, definitely, he should not eat or drink anything given him in this house.

But Montrose had no intention of leaving empty-handed, and it

would have been rude to refuse Winthrop's hospitality, so he accepted
the cup placed before him and one of the shortbread cookies Winthrop
also offered. The tea and the cookie were remarkably bland—flavorless,
to be honest—but when swallowed they produced a mild intoxication,
a torpor of reason that allowed him to embrace a parley with a dead
man as part of the natural order of things.

"Henry Winthrop," the dead man said. "It's been a long time
since anyone's called me that. You say Braithwhite sent you? Samuel
Braithwhite?"

"His son, Caleb. Samuel Braithwhite is dead."

"Really?" Winthrop said. "I hadn't heard that." He looked distract-
edly out the window. "We don't get much news, here."

"No," Montrose said, his own gaze straying to the calendar above
the mantelpiece. "I don't suppose you do. But about my son, Mr. Winthrop . . ."

"Braithwhite has designs on him, you said. What sort?"

"I don't entirely know. Braithwhite's father wanted to use Atticus as
a sacrifice in a ritual. Caleb's more subtle—for now he wants to keep
Atticus around, I think as a sort of trophy to impress his other sorcerer
friends. But in the long run, I expect he'll come up with some ritual of
his own. I want him gone before that happens."

"You want to kill him?"

"I would if I could. But he's charmed, somehow, and I can't raise a
hand against him. Braithwhite calls it immunity."

Winthrop nodded. "My father had that, too. It was frustrating."

"Is there a way around it?"

"A number of ways," Winthrop said. "But I don't know what any of
them are."

"You know anyone who does?"

"No one living."

"What about your father's notebooks?" Montrose said. "That's what
Braithwhite sent me here to get, and he was very particular about not

wanting anyone else to have them. Could there be something in them, you think, about revoking immunity?"

"There might be."

"Would you be willing to part with them?"

Winthrop shrugged noncommittally. "I suppose I could let them go. God knows they aren't doing *me* any good. Of course," he added, "there would have to be a fair exchange."

"I have money," Montrose said. "It's back in my car—"

"No, not money. Money's no use to me."

"What, then?"

"Feeling," Winthrop said.

"I don't understand."

Winthrop looked out the window again. "It's not just news we lack for, here," he said. "It's everything. All that sunshine . . . But I'm never really warm." He turned back to Montrose. "Or cold, either. And this—" Gesturing at the tea and shortbread. "Unsatisfying. No sweetness in the sugar. No savor, in salt. And it's the same with emotion. Oh, we can pretend, but it's just faded echoes. To really feel something again, to experience strong emotion, even for a moment . . . That would be a good trade."

The look of naked craving on Winthrop's face reawakened that inner voice. Get out, it told Montrose. This ain't a man, it's a vampire and it's starving, get away from it.

"I still don't understand," he said. "How can I make you feel something?"

"Tell me a story," Henry Winthrop said. He raised his head up like an animal scenting prey. "Tell me about your father."

"No," said Montrose. "No, I won't do that."

But the dead man wouldn't hear no.

"Rowland, was it?" he said. "Was that his name? Dick Rowland?"

Montrose shook his head, that inner voice saying: Run. "My father was Ulysses."

"So who was Dick Rowland?" Winthrop demanded.

Montrose tried to get up then, but the torpor had settled in his legs, trapping him in the chair.

"Who was he? Tell me."

Nothing for it but to answer. "He was a bootblack," Montrose said. "A shoe shiner."

"Did he and your father work together?"

"No. My father had his own store. He and Rowland didn't know each other, not to speak to anyway."

"But there was a connection between them," Winthrop insisted. "What was it? What happened?"

"Rowland was accused," Montrose said, after trying once more, unsuccessfully, to stand.

"Accused of what?"

"The usual," Montrose told him, and with the sudden kindling of anger in his breast he lost his reluctance to speak. "It was Memorial Day, 1921," he said. "Dick Rowland went into the Drexel Building in downtown Tulsa to use the colored restroom on the top floor. He stumbled and fell against the elevator operator, a white girl named Sarah Page. She said he attacked her."

"And did he?" Winthrop asked.

Montrose threw him a look of disgust. "Broad daylight in a public building on Main Street, he's going to attack a white girl? How suicidal would a man have to be? But it didn't matter: She screamed and he ran, and from that moment on he was guilty.

"Cops arrested him early the next day. That afternoon, the *Tulsa Tribune* ran an article about the 'attack,' claiming the girl's clothes were torn. They admitted later they'd made that up, but of course as soon as the paper hit the street, the lynch talk started.

"The sheriff had Dick Rowland in the jail at the county courthouse. By nightfall there was a huge mob of white people gathered outside. But the Negroes who lived up in the Greenwood section had heard about the lynching too, and some of the men decided to get their guns and go down and put a stop to it. My father was one of them. I never got a chance to ask him what happened, but the story I heard later was that one of the whites at the courthouse tried to take a pistol away from one of the Negroes. War broke out.

"The Negroes were outnumbered something like twenty to one, so the ones who survived the initial gunfire fell back towards Greenwood. The whites followed after, but they stopped along the way to get more guns and ammunition. They broke into hardware stores and pawnshops, took everything that wasn't nailed down.

"My father got back to our house around eleven o'clock. His arm was cut and there was blood all down his sleeve, but I don't think he even knew it. He told my mother to start packing the car with anything she couldn't bear to lose. He said he was going back out—the Greenwood men were setting up a defensive line at the railroad tracks, to turn back the white mob—but if that failed, we had to be ready to leave in a hurry.

"My mother didn't want him to go, but he didn't see there was any choice. He said: 'They're looting their own people's property, what do you think they're going to do if we let them get up in here?'

"I told my father I wanted to come with him to help defend the neighborhood. Seven years old, I thought I was a big man already. My father said no of course, and with him, one no was all you ever got. But I got excited and tried to argue, and that's when he gave me this." He tilted his head and pointed to a scar by the corner of his left eye. "Cut me with his ring.

"My father had a reputation as a violent man, and he *could* be violent, but it was always controlled. He'd hit me if I needed it, but he never left a mark on me before, and he didn't mean to that night. When I felt the blood trickle down my cheek, that's when I realized how scared he was. How bad a fix we were in.

"And *then*," Montrose said, "my brother George stepped up and said he needed to go out and get my great-grandmother's book . . ."

"Her book?" Winthrop said.

"An accounts ledger," said Montrose. "It was in the safe at my father's shop. My father told George if worse came to worst, he'd save the book himself, but George insisted it was his responsibility. I expected George to get smacked down too about then, but my father said OK. I couldn't believe it—when my mother jumped in and tried to forbid George to go, my father told *her* to be quiet.

"So my father and George went out together, and after that my mother was all business. She had me and my sister running around the house, gathering things together. Packing wedding dishes. I was so mad. George gets to go to the front line, I get *wedding dishes*.

"As we were bringing things out to the car, we could hear gunshots off in the distance. My mother got real agitated and I did too, but for different reasons. We got the car pretty well stuffed, and then there was this moment when my mother and Ophelia were inside the house trying to decide what else to take, and I was outside, alone, listening to those gunshots, and I couldn't hold myself back anymore. I'd just put my father's toolbox in the car, so I grabbed this big old claw hammer and started running towards the battle.

"When I got to Archer Street I could barely recognize it. The Greenwood defenders had shot out all the streetlights and they had snipers up overlooking the railroad tracks. The whites couldn't see the snipers, but a few of them had managed to sneak across with oil rags and lighters. All the shanties on the Greenwood side of the tracks were on fire, and some larger buildings too.

"So I was out there in the street with my hammer, with the fire and the smoke and the darkness, bullets flying by in both directions. Men were shouting at me to get the hell out of there, but I just started wandering down the street, in a daze, looking for my dad.

"I saw a car full of white men drive across the tracks and come under fire. The headlights and the windshield just exploded. The driver threw it into reverse and backed out in a hurry. I was jumping up and down, hollering—we were winning! Then my father swooped out of nowhere and grabbed me. He didn't hit me this time. He picked me up and shook me"—Montrose raised his hands above his head—"like *this*.

"I heard a big bang like a bomb going off. My father stopped shaking me and he hugged me to him and he started running. And you know, it's funny, but once we got away from the smoke and the flames, it was almost nice, him carrying me like that . . . I dream about it sometimes, and in the dreams there's no gunfire, it's just an ordinary spring night and my dad's carrying me home, like from a movie or a ball game. Like he should have been.

"We must have been about halfway home when a car came up behind us, moving fast. As it got close I saw it was all shot up, bullet holes in the hood, glass all knocked out, and I opened my mouth to say something, but there was no time. A white man leaned out of the back with a pistol and fired two shots. Then the car was past us and gone into the night—I never knew what happened to it, or who that man was.

"I thought the shots had missed us. I knew I wasn't hit, and my father didn't break stride. He ran on for another block or so and then he just stopped. He put me down, careful, put a hand on my shoulder like to steady himself. Then he fell over.

"We were on the grass in front of someone's house. The people inside heard me yelling and the porch lights came on. I saw my father had been shot in the side and there was blood coming out of his mouth. He had this look on his face. Horror. Horror at the universe. I was too young to understand it. I thought he was afraid because he was dying, but that wasn't it at all. It wasn't until I had a son of my own—a son who wouldn't listen—that I understood what he felt.

"He wasn't afraid for himself. He was afraid for me. He wanted to protect me. He had: He saved my life, getting me away from that gunfight. But the night wasn't over and he knew he wasn't going to be there to see me through it. That's the horror, the most awful thing: to have a child the world wants to destroy and know that you're helpless to help him. Nothing worse than that. Nothing worse."

Eyes suddenly wet, Montrose looked up, as though waking from a trance, and saw the woman in the kitchen doorway with the boy held tight in her arms. Seeing her stricken expression, Montrose wanted to apologize for bringing such a tale into her house, but her husband leaned forward, still hungry, and determined to lick every last crumb from this particular plate.

"And then he died?" Henry Winthrop said.

"Yeah," said Montrose. "Then he died."

Outside the window it was still summer, but the color of the sky had changed to pink and gold and the shadows on the grass were growing long. Montrose, still lost in the burning night of Tulsa, did not find it strange that evening should already be drawing on here.

Henry Winthrop said: "I wish I had a father like that."

"I *don't* have a father like that," Montrose said. "That's the damn point." He swiped his eyes with the heel of his hand. "So what's your story? What was your father like?"

"Curious," Winthrop replied. "There are other words I could use to describe him, but to understand him you'd have to start with that: his insatiable curiosity. He wanted to know everything about everything, which is a lot to know. Much more than could be learned in a single human life span. So to give himself the time he needed, he decided to become immortal—and as close to omnipotent as it was practical to get.

"On one level it was comical. The men my father associated with thought of themselves as rationalists. Scientists. *Natural* philosophers. To speak of the supernatural was a sign of simplemindedness. They wanted to become gods, but rejected the concept of God as vulgar superstition.

"My father was less orthodox than most. He didn't mind vulgarity if it got results. It's what led him to my mother. She was a witch," Winthrop explained. "Called herself that, unselfconsciously. She believed in gods, and miracles, and magic, and she showed my father that what he wanted was at least theoretically possible. She paid for it, too—first with her health, then with her life."

"The story is she had polio," Montrose said.

"That was the story," Winthrop agreed. "But it wasn't a disease that put my mother in a wheelchair, it was a mistranslation. A cosmic pun. Are you familiar with the language of Adam, Mr. Turner?"

"Acquainted with it," Montrose said cautiously.

"There's a line in Matthew's Gospel that says if you ask God for bread, he won't give you a stone," Winthrop said. "That's because the God of the New Testament is a person—a father—who cares about you. But when you invoke the language of Adam, you're addressing nature, and nature doesn't care, it just does what it's told. If you garble your instructions—transpose a letter, stress the wrong syllable—you'll get what you ask for, but it might not be what you want."

"What did your mother ask for?"

"A doorway," Winthrop said. "One challenge my father faced in understanding the universe was that most of it was beyond his reach. With my mother's help, he set out to find a means of bridging distant points in space. They succeeded, but one of their experiments left my mother crippled. She asked nature for the power to walk between worlds, and nature gave her legs of stone.

"After the accident, my father became more cautious. He had a deep respect for technology and already employed machines in the pursuit of his art. He began to invest more heavily in their use. He wanted to insure that in future mishaps, the harm would fall on something other than himself. Machines made good surrogates—and for situations where they weren't sufficient to absorb the risk, he also cultivated a pool of young, overeager apprentices.

"My mother continued to help my father with his research, but their relationship changed. At first she'd thought it was just bad luck that she was the one who'd gotten hurt. But seeing how he used his new assistants to shield himself from danger, she began to wonder."

"These apprentices," Montrose said. "Were you one of them?"

"No. My mother was adamant about that. She made my father promise never to involve me in his work, and because she was still very useful to him, he kept his word. Of course, I wanted to help him. What boy doesn't want to work with his father? But she made me promise, too. And any time I started showing interest in natural philosophy, she'd uncover her legs."

"How'd she die?"

"Trying to fix herself," Winthrop said. "When I was fifteen, she decided to leave my father—but in order to get free of him, she first had to get free of the wheelchair. I was away at boarding school when she performed a ritual of regeneration. She asked nature to give her her legs back; nature gave her legs. I don't know the exact count, but it was more than her heart or her nervous system could handle. My father claimed she didn't suffer for long.

"The funeral was closed casket. Afterwards we went home to a new house. My father talked about making a fresh start. He said he wanted to make me a partner in his research. But it was too late by then. While he'd been off chasing the ancient mysteries of the universe, I'd been studying a different, more modern sort of philosophy at school. My father was furious. He said he hadn't paid all that tuition to have me turned into a socialist. He blamed my mother, who'd chosen the school, for deliberately corrupting me. He was right about that.

"What he didn't know was that my mother had written me a letter before she died. She knew she might not survive the ritual. She wanted to make sure I survived my father. So she sent me detailed instructions on how to run away: where to get the money I'd need; how to forge a new identity; and how to hurt my father, for her, on my way out the door.

"It was another year before I left. I needed time to get ready, and I was afraid. My father was keeping a close eye on me. He refused to let me go back to school. Instead he hired a tutor, this crusty old Prussian . . . I spent months cooped up in our new house. That's how I got to know Pearl. We would sneak up to the roof together when I was supposed to be studying."

"It ever occur to you," said Montrose, unable to help himself, "that involving a maid in your family drama might not be right?"

"We were young and in love," Winthrop said. "And to my way of thinking at the time, I wouldn't have been doing her a favor to leave her in my father's service. Pearl wanted to get away from that house as badly as I did. To see the world." He smiled and Montrose bit back a caustic remark; from the kitchen, unnoticed by either of them, came the banging of pots.

"We waited for a night when my father was out of town," Winthrop continued. "We slipped out after supper, went to Dearborn Station, and bought tickets to Los Angeles. We made sure the ticket clerk would remember us. But we never boarded the train. Instead we went to a garage where my mother's old car was stored. It hadn't been driven in more than a decade, but she'd paid to keep it serviced. The keys were in the glove box.

"We drove east. The first year we were in New York City. We were married there, and I became Henry Narrow. By the time Henry junior was born, we'd moved to Philadelphia. I got a job at a bookstore; Pearl worked as a nanny and taught Sunday school on the weekends. We had a good life there."

"Yeah?" Montrose said. "So what'd you come back to Illinois for?"

"Pearl missed her mother," Winthrop said. "Every Saturday in Philadelphia I'd get the previous Sunday's *Chicago Tribune* and look for news of my father. But his obituary had already come and gone, so it was years before I found out he was dead. When I told Pearl, she wanted to go back and look for her mom. I didn't think it was a good idea. Death, in my father's case, wasn't necessarily final, and even if he really was gone, he had friends and enemies who might still be looking for me, because of what I'd taken.

"But Pearl missed her mother. Without telling me, she'd contacted some of her other relatives to see if they'd heard from her; none of them had, and she was worried. Eventually we agreed on a compromise: We'd go back to the Midwest and set up somewhere quiet where my father's old associates wouldn't find us, but close enough to Chicago that I could slip in and look for Pearl's mother. Originally we planned to rent a place farther north, but on the way out from Philadelphia we stopped over in Paducah to visit one of Pearl's cousins. She really seemed to enjoy the reunion, and while we were there I happened to see a listing for this house, just a short drive across the river. And we had the money, so I thought, why not?"

"Why *not*?" Montrose said. "After what Mr. Landsdowne told you? What in God's name were you thinking?"

"I thought we were protected," Winthrop said simply. "My mother's last letter included instructions for two enchantments. One to confound pursuers when I was on the move. The other to be used on any house I chose to dwell in, to ward off those who would do me harm. They were the only spells I ever knew, but I didn't really understand how they worked—and my mother didn't know about Pearl. She assumed I'd be running on my own and that the main threat to me would be my father and men like him."

"Sorcerers," said Montrose. "The ward on the house only protects against sorcerers?"

"That would be my best guess," Henry Winthrop said. "Even now I don't know for sure. But my real failure of understanding was more fundamental. I made the same mistake my mother made: I asked for something without grasping the true nature of my request.

"My father was my protector too, you see. He didn't protect me the way your father protected you, out of love. He protected me incidentally, as a function of who and what he was. So long as I was under his roof, the only thing I had to fear was him. In seeking to free myself from him, I was also seeking to make myself vulnerable to the world, but I didn't appreciate that. I thought free meant free to do as I pleased. I thought . . . I thought *I* had immunity."

"Every boy thinks that," Montrose said. "But then you got out in the world, and her with you . . . You didn't see it was otherwise?"

Winthrop shook his head. "No one ever bothered us in Philadelphia. Oh, maybe now and then someone would say something rude—Pearl was much more sensitive to that than I was. But no one ever *attacked* us. I assumed my mother's spell was working. I saw no reason it shouldn't work just as well here."

"You were a goddamned fool, is what you were."

"Yes, I was a fool," Henry Winthrop agreed. "That was the problem. I had charms to protect me against philosophers and wise men, but not against my own foolishness . . . or the hands of the simpleminded."

"Narrow!"

The call came from outside, where night had fallen. A particular night. Montrose looking out the window saw three cars drawn up on the lawn and a dozen men milling in the headlights. A mob of simpletons, but armed. "Narrow!" their leader cried. "You and your two niggers come out here!" In the summer darkness across the street more people were gathered, spectators, women and children among them.

One of the men on the lawn thumbed the wheel of a lighter and touched the resulting flame to a rag stuffed in the mouth of a gasoline-filled Coke bottle. Montrose watched the bottle come tumbling towards the window until at the last second the strength returned to his legs and he shoved back out of the way of the spray of window glass. The bottle flew across the room to dash against the foot of the hearth and the rug in front of the fireplace blazed up.

Henry Winthrop, who hadn't moved, sought Montrose's gaze from across the table. His expression was mournful and self-pitying. "I didn't know," he said. "I swear I didn't know." Then a pistol cracked out in the night and Winthrop's head snapped back; he slumped, lifeless, in his chair. Montrose stood up, kicking his own chair away, and put his back against the wall beside the window.

The spreading fire had cut off the doorway to the kitchen and smoke from the burning rug was billowing across the ceiling. Montrose covered his mouth and nose with a handkerchief. He was preparing to leap the flames when he suddenly saw the woman and the boy standing side by side on the hearth, posed like corpses with their eyes closed and their arms crossed in front of them.

More shots were fired from outside. Montrose ducked reflexively. When he recovered himself, the woman and the boy were gone, and in their place, standing directly in the fire, was a large, dark-skinned colored man. The man's eyes were open and filled with a bitter rage almost as familiar to Montrose as his own.

"Dad?" Montrose said, lowering the handkerchief. "Daddy?"

Ulysses Turner moved his lips urgently, but whatever words passed between them were swallowed by the flames. Montrose leaned forward, straining to hear, but the heat held him back and so he stood there helpless and uncomprehending while the room filled with smoke and the sound of bullets launched by the hands of simple men.

"**P**op?"

Atticus followed his father's tracks in the snow to the back of the Narrow house and climbed up to the porch, stepping carefully over a gap in the boards. Two planks were nailed across the back doorway but the door had been forced open, so by crouching he was able to enter.

"Pop?" he called, standing in the ruined kitchen.

"In here."

The section of floor in front of the parlor fireplace had fallen in, as had the ceiling above it. By the light shining in through gaps in the boarded-up windows, Atticus could see his father on the far side of the room, sitting precariously in a chair that was missing one of its back legs. Montrose was hunched forward with his arms outstretched, gripping some sort of package.

"Pop? How'd you get over there?" No answer. Atticus went back through the kitchen and found his way up a central hall to the parlor's other entrance. Standing before his father, he saw that the package in Montrose's hands was a set of notebooks, squared up and tied with heavy twine. The books were coated with ash but the twine looked clean and new.

"What you got there, Pop?" Atticus said. "Is that—"

Montrose stood up, sending the rickety chair toppling over backwards. *"Nothing,"* he said, looking his son in the eye with a furious urgency. "We found *nothing.* The Narrows are dead, their house is burnt, and we didn't find a damn thing. That's what we're going to tell Braithwhite. And that's what we're going to *believe,* so if he looks inside our heads he doesn't see different. You understand me? You listening?"

"Yeah, Pop, I get it."

"You'd *better,"* Montrose said, and he sighed, wearily, feeling the weight of every one of his Jim Crow years . . . but still, feeling. "We need to go now," he said. "This is a place for the dead, and we don't belong here." He hugged the notebooks to his chest. "Not yet."

HORACE AND
THE DEVIL DOLL

❦

The specimen, as West repeatedly observed, had a splendid nervous
system.

—*H. P. Lovecraft, "Herbert West—Reanimator"*

"**T**he lady sounded like she was possessed," Neville said. "Like that
time on *The Mysterious Traveler*, when the demon took control of the
archaeologist's girlfriend, the way her voice changed? It was just like
that, except she used words you can't say on the radio."

His grandpa Nelson down in Biloxi had turned fifty-five, he explained. The family was going to call to wish him happy birthday in the
evening after the rates went down. But then during dinner Neville's
sister Octavia broke a glass and cut her foot. Neville's parents took
Octavia to the emergency room, leaving Neville home to watch his
other sister. Neville got it into his head to call Grandpa on his own, to
let him know they hadn't forgotten him. It was a foolish thing to do—
his father would be mad about having to pay for two calls, even at the
lower rate—but Neville had never placed a long-distance call before,
and having just turned thirteen himself, he was anxious to start doing
adult things.

So he picked up the telephone and got connected to the operator
in Biloxi. This is Neville Porter calling person-to-person for Mr. Porter,
Neville said. The operator, a white woman who sounded old and was
perhaps hard of hearing, said, What's the name of the party you wish to

speak to? Mr. Porter, Neville repeated. His *first* name, said the operator. It's OK, Neville told her, it's a private house. There's only one Mr. Porter there.

Which is when the demon came out.

Now you listen to me good, you goddamned pickaninny, the demon said. If you think I'm going to call a nigger "Mister," you've got another think coming. What's his *name*? N-N-Nelson, Neville said. The demon mocked his stammer, then made him apologize and address her as "ma'am" before finally putting the call through. By then, Neville didn't even want to talk to his grandpa anymore. Didn't want to talk to anybody.

"Why didn't you just hang up?" Curtis asked. "On the operator, I mean, not your grandpa."

"I couldn't," said Neville. "It would have been disrespectful."

"So? She was disrespectful to you. And what's she going to do about it anyway, from a thousand miles away?"

"She's not a thousand miles from my grandpa. What if she really got mad and talked to the other operators down there? You think he'd ever get a phone call again?"

Curtis reared back in outrage. "They can't do that!"

"It's Mississippi, stupid," Neville said. "They can do whatever they like."

Horace, walking beside them, nodded his head in agreement. "My dad was telling me about this one town down South? One year, the Negroes started up a drive to get people to vote, so the highway department shut down all the roads between the colored section and the courthouse. Cutting off someone's phone would be nothing compared to that."

"Well, I'd sue if they cut off my phone," said Curtis, whose father was a personal injury lawyer.

"Sue?" Neville said. "You think you could *sue*? My God, how ignorant are you?"

"You can always sue!" Curtis insisted.

"Not in Mississippi, you can't. The law's not *for* colored people, not down there . . . Sue!" Neville shook his head in disgust. "Wind up hanging from a telephone pole, most likely."

"Well you don't have to sound so happy about it!" Curtis said.

"I'm not *happy*, I'm *wise*," Neville replied. "You should try it some time."

In the distance now they could see a bright yellow awning that marked their destination, White City Comics Emporium. Neville, continuing to shake his head and muttering "Sue!" sped up, running to catch two other boys who were making the same after-school pilgrimage.

Horace stayed with Curtis. "Don't let Neville make you feel bad," he said. "I hear these kind of stories all the time from my dad, and I know they're true, but some of them are so crazy, it's like I don't even want to believe it . . . You know Joe Bartholomew?"

"Pirate Joe?" Curtis nodded. "Sure."

"You know he lost his eye in a car accident when he was little. Lost his mom, too. And my dad, he told me Mrs. Bartholomew probably didn't have to die, but the hospital where they lived in Alabama wouldn't treat colored people. They had to call an ambulance from another hospital, like seventy miles away, and by the time it got there it was too late."

"For real?" Curtis said. "I mean, I know it's all segregated and everything, but, even if you're dying?"

"That's what I asked my dad," Horace said. "You know, did they at least *try* calling the white hospital, just to see if they'd make an exception? Pirate Joe's mom was a schoolteacher, so I thought, maybe . . . But my dad said Jim Crow doesn't work like that."

"Man." Curtis fingered his coat above his appendix scar. "You ever been, yourself?"

"Down South? No, never yet."

"That's kind of funny, in a way. Your dad being a travel agent and all."

"A *safe* travel agent," Horace reminded him. "I tried to go. A couple years back, my dad went down to Atlanta on business, and I asked to come along, but my mom said no."

"She was probably worried about what would happen if you got in a car wreck. Or if your asthma acted up."

"One day I'll go," Horace said. "Before I move to New York and start working in comics, I want to see the South for myself. You could come with me if you like."

"Meet Jim Crow face to face? No thanks. I think I'd rather stay home and be ignorant."

"Hey! Hey you kids!"

The call, raspy and low, came from a boarded-up storefront they'd just passed. A white man stood grinning in the open doorway; he wore a rumpled suit and sported a five o'clock shadow, like a businessman who'd started to go feral. "You kids want to make some money?" he said. "One of you come here a second, I'll give you a dollar."

"A dollar for what?" said Curtis.

"I want to rub your head."

"What!?" Horace squawked.

"Just come here and let me rub your head." The man held up his right hand, curled loosely into a fist, and shook it; they heard the rattle of dice. "For luck."

Neville, who hadn't abandoned them after all, came rushing back. "Be *wise*," he hissed, pulling Horace and Curtis away. "Don't *stop*."

"**Y**ou're really not coming in?" Neville said.

"I can't," Horace said. "I promised my dad."

Looking through the front window of the Comics Emporium he could see that Mr. D'Angelo was back minding the store. A week ago when Horace had come here with Reginald Oxbow, Mr. D'Angelo had been out sick, and the substitute clerk had stared at them the whole time they were in the store. Then, when they'd come up to the cash register to make their purchases, he'd made them take their coats off to prove they weren't shoplifting.

That evening Horace's uncle had come over, and during dinner Horace mentioned what the clerk had done. Uncle Montrose was incensed: "You still bought comics from this guy after he treated you that way?"

"Well, yeah," Horace said, then tried to explain that since the clerk didn't own the store, they weren't really buying from *him*. But the distinction was lost on Uncle Montrose, who shot Horace's father a look that said, What are you teaching this boy?

So now the shop was off-limits until his father found time to come down and have a talk with Mr. D'Angelo about his employee. Horace knew it could have been worse: Uncle Montrose would have skipped the talk and gone straight to a permanent boycott.

"If you could go in," Curtis asked him, "you know what you'd want to get?"

Horace shrugged. "I was thinking the new *Superboy*."

"I was thinking about getting that too," Curtis said nodding. "Anything else?"

"Mostly I just wanted to look around, you know, see what came in this week."

"Watch us through the window, then. If I see anything good, I'll hold it up."

Neville and Curtis went inside, and Horace stood by the window, stamping his feet to keep warm. He hadn't been standing there long when he heard someone come up behind him. Thinking it might be the dice man, Horace raised a protective hand to his scalp, but when he turned around, there were two white men there, both clean-shaven. The one on the left opened his coat to show the police star on his vest.

"Horace Berry?" he said. "I'm Detective Noble, and my partner here is Detective Burke. We have some questions for you."

They took him to a diner down the street. Dismissing the waitress with a flash of their police stars, the detectives sat Horace in a U-shaped booth and crowded in beside him, Detective Noble on his left and Detective Burke on his right, close enough that he couldn't move without bumping into one of them yet far enough apart that he had to constantly swivel his head to maintain eye contact with whichever of them was speaking. Adding to his discomfort was a customer with a cigar who was sitting at the counter directly across from the booth. When Horace noticed the cloud of smoke rising above this man's head, he felt his lungs start to clench up and knew that to avoid an asthma attack he'd need to breathe slowly and keep calm. Difficult under the circumstances.

"So, Horace," Detective Noble began, "the reason we wanted to talk to you—"

"—is because we think you can help us with an investigation," Detective Burke said.

"We'd like to know what you can tell us about this." Detective Noble placed a copy of *The Interplanetary Adventures of Orithyia Blue* on the table. "You recognize it?"

Horace picked up the book. It was issue #11: the Christmas special. It was wrinkled and torn and the ink on the front cover had smeared. The back cover was soiled with a muddy tire track.

"It was found at the scene of an accident," Detective Noble said.

"Accident! Is my mom OK?"

"Your mom?" said Detective Burke. "She's fine, as far as we know."

"What makes you ask about her?" said Detective Noble.

"Nothing," said Horace. He lowered his eyes and pretended to be interested in the tire track.

Detective Noble jabbed two fingers under Horace's chin and tilted his head up. "Horace, listen to me," he said. "You don't want to lie to us."

"You really don't," Detective Burke agreed. "There's no future in it."

"I'm going to let you in on a little secret," said Detective Noble. "Cops—*smart* cops—a lot of times when we ask a question, we already know the answer. But we ask anyway, because we like to know whether the person we're talking to is cooperating—"

"—or trying to fuck us," Detective Burke said.

"You're not trying to fuck us, are you, Horace?" Detective Noble said.

"No!" Horace said. "But I don't . . . I don't know what this is about."

"You don't need to know what it's about," Detective Burke said. "You just need to answer our questions."

"But," added Detective Noble, in a gentler voice, "we could probably tell you a little, just to get things off on the right foot." He looked at his partner. "We can tell him a little, can't we?"

Detective Burke shrugged. "Maybe a little."

"Sure." Detective Noble turned back to Horace. "It's about connections," he said. "The past few months, Detective Burke and I have been running a surveillance detail. You know what that is?"

"You're watching somebody?"

"That's right. A man named Caleb Braithwhite. You familiar with that name, Horace?"

Horace shook his head, conscious of the two detectives studying him very intently now.

"Well," Detective Noble said, "we've been keeping an eye on Mr. Braithwhite and on people he associates with. People like your cousin Atticus, and your uncle Montrose, and your dad."

"My dad? What—"

"And because we like to be thorough," the detective continued, "we've also been looking at people who *might* be associated with Mr.

Braithwhite, even if we've never actually seen them together. Your mom, she'd be in that category. So that's the first thing."

"The second thing," said Detective Burke, "is this accident . . ."

"A shooting accident," Detective Noble said. "But with complications."

"Yeah, weird ones," said Detective Burke. "Three men dead, two more missing, and signs of at least one other person who fled the scene. And this"—tapping a finger on the comic book—"was on the ground near the victims."

"Now this happened in Wisconsin, outside our jurisdiction," Detective Noble explained. "But the authorities who are looking into it are friends of our boss, and they like to trade favors and share information, so they ended up showing him this comic book, which they couldn't make heads or tails of."

"Ordinarily it wouldn't have meant anything to us, either," Detective Burke said. "But this is where the part about the connections comes in . . ."

"Orithyia Blue, that's an unusual name," said Detective Noble. "Orithyia was a queen of the Amazons. Not a very famous one, though. These days, the only Amazon most people have heard of is Wonder Woman. And if they know an Amazon queen, it's probably Wonder Woman's mom. What was she called again?"

"Hippolyte," Detective Burke said.

"That's right, Hippolyte, with an 'e' on the end. But you can also spell it with an 'a.'"

"Orithyia Blue," Detective Burke said. "Hippolyta Berry. Interesting coincidence."

"And it gets more interesting," Detective Noble said, "if you know, like we do, that your mother used to be Hippolyta Green."

"Blue and Green." Detective Burke grinned. "Both colored women."

"We also know your mother goes on a lot of road trips," Detective Noble said, "and we know she was out of town on the night of

December twenty-first, which is when this thing in Wisconsin happened. We wouldn't have figured her for a comics fan, but then your teacher Mrs. Freeman told us—"

"You talked to Mrs. Freeman?"

"Like I said, we're thorough. Mrs. Freeman told us you're quite the little artist. So you see where this takes us," Detective Noble concluded. "And now that we've shared all this with you, Horace, it's time for you to start sharing back. This *is* your work, right?"

No point in denying it. "Yes, sir."

"You gave this to your mother before she left on her trip?"

Horace nodded.

"Do you know where she went?"

"Minneapolis."

"So she would have driven through Wisconsin."

"I guess."

"And what happened?"

"I don't know." As Detective Burke suddenly leaned into him: "I don't!"

"You know *something*," Detective Burke said.

"She said . . . she said she lost it!"

"When?"

"When she got back," Horace said. "At Christmas. She asked me if I took the book out of the car, and I said I didn't, and she said she must have lost it. She was worried." He regretted the words as soon as they were out of his mouth. "But she wouldn't . . ."

"Wouldn't what?"

"Wouldn't do anything bad!"

"Maybe not on her own," Detective Noble said. "But if Mr. Braithwhite asked her to do something for him—"

"I don't know any Mr. Braithwhite! I—"

"Calm down, Horace, we believe you. But see, now we've got this problem. Detective Burke and I need answers. We could just go ask your mother directly, but if she *is* working for Mr. Braithwhite, she might not want to talk to us—"

"And that could get ugly," Detective Burke said. "Fast."

"We'll do what we have to do," Detective Noble said. "But what I'm thinking, maybe you could talk to your mother for us. Be subtle about it: Ask her if she ever found that missing comic book, and then see if you can get her to tell you about her Minneapolis trip."

"And when you've gotten what you can about that," Detective Burke added, "try mentioning Mr. Braithwhite's name. Maybe say you over-heard your dad talking about him. See how she reacts."

"And then come back to us," Detective Noble said. "And tell us all about it. What do you say, Horace? You think you could do that?"

He wanted badly to say no. Beyond not wishing to betray his mother's confidence, Horace sensed that this was all a play-act, and that the detectives had already decided what they were going to do. If their plans included hurting Horace's mom, nothing he did or didn't agree to would change that. In which case he should refuse them and suffer the consequences with his dignity intact. But he wasn't nearly brave enough to do that, and just the thought of saying no triggered another warning spasm in his lungs.

"I can try," he said, the words coming out wheezy. "I can try talking to her."

Detective Noble looked sad. "Oh, Horace," he said. "You disap-point me."

"We warned you not to lie, Horace," Detective Burke said.

"I'm not lying!" Horace said. "I'll talk to my mom. I'll—" But then he broke off, coughing. The customer with the cigar had gotten up from the counter and was approaching the booth, preceded by a heavy reek of smoke.

"So?" the cigar man said.

"Sorry, Captain Lancaster," Detective Noble told him. "I don't think Horace is going to play ball with us."

"He thinks he can pretend to go along," said Detective Burke. "Trick us into letting him go, then run home to warn Mommy and Daddy."

"All right, then," Captain Lancaster said. "We'll do it the other way." He drew on the cigar, and as the tip flared, Horace felt a twitch start in his left eye. "Stand him up," the captain said.

The detectives grabbed Horace's arms, lifting him out of his seat and over the top of the table. Horace kicked and tried to scream, but his lungs wouldn't give him the air, and then as he was set down on the floor outside the booth he saw it didn't matter anyway: The waitress and the diner's other customers had all disappeared. He was alone with the detectives, the captain, and the burning cigar tip.

Horace whipped his head around until he was dizzy, determined to present a moving target, but Lancaster's intent wasn't to blind him. Instead he held the cigar in his right hand and spat thickly into his left. He jammed the cigar back between his teeth, then clapped his hands and began rubbing them together briskly. Horace stopped moving as he saw what looked like steam jetting from between the captain's palms.

Then the captain said, "Hold his head still," and Horace started struggling again. But Detective Burke dug his fingers into the back of Horace's skull, and the captain reached out with his hot, spit-slicked hands and massaged Horace's scalp as though determined to rub away every last ounce of luck he possessed.

That night he had the dream about the heads.

It was an old dream. Back when Horace was seven, he'd taken a ride with his uncle to a warehouse in Gary, Indiana. The place was a giant junk shop that specialized in secondhand industrial equipment, and Montrose's bosses had sent him to look at a used printing press.

While Uncle Montrose conducted his business, Horace explored the warehouse's collection of spare machine parts. Larger items sat out openly on shelves, or on the floor, while smaller objects were gathered in wooden crates. The crates were themselves secondhand, and some still bore the labels for the produce they had originally contained. As he wandered, Horace began making up a story about a grocery store for robots, a "metalgrocer" that sold lettuces made of fan blades and stone fruits that were vacuum tubes.

In the shadows at the back of a low shelf he spied a crate labeled GEORGIA NIGGER HEADS; the words were accompanied by a cartoon of a freckled and bucktoothed Negro boy. In what might have been someone's idea of a joke, the portion of the label showing the boy's body had been torn away, leaving only the grinning head and the wide-brimmed straw hat.

A white man hunting for something along the same row of shelves saw Horace staring at the crate. "They're watermelons," the man told him. "Little watermelons, about the size of your noggin. With dark rinds, and woolly bits around the stems. So that's what they call them, nigger heads. You can eat the seeds."

Riding home that day, Horace fell asleep in the car and dreamed that he was in the produce section of a big supermarket, facing a display stand on which colored boys' heads were stacked in a tidy pyramid.

The heads themselves were not that scary. They weren't *severed* heads, just heads that lacked bodies. They were alive and didn't appear to be suffering; most of them looked bored, or were asleep. The unnerving thing was that none of the customers in the store seemed to find them at all remarkable. They pushed their carts past the display without a glance, or if they did look, they regarded the heads with indifference, as if they really were nothing more than a bunch of watermelons. Horace kept wanting to speak up, to point out that no, in fact, these were *boys' heads*. But at the same time he was afraid to draw attention to himself, certain that something awful would happen if he did.

The dream had recurred many times since then, usually when he was anxious about something. In more recent versions, his own head was often part of the display.

This time Horace's head remained on his shoulders, but the faces of Neville, Curtis, and the Reverend Oxbow's son Reggie all looked out from the pile.

It was after hours. The supermarket's lights were turned down low and there were no customers, which Horace couldn't recall ever having been the case before. Nervously he looked towards the rear of the store. There was something moving around back there, making furtive noises in the shadows. Whatever it was, Horace knew instinctively that he didn't want to meet it face to face. He needed to get out of here.

But when he looked to the front of the store, there was no exit door, just a line of opaque, milky-white windows. Lights shining from outside cast the silhouettes of two men against the glass. The detectives, Burke and Noble, waiting in the parking lot: If he broke a window to escape, they'd grab him.

Just get a good running start, Horace told himself. Bust right on through and keep going; they won't expect that. He took his mark and was about to go when something made him glance at the heads again. Neville and Curtis and Reggie were all looking at him imploringly. Don't leave us, their faces said. Don't leave us behind.

The thing from the back of the store was coming closer now, scuttling up an aisle towards the produce section. Horace searched frantically for something to carry the heads in. On a low shelf underneath a counter heaped with peaches he saw a wicker basket. But when Horace tried to grab it, it slid back out of his grasp. He crouched and leaned forward, cheek pressed against the front of the counter, arms reaching blindly into the shelf.

The lights went out. Something shifted above him and a peach tumbled down and burst, rotten and slimy, on his shoulder. Horace gave a cry of disgust and scrambled backwards to escape the avalanche of peaches that followed. He raised his arms defensively, expecting something to come flying at him out of the darkness. Then he realized there was a weight on his shoulder that was more than just the remnant of the burst peach—a weight on *both* his shoulders. Strong hands reached up from behind and clapped over his ears, gripping tight. Twisting. Horace screamed himself awake then, but not before feeling his head turned completely around and yanked from the top of his spine, as neatly as a ripe piece of fruit being harvested from the vine.

When he came out to breakfast, his parents were arguing. Horace's mom had made last-minute plans to drive to New York to see her mother over the weekend. But Horace's dad had been counting on her to fill in for Victor Franklin at the Grand Boulevard travel office while Victor was in Philadelphia at his sister's wedding.

Ordinarily Horace would have stayed out of it. But if Mom was going out of town alone—which it sounded like she was determined to do—he needed to warn her about the police being after her.

He'd tried to tell her yesterday. After the detectives had let him go, he'd run straight home. His scalp had been on fire, as if the captain's spittle were laced with battery acid, and as soon as he got in the apartment he'd stuck his head under a cold faucet. The burning subsided, but there was a residual itch that no amount of soap and water could get rid of.

The itch in his scalp was mirrored by an itch in his throat and lungs. As he discovered over the course of the evening, any attempt to tell his mother or his father about his encounter with the police caused the itch to flare up. He'd get a few words out at most and then start coughing. The more he tried to talk, the harder he coughed, until he was hacking like a hairball-sick cat.

He'd hoped a night's sleep might cure him. Instead, the itch seemed to have progressed to a more advanced stage, where even *thinking* about talking was enough to set it off.

"I don't see why it has to be me," his mother was saying. "Can't you get Atticus to do it?"

"Atticus won't be back from Michigan until tomorrow morning," his father said, "and I imagine he's going to want to sleep when he gets in."

Cough.

"What about Quincy, then?"

"I need Quincy at the Douglas office. Why can't you just wait for Victor to get back on Tuesday and go see your mother then?"

"Because the weather's supposed to turn next week and if there's a blizzard I can't go anywhere."

Cough, cough. Horace reached for his drinking glass.

"George," his mother said, "I just need to be on the road awhile. You know how I get. I've been feeling cooped up lately."

"You've definitely been feeling *something*, and not just lately," his father said. "Is there something you haven't—"

Horace coughed explosively, spraying milk all over his scrambled eggs and a good portion of the table besides.

"Good *Lord*," his mother said.

"Horace," said his father. "You all right?"

No, he wasn't. But it was beginning to sink in that he wasn't allowed to say so.

Horace was one of a rotating crew of boys who ran deliveries after school for Rollo Danvers's corner grocery. He worked three or sometimes four days a week, earning a flat nickel for each delivery run plus whatever he got in tips. Usually he tried to get in quick and snag the first run of the afternoon, but today Horace let the other boys go ahead of him, so he could have some time to finish up a project he'd started in class.

His parents had reached a compromise: His mother was minding the Grand Boulevard office today and tomorrow and would leave for New York tomorrow night, while his father got someone else to fill in on Monday. Meanwhile Horace, seeking to pass a warning to his mom without speaking it aloud, had decided to encode his message in a comic. A straightforward note might have seemed more sensible, but Horace was used to communicating this way.

He didn't have time to do a complete book, so he'd concentrated his effort on a single page-sized illustration. Orithyia Blue was front and center, cruising through open space, distracted by the contents of the as-yet-unfilled thought balloon beside her head. Following close behind her, plain to see if only she'd look in the rearview, were a pair of vicious bounty hunters. Horace had spent a lot of time on the bounty hunters' faces.

The artwork was done. What he still had to figure out was what the two bounty hunters were saying—and what Orithyia was thinking. He sat in the little back room of the grocery, sketchbook on his knees, trying to come up with the right words, always the hardest part for him. His scalp continued to itch, which made it difficult to concentrate. He scratched his head furiously to buy himself a few seconds' relief and lowered the tip of his pencil to Bounty Hunter Noble's dialogue balloon.

Horace.

He looked up, thinking Rollo had spoken to him. But Rollo was at the front counter, talking to a customer on the phone, and there wasn't anyone else in the store right now. Horace looked back down at his sketchbook.

And looked up again. This time it wasn't a sound, but a feeling— the uncomfortable sense of being stared at.

A high shelf on the wall opposite him held rags, brushes, and a variety of cleaning products, including a canister of Old Carolina Metal Polish that Rollo used to shine the cash register. The canister was illustrated with a drawing of a Negro butler, a lesser sibling of Uncle Ben and Aunt Jemima whom Horace had dubbed Cousin Otis. There was something *wrong* about Otis, something vaguely sinister in the geometry of his face that suggested, to Horace at least, that behind his servile grin he was plotting to do away with the family whose silverware he cleaned. Horace had used a sketch of Otis as the basis for Iago, the homicidal android bellhop from *Orithyia Blue #9*.

Today Otis seemed to have a bit more life in his eyes, and his gaze, ordinarily focused on the sparkling teapot in his hands, was directed outward, so that the weight of his grinning malice fell on Horace.

Ridiculous. But once the thought was in Horace's head he couldn't get it out: Otis was eyeballing him.

Horace turned his chair around and scooted it back beneath the overhang of the shelf. He resettled the sketchbook on his lap and tried, again, to concentrate.

He'd just gotten an idea and was touching pencil to paper when he heard a soft scraping on the shelf above him. A trickle of dust sifted down onto the sketchbook, speckling the page. Horace stared at the specks while his scalp crawled with imaginary dust mites. Then the scraping came again, louder. Horace tilted his head back, lifting a hand to shield his eyes, and a bottle of drain cleaner hit him in the chest.

He jumped out of the chair, dropping his sketchbook and pencil on the floor, and flattened himself against the far wall. Up on the shelf, Cousin Otis's canister remained exactly where it had been—though Otis's grin seemed just a bit wider, as if to say, What's got into *you*, boy?

"Horace!" Rollo called. "You're up!"

Outside in the cold, the itch in his scalp turned to an icy prickling that generated waves of free-floating paranoia. As Horace lugged his delivery basket down streets stained pink by the lowering winter sun, he found his anxiety fixating on seemingly random objects, like a playground seesaw whose lengthening shadow resembled that of an emaciated and headless giant.

Rollo had given him four deliveries to make, the last of which was to Mrs. Vandenhoek, a ninety-year-old Dutchwoman who'd been in

Washington Park since back when it was still a mostly white neighborhood. She lived alone in a house surrounded by brick tenements.
Delivering to her was an exercise in patience. She seemed to spend
most of her time upstairs, and when you rang the buzzer, she'd throw
up a window and peer out, not speaking, just squinting suspiciously,
like a nearsighted castle guard deciding whether to lower the draw-
bridge. Eventually she'd come down and unlock what sounded like half
a dozen deadbolts on the front door. She never brought money with her
on the first trip, and no matter the weather she wouldn't let you in the
house. Instead, she'd make you wait outside while she put her groceries away and went to whatever remote hiding place she kept her cash
in (Horace imagined a cellar vault, three or four levels down, guarded
by Dutch-speaking trolls). After you'd had a chance to reflect on the
fleeting nature of youth, she'd return to the door, opening it this time
with the chain on, and hand you what she owed for the groceries, plus
a dime tip.

Today, conscious of the rapidly approaching sunset, Horace broke
protocol and asked Mrs. Vandenhoek if she'd like him to bring her groceries inside for her. She gave him one of her squinty-eyed looks, like
he'd offered to come in and cut her throat, and then carried on as she
always did. As she headed for the vault, Horace put down his basket
and turned nervously in place, scratching his head, until his anxiety
found a new target to seize on: Mrs. Vandenhoek's Christmas display.

The display, which appeared in Mrs. Vandenhoek's yard in late
November and typically remained out all winter, consisted of a
wooden manger scene, warped by time and weather, and a knee-high
statuette of the Dutch Santa, Sinterklaas, who rode a white horse
and had a hat shaped like the pope's. In between Sinterklaas and the
manger was a second statuette that could have been mistaken for
a lawn jockey in Renaissance garb. This was Black Pete, the dark-
skinned elf who worked as Sinterklaas's enforcer, spying on and pun-
ishing bad children.

Horace had learned about Black Pete not from Mrs. Vandenhoek but from Rollo, who'd served in World War II and had traveled around Europe after the fighting ended. In December 1945 he'd been in Amsterdam, and had awakened one morning to find the streets swarming with men in blackface. "They were hitching rides on military jeeps," Rollo said, "so it's like the Army of Minstrelsy invaded."

Mrs. Vandenhoek's Black Pete looked like an actual Negro, not a minstrel player, but he also, Horace noted now, looked a lot like Cousin Otis, around the eyes and mouth at least. After trying and failing to unsee the resemblance, Horace shifted position until his view of Black Pete's face was eclipsed by the head of Sinterklaas's horse.

A minute passed. Horace stamped his feet and blew into his hands and scratched his head and wished Mrs. Vandenhoek would hurry up.

Then he felt eyes on him again. He looked at the Christmas display and saw that Black Pete had come out from behind the horse. Horace tried to convince himself that *he* was the one who had moved, but the problem with that was that Pete hadn't just shifted back into view, he'd also *turned*, so that instead of facing the street as he normally did he was now staring—and grinning—directly at Horace.

The sudden blare of a car horn made Horace look away. It was only for a second, but when he looked back, Black Pete wasn't there anymore.

The prickling on his scalp crept down to the back of his neck. He started to turn around, and something that felt very much like a tiny leg hooked him behind the ankle; he toppled over backwards and sprawled, shrieking, on Mrs. Vandenhoek's front walk. The front door of the house popped open and there stood Mrs. Vandenhoek, squinting angrily, her fist clenched tight around the grocery money and the dime tip that, Horace strongly suspected, he wasn't going to get now.

As for Black Pete, he was back beside Sinterklaas, his face all innocence except for the faint hint of a smirk that only Horace's eyes could see.

⊰╫⊱

On Saturday, Curtis and Neville brought the devil doll to the church.

The Mount Zion Church had been a synagogue before the neighborhood changed, and before that it had been a meetinghouse for some austere denomination of white Protestants. The building lacked a steeple but it did have an attic, accessible through a steep, narrow stairway behind the altar. Too low-ceilinged to be useful for anything but storage, for years the attic had been abandoned altogether, until Reggie Oxbow prevailed upon his father to let him turn it into a clubhouse.

The attic was Reggie's personal fiefdom, but his lordship came at a price: He was expected to look after his little sister, June, whom everyone called Bug. Bug and her friends were allotted a small portion of the attic near the stairs, while the rest of the space was reserved exclusively for Reggie and his friends.

They played a lot of games up there. Mrs. Oxbow ran the charity shop in the church basement, and Reggie and Bug got first crack at any toy donations. Reggie had amassed an impressive collection of used board games. The boys made up games, too, scrounging pieces from duplicate Monopoly sets.

For the past few weeks they'd been obsessed with a game they called Kreeg. Kreeg was short for *Das Kriegsspiel*, "The War Game." Horace had found the manual in a box of foreign-language books at Thurber Lang's bookstore. The text was in German, but from the illustrations he'd deduced that this was a set of rules for reenacting the campaigns of Napoleon with dice and tin soldiers.

Horace had enlisted Rollo, who still had some German from his own time at war, for help with the translation. He took the translated rules to Reggie, who was initially cool to the idea, saying, without irony, that he wasn't interested in playing Napoleon. It was Curtis who'd turned Reggie around, by pointing out that they could keep the bones of the rules intact while changing the game's subject matter. And so the war horses and ships of Europe became thoats and fliers of Barsoom, and the Continental Powers became various races of Martian; and Kreeg was born. Their first game had the Red Martians under John Carter defending the twin cities of Greater and Lesser Helium against a combined force of Green, Yellow, and Black Martians. It was a lopsided battle, but it was also a big hit, especially with Reggie, whose Green Martians spearheaded a crushing victory over Neville's Reds.

That Saturday when Reggie and Horace came up the stairs to the attic, they found Neville and Curtis putting the finishing touches on a new scenario. Set up on and around the cardboard boxes they used to represent the Martian terrain was a combined force of plastic army men, toy vehicles, chess pieces, checkers, and Monopoly and Parcheesi tokens. Ordinarily these would have been broken out into separate, opposing battle groups, but today they were united against a singular foe, an ugly black doll that Horace had never seen before.

"What the heck is *that*?" Reggie said.

Behind him, Bug looked up from a solitaire game of Chutes and Ladders and intoned solemnly: "It's the *devil*."

According to the box in which it had come (and on which it now stood, like a splay-toed statue on its pedestal) it was a Fully Poseable African Pygmy Devil Doll: a midget witch doctor, eighteen inches in height, its oversized head accounting for at least a third of that. The doll's hair was woven into short braids weighted with bits of bone, and another, larger bone was shoved sideways through its nose. Its eyes were deep-set under woolly brows, and its mouth was open in a thick-lipped, toothy leer from which a sharp red tongue protruded. Its bare arms and chest were covered in ritual tribal scars. A miniature skull hung on a thong around its neck, and another capped the medicine stick it wielded; and dangling like a pocket watch from the belt of its grass skirt was a tiny shrunken head.

It was hideous to the point of being comical, but in the manner of a clown, that might not be so funny after dark. Indeed, Horace's first thought on seeing it was to imagine what it would be like to find the doll hiding under his bed or lurking in a closet; probably not funny at all, in that circumstance.

"Isn't it cool?" Neville said. "I dug it out of a trash bin behind the thrift store near my house. Didn't cost me a nickel."

"What'd you bring it *here* for?" Reggie said. "You forget this is a house of God?"

Neville rolled his eyes. "Church is *downstairs*," he said.

"Besides," added Curtis, "this isn't really a devil. It's a robot."

"A what, now?"

"A robot," Neville said. "Built by Ras Thavas"—the mad Red Martian scientist—"to fool the Green Martians. It's made up to look like a giant Martian tribal spirit, but Tars Tarkas figures out it's really a machine, and he gets John Carter to round up all the other Martians to go fight it."

"It's got 350 battle points," Curtis explained. "So it's real hard to kill. And it's got all kinds of special weapons—"

"—like disintegrator rays out its eyes," said Neville. "And a *death stomp*."

"What are you talking about?" Reggie said.

"It's a battle," Curtis said. "A new one. We made it up."

"No, no, no . . . We're not doing any *new* battle today, especially not with some devil doll. We're doing the Siege of Helium."

"We've *done* that one. Like a million times."

"Yeah, because it's fun."

"Fun for you, maybe," said Neville. "I'm sick of it."

"Yeah, Reggie," Curtis said. "Let's try this today. It'll be good, you'll see."

"Nah. No way." Reggie stepped onto the battlefield, scattering Martian infantry with his own version of the death stomp. "Let's get this set up for Helium. And get that devil doll out of here."

"Uh-*uh*," said Neville, and then he and Reggie were bumping chests and yelling while Curtis tried to separate them. Ordinarily

Horace would have been in the middle too, but not this time. He was too busy staring at the devil doll.

Neville had nudged the devil doll's box in passing and the doll had tottered and nearly fallen over. It didn't just not fall, though; it *caught itself*, ankles and knees flexing beneath the grass skirt to bring it back into balance. As the boys shouted at each other, the doll swiveled its big head around to glare at Neville's back, and raised its medicine stick as if to hex him.

"Hey guys," Horace tried to say, "the devil doll's *moving*," but what came out of his mouth was a wordless wheeze. The doll heard him, though, and swung its head back his way. As it locked gazes with him, he saw what looked like sparks dancing around its eyes, precursor to a disintegrator blast, perhaps; and then his scalp was burning again, worse than ever, and his lungs were burning too.

Curtis was the first to notice his desperate whoops for breath. "Horace?" he said, while Horace clutched at the roof beam above his head and with his other hand tried to point, thinking, Look, look, *look at the doll* . . . But none of them would look, except maybe Bug, who he thought he heard gasp right before he passed out.

Then the devil doll wagged its medicine stick and its eyes flashed. Horace's own eyes rolled up in his head and he swooned, crushing armies beneath him as he fell.

He woke up in a hospital bed. It was dark outside the window and the only light on in the room was a small bedside reading lamp. Horace, at first seeing only the dim ceiling above him, feared he was back in the supermarket with the heads. He sat up gasping.

"Easy," his father said. He leaned over from his chair beside the bed and squeezed Horace's shoulder. "How you feeling?"

"Weird." His lungs felt raw, but he touched the top of his head, as if the true discomfort were there. "What happened?"

"You choked up and nearly stopped breathing," George said. "Reverend Oxbow decided not to wait for an ambulance. He threw you in his car and got you to the emergency room double quick."

Horace nodded, flashes of memory coming to him now: of being carried semiconscious through the cold; of concerned faces leaning over him; of a needle going into his arm and a mask being placed over his face. Then he remembered the devil doll.

"Horace?" his father said, alarmed by the expression on his face. "Horace, you OK?" He reached for the buzzer to call the nurse.

"I'm all right!" Horace said. "I'm sorry . . . I just . . . I'm OK."

"You sure?"

Horace made himself nod. Then he asked: "Where's Mom?"

"On her way to New York."

"Already?" He started to get agitated again. "I thought she wasn't leaving till tonight."

"She wasn't. But this morning we had another conversation, about whether the Grand Boulevard office *really* needed to be open today . . . She'd been gone about an hour when the Reverend called me."

"Did she take the drawing I made for her?"

"I don't know. I didn't pay attention to her packing."

"We should go home," Horace said. "We should be there in case she calls."

"Whoah!" George put a hand on Horace's shoulder again. "Doctor wants you to stay here overnight, just in case."

"But if Mom tries to call us . . ."

"She's not going to call tonight. You know your mother: It's when the phone *does* ring that you got to worry. She'll check in tomorrow sometime, and you'll be home by then."

Someone went running by in the hall outside. Horace turned his head at the sound. "You're staying here with me tonight, right?"

"Yeah, of course . . . Horace? You sure you're OK?"

"I'm fine," Horace said, continuing to stare into the hallway. "I'm just tired."

He went home in the morning. Curtis and Neville came by to see him after church. They brought a get-well card from the Oxbows and a bag of Mrs. Oxbow's ginger cookies. "Reggie would have come over too," Curtis said, "but he's grounded."

"Grounded for what?" Horace asked.

"He hit Bug and knocked her down the stairs," Neville said. "She's OK, just a little bruised up, but the Reverend was not happy."

"What did Reggie do that for?"

"Bug wrecked the clubhouse," Curtis explained. "Neville and I took a look, and we could see why Reggie was mad: It's like she went crazy up there. *All* the games dumped out on the floor, kicked around and stomped on. She even busted out one of the windows."

"That doesn't sound like Bug," Horace said.

"Yeah, she says she didn't do it. Or any of her friends, either. But who else?"

"Of course, Bug might not have done *all* of it herself," Neville added.

"What do you mean?"

"The devil doll," Curtis said. "It's gone. Reggie says Bug stole it."

"But that's not what happened," said Neville. "Reggie just didn't want to play that battle. He must have got rid of the doll after we left yesterday, then decided to blame it on Bug after what she did."

They stayed for an hour. Horace spent the rest of the day reading and from time to time getting up to stare out the front window at the street below.

That night his mother called from New York. Her trip had been un-eventful. She *had* taken the comic that Horace had made for her, though she hadn't looked at it yet—but she'd read it on her way home, she promised. She felt guilty for not being there when Horace was sick, and said she was thinking of cutting her trip short. Horace was torn on that, part of him wanting her to come home right away, another part wanting her to stay where she was safe. "I'm OK," he told her. "Don't worry about me."

It wasn't even eight o'clock yet when he got off the phone, but his father told him it was time for bed—he needed his rest. Horace got into bed but he didn't sleep. He lay in the dark with his eyes open until he heard his father go into his own room. Then he got up, quietly, and went to check that both the kitchen door and the front door were locked and bolted. He went to the parlor window and looked down at the street again. He looked for a long time.

Eventually Horace slept, but he dreamed that he didn't—that he just went on checking doors and windows all night. By the time morning arrived he was exhausted. His father, seeing how tired he was at breakfast, offered to let him stay home from school. But Horace thought it would be more restful to be out among other people than home alone; he told his dad he wanted to go.

"All right, but you take it easy," George said. "No deliveries today. You come straight home."

At school he tried to talk to Reggie about the devil doll. But Neville and Curtis must have gotten to Reggie first, because he was in no mood to discuss it. "It wasn't me, it was Bug!" he said. "Now leave me alone!"

That evening his father had a Freemasons meeting to go to. "I was thinking of skipping it," George explained, "but your uncle Montrose has something he wants to talk to me about. We might go out, after. I got Ruby coming to stay with you while I'm gone. I don't want any arguments—I know you think you're too old for a sitter, but I don't want you by yourself tonight."

Horace didn't make any arguments.

Ruby came over at seven. Horace was glad to see her, and not just because he didn't want to be alone. He'd always liked Ruby. He felt like she was one of the few adults other than his parents who took his artistic ambitions seriously, neither dismissing them as fantasy nor offering false assurances. Making a living at comic books would be hard, she said, and he might well fail, but if it was what he wanted to do with his life, he shouldn't let anyone talk him out of trying.

They sat in the kitchen and drank hot chocolate and played Scrabble. Ordinarily this would have been heaven, but Horace couldn't stay focused. He kept getting up to go check the front door and look out the parlor window, and the third time he was gone long enough that Ruby called out to make sure he was OK.

He came back to the kitchen and managed to sit still for ten whole minutes. But then he thought he heard something out on the fire escape. He got up and opened the door and poked his head out. There was nothing there. Nothing in the alley, either—not that he could see.

When he sat back down at the table, Ruby said, "What's got into you?"

Horace looked at her. His lungs were fine right now, but he could feel the asthma just waiting to rise up and stifle him the minute he said the wrong thing.

"Horace? Is there something you want to tell me?"

Horace breathed in, and breathed out. He shook his head.

He looked down at his tile rack:

OELCZPI

He shuffled the letters around:

POLICEZ

He breathed in, and breathed out. He looked up and saw that Ruby was still watching him and without pausing to think about it he said, "Ruby can I tell you a secret?" His lungs tightened up at the end of "secret" but the question was already out.

"Sure," Ruby said. "You can tell me a secret. You can tell me anything you like."

For the next thirty seconds or so he couldn't do anything but concentrate on getting air. Then his lungs unclenched, but not all the way, and Horace knew if it happened again it would be much worse.

He kept his tongue still. He removed the z from the tile rack and turned the rack around so Ruby could see the other letters.

"That's what your secret's about?" Ruby said.

Horace breathed in, and breathed out. He nodded.

Ruby lowered her voice and asked: "You worried somebody might be listening?"

Horace shook his head.

"But you don't want to say it out loud?"

Horace nodded.

"All right . . ." Ruby dumped her own tile rack on the board, and dumped out the tile bag, too. Then she shoved all the letters over to Horace's side of the table. "Spell it out for me."

It didn't take very long. He spelled out DETECTIVES and ASKED ME and MOMS XMAS TRIP and WISCONSIN and a few more words and phrases, but as soon as he got to BRAITHWHITE they switched to a Twenty Questions format, with Ruby, who had always been a good guesser, seeming to know exactly what to ask. Horace nodded fervently, shook his head a few times, did a couple more spell-outs, and then, the bulk of the secret having been spilled, he felt his asthma back off and found that he could speak. He filled in a few more details.

He didn't tell her everything. He told her about Captain Lancaster rubbing spittle on his head and some of how that had affected him, but when he came to the part about Cousin Otis, and Black Pete, and especially the devil doll, Horace balked, thinking it would sound too crazy. So instead he just said that in addition to his asthma problems, he'd been "feeling strange" and "having weird dreams."

"You believe me, right?"

"Yeah, of course I believe you," Ruby said.

Horace slumped with relief. Then he said: "What am I supposed to do? I want to help Mom, but I don't even know what this is about."

"You just sit tight," Ruby told him. "I know someone who can help."

"You do? Who?"

But Ruby shook her head. "That's going to have to stay between me and me, for now. When's your mom get back from her trip?"

"She hadn't decided, last I talked to her. Maybe tomorrow night."

"All right, so you don't need to worry about her," Ruby said. "You just keep your own head down. Once your daddy comes home, I'll get in touch with my . . . friend. I should be able to reach him tonight, but if not, I'll be talking to him tomorrow for sure."

"And he'll know what to do?"

"He'd better," Ruby said. "You just be careful going to school tomorrow, and after—"

"After, I got work," Horace said. "I had to skip today, but I promised Rollo I'd be in tomorrow."

"All right, tell you what," Ruby said. "You go to Rollo's, and I'll meet you there. But you keep your eyes peeled on the street, Horace, and if you see those two detectives coming, or that Captain Lancaster, you run the other way. Don't worry about getting in trouble, either—just do what you need to to get clear and we'll sort it out later. OK?"

"OK." Suddenly Horace was blinking back tears. "Thank you, Ruby. I've been so scared about this, and I didn't know what I was going to—"

This time they both heard it: a thump like a heavy footfall, out on the fire escape. Ruby put a finger to her lips and pointed at the switch on the wall behind Horace. He got up and flipped the lights off. Ruby rose silently and went to the sink, leaning forward to look out between the burglar bars that covered the window.

"What is it?" Horace whispered, but Ruby gestured for silence. She grabbed a knife from the drying rack and stepped to the door, at the same time motioning Horace back into the hall. She opened the door and went out, and Horace covered his face with his hands. But after a moment Ruby came back inside, shaking her head.

"Nobody," she said. "Nobody there."

By six thirty the next evening Ruby still hadn't showed.

Horace had finished his last delivery run twenty minutes ago. Rollo told him he could go home, but he lingered instead, loitering at the front of the store so he wouldn't have to play stare-down games with Cousin Otis—and so he could keep an eye on the sidewalk. Coming back from this last run, he'd caught a glimpse of a small black creature— something that might have been a cat, or a large rat—darting underneath a parked car half a block behind him. Now, staring out the window, he found himself fixated on a patch of darkness beneath a blown streetlamp across the way.

"You plan to keep fidgeting like that?" Rollo said, looking up from the Zane Grey novel he was trying to read.

"Sorry," Horace said. "Can I use the phone, Rollo?"

"Long as it's local."

He dialed the number Ruby had given him but it just rang and rang. Then on impulse he called home, but there was no answer there, either. He tried the travel office number and got the after-hours answering service. "No message," he told the woman.

He hung up and stood gnawing his lower lip. His father had mentioned that he might go run an errand after work. Horace hadn't thought much of it, because he'd assumed Ruby would be with him, but now his imagination went to work, and he pictured going up the stairs to the dark apartment, alone.

The phone rang, making Horace jump.

Rollo gave him a look and picked up. "Danvers Grocery, Rollo Danvers speaking." He listened a moment and reached for his order pad. "Yeah, we deliver there," he said, scribbling down an address. "Is that a house or an apartment? . . . OK . . . And that's all you want? . . . Sure, no problem . . . And what name is this order for? . . . Hello?" Rollo frowned, then shrugged and hung up.

Rollo tore the top sheet from the pad and reached behind him to get a pack of Chesterfields. He slid the paper and the smokes across the counter. "Delivery over on South Park Way," he said. "You can just go home, after, and bring me the money tomorrow."

Horace stared at the cigarette pack, his mind on the dead streetlamp outside. "I don't know, Rollo," he said.

"You don't know *what?*" said Rollo.

Horace raised a hand to his head. Scratched. "Nothing," he said.

Fifteen minutes later, he stopped beneath a streetlamp to check the address on the order sheet. To his left, across a two-lane avenue, stretched the 370-acre park that gave the Washington Park neighborhood its name. A few sparks of illumination were visible back among the trees, but this section of the park was mostly unlit, and the impression was that of standing by the shore of a vast dark lake.

It wasn't the park he was concerned about. As he returned the paper to his coat pocket, he looked back along the sidewalk in the direction he had come, paying particular attention to the curbline beside the parked cars.

Like the last dozen times he'd checked, there was nothing to see.

He continued walking south, scanning a row of narrow townhouses. At the end of the row he found the number he was looking for. It was spray-painted on a plywood slab that had been used to board up the house's front door. Horace stared at the CONDEMNED notice pasted to the wooden slab and thought: Maybe Rollo wrote the number down wrong. But the prickling of his scalp told a different story.

With a glassy *pop!* like a flashbulb exploding, the streetlamp he'd just been standing under blew out. Horace turned towards the sound, his gaze going automatically to the curb by the foot of the lamppost. Nothing there. But then he lifted his head and raised his hand and scratched, and for a moment his vision blurred; and when it cleared again, he saw a red eye glowing in the darkness.

No, not an eye: a cigar. Captain Lancaster was standing beneath the lamppost, his brutish face wreathed in smoke and illuminated by the glowing coal. There was something unreal about him, a waxwork stiffness that made him seem less a man than a mannequin. But he was no less frightening, for that.

Run the other way, Horace heard Ruby say. He turned around and the streetlamp on the corner to the south went out. As if the light had switched on rather than off, another figure sprang into view: Detective Noble.

Horace.

He jerked his head to the right. Detective Burke had materialized on the front steps of the condemned townhouse, almost close enough to touch. Like Lancaster he seemed posed, stiff as a scarecrow, but there was life in his eyes and he was grinning Cousin Otis's grin, the expression even more disturbing on a white face.

Horace retreated in the only direction he could. As he backpedaled into the street, headlights washed over him, but his eyes remained fixed on Detective Burke. Then the driver of the car speeding towards him leaned on the horn, and Horace whirled and leapt out of the way, his book bag flying up behind him. The car, which never slowed, clipped the book bag in passing, sending it whipping around to smack Horace in the face. He staggered across the far curb and into the park.

From under the trees he looked back. The captain and the two detectives had been swallowed up by the gloom, and Horace could see nothing moving on the darkened street. But there was definitely *something* there, making furtive noises in the darkness. Coming closer.

He turned and sprinted deeper into the park, making for a spark of lamplight up ahead beyond the trees. By the time he reached it he was winded and overheating. Horace shrugged off his book bag and leaned against the lamppost, which cast its icy white light over a frozen playground set. He unzipped the front of his coat. He breathed in, and breathed out, hearing nothing now but the sound of his own labored respiration.

With a creak of wood and metal one of the seesaws moved, an invisible weight pushing one end down, a clump of snow sliding off the other end as it rose up. As Horace came off the lamppost, a wind he couldn't feel set the swings moving.

The roundabout was next. With a groan it started turning on its own, slowly at first, shedding chunks of snow and ice as it picked up speed. Horace stared at it, transfixed by the moving shadows of the metal grab bars.

Something landed with a thump on the far side of the rotating platform. Horace watched the devil doll come riding around, its little hand clinging to one of the grab bars. As it jumped down, he took a step backwards and tripped over his book bag.

He fell on his back in the snow and for a moment he was eye level with the devil doll now running straight towards him. He rolled and kicked away the book bag and scrambled back up.

A footpath ran beside the playground and on the other side of it was a little cement blockhouse marked RESTROOM. Horace made a dash for it, praying that it wouldn't be locked. It wasn't, but when he got inside, he discovered that that was because the lock was broken. He put his back against the door and braced himself, at the same time casting around wildly for a weapon or a way out.

He found neither. The restroom was a windowless concrete cell, just large enough for a sink, a urinal, and a toilet stall. It was lit by a yellow incandescent bulb set above the empty mirror frame over the sink. The bulb flickered as Horace looked at it.

A heavy blow struck the door at Horace's back. He dug in his heels. More blows fell, making the door jump in its frame, but Horace held firm and it didn't open. There was a pause.

What came next was a light scratching: A small sound, but like fingernails on a blackboard it sent shivers up his spine and set his scalp crawling. Horace gritted his teeth and shut his eyes. Not getting in! he thought.

The scratching stopped. He opened his eyes.

There was someone in the toilet stall. Beneath the wooden partition Horace could see a pair of men's shoes and a frayed pair of trouser cuffs. *"Hey kid,"* a voice said, raspy and low, *"you want to make a dollar?"*

No way, Horace thought, uh-uh, but the stall door creaked open and there stood the dice man. His five o'clock shadow had become a patchy beard, matted with filth; his hair and clothes were filthy too, and he reeked, as if he'd crawled up a sewer pipe to get in here. His skin was red and cracked and covered in scabs. "Let me rub your head," he said, holding out a diseased hand. "For luck."

Horace shrank back. "You're not real," he wheezed, but the dice man took a shambling step towards him, and Horace rounded in a panic and tried to push out through the door, forgetting that it opened inward. Then he heard another step behind him, felt scabby fingers brush his scalp, and he yanked the door wide and bolted into the open air.

He was barely through the doorway when his feet tangled and he belly-flopped. He banged his chin on a hard patch of ice, sending sparks shooting up behind his eyes. More ice and snow pressed against his sweat-soaked shirt, instantly sucking the heat from his body. But it wasn't just the cold ground that froze him: As his vision cleared, he found himself practically nose to nose with the devil doll.

In the stark white lamplight its skin looked pale, and its tribal scars stood out in sharp relief; the bones in its hair gleamed. Its eyes glowed a dull red, and as it caught and held Horace's gaze it began to sway in a sort of dance, a hypnotic witch-doctor dance.

Get up, Horace told himself. It's just a stupid doll, you're a *giant* compared to it . . . Get up! Get up and stomp on it! But he couldn't move, not a muscle, and he wondered whether the devil doll would stop his heart now, or just hold him like this until he froze for real.

Then the doll raised its medicine stick, holding it overhand with the bottom end pointed at Horace's face like the tip of a stabbing spear. Horace felt that twitch start in his eye again. He thought of Pirate Joe, sitting half-blind in a car wreck in the land of Jim Crow, his mother dying beside him and help not coming—not in time, not in that country. A despair colder than the ground on which he lay engulfed him, but he felt a hot spark of anger too, at the unfairness of it, and as rage displaced his fear, the spell holding him weakened. In that same moment he became aware of the chunk of broken brick under his right hand.

The devil doll danced towards him, jabbing at his eyes, and Horace brought his arm around and smashed it with the brick. The doll went flying and the spell was broken. Horace sprang to his feet, clutching the brick and ready to do battle; but the doll, already recovered, looked up at him and *hissed*. Horace's anger turned to ash and his courage blew away like smoke.

And then he was running again, racing down the footpath with the devil at his heels. He could feel his lungs puffing up and he knew where this was going, but he couldn't stop.

The path curved sharply and Horace saw streetlights up ahead. He'd looped back around to South Park Way. Thoughts of home, where his father and perhaps even his mother would be waiting by now, filled him briefly with hope.

But another figure loomed in the path: a white policeman. Not a captain or a detective, but a uniformed beat cop, his beady eyes fixed on Horace running towards him. "Hey, champ," the policeman said. "Where are you going so fast?"

Not real, Horace thought, and kept running. But the policeman stuck out a foot and sent Horace sprawling.

"I *said*, where's the fire?" The policeman stood over him as he lay gasping on the path. "Where you running from, huh? What did you do?"

Horace flopped onto his side. He saw the devil doll, standing in a circle of lamplight back at the bend in the path. He tried to point, but the policeman grabbed him roughly under the arms, lifting him up and slamming him back against a tree. "What are you running from?" the policeman demanded. Horace, unable even to wheeze, now, raised his arm and gestured feebly, thinking, Look, look, *look* . . . But the policeman went on asking the same question, getting more and more angry.

The doll tilted its head to one side, and Horace saw the policeman tilt *his* head to one side. The doll lowered a hand to grip the shrunken head dangling from its skirt; the policeman dropped a hand to his belt and unsnapped his gun holster. Then Horace's full attention was on the policeman as he drew his revolver and cocked it.

"I'm going to ask you one more time," the policeman said. "What did you do?"

Horace's mouth opened and closed, uselessly.

The muzzle of the revolver became the center of the world.

Then the scene seemed to telescope, as an invisible cable attached to the policeman's back yanked him into the air and sent him flying into the trees on the far side of the path. Horace slid to the ground. He still couldn't breathe, and he wondered, a blackness darker than night boiling across his vision, whether he'd been shot after all, if this was what that felt like.

A warm hand pressed against the center of his chest and his lungs unclenched. He jerked upright, drawing in air in a ragged gasp. Another white man was crouched beside him, a young man in a suit.

"Easy," the man said. "Easy, now . . . Sorry to put you through this, but I needed to lure it out into the open." Shifting his hand slightly, he patted the cigarettes in Horace's coat pocket. "Hang on to these for me."

He stood up, leaving Horace at the base of the tree still sucking in fresh oxygen, and turned towards the devil doll, which had come down the path and now stood less than a dozen feet away. The doll had its arms up and was waving its medicine stick menacingly, but the white man seemed more amused than threatened. He bent down and picked up the doll by its braids and held it suspended in the air with its legs kicking.

"Fascinating," Caleb Braithwhite said, and then gripping the devil doll with both hands, he ripped off its head.

Once again, Horace was made to hold still while a white man massaged his scalp. At least he was in more pleasant surroundings this time: at home, in the kitchen, with his dad sitting at the table beside him and his mom standing by the sink with her arms crossed.

Caleb Braithwhite finished his examination and sat back. "It's a mark, all right. Surprisingly high level of artistry, too."

Horace's mother didn't care about the level of artistry. "Someone put a mark on our son's head?"

Braithwhite nodded. "There's a branch of the art that deals with bringing inanimate objects to life: dolls, statues, corpses occasionally. It's not one of my specialties, but I know Hiram Winthrop made a study of it. It looks like Lancaster has, too. This is more than I would have expected of him."

"I don't understand," Horace's father said. "What's any of that got to do with a mark?"

"The mark is a catalyst," Braithwhite explained. "You could think of it as a kind of opportunistic curse: It uses the subject's own senses and emotions to find an object to animate—ideally, something the subject is afraid of."

"And what it animates tries to kill you?" Horace said.

"That's the general idea. You're lucky Lancaster made the mark with saliva," Braithwhite told him. "Marks made in blood are much more potent, and almost impossible to remove." He reached into the bag he'd brought with him and pulled out a silver flask. He uncapped it and soaked a handkerchief with the contents; a sharp vinegary smell filled the room. "This will sting a bit." He leaned forward and scrubbed Horace's scalp with the handkerchief. It *did* sting, but it also made Horace feel better; he breathed easier than he had in days.

"But why?" George wanted to know. "Why would Lancaster go after Horace?"

"It's his way of sending me a message," Braithwhite said. "Lancaster thinks I'm planning to betray him, and he's right—but as it happens, the particular incident that set him off had nothing to do with me." He glanced over at Horace's mom. "On Solstice Night, your wife trespassed on a piece of property controlled by an Ancient Dawn lodge in Wisconsin. Apparently Lancaster thinks she was acting on my orders."

George turned to his wife. "Hippolyta? What's he talking about? What did you do?"

"Don't you look at *me* that way, George Berry," Hippolyta replied. "How long have you known Mr. Braithwhite here and not said anything?"

George opened his mouth, and shut it again. "We'll talk about this later," he said.

"Yes," Hippolyta said, "we will."

"The point is," said Braithwhite, "Lancaster thought I was making a move. When he couldn't get your son to act as his spy, he decided to kill him—in part to punish your wife for conspiring with me, but more as a way of letting me know that he was on to me. Which is good news."

"How do you figure that?" George said.

"If Lancaster were really worried, he'd have tried to kill me, not your son. The fact that he's playing games means he thinks he can still dominate me." Braithwhite smiled. "He's made the same mistake about me that Hiram Winthrop made about my father. He's underestimated me."

"So now what? You're going to kill him?"

"Not me," Braithwhite said. "Us."

THE MARK OF CAIN

They gathered at the Freemasons' temple in the late evening, under cover of a light but driving snowfall. George and Hippolyta and Horace were the first to arrive. His parents' attitude was solemn, but Horace could barely contain his excitement at being admitted to the secret meeting room; he gazed in wonder at the two Solomonic pillars, the altar with its copies of the Holy Bible and the Koran laid out side-by-side, and, sitting forgotten and gathering dust in a corner, the scale model of King Tut's tomb. "Is this a game?" Horace asked, of the model. But his father didn't answer and his mother said only, "Remember what I told you."

Pirate Joe and Abdullah came next, followed by Mortimer Dupree. Atticus, Letitia, and Montrose showed up together a few minutes later. Last to arrive was Quincy Brown, the lodge door-warden, who took up his post outside the room, armed with a sword. The sword was ceremonial, but Quincy, who'd been captain of the saber team at Wayne State, could handle himself quite well with it—and tonight he had a pistol in his pocket for good measure.

The others sat facing one another beneath the pillars of Solomon, like wizards embarking on a ritual whose outcome was far from certain.

Montrose went first. He told the story of how Caleb Braithwhite had contacted him last June, and how he'd been lured to Ardham and chained up in a cellar. Then Atticus took up the tale, describing his own journey to Ardham with George and Letitia, and what happened when they got there.

When Samuel Braithwhite and the Sons of Adam had been reduced once more to piles of ash, Letitia took her turn, explaining, with no small amount of pride, how she'd come to be the landlady of a haunted house. Her mood soured when Atticus added his coda about who the Winthrop House really belonged to; Letitia had learned the truth herself less than twenty-four hours ago, and she was still upset that Atticus hadn't told her sooner.

She wasn't the only one angry at having been kept in the dark. Hippolyta fumed as George recapped the Freemasons' trip to the museum to retrieve *The Book of Names*. But she was revenged a few moments later with the telling of her own story, which no one but George had heard yet; he wisely kept quiet as she told it, leaving it to Montrose to ask, "You went there alone in the middle of the night?" while Horace said, awestruck, "Another planet? For *real*?"

Though reluctant even now to betray her vow of silence to Ida, Hippolyta told them everything, for that was the point of this exercise: to share all, as any detail might prove important. In the end, the matter of most immediate concern to her listeners was not the old woman stranded at the far end of the universe, but the five dead white men.

"Holy God," Mortimer Dupree said.

"Yeah," George added, breaking his silence. "You can see why Lancaster might be feeling paranoid, if he thought Braithwhite was behind that."

"It's not just paranoia, though," said Montrose. "Braithwhite really is double-dealing . . ." And he told the story of the trip to the Narrow house. Hippolyta took the news of Pearl and Henry junior's fate hard. "That poor child," she said. "Poor Ida."

Then it was Horace's turn. As he described how he'd been cursed, stalked, and nearly killed, his excitement once more got the better of him, so that he sounded more thrilled than terrorized by the experience. But the adults' expressions were grave.

George finished up, recounting how Braithwhite had cleansed Horace of Lancaster's mark, and what he'd said afterwards. "So that's where we're at," George concluded. "Braithwhite's going to war, and he wants our help."

"He doesn't *want* our help," Montrose corrected his brother. "He *expects* it. Braithwhite thinks he owns us."

"Yeah," Atticus said, "and even if he does beat Lancaster, that won't be the end of it. He *says* he'll leave us alone, after, but . . ."

"Has he told you what his plan is?" Abdullah asked.

"Not yet," George said. "But he's sending someone, to give us our marching orders." He checked his watch. "They should be here any minute."

Soon enough, there was a knock at the door. George answered it, and Quincy stuck his head in and whispered something that made George say, *"Who?"* Then George stepped back, opening the door wide to admit Braithwhite's messenger.

"Ruby?" Letitia said.

So they listened to one more story. Ruby described how she'd lost her job, and how on New Year's Eve, seemingly by chance, she'd met Caleb Braithwhite.

"And you went off nightclubbing with him?" Letitia said. "That's why you didn't come to my party?"

Ruby gave her sister a look. "Tell me again how *God* wanted you to have the Winthrop House," she said.

Ruby's account of the rest of New Year's Eve was heavily abridged and revised. There was dancing and some drinking, but no kissing, and while the night culminated in a job offer, there was no magic potion. "He said he worked for the government and he was in Chicago on a special assignment. He said he needed a housekeeper for this safe house he'd set up—someone who'd be discreet and not mention his name to anyone." Ruby shrugged. "It was work, and it paid well."

Her description of the job itself was as close to the truth as she could make it without mentioning Hillary. She even told them about some of the errands Braithwhite had sent her on, though in this version of the story they were "patriotic missions" whose significance Ruby was left to guess at. "The men he had me spy on looked like gangsters, so I figured he must be with the FBI." She finally did get suspicious, though, after he started asking her questions about Letitia. And then a few days ago, while Braith-white was out of the house, she found the basement door unlocked . . .

Her description of Braithwhite's workshop omitted the glass coffin in favor of a vague assortment of strange devices that seemed more suited to devil worship than government work. "There were files, too," Ruby said. "He had a folder with Atticus's name on it, and another that was all about the Winthrop House. I'd only started to look at that when Braithwhite came back and caught me. Scared me near to death, but he wasn't mad. He said he'd be needing more of my help soon, and it'd be easier if I knew the truth . . . So he sat me down and told me his story, his *real* story. It sounded crazy, like something out of one of Horace's comic books, but he got me to believe it." She looked around the circle. "I guess you all believe it, too."

"So you know what he's up to?" George said. "What he wants from us?"

Ruby nodded. "Right about now, he's on the phone to Captain Lancaster, setting up a parley to work out their differences. There's a country club up in Forest Glen that belongs to Lancaster's coven, and Braithwhite's going to offer to meet there, tomorrow night. He wants to bring Atticus with him."

"What for?" Atticus said.

"That's easy," said Montrose. "You're the peace offering."

Ruby nodded again. "Something like that." She looked at Atticus. "He's not really going to offer you up, though. That's just a ruse, to get Lancaster to lower his guard a little . . . And that's where the rest of you come in." She opened her purse and pointed to the altar. "May I?"

George and Abdullah moved the holy books aside. Ruby unfolded a map that showed the layout of Lancaster's club and the surrounding grounds. For the next ten minutes, she explained Braithwhite's plan.

"That's a lot of moving parts," Pirate Joe said when she'd finished.

"Yeah, and if one thing goes wrong, we're all cooked," said Mortimer.

"We're cooked either way," Abdullah pointed out. "Even if the plan works, all we've done is give Braithwhite a clear field."

"I think it will work," Ruby said. "I haven't known Mr. Braithwhite as long as some of you, but I've seen enough of him to know he's good at getting what he wants. But I've also seen enough to know that what he wants, can't be good. He's likable enough, for a white man. But he's—"

"Evil," Montrose said.

"Yeah," Ruby said. She gestured at the map. "So you're right, this isn't enough. We need to get rid of him, too."

"I think we'd all be on board with that," George said, "if we knew how. The problem is that damn immunity of his. If we could get around that . . ."

"I don't know how to get around it," said Ruby. "But I know where it comes from." She told them about Braithwhite's mark.

Letitia's eyes narrowed. "A tattoo on his chest?" she said. "How would you know about *that*?"

"I'm the help, not a big-shot landlady," Ruby replied. "You think he's going to throw a shirt on just because I come in the room? I saw it once when he was shaving, and that's what he said, that it was his mark of Cain and that it protected him. I thought he was joking, but when I found out he was a warlock—"

"This tattoo," said Atticus. "It's red? Like blood?"

"Yeah."

Atticus looked at George. "What did Braithwhite say to you? Marks made with blood are more potent . . ."

" . . . and almost impossible to remove."

"*Almost* impossible," Hippolyta said. "Which means it's possible."

"Yeah, OK," said George. "But we still don't know how."

"No, we don't," agreed Montrose, suddenly thoughtful. "But I've got an idea who we can ask."

The snow continued to fall. The street outside the Winthrop House was hushed as Atticus and Letitia and Montrose drove up.

Inside was a different story. Mr. Fox was on the phone in the atrium, shouting to be heard over a bad connection and over the sound of his daughter skipping rope just a few feet away. In the dining room, Charlie Boyd and a group of friends were engaged in a boisterous card game. Meanwhile Mrs. Wilkins, awakened not by the noise but by thoughts of her late husband, was wandering perplexed along the gallery, trying to remember where she was.

"Mrs. Wilkins?" Letitia called up to her. "You all right?"

"Jeffrey?" Mrs. Wilkins responded, her rheumy eyes focusing not on Letitia but Montrose. "Jeffrey, are you *home*?"

"This is Mr. Turner, Mrs. Wilkins," Letitia said. "Wait here," she told Montrose and Atticus. "She's been getting this way after dark lately . . ." She started for the stairs.

Atticus turned to his father. "So where do you want to do this, Pop? Basement?"

"It's not up to me," Montrose said, looking at Hecate. He held up the satchel he'd brought with him as if to present it to the statue. "Mr. Winthrop? I got something here that belongs to you." He undid the catch and opened the satchel, sending a puff of ash up into the air.

"Got some bad news about your son, too . . ." He drew out the note-books, sending more ash flying.

The motion of the ashes caught Atticus's eye and he watched, mes-merized, as they whirled more and more slowly in the light and then stopped completely, frozen in midair. Looking past them he saw the girl, Celia, frozen too, both feet off the floor while a blur of rope hung beneath them. Behind her, her father posed motionless with the phone against one ear and a hand pressed to the other. In the dining room Charlie Boyd, mouth open in a now-soundless laugh, was caught in the act of slamming a pair of aces down on the table. Letitia's foot hovered over the top riser of the stairs, while Mrs. Wilkins stood paralyzed in confusion on the gallery.

"Pop?" Atticus said, spooked by the sound of his own voice in the abrupt stillness. "Are you—"

"Yeah, I'm still here," Montrose said, looking around at the frozen tableau. "Guess we don't have to worry about anyone eavesdropping on our parley."

They heard the elevator rising out of the basement. It stopped on the first floor and the gate rattled open. Atticus circled the fountain and approached the empty elevator car. The interior was lit by an over-head lamp that he'd rewired himself, but as he got closer he noticed another light, tinged red and flickering like hellfire, shining up from below and visible in the gap between the car and the shaft—and that corresponded to no device *he'd* had anything to do with. "Uh, Pop . . ."

"It's all right," Montrose said, stepping past him. "I've been down this road before. Just don't eat or drink anything, you'll be fine."

The next night was cold but clear. Braithwhite picked Atticus up out-side the Winthrop House at the appointed time and they headed for the Northwest Side. They spoke very little during the journey. Braith-white kept his eyes on the road ahead and grinned in self-satisfaction, as if his victory over Lancaster were already accomplished. Atticus, more somber, kept looking into the Daimler's backseat as if checking for followers on the road behind them.

The moon was just beginning to set as they drove up to the front gate of the Glastonbury Country Club with its prominent MEMBERS ONLY sign. The guard in the stone gatehouse acknowledged their arrival by picking up a telephone, but then for a long while nothing else happened. Braithwhite took the delay in good humor, his only sign of impatience a light drumming of his fingers on the steering wheel. Atticus looked into the backseat again.

Finally the guard came out and opened the gate for them. Braithwhite drove forward, but almost immediately found the way blocked again, this time by Detectives Burke and Noble. Adopting an impish expression, Braithwhite goosed the accelerator pedal, forcing the detectives to duck aside as the car lurched towards them. Noble managed a graceful sidestep, but Burke slipped on a patch of ice and nearly went down.

Atticus, knowing who would suffer for the detectives' displeasure, gave Braithwhite a side-eyed look that said, Was that really necessary? But then a thought struck him. "They're not immune."

"Lodges that know the secret of immunity tend to reserve it for the senior membership," Braithwhite said. "Keeps the neophytes in line." He added: "Don't forget you're not immune, either."

"I'm not the one making trouble," Atticus reminded him.

Noble was at the driver's door now, rapping impatiently on the glass. Braithwhite rolled his window down. "Good evening, officer," he said. "How can we help you?"

"Get out of the car," Noble said. Bending down to look in at Atticus: "Both of you."

They got out. Burke was waiting on the passenger side to slam Atticus up against the car and frisk him. Noble looked as though he would have liked to give Braithwhite the same rough treatment, but because of Braithwhite's immunity, he couldn't just lay hands on him. "If you wouldn't mind," he said, and Braithwhite raised his arms and consented to be searched.

Burke shoved Atticus aside and shined a flashlight around the Daimler's backseat. Detective Noble opened the trunk. "What's this?" Noble said, lifting up a dictionary-sized object wrapped in gift paper.

"A peace offering," Braithwhite said. "I told Lancaster I'd bring him Hiram Winthrop's lost notebooks."

Noble tore open the wrapping paper. "Peace offering, huh?"

"What is it?" asked Burke. Noble showed him, and Burke laughed and said to Braithwhite: "Do you have a fucking death wish?"

"If I do," said Caleb Braithwhite, "you won't be the one to grant it."

"No," Noble agreed, "Lancaster will want to do the honors himself." Then he shrugged. "It's your funeral . . . Leave the keys in the car, I'll walk you in."

"Mind you don't scratch it," Braithwhite said to Burke.

"Death wish," Burke replied. He slammed the trunk shut, then came back around the passenger side, meaning to give Atticus another shove. But Atticus, not wanting to be tempted to hit Burke now that he knew he could, had already started for the clubhouse.

As Noble and Braithwhite and Atticus went inside, Burke remained standing by the Daimler, rubbing his chin thoughtfully.

"Sir?" said the gate guard. "Is everything all right?"

"No," Detective Burke said. "I don't think so." He nodded at the Daimler. "Get this parked, then get on the phone to the house and get some more men out here. Back gate, too . . . I'm going to take a walk around the grounds. That asshole's up to something."

Hippolyta emerged from the trees as the moon slipped below the horizon. For the last twenty minutes she'd been making her way through the woods that bordered the country club's golf course. She'd stumbled more than once in the dark but her sense of direction had held true, and now looking south across a snow-covered fairway she could see the clubhouse and, closer to hand, the small outbuilding that was her destination.

She heard footsteps at her back as the white woman who'd accompanied her emerged from the woods as well. The woman's name was Hillary, and she worked for Braithwhite. Hippolyta would much rather have had Letitia or Ruby with her, but Letitia had been assigned a different task, and Ruby was back in town somewhere, performing some other errand which she wouldn't describe, but which, she'd said, was absolutely essential if Braithwhite wasn't to become suspicious.

Hippolyta felt for the pistol in her coat pocket and started across the fairway, Hillary at her side. Soon they were close enough to read the sign on the outbuilding: POWER & UTILITY—NO ADMITTANCE.

According to Braithwhite, there would be at least two men inside, stationed in a control room on the second floor. They'd have a phone to the main house and probably a radio as well, and the danger was that in the event of a commotion they'd have time to raise an alarm. Hence the white girl.

"OK," Hippolyta said, as they sheltered on the north side of the building, out of sight of the upstairs windows. "You know how you're going to get them to open the door for you?"

"I *could* just knock and ask," Hillary said. "But if they're being careful they might make me wait outside while they call it in. We need to make it so they don't stop and think. So . . ." She shrugged off her coat, revealing a sleeveless black dress more suited to a cocktail party than a trek through the woods. She bent down and tugged off her boots as well, and then standing in the snow in her stockinged feet gripped her dress with both hands and tore it.

"Yeah," Hippolyta acknowledged, seeing where she was going. "That'll work."

⸬

The gate guard set the Daimler's parking brake and got out. A ten count after the door slammed shut, there was a soft click of a latch and the rear seat's back cushion swung down, exposing the narrow compartment between the seat and the trunk in which Letitia lay hidden.

She got out of the car and crouched beside it as she loosened the drawstring on a velvet bag. Inside was a tapered ebony wand about a foot long, carved with Adamite letters. Its narrow end was tipped with a small silver dragonfly that Letitia was careful not to touch.

Staying low, she went after the guard, who had nearly reached the gatehouse. She let him get inside, then ran up and banged on the door. When he stuck his head back out, saying, "Mr. Burke?" she swiped his cheek with the dragonfly. It was the barest of caresses, but the guard's eyes rolled up instantly and he crashed to the ground, unconscious.

"Interesting," Letitia said.

Detective Noble led Braithwhite and Atticus to a large parlor at the west end of the clubhouse. There they were made to wait again. Braithwhite helped himself to scotch from the bar and sat in one of two chairs arranged in front of a roaring fireplace. Atticus, not needing to be told the amenities weren't for him, remained on his feet, scanning the shelves of a pair of ceiling-high bookcases. Unfortunately, this was one of those decorative pseudo-libraries whose contents appeared to have been chosen purely for the look of the bindings.

The hallway door opened and Lancaster entered in a swirl of cigar smoke.

"Nice of you to join us," Caleb Braithwhite said.

"Really?" said Lancaster. "That's the attitude you want start with?" He waited for Noble to hand him a scotch, then took the other seat by the fire. "So," he said. "Did you bring that thing you promised me?"

Detective Noble cleared his throat. He picked up Braithwhite's present from the bar and brought it over to Lancaster. Lancaster set down his drink and put the cigar in his mouth and took the book—a single leather-bound volume—in both hands. As he read the gilt lettering on the cover—*A COMPREHENSIVE ENCYCLO-PEDIA OF HEBREW KABBALAH, by Mordecai Kirschbaum*—his expression grew pained. He gave the book back to Noble and took the cigar out of his mouth and stared into the fire, working his jaw side to side as if trying to find a comfortable position for it. "Wow," he said finally. "You are just bound and determined to piss me off, aren't you?"

"I couldn't bring you Winthrop's notebooks," Braithwhite told him. "I don't have them."

"I don't fucking believe you," Lancaster replied. "And even if I did, it wouldn't excuse this sort of bullshit. Or *this*," he added, reaching into his jacket. He brought out a coin-sized disk of bone, engraved with the image of an owl, and tossed it on the hearth.

"Turnabout," Braithwhite said. "You've been spying on me too."

"I've been watching your ass, because I know you can't be trusted."

"And you're saying I could trust you?"

Lancaster reared his head back. "Unbelievable," he said. "You try to fuck me over, and it's *my* fault? . . . I dealt square with you, asshole. I welcomed you into my city. I was willing to work with you."

"Of course you were," Braithwhite said. "As long as I stayed in my place."

"What were you expecting? You're a *kid*, for Christ's sake, not even half my age . . . You think I'm going to bend my knee to you just because you've got a little talent? Who the fuck do you think you are?"

"A better natural philosopher then you'll ever be," said Caleb Braithwhite.

Lancaster laughed. "Is this the kind of lip you gave your old man? It's a wonder he didn't kill you first. I'll tell you something else, too: I didn't know your father, but Bill Warwick? He was one of Winthrop's apprentices, back in the day, and he was there when Winthrop and your dad had their thing. He told me some stories about what a snot-nose Sam Braithwhite was. So congratulations: You may have hated your father's guts, but it sounds like you're just like him."

Atticus had been doing his best to act invisible. But now, seeing Braithwhite's reaction to Lancaster's comment, he allowed himself to smile. Lancaster stiffened and turned to glare at him as if he'd laughed aloud.

"Sorry," Atticus said. "Why don't I wait outside while you gentlemen—"

"No, you stay right where the fuck you are," Lancaster told him. Turning back to Braithwhite: "Both of you."

The guard at the back gate had stepped outside to urinate in the bushes beside the gatehouse. He was zipping up his trousers when a silver dragonfly landed on the back of his neck and he collapsed. Letitia stood over him with her arms raised in a prizefighter's stance. Then she went to open the gate.

A van marked SHADOWBROOK BAKERIES that had been waiting down the road drove up and stopped inside the gate. Montrose and George jumped out. They picked up the unconscious guard and put him in the gatehouse. "How long is this guy supposed to be out for?" George asked.

"Mr. Braithwhite said he should be dead to the world for three or four hours at least," Letitia told him. "And when he wakes up, he won't remember anything he's seen or done tonight."

Abdullah had turned the van around and was backing it up to the loading dock behind the clubhouse kitchen. As he switched off the engine, a door at the side of the loading dock swung open and a dark-suited white man came out.

"Oh, shit," Montrose said. But it wasn't the van that had brought the white man outside—he had a cigarette between his lips, and his attention was focused on a lighter cupped in his hands.

"Don't worry," Letitia whispered, brandishing her wand. "I got this."

"Oh God, sir, please help me!" Hillary said, and as the guard threw the door open she pretended to swoon and fell into his arms. He stumbled back a few paces, regained his balance—and froze, feeling the muzzle of the gun pressed up under his chin. "Shh," Hillary said, while Hippolyta stepped through the open doorway and moved quickly to the foot of the stairs.

"Bobby?" a voice called down from above. "Who is it?"

Two minutes later Hillary was handcuffing both guards to a pipe in the ground-floor generator room. She tried to act surprised when she turned around and found Hippolyta's pistol pointed at her. "Now you," Hippolyta said, holding up another pair of cuffs.

Without waiting to be told, Hillary tossed her own gun into a far corner of the room. She took the cuffs and had begun to lock herself to a different pipe when one of the guards snickered and said, "That's what you get for trusting a nigger, sweetheart."

"You shut your mouth!" Hippolyta said, and then blinked, realizing that Hillary had said it too, in the exact same tone of voice.

Hillary answered Hippolyta's look with a shrug. "Go on upstairs and don't worry about me," she said, clicking her handcuffs closed. "George and Montrose will be giving the signal any time now."

Pirate Joe, Abdullah, and Mortimer made their way through the clubhouse kitchen, stepping over the unconscious bodies of security guards. They paused to rebalance their burden—a large, flat object wrapped in furniture pads—and headed for the ballroom. Another guard appeared out of a side corridor, but Letitia was right behind the man and she zapped him before he could do anything.

The ballroom was unoccupied. They maneuvered past the tables to the open space beneath the chandelier. While Pirate Joe and Abdullah undid the furniture pads and Mortimer reviewed a diagram on a creased piece of drafting paper, Letitia continued to the far end of the room. The display case had been removed, but the painting remained, and when Letitia pressed the hidden catch on the bottom of the frame, it swung out to reveal a large wall safe. She studied the combination dial and rubbed her fingers together, as if preparing to crack it.

Instead she returned to the Masons. "OK," she told them, "I'm going back out to make sure I didn't miss anybody. You boys be all right on your own for a few minutes?"

"Yeah," Pirate Joe said, grinning. "We should be fine until the shouting starts. Be careful."

Lancaster sipped his scotch reflectively. "So what do we do now, huh?" he said. "I suppose I could just send you packing, and keep *him*." He waved his cigar in Atticus's direction.

"You could try to do that," Braithwhite said.

Lancaster smiled. "You think I couldn't run you out of town if I wanted to? But it'd be a shame, to lose you now. You've got skill, I grant you that. And a way with words. You could be very useful, come Midsummer's Day. If only I could turn my back without worrying you'd stick a knife in it."

"That is a problem."

"Yeah, but maybe I have a solution. Tell me, that mark I put on the boy, what did you think of that?"

"Technically impressive," Braithwhite acknowledged. "Was it really your work?"

"I picked up the basic principles from Bill Warwick," Lancaster said. "But the execution was all mine."

"So what's your plan? You want to send a toy to chase after me, now?"

"No, I've got a different mark in mind, for you. Something else Bill was working on. I found it in his files, after he disappeared. He called it 'the mark of the beast.'"

"As in St. John's Revelation," Braithwhite asked, "or a livestock brand?"

"Well, they're kind of the same thing, aren't they?" Lancaster said. "Bill was always worried about who he could trust. I think that's why he went into Winthrop's treasure chamber alone, too bad for him . . . Anyway, this mark, the idea is you put it on people whose loyalty you want to insure. Then all you have to do is think about them, and you know exactly where they are and what they're up to. And if they're up to no good, you just think a little harder, and they die. And the best part? The mark works on people with immunity."

"So no one can kill your servants but you," Braithwhite said. He glanced over at Noble. "And you know how to do this?"

"Bill was still working on the mark when he disappeared," Lancaster said. "I *think* I've got the last few kinks worked out. There are a couple of questions I was hoping Winthrop's notebooks might help me with, but that's just being conservative. I'm ready to make a live test right now."

Braithwhite's smile became dangerous. "And you think you can force me to sit still for that?"

"Not me," Lancaster said. "Us."

Noble opened the hallway door to admit a procession of white men wearing silver signet rings. Atticus recognized one of them as a former city alderman, and there were others, more vaguely familiar, whose faces he must have seen in newspaper photographs.

There were thirteen men in all. They formed up in two rows, like an odd-numbered jury.

"So," Lancaster said, looking from Braithwhite to Atticus and back again. "Who wants to be first?"

Montrose and George had gotten onto the roof through a trapdoor in the kitchen. The chimney they wanted was at the far end of the building; their route to it was a two-foot-wide walkway running just below the line of the roof peak. It would have been an exciting hike even in summer, but now the walkway was slick with snow and ice.

"Santa's little helpers," George muttered nervously, to which Montrose replied, "Don't go all Berry on me." Montrose started off, George followed, and soon, thanks in no small part to the power of sibling rivalry, they were moving along the roofline with the sprightliness of boys. In moments they stood above their destination. Montrose tied a rope to the walkway and they eased themselves down the slope of the roof until they were braced against the chimney's side. Then George took a flashlight from his pocket and looked towards the outbuilding where Hippolyta was waiting to cut the power. Montrose unslung a bag from around his neck and took out a glass bottle filled with a milky white potion.

The potion was a concoction of Braithwhite's, but the specific choice of container had been Montrose's idea.

"No volunteers?" Lancaster said. "Fine then, we'll start with you, Braithwhite."

He put down his empty glass and tossed his cigar butt into the fire. Noble brought him a knife from the bar, then returned to stand by the door. The men of the Chicago lodge all fixed their eyes on Braithwhite; the atmosphere in the room grew charged. Atticus tensed, preparing for action. Only Caleb Braithwhite remained relaxed, or seemed to, until suddenly he leaned forward in his chair, stuck two fingers in his mouth, and let out a piercing horse whistle.

As the whistle died away, Lancaster sat with his head cocked and the blade poised over his left palm. "What was that?" he said. "Calling for your magic pony?"

A Coca-Cola bottle came flying down the chimney and shattered. The fire was instantly doused and white smoke jetted from the hearth. At the same moment, the clubhouse's electricity went out.

At the sound of Braithwhite's whistle, Atticus had turned to face the door and committed everything he could see to memory. Now, though blinded by smoke and darkness, he knew exactly what combination of steps would get him out of the room.

There was only one obstacle in his path, and it didn't have immunity.

As Hippolyta emerged from the powerhouse she had the wind knocked out of her. For one brief, confused moment she thought she'd just run down the stairs too fast, but then the second punch landed on the side of her head and she realized she was in trouble.

She fell on her side in the snow and tried to reach for the pistol in her pocket, but Detective Burke grabbed her wrist and twisted her arm up and got the gun first. He kicked her in the ribs, flipping her onto her back, and stood watching while she writhed and tried to catch her breath.

"Well, well, Orithyia Blue," Burke said. "What are you doing here?" He gave her another jab with the tip of his boot. "Who else is with you, huh? George around here somewhere? You didn't bring Horace, did you?" He smiled at her reaction to her son's name. "No, I guess not— you probably left him with a babysitter tonight. Don't worry, though, I'm going to go check up on him after we're done here."

Time doubled back to Solstice Night in Wisconsin, Hippolyta hearing again that funny double pop as the two dark coats collided with each other. Burke's smile grew puzzled and he turned towards the open doorway of the powerhouse, even as Hillary stepped up and shot him a third time at close range. Then Burke was on the ground and Hillary was standing over him, gooseflesh breaking out on the freckled skin of her arms.

"You all right?" she asked Hippolyta.

Hippolyta, still short of breath, stared in mute fascination at Hillary's bare wrists.

"Yeah," Hillary said. "I brought a spare handcuff key. Thought I might need it."

Hippolyta sat up and pressed a hand to the side of her jaw. Something about Hillary seemed terribly familiar to her in that moment. "Who . . . who are you?"

"Nobody you need to worry about," said Hillary. "But can you do me a favor? When you see Mr. Braithwhite, tell him I quit."

Then she was gone, running in her stockinged feet through the snow to where she'd left her boots and her coat.

Caleb Braithwhite, exiting the parlor a few seconds after Atticus, slammed the door shut behind him and did something that made it not want to open again. As they dashed away down the hall, Atticus could hear the doorknob rattling and fists pounding against the wood.

Then the pounding ceased, and a powerful force blew the door straight off its hinges. Lancaster came out, waving away smoke. Noble, blood streaming from his broken nose, was right behind him. Then came the other lodge members, scattered at first but quickly reforming into a tight group that followed on Lancaster's heels.

They proceeded swiftly down the hall, chasing the sound of running footsteps in the darkness. The sound had just faded away when they stumbled over one of the downed security guards. "Quiet," Lancaster hissed.

From not far ahead came the sound of an avalanche of pots and pans hitting the floor. Noble started for the kitchen, but Lancaster said,

"Wait," and then, turning, stepped over to the doors of the ballroom and shoved them wide.

At the far end of the room, Atticus was holding a lighter up to the exposed wall safe, while Braithwhite manipulated the dial. They both looked around as Lancaster burst in.

"You just couldn't resist, could you, you stupid son of a bitch?" Lancaster strode forward, unbuttoning his cuffs and rolling up his sleeves. "Well, you can forget all about the book, now. Forget about being my pet researcher, too. I'm just going to take your fucking head and be done with it. And after Midsummer's Day, when I'm running the show? I'm going to make a special trip to Ardham and burn the whole fucking village down."

Braithwhite turned and walked forward as though intending to meet Lancaster and his entourage in the middle of the room. He moved more slowly than they did, though. His arms were loose at his sides, and his fingers waggled. He might have just been flexing them, limbering up, but viewed from a different angle the motions were a lot like those a puppeteer would make.

As Lancaster passed beneath the chandelier, the tablecloth on one of the tables behind him flipped up and Mortimer Dupree rolled out from under it. He scrambled forward, unnoticed by the Chicago lodge men intent on Braithwhite, and used a piece of silvered chalk to make a short, precise stroke on the floor. Changing a letter.

Lancaster and Noble and the men of the lodge all stopped short. Like passengers on an L train whose emergency cord had been pulled, they rocked forward and then back, fighting for balance. Even as they steadied themselves, their feet became rooted to the floor.

"Braithwhite!" Lancaster roared. "What the fuck is th—"

Mortimer made another stroke with the chalk. Lancaster's lips continued to move, but his tongue was stilled.

Two more tablecloths flipped up. Pirate Joe and Abdullah stood and switched on electric lanterns, illuminating the great chalk circle that surrounded Lancaster and his companions—and the larger pattern of which it was a part. To their right, parallel lines connected the big circle to a smaller one ringing the freestanding door that the three Masons had carried in from the van. To their left, a single line—straight at the ends, but zigzagging in the middle—linked to another small circle, currently unoccupied. And stretching out ahead of them, two more parallel lines, drawn so close together that they seemed like one, reached all the way to the base of the wall beneath the safe.

"I'd say something clever and pithy now," Braithwhite told Lancaster, "but I've always been more of a doer than a talker." He took a piece of chalk and drew an outline around the safe door, connecting it to the parallel lines on the floor. Then he went over to the empty circle, where Atticus was waiting with a knife and a rolled-up parchment. But when he tried to take these implements from Atticus, Atticus shook his head.

"I'll do it," Atticus said, and stepped into the circle. He cast a dark look at Lancaster. "I owe him, for Horace."

Braithwhite hesitated, a glimmer of suspicion in his eyes. "This ritual isn't without risk," he said.

"What, as opposed to the rest of the evening?" said Atticus. "Do me a favor."

Still Braithwhite hesitated. But he could see no angle here, and for once, and not by accident, his intuition failed him.

"All right," he said. "But the rest of you should clear out, just in case." Pirate Joe, Abdullah, and Mortimer went out into the hall. Atticus slit his palms. Braithwhite squatted down and made two strokes with the chalk, granting Atticus the power to both read and utter the language of Adam.

The spell was different this time. What came out of the doorway was not light, but darkness—a living dark, like the creature that haunted the Sabbath Kingdom Wood. It swallowed up Lancaster and

Noble and the rest of the Chicago lodge, and shot out a thin tendril of shadow to pop open the safe. And then it withdrew, back into the doorway, leaving not even ashes behind.

"Almost too easy," Braithwhite said, rubbing his hands together as he went to claim his prize. "Midsummer's Day, now, that's going to be a real challenge for us . . ."

Atticus dropped the bloody parchment to the floor. He raised his left arm and stripped down his sleeve, exposing the Adamite letters written on his skin. The black ink he'd used was barely visible, but he could read it just fine now, and he recited the incantation in his head, committing it to memory as he had the layout of Lancaster's parlor. Holding it firmly in mind, he stepped out of the circle.

Braithwhite removed *The Book of Names* from the safe and verified that it hadn't been damaged. "All right, then," he said. "Let's get the rest of the family together and get—" As he turned around, he was surprised to find Atticus right behind him, but secure in his immunity he didn't try to duck away, even when Atticus reached out with a bloody palm. "What's this, now?"

Atticus answered in the language of Adam. As he uttered the first syllable, he placed his hand on Braithwhite's chest. A great heat burned through the fabric of Braithwhite's shirt. Braithwhite cried out and dropped *The Book of Names*; he tried to pull away, but the two of them were already fused together, skin to skin, palm to chest, blood to mark. Atticus went on speaking, while Braithwhite howled and clutched at Atticus's forearm.

Atticus finished the incantation. The heat and the pain faded. When Atticus pulled his hand away, there was still a mark on Braithwhite's chest, and it was still a mark of Cain—but a *different* one, the new a pun upon the old.

Braithwhite fell back against the wall, saying, "What? . . . What did you?" and then his legs buckled under him and he slid helpless to the floor.

The ballroom doors opened. Montrose and George and Letitia came in, and Hippolyta, and Pirate Joe and Abdullah and Mortimer. They came and stood beside Atticus, looking down, while Braithwhite jerked and trembled like a man having a seizure. "You can't," he gasped, fighting to get the words out. "You can't . . . kill me . . ."

"We're not killing you," Atticus informed him. "We're kicking you out."

They cleaned up before they left. Mortimer mopped the ballroom floor while Pirate Joe and Abdullah put the props and equipment away. Hippolyta led a delegation out to the powerhouse: Letitia swatted the two guards with her wand of sleep and forgetting, and Montrose and George, after a brief discussion, wrapped Detective Burke's body in a furniture pad and put it in the trunk of Braithwhite's Daimler. They loaded Braithwhite into the back of the van.

They got on U.S. 41 and drove south. It was after midnight when they crossed the Calumet River and came to a double road sign reading:

NOW LEAVING CHICAGO

and

WELCOME TO INDIANA!

There they turned left, driving onto an open stretch of ground between Indianapolis Avenue and the Pennsylvania Railroad tracks. They drew up the van on the Illinois side of the border. Letitia parked the Daimler just across the state line and left the keys in the ignition. Atticus and Montrose dragged Caleb Braithwhite out and dumped him unceremoniously beside his car. As soon as he was beyond the Chicago city limits, Braithwhite began to recover his strength, and within moments he was standing up on his own.

Hippolyta retrieved a road atlas from the van's glove compartment. She handed it to Atticus, who walked it over to Braithwhite. "Horace couldn't be here to say goodbye," Atticus said, "but he made you a going-away present."

"From now on," George explained, "you'll want to steer clear of the areas marked in red."

"It shouldn't be too much of a burden," added Hippolyta. "Most of the country's still open to you. As long as you don't make any detours through Detroit or Philadelphia or Harlem, you should get home just fine."

Braithwhite was shaking his head. "You can't," he said. "You can't do this to me."

"Can and have done," Atticus said. "Mr. Winthrop sends his re-gards, by the way. He was very grateful to get his notebooks back."

"Winthrop?" Braithwhite said. "*Winthrop* told you how to do this?"

"Yeah," Atticus said, "and you should be grateful too—my pop had a different end in mind for you, and I was leaning that way myself."

"I'll show you gratitude," Braithwhite promised. He turned to Leti-tia. "You and your tenants are going to have to find a new place to live. As soon as I get to a pay phone I'm calling in a demolition crew to turn the Winthrop House into a pile of rubble."

"Oh, I don't think so, Mr. Braithwhite," Letitia said. "It's not your property anymore."

"She's right," said Atticus. "I stopped by Mr. Archibald's office this afternoon. Paid off Letitia's contract, in cash."

"You paid it off." Braithwhite looked at George. "With the money I gave you?"

"With our money, Mr. Braithwhite," George said. "*Our* money."

For a moment then Braithwhite was speechless with anger; his face reddened and his hands holding the atlas trembled. But he mastered himself quickly. "Fine," he said. "Keep the house. Keep the money. But the book . . ." He looked at Atticus. "Let me have *The Book of Names*."

"I don't think so," Atticus said. "Abdullah?"

"No," Abdullah said flatly.

"I'll pay you for it," Braithwhite said. "Name a price."

"Not for every last dollar you have," Abdullah told him. "It's for the flames."

"There you go," said Atticus. "But don't feel too bad, Mr. Braithwhite. The truth is, the book wouldn't do you any good, anyway. That new mark on your chest? It doesn't just bar you from physical locations. You're out of the brotherhood, as well."

"What are you talking about?"

"You're not a sorcerer anymore. You still have your immunity—in a more limited form—but you'll find your other powers are gone, and trying to get them back or learn new ones will only make you very sick. You're allergic to natural philosophy."

Braithwhite refused to believe him at first, but then he looked inside himself and tried to call up some of those other powers, and his expression changed from denial to dawning horror and desperation. *"No,"* he said. "No, Atticus . . . Atticus, come on! You *can't—*"

"Can," Atticus said. "And have done."

He turned to go. Braithwhite made a grab for his arm, but Atticus pulled free easily, and then a wave of weakness and nausea sent Braithwhite stumbling backwards. "Atticus!" he cried. "Atticus, please . . . ! You *need* me, Atticus!"

Standing once more among his family and his friends, Atticus looked back and lofted an eyebrow. "I *need* you?" he said. "I think you might want to check a dictionary, Mr. Braithwhite."

"You think this is over, just because Lancaster's lodge is destroyed?" Braithwhite said. "It's not over! There are other lodges, all over America. They know about you, now. And they'll be coming for you, but not like I did. They won't think of you as family, or even as a person, and they won't leave you alone until they get what they want from you. No matter where you go, you'll never be safe. You—"

But he had to break off, for suddenly Atticus burst out laughing. Letitia and George and Hippolyta and the others laughed, too—even Montrose, who up to now had been feeling surly about the fact that Braithwhite was getting away alive. They *roared* laughter.

"What?" Braithwhite shouted, looking at them as if they were crazy. "What's so funny?" But for a long while they were laughing too hard to answer.

"Oh, Mr. Braithwhite," Atticus said finally, wiping tears from his eyes. "What is it you're trying to scare me with? You think I don't know what country I live in? I know. We all do. We always have. *You're* the one who doesn't understand."

Still laughing, they got into the van and drove away. Caleb Braithwhite remained standing out in the cold long after their taillights had vanished into the distance. Half an hour later when the Indiana state trooper rolled up, he was still standing there, slack-jawed in the dark with a map book in his fist, like a lost traveler trying to work out just where and how he'd gone wrong.

EPILOGUE

Nineteen fifty-five! A new year is upon us, and as always we pause to give thanks for the advances of the last twelve months: the just ruling of the Supreme Court in Brown v. Board of Education; news that the desegregation of our armed services is, belatedly, completed; and other victories, less heralded but no less vital. We continue to look forward to the time, not far off now, when all travelers are treated as equals. And until that glorious day, we resolve to stride forth boldly, prepared for whatever challenges the road ahead may bring . . .

—The Safe Negro Travel Guide, *Spring 1955 edition*

"**S**ure, I can ask him," Letitia said. "But I can't promise he'll do it."

"I'd be willing to trade favors with him, within reason," said Hippolyta.

They were sitting in Hippolyta's kitchen on a morning in early March. On the table between them lay a sheet of paper on which Hippolyta had drawn an eight-by-eight array of boxes. A handful of the boxes had been filled in with numbers—tentatively, in pencil—but most were still blank.

Letitia touched a finger to the paper. "You sure about this? The woman did try to kill you."

"She was trying to protect her daughter."

"And you think she's going to thank you for bringing her the truth about what happened to Pearl?"

"No, probably not," Hippolyta acknowledged. "But it doesn't seem right to just leave her out there."

"Maybe," Letitia said. She glanced at the other papers on the table: brochures and application forms for the University of Chicago and two other schools, farther afield, that offered courses on astronomy. "Tell me something, though. How much of this is just you wanting another crack at that machine?"

Hippolyta smiled. "If I could have that portal here in the house, with no guards around it . . ." She paused, recalling a harsh red alien sunrise. And Scylla. "Well, I'd still need to be careful, but in that case, sure, I'd love to do some exploring. As it is, I can't see making a habit of it. Just one more time."

Letitia was skeptical, having heard those words on other people's lips, but she said: "All right. I'll talk to Mr. Winthrop, see if he'll give me the combination."

"Thank you," Hippolyta said. "I'd appreciate it if you didn't mention it to George."

"Yeah, I figured. Don't worry."

Hippolyta got up to pour herself more coffee. "So how's Ruby doing?"

"If you see her, maybe you can tell me," Letitia said.

"She hasn't been around?"

"She was in church last Sunday, but she ran out at the end of the service before I could talk to her. I think she's mad at me."

"What about?"

Letitia shrugged. "She's feeling sorry for herself, I guess. Getting rid of Mr. Braithwhite cost her another job, so it's like she got punished for doing what had to be done."

"She got punished, and you got the Winthrop House."

"I *told* her I'd share it with her," Letitia said. "But Ruby didn't want that. Ruby doesn't know *what* she wants, that's the real problem . . . But that's not *my* fault. Life's just not fair sometimes, you know? It's not fair, but what are you going to do?"

꧁꧂

She waited in the building lobby at noon, her red hair freshly cut in a modified Amelia Earhart style. She wore stockings this time, along with a new dress and shoes bought specially for the occasion. In her purse was a new set of ID that she'd obtained, at no small expense, through a former business associate of her father's.

"Miss Lightbridge?" she said, as the woman stepped off the elevator. "Excuse me, Miss Lightbridge?"

Joanna Lightbridge looked warily at this stranger smiling at her like an old friend. "I'm sorry, have we met? Miss . . ."

"Hyde. Hillary Hyde. And no, you don't know me. I'm sorry to ambush you like this. I tried to make a regular appointment, but your receptionist told me I'd have to meet with one of your assistants, and while I'm sure they're very good, it's you I wanted to talk to." She opened her purse and brought out a folded newspaper clipping. "I read the interview you did with the *Tribune* last month. It was very inspiring."

"*I* certainly wouldn't call it that," Miss Lightbridge said, her expression souring. "I'm not sure I'd even call it an interview."

"The reporter was very rude to you. Those questions about why you weren't married, I thought that was inappropriate. But your answers were good, and I could tell there was more you were trying to say—maybe more that you *did* say, that he just didn't write down." A postman entered the lobby from the street, pushing a hand truck loaded with packages; the two women moved aside to make way for him and ended up standing closer together. "Miss Lightbridge, I lost my mother a little over a year ago," she continued, "and since then I've been through some other changes, I won't bore you with the details, but it's made me realize I'm just not satisfied with the kind of work I've been doing. I'm not married and I'm not looking to start a family anytime soon. I know a lot about what I don't want, but not much about what I do—and it seemed to me, reading your interview, that you'd been through something similar in your life. Now I know you're very busy, but I was hoping you could spare me just a little time, to maybe point me in the right direction, give me a sense of how to start looking for what I'm looking for . . ."

Joanna Lightbridge was smiling now. "Miss Hyde, is it?" she said.

"Hillary, please."

"Hillary . . . Have you eaten?"

"No, I haven't. I'd be happy to buy you lunch."

"That's all right, Hillary. Lunch is on me."

George had thought at first to go with something bulky and obvious, the kind of safe that takes a team of men to move, but Montrose pointed out that even inch-thick steel won't stop a thief from putting a gun to your head—or your family's heads—and demanding the combination. So George had let Montrose take one of his filing cabinets over to a machine shop and trick it out. The top two drawers still functioned normally (they contained the field reports for West Virginia, Wisconsin, and Wyoming), but the bottom two were a false front: a hinged panel that swung open to reveal a two-and-a-half-foot-tall safe bolted to the floor.

"Is that really three hundred thousand dollars?" Horace said as he stared at the stacks of bills in the safe.

"Less than that, now," George told him. "But still plenty to pay for your college, and Ophelia's kids' college too."

"And yours," Montrose said, looking pointedly at Atticus.

"And Mom's," Horace put in.

"Yeah, hers too," said George. "And whatever's left after that, well we'll see, but if you still want to be a comics publisher when you get done with school, maybe we'll arrange a business loan."

"Really?"

"We'll talk after you've got your diploma," George said. "But until then, Horace, you can't tell a soul about this, understood?"

"Understood," Horace said.

George closed up the safe and the false panel and the four of them returned to the front office. Cartons containing the Spring 1955 edition of *The Safe Negro Travel Guide* were stacked up against the wall. George thumbed through a loose copy, inhaling fresh ink and wondering, as always, how much longer it would be before he could cease publication and change the name of the business to the plain old Berry Travel Agency.

A few more years, probably.

"Before you go," he said, turning to Atticus, "I've got some new leads I'd like you to check out."

"Where at?"

"Memphis. Plus a tourist home across the river in Arkansas."

"Sure," Atticus said. "I can take a run down this weekend."

"Can I come?" Horace said.

"I don't think so," said George. "You've got homework this weekend, don't you?"

"I can do it in the car."

"Also, it's Jim Crow country."

"I know," Horace said.

"Jim Crow ain't an amusement park ride," Montrose said, recognizing the boy's tone.

"I know," Horace said. "But I've got to see it sometime." He looked at his father. "I'll be thirteen next month."

George and Montrose exchanged glances. Then Atticus spoke up: "I'd be willing to take him, if you'll let me. And you could come too, Pop."

"Me?" Montrose said.

"Yeah, you," said Atticus. "You can make sure Horace draws the right lessons from what he sees. Like you did for me. And I know I'd enjoy the company."

Montrose scowled. But he didn't say no.

"I'd feel better if you did go," George offered. "I'd come too, if I weren't busy."

"Come on, Pop," Atticus said.

"Yeah, all right," Montrose said. "But I'm driving . . ."

ACKNOWLEDGMENTS

This novel had a longer gestation than most. The first seeds of inspiration were planted almost thirty years ago, in conversations with Joseph Scantlebury and Professor James Turner at Cornell University. More recently, but still a while back, I happened on Pam Noles's essay "Shame," about the peculiar difficulties of being a black science-fiction fan. And James W. Loewen's *Sundown Towns* introduced me to Victor H. Green's *Negro Motorist Green Book*, at which point the story began to take shape.

I am indebted as always to my wife, Lisa Gold, and my agent, Melanie Jackson. Thanks are also due to Jonathan Burnham, Maya Ziv, Lydia Weaver, Tim Duggan, Barry Harbaugh, Jennifer Brehl, Karen Glass, Caitlin Foito, Amy Stolls and the National Endowment for the Arts, Alix Wilber and Richard Hugo House, Neal Stephenson, Karen Laur, Greg Bear, and Peter Yoachim.